Three Bags Full

Three Bags Full

A Sheep Detective Story

Leonie Swann

Translated by Anthea Bell

DOUBLEDAY
FLYING DOLPHIN PRESS
New York London Toronto Sydney Auckland

For M.,
without whom the whole story would never have come out

PUBLISHED BY DOUBLEDAY/ FLYING DOLPHIN PRESS

First published in 2005 by Wilhelm Goldmann Verlag, Munich, part of the Random House Group. Published in 2006 in the United Kingdom by Doubleday, a division of Transworld Publishers.

Copyright © 2005 by Leonie Swann
English-language translation © 2006 by Anthea Bell
Sheep arrangement by Wiebke Rossa

All Rights Reserved

Published in the United States by Doubleday/Flying Dolphin Press, an imprint of The Doubleday Broadway Publishing Group, a division of Random House, Inc., New York.
www.doubleday.com

DOUBLEDAY/FLYING DOLPHIN PRESS and its colophon are trademarks of Random House, Inc.

This book is a work of fiction. Names, characters, businesses, organizations, places, events, and incidents either are the product of the author's imagination or are used fictitiously. Any resemblance to actual persons, living or dead, events, or locales is entirely coincidental.

Book design by Falcon Oast Graphic Art Ltd.

Cataloging-in-Publication Data is on file with the Library of Congress

ISBN 978-0-385-52111-6

PRINTED IN THE UNITED STATES OF AMERICA

10 9 8 7 6 5 4 3 2 1

First U.S. Edition

DRAMATIS OVES

in order of appearance

MAUDE (1)	has a very good sense of smell and is proud of it.
SIR RITCHFIELD (2)	the lead ram, not as young as he used to be, rather hard of hearing and has a poor memory, but his eyes are still good.
MISS MAPLE (3)	the cleverest sheep in the flock, maybe the cleverest sheep in Glennkill, quite possibly the cleverest sheep in the whole world. Has an enquiring mind, never gives up, sometimes feels a sense of responsibility.
HEATHER (4)	a lively young sheep, doesn't always think before she speaks.
CLOUD (5)	the woolliest sheep in the flock.
MOPPLE THE WHALE (6)	the memory sheep: once he has seen something he never forgets it. A very stout Merino ram with round spiral horns, almost always hungry.
OTHELLO (7)	a black Hebridean four-horned ram with a mysterious past.
ZORA (8)	a Blackface sheep, with a good head for heights, the only ewe with horns in George Glenn's flock.
RAMESES (9)	a young ram whose horns are still rather short.
LANE (10)	the fastest sheep in the flock, a pragmatic thinker.
SARA (11)	a mother ewe.
A LAMB (12)	who has seen something strange.
CORDELIA (13)	likes unusual words.
MELMOTH (14)	Sir Ritchfield's twin brother, a legendary ram who disappeared.
MAISIE (15)	a naïve young sheep.
THE WINTER LAMB (16)	a difficult lamb, a troublemaker.
WILLOW (17)	the second most silent sheep in the flock; no one minds that.
GABRIEL'S RAM (18)	a very odd sheep.
FOSCO (19)	correctly thinks himself clever.

The trail wound here and there
as the sheep had willed in the making of it.

Stephen Crane, *Tales of Adventure*

1

Othello Boldly Grazes Past

"He was healthy yesterday," said Maude. Her ears twitched nervously.

"That doesn't mean anything," pointed out Sir Ritchfield, the oldest ram in the flock. "He didn't die of an illness. Spades are not an illness."

The shepherd was lying in the green Irish grass beside the hay barn, not far from the path through the fields. He didn't move. A single crow had settled on his woolly Norwegian sweater and was studying his internal arrangements with professional interest. Beside the crow sat a very happy rabbit. Rather farther off, close to the edge of the cliff, the sheep were holding a meeting.

They had kept calm that morning when they found their shepherd lying there so unusually cold and lifeless, and were extremely proud of it. In the first flush of alarm, naturally there had been a few frantic cries of "Who's going to bring us hay now?" and "A wolf! There's a wolf about!," but Miss Maple had been quick to quell any panic. She explained that here on the greenest, richest pasture in all Ireland only idiots would eat hay in midsummer anyway, and even the most sophisticated wolves didn't drive spades through the bodies of their victims. For such a tool was undoubtedly sticking out of the shepherd's insides, which were now wet with dew.

Miss Maple was the cleverest sheep in all Glennkill. Some even claimed that she was the cleverest sheep in the world, but no one could prove it. There was in fact an annual Smartest Sheep in Glennkill contest, but Maple's extraordinary intelligence showed in the very fact that she did not take part in such competitions. The winner, after being crowned with a wreath of shamrock (which it was then allowed to eat), spent several days touring the pubs of the neighboring villages, and was constantly expected to perform the trick that had erroneously won it the title, eyes streaming as it blinked through clouds of tobacco smoke, with the customers pouring Guinness down its throat until it couldn't stand up properly. Furthermore, from then on the winning sheep's shepherd held it responsible for each and every prank played out at pasture, since the cleverest animal was always going to be the prime suspect.

George Glenn would never again hold any sheep responsible for anything. He lay impaled on the ground beside the path while his sheep wondered what to do next. They were standing on the cliffs between the watery-blue sky and the sky-blue sea, where they couldn't smell the blood, and they did feel responsible.

"He wasn't a specially good shepherd," said Heather, who was still not much more than a lamb and still bore George a grudge for docking her beautiful tail at the end of last winter.

"Exactly!" said Cloud, the woolliest and most magnificent sheep ever seen. "He didn't appreciate our work. Norwegian sheep do it better, he said! Norwegian sheep give more wool! He had sweaters made of foreign wool sent from Norway—it's a disgrace! What other shepherd would insult his own flock like that?"

There ensued a discussion of some length between Heather, Cloud, and Mopple the Whale. Mopple the Whale insisted that you judged a shepherd's merits by the quantity and quality of the fodder he provided, and in this respect there was nothing, nothing whatsoever, to be said against George Glenn. Finally they agreed that a good shepherd was one who never docked the lambs' tails; didn't keep a sheepdog; provided good fodder and plenty of it, particularly bread and sugar but healthy things too like green stuff, concentrated feed, and mangel-wurzels (for they were all very sensible sheep); and who clothed himself entirely in the products of his own flock, for instance an all-in-one suit made of spun sheep's wool, which would look really good, almost as if he were a sheep himself. Of course it was obvious to them all that no such perfect being was to be found anywhere in the world, but it was a nice idea all the same. They sighed a little, and were about to scatter, pleased to think that they had cleared up all outstanding questions.

So far, however, Miss Maple had taken no part in the discussion. Now she said, "Don't you want to know what he died of?"

Sir Ritchfield looked at her in surprise. "He died of that spade. You wouldn't have survived it either, a heavy iron thing like that driven right through you. No wonder he's dead." Ritchfield shuddered slightly.

"And where did the spade come from?"

"Someone stuck it in him." As far as Sir Ritchfield was concerned, that was the end of the matter, but Othello, the only black sheep in the flock, suddenly began taking an interest in the problem.

"It can only have been a human who did it—or a very large

monkey." Othello had spent his youth in Dublin Zoo and never missed an opportunity to mention it.

"A human." Maple nodded, satisfied. "I think we ought to find out what kind of human. We owe old George that. If a fierce dog took one of our lambs, he always tried to find the culprit. Anyway, he was our shepherd. No one had a right to stick a spade in him. That's wolfish behavior. That's murder."

Now the sheep were feeling alarmed. The wind had changed, and the smell of fresh blood was drifting toward the sea.

"And when we've found the person who stuck the spade in," asked Heather nervously, "then what?"

"Justice!" bleated Othello.

"Justice!" bleated the other sheep. And so it was decided that George Glenn's sheep themselves would solve the wicked murder of their shepherd.

First Miss Maple went over to examine the body. She did it reluctantly: in the summer sun of Ireland, George had already begun to smell bad enough to send a shudder down any sheep's spine.

She started by circling the shepherd at a respectful distance. The crow cawed and fluttered away on black wings. Maple ventured closer, inspected the spade, sniffed George's clothes and face. Finally—as the rest of the flock, huddling together at a safe distance, held their breaths—she even stuck her nose in the wound and rooted around. At least, that was what it looked like from where the others stood. She came back to them with blood on her muzzle.

"Well?" asked Mopple, unable to stand the suspense any longer. Mopple never could stand strain of any kind for long.

"He's dead," replied Miss Maple. She didn't seem to want to

say any more just now. Then she looked back at the path. "We have to be prepared. Sooner or later humans are going to turn up here. We must watch what they do. And we'd better not all stand around in a crowd; it looks suspicious. We ought to act naturally."

"But we are acting naturally," objected Maude. "George is dead. Murdered. Should we be grazing right beside him where the grass is spattered with his blood?"

"Yes, that's exactly what we ought to be doing." The black figure of Othello came between them. His nostrils contracted as he saw the horrified faces of the others. "Don't worry, I'll do it. I spent my youth near the carnivores' enclosure. A little more blood won't kill me."

At that moment Heather thought what a particularly bold ram Othello was. She decided to graze near him more often in future—though not until George had been taken away and fresh summer rain had washed the meadow clean, of course.

Miss Maple decided who would keep watch where. Sir Ritchfield, whose eyesight was still good in spite of his advanced age, was stationed on the hill. You could see across the hedges to the paved road from there. Mopple the Whale had poor eyes but a good memory. He stood beside Ritchfield to remember everything the old ram saw. Heather and Cloud were to watch the path that ran through the meadow: Heather took up her post by the gate nearest to the village; Cloud stood where the path disappeared into a dip in the ground. Zora, a Blackface sheep who had a good head for heights, stationed herself on a narrow rocky ledge at the top of the cliff to keep watch on the beach below. Zora claimed to have a wild mountain sheep in her ancestry, and when you saw how confidently she moved above the abyss you could almost believe it.

Othello disappeared into the shadow of the dolmen, near the place where George lay pinned to the ground by the spade. Miss Maple did not keep watch herself. She stood by the water trough, trying to wash the traces of blood off her nose.

The rest of the sheep acted naturally.

A little later Tom O'Malley, no longer entirely sober, came along the footpath from Golagh to Glennkill to favor the local pub with his custom. The fresh air did him good: the green grass, the blue sky. Gulls pursued their prey, calling, wheeling in the air so fast that it made his head spin. George's sheep were grazing peacefully. Picturesque. Like a travel brochure. One sheep had ventured particularly far out, and was enthroned like a small white lion on the cliff itself.

"Hey there, little sheep," said Tom, "don't you take a tumble now. It'd be a shame for a pretty thing like you to fall."

The sheep looked at him with disdain, and he suddenly felt stupid. Stupid and drunk. But that was all in the past now. He'd make something of himself. In the tourism line. That was it, the future of Glennkill lay in the tourist trade. He must go and talk it over with the lads in the pub.

But first he wanted to take a closer look at the fine black ram. Four horns. Unusual, that. George's sheep were something special.

However, the black ram wouldn't let him close enough, and easily avoided Tom's hand without even moving much.

Then Tom saw the spade.

A good spade. He could do with a spade like that. He decided to consider it his spade in future. For now he'd hide it under the dolmen, and come back to fetch it after dark. He didn't much like the idea of going to the dolmen by night—

people told tales about it. But he was a modern man, and this was an excellent spade. When he grasped the handle, his foot struck something soft.

It was a long time since Tom O'Malley had attracted such an attentive audience in the Mad Boar as he did that afternoon.

Soon afterward, Heather saw a small group of humans running along the path from the village. She bleated—a short bleat, a long bleat, another short bleat—and Othello emerged rather reluctantly from under the dolmen.

The group was led by a very thin man whom the sheep didn't know. They looked hard at him. The leader of the flock is always important.

Behind him came the butcher. The sheep held their breath. Even the scent of him was enough to make any sheep go weak at the knees. The butcher smelled of death. Of screams, pain, and blood. The dogs themselves were afraid of him.

The sheep hated the butcher. And they loved Gabriel, who came right behind him, a small man with a shaggy beard, and a slouch hat, walking fast to keep up with the mountain of flesh just ahead. They knew why they hated the butcher. They didn't know why they loved Gabriel, but he was irresistible. His dogs could do the most amazing tricks. He won the sheepdog trials in Gorey every year. It was said he could talk to the animals, but that wasn't true. At least, the sheep didn't understand it when Gabriel spoke Gaelic. But they felt touched, flattered, and finally seduced into trotting trustfully up to him when he passed their meadow on his way along the path through the fields.

Now the humans had almost reached the corpse. The sheep forgot about looking natural for a moment and craned their necks to see. The thin man leading the humans stopped several lamb's leaps away from George, as if rooted to the ground. His tall figure swayed for a moment like a branch in the wind, but his eyes were fixed, sharp as pins, on the spot where the spade stuck out of George's guts.

Gabriel and the butcher stopped a little way from the body too. The butcher looked at the ground for a moment. Gabriel took his hands out of his trouser pockets. The thin man removed his cap.

Othello boldly grazed his way past them.

Then, puffing and panting, her face scarlet and her red hair all untidy, Lilly came along the path too, and with her a cloud of artificial lilac perfume. When she saw George she uttered a small, sharp scream. The sheep looked at her calmly. Lilly sometimes came to their meadow in the evening and uttered those short, sharp screams at the least little thing—when she trod in a pile of sheep droppings, when her skirt caught on the hedge, when George said something she didn't like. The sheep were used to it. George and Lilly often disappeared to spend a little time inside the shepherd's caravan. Lilly's peculiar little shrieks didn't bother them anymore.

But then the wind suddenly carried a pitiful, long-drawn-out sound across the meadow. Mopple and Cloud lost their nerve and galloped up the hill, where they felt ashamed of themselves and tried to look natural again.

Lilly fell to her knees right beside the body, ignoring the grass, which was wet with last night's rain. She was the person making this dreadful noise. Like a couple of confused insects, her hands wandered over the Norwegian sweater and George's jacket, and tugged at his collar.

The butcher was suddenly beside her, pulling her roughly

back by her arm. The sheep held their breath. The butcher had moved as quickly as a cat. Now he said something, and Lilly looked at him with tears in her eyes. She moved her lips, but not a sound was heard in the meadow. The butcher said something in reply, then he took Lilly's sleeve and drew her aside. The thin man immediately began talking to Gabriel.

Othello looked round for help. If he stayed close to Gabriel, he would miss whatever was going on between the butcher and Lilly—and vice versa. None of the sheep wanted to get close to the body or the butcher, which both smelled of death. They preferred to concentrate on the job of looking natural.

Miss Maple came trotting along from the water trough and took over observation of the butcher. There was still a suspicious red mark on her nose, but as she had been rolling in the mud she now just looked like a very dirty sheep.

". . . ridiculous fuss," the butcher was just saying to Lilly. "And never mind making a spectacle of yourself. You've got other worries now, sweetheart, believe you me." He had taken her chin in his sausagelike fingers and raised her head slightly so that she had to look straight into his eyes.

"Why would anyone suspect me?" she asked, trying to free her head. "George and I got along fine."

The butcher still held her chin in a firm grip. "Got along fine. So you did. That'll be enough for them. And who else got along fine with George? Wait for his last will and testament, then we'll see just how fine you two got along. I don't suppose that cosmetics stuff earns you a fortune, and you won't get rich sleeping around in this dump either. So you be nice to old Ham and you won't need to worry about this mess anymore."

Gabriel said something. Ham turned abruptly and marched back to the others, leaving Lilly where she was. She drew her shawl more closely round her shoulders, trembling. For a moment she looked as if she was going to burst into tears. Maple knew how she felt. Being touched by the butcher—it must be like having death grab you by the ear.

The four humans were exchanging words again, but the sheep were too far away to catch anything. There was a pointed, awkward silence. Gabriel turned and strolled back in the direction of the village, with the thin man close on his heels. Lilly seemed to think for a moment and then hurried off after the two men.

Ham took no notice of the others. He went right up to George. Slowly, he raised one of his great butcher's paws until it was hovering directly above the body like a fat bluebottle. With his fingers he traced two lines above George in the air. A long one from George's head to his stomach and a shorter one from shoulder to shoulder. When Gabriel called him again he went off in the direction of the village.

Later, three policemen came to take photos. They brought a highly perfumed woman journalist with them. She took photos too, far more photos than the policemen. She even went to the edge of the cliffs and photographed Zora on her rocky ledge, and later she took pictures of Ritchfield and Mopple grazing in front of the dolmen. The sheep were used to the occasional attention of tourists with backpacks, but all this press interest soon made them uncomfortable. Mopple was the first to lose his nerve; he ran uphill, bleating loudly. His panic infected the others, even Miss Maple and Othello. Within a few minutes they were all huddled together on the hill, feeling slightly ashamed of themselves.

The policemen took no notice of the sheep. They pulled the

spade out of George, wrapped both him and it in large plastic bags, crawled about on the ground a little more, and then disappeared into a white car. Not long after that it began to rain, and soon the meadow looked as if nothing had happened.

The sheep decided to go into the hay barn. They all went together, because just now, so soon after George's death, the barn seemed to them a bit gloomy and sinister. Only Miss Maple stayed outside in the rain a little longer, letting it wash the mud off her, and in the end it washed off the last small bloodstain too.

When she went into the barn, the sheep had gathered around Othello and were bombarding him with questions, but the ram was biding his time. Heather bleated in alarm, "How could you stand it, being so close to the butcher? I'd have died of fright. I almost did die of fright just watching him come down the path!"

Miss Maple rolled her eyes. But you had to give the black ram credit: he seemed unimpressed by the admiration of his flock. Sounding very matter-of-fact, he turned to Miss Maple.

"The butcher spoke first. 'Swine,' that's what he said."

The sheep looked at each other in amazement. No pig had ever set trotter on their pasture! The butcher's remarks made no sense. But Othello was very sure of himself.

"He smelled very angry. And frightened. But mostly angry. The thin man was afraid of him. Gabriel wasn't." Othello seemed to be reflecting on Gabriel's fearlessness for a moment. Then he continued.

"Lilly didn't say anything sensible. Just 'Oh, George.' And 'Why now?' and 'Why are you doing this to me?' Perhaps she didn't realize he was dead. Then the butcher pulled her away by her arm. 'No one's to touch him,' he said. So then she said quite quietly, 'Please, I only want a moment alone with him.'

None of the others said a word, only the butcher. 'If anyone had that right it'd be Kate.' He sounded nasty, and then he hauled her away."

The sheep nodded. They themselves had had a good view of it all. Suspicion instantly turned against the butcher. But Miss Maple shook her head impatiently, and Othello went on.

"The moment the butcher was far enough off, the thin man began talking to Gabriel. He smelled funny, of whiskey and Guinness, but not as if he'd been drinking. More on his body and his clothes. Specially his hands."

"He dunnit!" bleated Rameses, a very young ram with a lively imagination. "He poured whiskey over his hands because he couldn't stand the smell of the blood anymore."

"Maybe," said Miss Maple hesitantly.

Maude, who had the best sense of smell in the whole flock, shook her head. "Human beings don't scent blood the way we do. They can't really scent anything at all."

"We don't know whether the murderer had bloodstained hands or not," said Miss Maple. "We don't know anything much." She looked enquiringly at Othello.

"Then the thin man told Gabriel very quietly, 'He still had so much he was going to do, his head was full of crazy plans. I don't suppose anything will come of them now, do you?' He spoke very fast, so fast that I couldn't remember it all in one go. He kept on talking about George's plans. I think he wanted to worm something out of Gabriel. But Gabriel didn't reply."

Othello put his head thoughtfully on one side. "I'd say the thin man annoyed him. That's why Gabriel called the butcher back. When the butcher came closer, the thin man immediately stopped talking. Then they all started up again at the same time. Lilly said, 'Someone ought to tell his wife.' Gabriel said,

'Someone ought to fetch the police.' And the butcher said, 'I'll stay with him till they come.' Then the thin man said quickly, 'No one's staying here alone.' The other men stared at the butcher the way you stare another ram down before a duel. The butcher went very red in the face. But then he nodded."

Miss Maple started to collect questions. She told all the sheep to say what they didn't understand and what they'd like to know. She stood in the middle of the flock with Mopple the Whale beside her; when she thought a question was worth remembering, she looked at Mopple and nodded, and the stout ram memorized the question. Once Mopple had memorized something he never forgot it.

"Why did they take photographs of us?" asked Maude.

"Why did it rain?" asked Cloud.

"Why did George come to the meadow in the night?" asked Heather. Maple nodded at Mopple. Heather glanced proudly at Othello.

"Why did the butcher come here?" asked Maude.

"What does the butcher want from Lilly?" asked Othello. Miss Maple nodded.

"What's a Last Will and Testament?" asked Lane, and Miss Maple nodded again.

"When will we be able to graze where George was lying again?" asked Cloud.

"Are they going to drive pigs into our pasture?" asked Maude.

"Why use a spade? The murderer could have pushed him off the cliffs," said Zora. Miss Maple nodded.

"What about the wolf?" asked Sara. "Will he be a danger to the lambs—or us?" Miss Maple hesitated for a moment, but she gave Mopple no sign.

"Why doesn't someone murder the butcher?" asked Cloud. Several sheep bleated approvingly, but Miss Maple didn't nod.

"How long had he been lying in the meadow?" asked Mopple the Whale. Miss Maple nodded at him, and Mopple beamed.

A lamb trotted forward. He had no name yet: the sheep were given names only when they had lived through their first winter. "Will George's ghost come back?" asked the lamb shyly. Cloud leaned soothingly down to him and let him snuggle up to her thick fleece. "No, little one, George's ghost won't come back. Human beings don't have souls. No soul, no ghost. Simple."

"How can you say that?" protested Mopple. "We don't know whether humans have souls or not."

"Every lamb knows that your soul is in your sense of smell. And human beings don't have very good noses." Maude herself had an excellent sense of smell, and often thought about the problem of souls and noses.

"So you'd only see a very small ghost. Nothing to be afraid of." Othello leaned down to the lamb too, amused.

"But I've seen it already!" bleated the lamb. "It was very big, much bigger than me, and I have a very good sense of smell. It was shaggy and it danced. At first I thought it was a wolf's ghost, but now George is dead I know it must have been his. I was so scared, I thought this morning I must have been dreaming."

Miss Maple looked keenly at the lamb. "How do you know George was dead by then?"

"I saw him."

"You saw George dead and didn't tell us?"

"No, it wasn't like that." The lamb sniffed. "I saw the spade. But George must have been lying underneath it, mustn't he?" The lamb looked thoughtful. "Or do you think he fell on top of the spade later?"

There was no more to be got out of the lamb, who had slipped out of the barn in the night and couldn't say why. In the moonlight, he had seen the spade and the shaggy wolf's ghost, but he couldn't describe it in any more detail. He was so frightened that he fell asleep at once.

Now silence reigned. The sheep huddled closer together. The lamb buried his head deep in Cloud's fleece, while the others stared at the ground. Miss Maple sighed.

"Two questions for Mopple. Who is the wolf's ghost? And where's Tess?"

The sheep looked at each other. Where indeed was Tessy, George's old sheepdog, his most faithful companion, the one real love of his life, the gentlest sheepdog who had ever herded them?

When the others had gone to sleep Miss Maple quietly added another question to the list. She had told Rameses that she didn't know whether the murderer had bloodstained hands. The fact was, she didn't even know whether the murderer had hands at all. She thought George's face had looked peaceful, smelling slightly of Guinness and tea; his clothes were smoky; he was holding a couple of flowers in his fingers. That had struck her as a little strange, because George wasn't normally much interested in flowers. He had more time for vegetables.

But she had found something else, and it had made her push the bloodstained Norwegian sweater up a little way with her nose. There, on George's pale stomach, slightly above the place where the spade had gone in, was the print of a sheep's hoof—a single hoofprint, just the one.

2

Heather Suspects Something

Next day the sheep woke up to a new world, a world without any shepherd or any sheepdog. They hesitated for a long time before deciding to leave the barn. At last they ventured out into the open air, led by Mopple the Whale, who was hungry. It was a beautiful morning. Fairies had danced on the grass overnight and left thousands of dewdrops behind. The sea looked as if it had been licked clean, blue and clear and smooth, and there were a few woolly little clouds in the sky. Legend said that these clouds were sheep who had simply wandered over the cliff tops one day, special sheep who now went on grazing in the sky and were never shorn. In any case, they were a good sign.

A mood of tremendous high spirits came over the sheep. They had spent a long time standing around yesterday, their sinews aching with tension; today they gamboled over the meadow like March lambs, galloping toward the steep cliffs, stopping just before the land dropped away and then racing back to the hay barn. Soon they were all out of breath.

That was when Mopple the Whale had the idea of the vegetable garden. Behind the hay barn stood the shepherd's caravan, a rickety vehicle in which George Glenn once used to go around the countryside with another flock of sheep. Recently he'd just kept a few odds and ends in it. Behind the caravan George had laid out a little vegetable garden, growing lettuces, peas, radishes, cress, tomatoes, endives, buttercups, and a few chives.

He had fenced it in. The vegetable garden was in the meadow, but the sheep weren't allowed into it. This ban was hard on them, especially as the fence in itself presented no real problem. But George's watchfulness had kept them from harvesting the produce of this vegetable paradise in their own sheepy way. Now George was gone. Lane pushed back the bolt with her muzzle, Maude started grazing the buttercups, Cloud set to work on the peas and Heather on the tomatoes. After a few minutes there was nothing left of the neatly planted beds.

Gradually all fell silent. The sheep looked at one another, feeling ashamed. One by one they trotted back to the meadow. Othello, the only one who hadn't taken part in their raid, was standing by the gate. He signaled to Miss Maple, who followed him to the back of the caravan, where the spade that George used for working in the vegetable garden usually leaned. Today, however, there was nothing to be seen but the whitewashed side of the caravan and a few flies basking in the sun. Othello looked inquiringly at Miss Maple.

Miss Maple looked thoughtfully back.

The sheep spent the rest of the morning feeling remorseful. Mopple had eaten so many slugs along with the lettuce that he didn't feel well. One of the lambs had a sharp piece of wood stuck in one hoof and was limping. They thought about George.

"He'd have been very cross," said Ritchfield.

"He could have made that hoof better," said Cloud.

"He used to read us stories," said Cordelia.

That was true. George had spent a lot of time in the meadow. He would turn up early in the morning when they were still deep in their sheepy slumber, huddled close together. Tess, herself still drowsy at that hour, had to drive them apart. George would laugh. "You lazy creatures!" he would say. "Come on, get down to work!" They felt slightly injured every morning. They grazed while George worked in the vegetable garden or did a few repairs.

Their sense of injury would wear off by the afternoon. Then they gathered in front of the steps of the caravan, and George read to them. Sometimes from a fairy tale which told them how dew falls on the meadows; sometimes from a book about the diseases of sheep, which scared them; once from a detective story, which they didn't understand. George probably didn't understand it either, because he threw the book away when he was halfway through it, and they never did find out who the murderer was.

But mostly old George Glenn read love stories, slim volumes printed on grayish paper in which the heroines were all called Pamela and had red hair "like a sunset in the South Seas." George didn't read these stories because he was the romantic sort or because he had poor literary taste (which he certainly did; the book about the diseases of sheep had tried their patience sorely), he read to them to let off steam. He read how the redheaded Pamelas lured innocent pirates, doctors, or barons into their clutches, and he got very worked up, saying bad things about all the redheaded women in the world, particularly his own wife.

When George revealed details of his home life, the sheep listened in astonishment. She had been the most beautiful woman in the village, his own personal Pamela, and at first he could hardly believe his luck. But as soon as they were married Pamela (whose real name was Kate) started baking juicy apple pies and got fat. George stayed thin and his manner became increasingly dry. He had dreamed of traveling all over Europe with a flock of sheep, and apple pie was no substitute. At this point the sheep usually bowed their heads. They would have loved to travel to Europe, which they pictured as a huge meadow full of apple trees.

"Now we'll never go to Europe," said Zora.

"We'll never even go to the other pasture again," said Heather.

"Today would have been the day for our tablets." Only Lane was sorry George wasn't here to force their weekly calcium tablets into their mouths. She loved the taste. The other sheep shuddered.

Mopple felt emotional. "We shouldn't forget him," he said. "And we shouldn't have eaten those vegetables."

"Why not?" Zora said casually, staring in the direction of the sea. Mopple chewed his last lettuce leaf vigorously. When Zora said something that sounded casual, he was always struck as if by lightning.

"How are you going to put it right?" asked Cloud.

They decided to devote a small section of their meadow to George's memory. Not in the vegetable garden, which was past praying for anyway. At the foot of the hill, however, they found a patch where many of their favorite herbs grew, and they decided that no sheep was to graze there anymore. They called it "George's Place." Suddenly they felt relieved.

Miss Maple watched from a distance as her flock founded George's Place. She thought of George reading them stories; it also occurred to her that he had turned up less and less frequently over the last few weeks. Often he hadn't come to the meadow to see them at all, but just drove quickly past in his stinking car. Tess would jump off the passenger seat and shoo them into action in the morning, and she and George came back in the evening to count them. But they were away all day long. At first George had tried to teach Tessy to herd them when he wasn't there, but the sheepdog was convinced that her main job was to herd George. She herded the sheep only as a favor to him.

Miss Maple thought about Tess. Had she run away? If so, then it must have been something very terrible that had killed George. The dog was as faithful as a mother ewe. She would have done anything for George. But George was dead, and now Tess had disappeared.

Moving with unusual rapidity, Mopple broke away from the group admiring George's Place and began to feel hungry for the very herbs that grew there. He trotted toward Miss Maple, but Sir Ritchfield suddenly barred his way. Miss Maple couldn't tell where he had come from all of a sudden. Ritchfield looked menacingly at the younger ram, and Mopple trotted away again, not back to George's Place but over to the cliffs, where he could gaze thoughtfully down at the beach.

"Sometimes you have to make the young 'uns respect you," Ritchfield said, "or they'll end up like Melmoth."

Miss Maple did not reply to this. No sheep could have been less like Melmoth than Mopple.

Gradually the enthusiasm for George's Place died down. The sheep set about their usual occupation of grazing, while Miss Maple looked on. It was a good thing they had calmed down. When they were full of grass and less excited, they'd regain their curiosity about the murderer. They would take comfort breaks for eating, but they wouldn't let up on the job. Maple knew them all; she had seen the younger sheep grow up; she herself had grown up with the older sheep. When she was still a lamb the escapades of Ritchfield and his twin, Melmoth, had kept the flock all agog. It was so long since Ritchfield last mentioned him that Maple had thought he'd forgotten him. Now she felt uneasy. The air was perfect: a cool wind blew off the sea, the meadow was fragrant. All the same, the whole place suddenly smelled of death, new death and old, almost forgotten death. Maple began to graze.

The flock had human visitors again that afternoon. A plump woman and a black-clad man with a stiff collar round his neck and a strikingly long nose came up from the village. The woman wore black too, but with her fiery red hair, blue eyes, and rosy cheeks she looked colorful to the sheep. She smelled of apples, such a nice smell that this time there were five observers listening in on the two of them at the same time: Miss Maple, Othello, Heather, a young sheep called Maisie, and Mopple the Whale.

When the humans came to the dolmen they stopped.

"Was it here?" asked the woman. The man nodded. The brightly colored woman stared at the ground. The rain had washed away the mark where the spade went in, so she was staring at the wrong spot.

"It's so terrible," she said in a thread of a voice. "Who'd do a thing like that? I mean, who'd do it?" The sheep pricked up their ears. Perhaps the tall man in black was going to provide the answer. But he said nothing.

"I didn't always have an easy time with him," added the woman.

"No one had an easy time with George," said the long-nosed man. "He was a lost soul, a lamb gone astray, but the Lord in his infinite mercy has taken him home again."

The sheep looked at one another in surprise. Cloud bleated.

"I wish I'd known him better," the woman went on. "He was so strange recently. I thought it was old age coming on. He went out in the car so much, he had letters that I wasn't allowed to open, and," she said, stretching up a little way to whisper in the tall man's ear, but the sheep heard her all the same, "and I found out that he was reading novels in secret—love stories, they were." She went red. It suited her. The man looked at her with interest.

"Really?" he asked.

They moved slowly toward the shepherd's caravan. The sheep felt nervous. Any moment now the damage they'd done to George's vegetable garden would be revealed.

The woman's eyes wandered over the caravan, the vegetable beds stripped bare, the tomato plants pulled up.

"It's so beautiful here," she sighed.

The sheep couldn't believe their ears.

"Perhaps I ought to have come up to see him here sometimes. But he didn't want me to. He never let me. I could have brought him apple pie. Too late for that now." She had tears in her eyes. "I never took any interest in the animals. George brought the wool home, and then I took over. Lovely, soft wool . . ." She sobbed.

"What will happen to the flock now, Kate?" asked the long-nosed man. "This is a fine piece of grazing land, so it is, and someone must care for the sheep."

Kate glanced round. "They don't seem to need anyone to care for them. They look perfectly happy to me."

The man's voice was tart. "A flock needs a shepherd. I daresay

Ham would buy them if you don't want to be troubled with them."

The sheep froze with horror, but the woman shrugged her shoulders.

"Ham's no shepherd," she said. "He wouldn't *care for them.*"

"There are different ways of caring for someone. With love and with rigor, with the word and with the sword. So the Lord has told us. Order, that's what matters." The black-clad man's big nose was pointing at the woman's face in a reproachful way. "If you feel awkward about approaching Ham yourself, I can do it for you," he added.

The woman shook her head, and the sheep sighed with relief. "No, all that business with Ham was over and done with long ago. But I don't even know if everything belongs to me anyway. There's a will. George left it with a lawyer in town. It must be a very unusual will, because he looked around for ages before he found the right lawyer. The will is sure to say who gets everything. I don't want it. I just hope he hasn't left anything to *her.*" Suddenly she didn't seem to think the meadow was so beautiful anymore. "Let's go."

The man nodded. "Be brave, my child. 'The Lord is my shepherd, I shall not want.' " And they marched off, right across George's Place, crushing several fresh shoots underfoot.

Othello ground his teeth. "I wouldn't want that lord of his to be *my* shepherd." The others nodded.

"I shall run away before they sell us to the butcher," bleated Mopple.

"I shall jump off the cliff," said Zora. The others knew that secretly Zora hoped to end up as one of those very special cloud sheep.

"You'll all stay here," said Miss Maple gently. "At least we've found out what a Last Will and Testament is. It says who George's things and his sheep belong to now."

"Yes, and it's been left in a laurel in town!" added Heather. "And it will tell that long-nosed man that George would never have sold us to the butcher!"

They were feeling very relieved.

"I hope they find it soon," said Lane.

"George was not a lamb," said Heather.

"That woman was too old to be his child," said Mopple.

"The tall man was lying," said Othello. "He didn't like George, not one little bit. And I don't like *him*. I don't like the sound of that other man either, the lord he was talking about."

"It was that lord who did it!" cried Heather suddenly. "He took George home with him. And then it happened. They quarreled, first with words and then with the sword. Only there wasn't any sword handy so he used the spade."

Mopple agreed with her. "They were probably quarreling about order. George never kept things in very good order. Except in his vegetable garden." He looked in the direction of George's Place, rather ashamed of himself. "The next thing we must do is find out who that lord is."

Maple looked at him skeptically.

Cloud had said nothing so far. But now she perked up. "The lord is a lamb."

The others stared at her in astonishment. Even Cloud herself looked surprised.

"No, the lord is a shepherd," Heather contradicted her. "A very bad shepherd. Much worse than George."

Cloud shook her head. "No, no. It wasn't like that. If I could only remember better . . ." Cloud stared at a tuft of grass in front of her hooves, but the sheep could tell that she was thinking of something quite different.

"That man . . . I know him. He came to our meadow once before, long ago. I was still a lamb. George had me in his arms—he'd just been trimming my hooves. Everything smelled of . . . of earth and sun . . . like a summer shower. Such a lovely smell, and then . . . something bitter. I could smell at once that George didn't like the man. The man was inviting George to something, but his voice was unfriendly. He said he wanted to give a blessing to the dumb animals. I didn't know what a blessing meant, but it sounded uncomfortable. I thought he meant me, because George had said I was a dumbo just before, because I wouldn't keep still. I was scared. George laughed. 'If you mean Ham, you give him your blessing every Sunday,' he said. The other man got very angry. I don't remember what he said, but he talked about the lord a lot and how he was going to divide the sheep from the goats."

The sheep bleated in alarm.

Cloud stared thoughtfully at her tuft of grass. Only when Zora nuzzled her side gently did she go on. "After a bit George got angry. He dumped me in the long-nosed man's arms. 'Give this dumb animal a blessing, then,' he said. The other man smelled bad, and I was scared. He didn't know how to hold me properly, but he took me away with him. His house was the biggest one in the village, tall and pointy and cold like the man himself. He shut me into his garden. All alone. There was an apple tree, but he'd put a fence round it, and the apples were just rotting on the ground."

Several of the sheep bleated indignantly. Cloud shuddered.

"Then a whole lot of humans came streaming into the house all at once. They brought dogs with them, and other sheep, and a pig. And I had to go in too. There was a terrible racket, but the man in black talked above it. 'Welcome to the house of God!' he said." She stopped and looked thoughtful.

"So his name is God," said Sir Ritchfield.

Othello made a strange face. "God?"

"Could be," said Cloud uncertainly. "But after a while I worked it out that they were worshipping a special lamb. I thought that was a nice idea. They called it 'the lord.' There was music, like on the radio . . . only not quite the same. I looked round a bit and got a nasty fright. There was a man hanging on the wall with no clothes on, and even though he was bleeding from lots of wounds you couldn't smell the blood." She wouldn't say any more.

"And there was a spade sticking into him, right?" asked Sir Ritchfield triumphantly.

"This God sounds rather suspicious to me," said Mopple.

"He's very powerful," Cloud went on. All the people went down on their knees in front of him. And he said he knows everything."

Maude thoughtfully chewed some grass. "I remember that time," she said. "Cloud was away for a whole day. Her mother was looking for her like . . . like a mother would."

"Why didn't you ever tell us about this before?" asked Zora.

"I didn't understand it," said Cloud quietly. She looked a little dreamy and began awkwardly rubbing her nose on one of her forelegs.

The sheep thought some more about God.

"He can't know everything," bleated Othello. "He didn't know that George reads those Pamela novels."

"Used to read them," said Sir Ritchfield drily.

"The murderer always returns to the scene of the crime," said Mopple the Whale. "And the long-nosed man *did* return to the scene of the crime." Mopple looked round proudly. That was the one useful fact they had learned from George's detective story. Mopple, of course, had remembered it. "What do you think?" he asked Miss Maple.

"It does seem suspicious." She nodded. "He didn't like George, and George didn't like him. He seems too interested in what's going to happen to us and the meadow. And when they were standing in front of the dolmen he looked at the exact spot, just where George was lying."

Impressed, the sheep said nothing. Maple went on. "But it could be just coincidence. He was looking at the ground the whole time. There are too many questions. What was the business with Ham that was over and done with long ago? Who is *she*—the person that Kate hoped George hasn't left anything to?"

"It isn't easy to understand humans," said Maude.

The sheep lowered their heads. They grazed a little, and they thought.

Mopple was thinking that he hadn't always understood even George, although George was quite easy to understand—for a human. He was interested in his vegetable garden, and he read Pamela stories to his sheep. He wasn't interested in apple pie. But recently George had been doing some odd things. Every now and then he got out the target.

When George marched across the meadow in his gum boots with the round, brightly painted target, Mopple felt an urge to find a safe place. The only safe place where you couldn't see the target was behind the shepherd's caravan, close to the vegetable garden. When George came out of the caravan for the second time with his gleaming pistol he would find Mopple there. Then he aimed it at Mopple and shouted, "Caught you in the

27

act! Hands up!" Mopple always ran for it, scuttling zigzag across the meadow, and George laughed.

The noise had always been unbearable, but once George had bought a silencer all you heard was a soft smacking sound, like a sheep biting into an apple. This sound, together with Mopple's fear, was the only perceptible outcome of George's enthusiasm for firing his pistol. There was no point in it. Mopple would have been delighted to produce the same sound, with real apples, but George wasn't giving up his target practice.

Miss Maple was thinking of the way Lilly's hands had wandered over George's jacket like insects trying to find something.

Zora was thinking how bad humans were about heights. As soon as they had tottered too close to the cliffs they turned pale, and their movements became even clumsier. On the cliff tops, a sheep was infinitely superior to any human. Even George could do nothing about it when Zora jumped down onto her favorite rocky ledge. He stayed a safe distance away. He knew that it was a waste of time trying to lure her back with blandishments, so he would call and begin throwing things at her, first dirty tufts of grass, then dried sheep droppings.

From the depths below, the wind sometimes carried back to him the sound of a thin, long-drawn-out curse. George's temper instantly improved. He would get down on all fours, crawl to the edge of the cliffs, and look to see tourists or villagers who had been hit on the head by his missiles. Zora saw them too, of course. Then they would look at each other—the shepherd, lying on his front grinning, and Zora, enthroned on her ledge like a mountain goat. At that moment they understood each other perfectly.

Zora thought that human beings would be a lot better off

if they could only make up their minds to go around on four legs.

Rameses was thinking of the story of the escaped tiger that Othello sometimes told to a marveling flock of lambs.

Heather was thinking of the road they took to the other pasture. Of the humming of insects, the noise of cars and their stinking fumes as they drove past the sheep, of the shining surface of the sea. In spring the air smelled of damp earth; in summer flocks of sparrows fluttered like leaves through the cornfields; in autumn when the wind shook the trees, acorns pattered down on the sheep; in winter the hoarfrost drew strange patterns on the asphalt. It was always a wonderful way to go, until they came to the place where the green men lay in wait. The green men had caps and guns and meant no good. When they came to the green men, even George felt nervous. All the same, he gave them a friendly greeting and made sure their dogs didn't get too close to the sheep. Without George they'd never have made it past the men. Heather wondered if they would ever see the other pasture again.

Cordelia was thinking how human beings can invent words, how they can line up their invented words side by side on paper. It was magic. And even that Cordelia knew only because George had explained what magic is. When George read aloud and came to a word that he thought the sheep couldn't understand, he explained it. Sometimes he explained words sheep knew anyway, words like 'prophylactics' and 'antibiotics.' You took prophylactics before you got ill; you took antibiotics while you were ill. They both tasted bitter. George didn't seem to know his way around this subject too well. He got involved in a complicated explanation. Finally he swore and gave it up.

But he was very pleased with other explanations, even if the sheep didn't understand a word he said. In such cases they were careful not to let George guess how little they had taken in. Sometimes, however, he really did teach them something new. Cordelia loved his explanations. She loved knowing words that belonged to things she'd never seen, even to things you couldn't see at all. She remembered those words carefully.

"Magic," George had said, "is something unnatural, something that doesn't really exist. If I snap my fingers and Othello suddenly turns white, that's magic. If I fetch a bucket of paint and paint him white, it isn't." He laughed, and for a moment it looked as if he felt like snapping his fingers or fetching that bucket. Then he went on, "Everything that looks like magic is really a trick. There's no such thing as magic." Cordelia grazed with relish. "Magic" was her favorite word—for something that didn't exist at all. Then she thought about George's death. That was like magic too. Someone had stuck a spade through the shepherd's body in the middle of their meadow. George must have screamed horribly, but none of his sheep in the hay barn, quite close, had heard anything, and then a lamb had seen a ghost. A ghost silently dancing. Cordelia shook her head. "It's really a trick," she whispered.

Othello was thinking of the cruel clown.

Lane was thinking of the strange humans who used to visit George from time to time. They always came by night. Lane slept lightly, and heard the crunch of the car tires when they turned off the paved road and onto the path through the fields. She sometimes hid in the shadow of the dolmen to watch. It was a show performed just for her. The headlights of the cars cut lines of light through the darkness or were caught in the mist and formed a glowing white cloud. The cars that came along the path through the fields were big, with purring engines, and they didn't stink nearly as badly as George's car, which he himself called the Antichrist. Then their lights were switched off, and one or two shadowy figures in long dark coats would approach the shepherd's caravan. They moved cautiously, taking care not to tread on any fresh sheep droppings in the dark. A hand knocked on the wooden door. Once, twice, three times. The door of the caravan was opened, cutting a rectangular space filled with a reddish glow in the darkness. For a moment the strangers stood in the doorway like huge, sharply outlined ravens. Lane had never seen their faces, yet by now they seemed to her almost familiar . . .

Something dark was moving along the path over the fields toward the meadow. It moved fast. There was a moment of panic among the sheep, who all galloped uphill without taking their eyes off the newcomer. God was back. He was pacing up and down the meadow like a hound on a trail, his long nose pointing to the ground.

He walked all round the dolmen and up the footpath to the cliffs. He almost fell over the edge, but at the last moment that nose shot up again and saw the great expanse of blue in front of it. Then the tall black body came to a halt. A sigh passed through the flock. The sheep had been watching God and the movements of his nose ever since the pair of them had started toward the cliffs.

The black-clad man glanced briefly their way. Othello lowered his horns menacingly, but God had already set off along the footpath toward the village. After three or four paces he heard something. He froze, then turned abruptly and fled along the footpath out to the moorland, his face pale and anxious.

The sheep heard it too—a humming, rushing noise. It

sounded like the noise they themselves had made when they invaded George's vegetable garden. It was coming closer. Now they heard dogs barking, and there were human voices too. The sheep saw exactly what the long-nosed man had been running away from. A flock was moving toward the meadow, a flock such as the sheep had never seen before.

3

Miss Maple Gets Wet

George had not liked other human beings. It was rare for any of them to pass the meadow—maybe a farmer now and then or an old woman who wanted a good gossip—and when they did, George got cross. He used to put a very loud cassette in his gray tape recorder and escape into the vegetable garden, where he worked on something as dirty as possible until the visitor had gone away again.

So the sheep had never seen a whole flock of humans before, and they were too surprised to panic. Later, Mopple claimed to have seen seven people in the flock, but he was shortsighted. Zora counted twenty, Miss Maple forty-five, and Sir Ritchfield lots and lots—more than he could count, anyway. But Ritchfield had a terrible memory, particularly when he was worked up. He forgot what he had counted already, so he counted everything and everyone twice or three times. He counted the sheepdogs too.

Mopple stared shortsightedly and morosely at the humans. Well, they could forget the theory of the murderer returning to the scene of his crime now. They had *all* come back to the scene of the crime, and the murderer must surely be concealed among them. With curiosity, the sheep watched the human flock moving on. It was led by neither the strongest nor the brightest among them but by Tom O'Malley. Then came the children, then the women, and finally the men, who were hanging back a little with their hands awkwardly thrust into their trouser pockets. Well behind them again came several very old folk, who could move only slowly and shakily.

Tom had brought a rusty old spade with him. He rammed it into the earth at least ten paces from where George had been lying. The people retreated, as if Tom had splashed them with cold water, and formed a circle at a respectful distance.

"It was here," shouted Tom. "Right here. The blood splattered all the way to here," he said, taking two long strides toward the dolmen. "And right here," he added, with three strides in the other direction, "is where I was standing meself. The moment I see it, I knew it was all up with old George. Blood everywhere. And his face all distorted, horrible it were, with his tongue bright blue and hanging out."

None of this was true. Miss Maple thought how odd that was. It should really have been just as Tom said: blood everywhere, a look of pain frozen on George's face. But George had been there on the meadow looking as if he'd just lain down to sleep.

The human flock retreated a little farther and uttered a strange breathy sound, somewhere between horror and delight. Tom went on shouting. "But your old friend Tom didn't panic, not him. He goes straight off to the Mad Boar to call the police—"

A grating voice interrupted him. "You bet your life! Our old friend Tom, he'll always find his way to the pub!" People laughed. Tom bent his head. The sheep up on their hill couldn't make out what he was saying anymore. Whatever remnants of order had still existed in the human flock now collapsed. Children were chasing around all over the place; grown-ups were forming little groups, bleating the whole time. The wind blew scraps of words up to the hill.

"Goblin King! Goblin King! Goblin King!" the children were singing.

". . . could be he left it all to the Church," said one red-faced farmer.

"That Lilly had a nervous breakdown when they found him!" twittered a chubby-cheeked woman. The man standing next to her held her hand and smiled.

A small man shrugged. "He was a sinner, what d'you expect?"

"And so are you a sinner too, Harry!" grinned an old woman with gaps in her teeth. "The Lonely Heart Inn . . . let's say no more! Your auntie can think herself lucky to have such a good nephew!"

The man turned pale and indeed said no more.

"They say he was worth a fortune," said a man with a prominent paunch.

"Old George had debts for sure, everyone knows that," said another.

". . . a little too fond of his sheep, was George," a very young man was telling two friends, "know what I mean?" He gestured. The other two laughed.

"A crime of passion among the sheep, eh?" cried the thinnest of them, so loud that a couple of women turned round. All three young men laughed their unpleasant laugh again.

"Must have taken him by surprise, so it must," said a man who smelled strongly of sweat, "and old George was damn hard to surprise."

"This is a disaster for the tourist trade," said another man in a high-pitched voice. "George really knew how to mess things up for us."

". . . he was going to sell everything to Ham—the sheep, the land, the whole lot!" said a woman with no neck.

"It was Satan himself who did it," whispered a mousy woman to two small, fair-haired children.

"God have mercy on his soul!" said another woman in a trembling voice. The sheep knew her: "Bible-thumping Beth" was George's name for her. Beth turned up regularly outside the shepherd's caravan to urge George to do something called good works. The sheep didn't know exactly what good works were, but they thought perhaps George was supposed to go and work in some other vegetable garden. But George had a garden of his own. The sheep could see why he didn't want to do as Beth said. Every time George said no, she pressed a bundle of thin pamphlets called tracts into his hand, with a view to converting his sinful soul. There was no knowing what happened to George's soul, always supposing he had one. But he was pleased to have those tracts, although he never read them aloud to the sheep. The evening after Beth brought them, George always had baked potatoes cooked over a small, flickering fire.

Suddenly the enemy raced into the middle of the flock—the ancient enemy. All you could do was run away. Until recently there had only been a couple of the enemy with the human flock, running round the meadow sniffing, whistled off by their masters now and then, told to lie down, trying to make for the wide open spaces. But the closer the whispering groups of humans came to the dolmen, the farther afield the dogs explored. They had now formed a small pack: three sheepdogs and another dog. The sheepdogs' eyes were shining. The dappled pattern of their coats glinted across the meadow. They were making for the hill, keeping close to the ground. The sheep bleated in agitation. Now they'd be herded this way and that, chased apart and brought back together again, driven by sheepdogs moving like beasts of prey. No sheep can stand up to that. They weren't really frightened—they'd been herded thousands of times before—but all the old discomfort had come over them.

Then they saw the way that other dog was moving, and their nervousness really did become fear. The gray wolfhound looked as if he were doing the same as the sheepdogs: crouching low before approaching. But something was wrong. He didn't bark, he didn't hesitate. For a moment the whole flock held its breath: they were being hunted for the first time in their lives. The dog began to run.

Unbridled panic broke out. The flock dashed off in all directions, carrying the startled sheepdogs away with it. Mopple ran right through the crowd of human beings and knocked Harry the Sinner over. Zora took refuge on her rocky ledge. From there, she was the only sheep who could see what was really going on.

The hill was empty. At its foot, close to George's Place, lay two dark bodies, Othello and the dog. They were both just rising to their feet again. Othello attacked first. Zora had never seen a sheep go on the attack before; Othello should have run for it. The dog hesitated. It was a moment before he recognized the black figure of Othello racing up to him as his prey. Then he took off. But before they collided he lost his nerve, braked, and swerved aside. Othello immediately changed direction, moved in a slight curve, and galloped back toward the dog again. Zora stared incredulously at the hill. It was clear to her that Othello was faster than the dog. The dog seemed to realize it too. He crouched on the ground, teeth bared, ready to leap at the ram from below.

Zora quickly closed her eyes and thought about something else. That was her way of dealing with the bad moments in life. She thought of the day when she brought her first lamb into the world, she thought of the pain, and the anxiety later, because the lamb had been brown as earth, even after she had spent ages carefully licking the blood off his coat. Brown as earth, with a black face. Later the brown would turn a woolly white, but Zora wasn't to know that at the time. She had wondered why she was the only sheep in the meadow not to have had a white lamb. But then the lamb had bleated, tiny and brown as he was, and he had a more beautiful voice than any of the other lambs. He had smelled good too. And Zora knew she would defend him against the whole world, whether or not he was the brown color of earth. She had taken him to the cliffs that very day to show him the gulls and the sea.

Zora relaxed. She had had three lambs so far, and they were the bravest and most sure-footed sheep anyone could imagine. She hadn't brought a lamb into the world this year, and hardly any of the other ewes had had lambs either. Zora realized why she had found meditating on her rocky ledge so hard recently, and why she was further than ever from becoming a cloud sheep. She'd missed the lambs all summer. Only two inexperienced young ewes had produced lambs, in an excited, clumsy sort of way, and George had sworn when each of those lambs appeared. And then of course there was the winter lamb . . . Zora's nostrils flared scornfully. She listened. She would have liked to hear a few young creatures bleating just now, but everything was unnervingly quiet, except for the cries of the gulls, and Zora did not take any notice of those anymore. The human beings were buzzing away in the distance like a lot of insects.

Zora heard a terrifying scream. Her eyes opened, even though she was trying hard to keep them closed. Instinctively she looked back at the hill. A dark body lay on the ground. Feet were twitching in the air as if they wanted to go on running. She shuddered. The dog had got Othello. Only a moment later did she see that it was the wolfhound lying on the ground. There was no sign of Othello.

The shaggy wolfhound was trying, unsuccessfully, to stand up. His master came along: one of the young men who had laughed in that nasty way. He was pale, and poked his dog with his foot. A farmer came to lift the animal and carry it away.

The humans were buzzing excitedly. None of them could explain what had happened to that fine, strong dog. When they saw the blood on his belly some of the women screamed. "Satan" and "Goblin King!" rang through the air again. Human mothers bleated till their children came back to them. The human flock went away in a hurry, as suddenly as it had come.

Only the spade was left.

Zora sat motionless on her rocky ledge, wondering if she might have been dreaming. Yes, that must be it. The grass around her was soft as a sheep's muzzle, and herbs that no one else could pull up grew here too. Zora called them "herbs of the abyss," and to her they tasted better than anything there was to eat in the meadow. The fresh sea air wafted up in cool, seaweed-scented gusts, and the gulls circled below her. It was a good feeling to have those screeching white birds lower down; it was good to be alone. No one could follow her here.

She saw the flock slowly calm down and begin to graze. Othello was with them. None of the sheep seemed to be taking any particular notice of him. Zora thought how little she really knew about Othello.

George had sometimes brought new sheep back with him. Usually they were newly weaned lambs, and were warmly accepted by the flock. As far back as Zora could remember, only two grown-up sheep had come from outside: Othello and Mopple the Whale. Mopple had arrived two winters ago, in George's noisy car. George transported single sheep on the back seat. That's where they had first seen him, a plump young ram staring in bewilderment out of the car window and eating George's road map. George had placed Mopple in front of them and made a little speech. Mopple was a ram from a meat breed, he said, but they weren't to worry—no one here was going under the knife—the idea was just to bring in a little fresh blood. The sheep hadn't understood, and were afraid of Mopple at first. But the young ram was friendly and seemed embarrassed. When Sir Ritchfield challenged him to a duel it turned out that Mopple was no danger to anyone.

Ritchfield had never challenged Othello to a duel, and none of the sheep had ever wondered why. More surprising was the fact that Othello had never challenged Ritchfield. Othello seemed to respect Ritchfield, although the harder of hearing and more forgetful he became, the less the other sheep could understand it.

None of the sheep had seen Othello arrive. He just appeared one morning, a full-grown ram with four dangerously curved horns. *Four horns!* They had never seen a four-horned sheep before. The ewes were impressed, and the rams were secretly envious. Zora remembered all that very well; it wasn't so long ago. George didn't introduce Othello. Instead he sang and whistled and danced. They'd never seen him so excited. He sang in strange languages, and spread some of the stinging ointment they feared on a narrow but impressive wound running right over Othello's forehead. The sheep shuddered, while Othello stood perfectly still. George jumped from one leg to the other until he had to take his woolly sweater off.

Zora trotted back to the other sheep. She wanted to ask if Othello had really just defeated a large gray dog. It seemed to her unlikely. She met Maude grazing near George's Place, so close to it that Zora had to bite back a remark in passing.

Maude was chewing, lost in thought.

"Maude," said Zora, "did you see how Othello fought that dog?"

Maude stared blankly at her. "Othello is a sheep," she said. "Excellent grass around here," she added invitingly. Zora turned. She'd ask Maple, or better still Mopple. If any sheep could remember peculiar things, then it was Mopple the Whale.

When she raised her head to pick up Mopple's scent, she noticed that Othello had joined the other sheep and was grazing by. He looked just the same as usual. Zora bent her head and began grazing too. It was best for sheep to forget confusing things as quickly as possible, before the world gave way beneath their hooves.

Sheep are not talkative folk. That's because their mouths are often full of grass, and sometimes they have nothing but grass in their heads. But all sheep love good stories. What they like to do best is listen, marveling—for one thing, because it is easy to

41

listen and chew at the same time. Something was missing in their lives now that George was not around to read stories aloud to them. So it sometimes happened that one sheep would tell the others a story. The story-telling sheep was very often Mopple the Whale, now and then Othello, very seldom one of the ewes.

The mother ewes mostly talked about their lambs, and that didn't interest the other sheep. Of course some lambs were legendary—Ritchfield had been one of those in his time—but the mothers of those lambs deliberately kept their mouths shut.

All the sheep were interested when Othello told a story, but they didn't really understand him. He told them about lions and tigers and giraffes, strange animals from countries where it was burning hot. There were often arguments, because each sheep imagined these animals differently. Did giraffes smell like rotten fruit, did they have bushy ears, did they have at least a little fleece? Othello didn't usually get any further than mere descriptions, and even these were enough to give the sheep a queasy feeling around the backs of their necks. Othello never talked about humans.

When Mopple told a story it was nearly always about humans. Mopple retold the stories that George had read aloud to them. He had remembered everything, and his stories could be almost as good as when they heard them the first time round. They were just shorter. At some point Mopple would feel hungry, and that was where the story ended. The better a story it was (that is to say, the more meadows, grazing, and fodder it contained), the sooner it was over. The real excitement now wasn't always in the stories themselves but in wondering how far they would get this time.

The prospects today looked poor. Mopple was telling the

fairy tale. In no other story were there so many meadows, so much grass, and so much fruit. Mopple's eyes shone as he told them about the fairy ball held every night on the frogs' meadow. His eyes went moist as he told them how envious goblins pelted the fairies with apples during the festivities. He told them about the appearance in the long grass of the Goblin King, who could raise the dead from their graves and send them to haunt the living. Then something unusual happened. Mopple was interrupted.

"Do you think the Goblin King really did it?" asked Cordelia hesitantly. All the sheep knew she was talking about George's death. Mopple quickly pulled up a tuft of grass.

"Or Satan?" added Lane.

"Nonsense." Rameses snorted nervously. "Satan would never do a thing like that."

Several of the sheep bleated in agreement. None of them thought Satan capable of such an act. Satan was an elderly donkey who sometimes grazed in the meadow next to theirs, and uttered bloodcurdling cries. His voice was truly dreadful, but otherwise he'd always struck them as harmless.

"I still think it was God who killed him," said Mopple, with his mouth full. "Beth thought so too." The sheep had a certain respect for Beth because she had invested so much time and trouble in such a doubtful item as George's soul.

"Why would *he* do a thing like that?" asked Maude.

"God moves in mysterious ways," explained Cloud. The others looked at her in surprise. Cloud realized that she had said something odd. "He says so himself," she added.

"Then he's a liar!" Othello looked furious. The eyes of the ewes were shining with admiration. Only Miss Maple was unimpressed.

43

"Was it high or low tide on the night George died?" she asked suddenly. For a second they were all silent.

Then Mopple and Zora bleated in unison, "High!"

"Why?" asked Maude.

Maple began walking up and down as she focused. "If George had been thrown over the cliff, the tide would have washed him away, maybe all the way to Europe. Then no one would have known what happened to him. This way, though, it was downright impossible for him *not* to be found. The murderer wanted George to be found. Why? Why do you want something to be found?"

The sheep thought long and hard.

"Because you want to please someone?" suggested Mopple hesitantly.

"Because you want to warn someone," said Othello.

"Because you want to remind someone of something," said Sir Ritchfield.

"Exactly!" Miss Maple sounded satisfied. "Now we must find out who's pleased, who's been warned, and who's been reminded of something. And what they've been reminded of."

"We can't find that out," sighed Heather.

"Maybe we can," said Miss Maple.

Without another word she began to graze. For a moment all the sheep were silent, thinking with some awe of the huge task ahead of them.

A lamb suddenly bleated out loud with fright and indignation. Its mother, Sara, set up an agitated bleat of her own. She was twisting and turning as if trying to shake an insect out of her fleece. Her lamb stood beside her, looking tearful. Then something small and shaggy shot past Sara's legs and ran off, zigzagging as it went.

The halfling. The milk thief. The winter lamb. He had taken his opportunity to steal Sara's milk while they were all busy thinking.

Every sheep knows that a winter lamb bodes no good to the flock. Winter lambs are born at the wrong season, in the cold, with twisted characters and nasty souls. Bringers of bad luck, who can tempt robbers to roam around freezing flocks of sheep at the lean time of year. And there had never been a worse winter lamb than the one who had plagued their flock since last year. He had been born at the darkest hour of the night. His mother had died and they'd expected him to die too. But he tottered after the flock, squealing, and the sheep reluctantly made way for him. This went on for two days. On the third day they had expected him to die at last, but George foiled them with a bottle of milk. When they bleated reproachfully at him, he muttered something about "brave little thing" and against all the dictates of reason he reared the lamb: a ruthless milk thief, as badly out of proportion as a goat, far too small for a lamb of his age, but tough and cunning. They tried to ignore him as far as they could.

So there wasn't much agitation among the sheep now. Once they were sure that the winter lamb really had run off to the edge of the meadow and was hanging around under the crows' tree, they acted as if nothing had happened.

They spent the rest of the day grazing (but not on George's Place), and digesting the grass comfortably in the evening twilight. Then they trotted off to the hay barn. Cloud had announced that it was going to be a rainy night.

They pressed close together, lambs in the middle, older sheep around them, full-grown rams on the outside, and went to sleep at once.

45

Miss Maple dreamed a dark dream, a dream in which you could hardly see the grass in front of your own sheepy nose.

The dolmen stood before her, bigger but flatter than it was in real life. Three shadowy human figures were standing on it. Maple felt their eyes resting on her. These humans could see in the dark.

Suddenly one of them moved toward Maple. His vague outline took on the shape of the butcher.

Maple turned and fled. The spade that she seemed to have been holding in one front hoof fell to the ground with a dull thud.

She heard the butcher's voice behind her. "A flock needs a shepherd," he whispered. Maple knew at this point that she didn't need a shepherd, it was a flock she needed. She bleated until the other sheep answered from the darkness. Stumbling forward, she found the flock and pushed her way into the safe, woolly tangle.

Something made her suspicious. Her flock smelled wrong— just why, Maple couldn't say. She heard the butcher coming closer and froze. Then a wind rose and blew away the darkness like mist. In the pale light Miss Maple could see that all the sheep in her flock had turned black. She was the only white sheep among them. The butcher was making straight for her, holding an apple pie.

Suddenly it was dark around her again. Miss Maple had woken up. She was about to snuggle up to Cloud, her favorite nighttime neighbor, but something was still wrong. The sheep round her smelled like her own flock, and yet they didn't. She could pick up the scent: Mopple, who still smelled slightly of lettuce,

Zora with her scent of fresh sea air, Othello's resinous ram smell. But it was as if other sheep had been mingling with them, incompatible sheep that didn't give anything away about their personalities. Half sheep, as it were. Miss Maple peered around, but it was at least as dark in the hay barn as in her dream. The rain was pouring down outside, and there were no other sounds. Maple suddenly felt sure that she had seen a movement close to the barn door. She pushed Cloud aside. Cloud began bleating quietly in her sleep, and other sheep joined in, making Miss Maple temporarily lose her sense of direction. She stood still. After a few moments the bleating died away, and she heard the rain again.

Outside, rain like stair rods was falling into the night. Maple sank up to her knees in mud. Her fleece soaked up the water, and she felt twice as heavy as usual. She thought of the lamb who had seen a ghost, and was going to make her way to the dolmen when she heard a sharp, ringing sound, like stone knocking on stone. It came from the cliffs. Maple sighed. The cliffs were certainly not the place she wanted to meet a wolf's ghost on a pitch-dark, rainy night. All the same, she moved on.

It was not as dark on top of the cliffs as she had feared. The sea reflected a little light, and you could see the coastline, shadowy but unmistakable. You could also see that there wasn't anyone there. Whoever had made the noise must have fallen off the cliffs. Maple felt her way cautiously up to the edge of the slippery slope with her wet hooves, and peered down. Of course she couldn't see anything, not even how far down the abyss went. She decided to retreat, and realized that it wasn't going to be easy. The grass was wet and slithery. Someone had set a trap for her, and she, Miss Maple, the cleverest sheep in

Glennkill and perhaps the world, had walked right into it. Maple waited for a hand or a nose to give a gentle but determined push and send her over the edge.

She waited a long time. When she realized that there was no one behind her she lost her temper. With a furious backward jump she made it to reasonably firm ground again and trotted back to the hay barn. She stopped at the door and took a deep breath of air. It smelled of her flock and nothing else. Maple puffed and panted with relief, and noticed that her legs were trembling. She searched for Cloud, who was still bleating softly somewhere, lost in a dream where there was no butcher and no apple pie, probably just a large green field of clover.

Suddenly one of her still-shaking hooves trod in something warm and liquid. The liquid was dripping off Sir Ritchfield. The old ram was standing there motionless with his eyes closed, as if he were fast asleep. He was soaking wet, like a sheep who has been dipped underwater for a very long time. Miss Maple laid her head on Cloud's woolly back and thought.

4

Mopple Squeezes Through a Gap

There was no wind the next day, and the gulls were not calling. Thick gray mist crawled back and forth over the meadow. No one could see more than two sheep's lengths ahead. For a long time they stayed in the hay barn, where it was warm and comfortable. Now that Tess and George weren't driving them out into the early-morning light anymore, they were choosier.

"It's damp," said Maude.

"It's cold," said Sara.

"It's too much to expect of us," said Sir Ritchfield. That settled the matter. The old ram hated mist. Ritchfield couldn't use his good eyes at all in mist. He realized that he wasn't hearing very well these days, and he very soon forgot which way he had come.

But there was another reason for the general hesitation too. The mist seemed to them sinister today, as if strange shadows were moving beyond its white breath.

So they stayed in the barn all morning. They got bored, they felt guilty, and finally they were hungry. But they remembered how George and Tess had annoyed them on days like this, and stayed put. A front line of white, thoughtful sheep's faces stared shortsightedly into the swathes of mist, while Mopple started forcing his way out into the open air through a gap in the back wall of the barn.

The wooden splinters of the rotten planks caught in his fleece and scratched his tender skin. When he had squeezed himself about halfway through he began to wonder whether his idea about that gap had really been a good one.

"If the head will fit through so will the rest of the body," George always used to say. Only now did it strike Mopple that he had been talking about the rats in the shepherd's caravan feasting on the contents of rusty cans.

Mopple had never seen a rat at close quarters. He wasn't so sure whether they really did look like small sheep. Mopple's mother had told him so when he was still a plump suckling lamb; she said that they were very small and very woolly sheep who ran through the stables and barns in flocks, taking dreams to the big sheep. As a grown ram he had wondered why other sheep kicked out at those little rat sheep. He concluded that they were probably sheep having bad dreams. Mopple couldn't complain of his own dreams. There wasn't much variety in them, but they were peaceful.

Mopple stopped to think about what most sheep looked like. Zora, for instance: elegant nose and velvety black face, grace-fully curved horns (Zora was the only ewe with horns in George's flock, and they suited her extremely well), large fleecy body and four long, straight legs with delicate feet. The head might be a sheep's most attractive feature, but it wasn't the widest part of its body.

Mopple twisted and turned uncomfortably, determined not to panic—at least, not straightaway. Was it right to go out through a gap in secret, behind the backs of the other sheep?

He had his reasons, but were they good reasons? For one thing, he felt hungry sooner and more often than the others. Not a bad reason. Mopple stretched his neck, got a tuft of grass between his teeth, and calmed down a bit.

The other reason was more complicated. The other reason was Sir Ritchfield or Mopple's own memory or Miss Maple, or rather all three of them together. A clue. There had been a great many clues in George's detective story, but George had thrown the book away. However, Miss Maple would know what to do with a clue. And Ritchfield would probably try to prevent Mopple from telling Maple. So Mopple had to get through this gap. To tell Miss Maple in secret. She wasn't in the hay barn, so she must be outside somewhere. Or maybe not?

Before Mopple started it had all seemed very simple, but now a sharp splinter of wood was sticking into his side, and he was terrified of puncturing himself and leaking out like Sir Ritchfield. The sheep all agreed that somewhere in Sir Ritchfield there must be a hole through which his memories leaked out and trickled away, but they ventured to say so only when he wasn't within hearing distance. These days it wasn't difficult to be out of hearing distance of Sir Ritchfield.

Mopple tried to make himself thinner. The sharp stabbing feeling went away. He took a deep breath, and the tip of the splinter stuck into his side again. Panic was very close now. He felt it breathing down his neck like a beast of prey. He was going to leak worse than Sir Ritchfield, he'd forget every-thing, even why he was in this gap, and then he'd be stuck here forever and die of starvation. Starvation—him, Mopple the Whale!

Mopple made himself so thin that he saw stars in front of his eyes, and kicked out frantically with his back legs.

*

Othello had spent half the night out in the meadow, dripping wet and in a state of feverish excitement. Would *he* come back? From the moment when Othello saw Sir Ritchfield he had secretly hoped so. He had feared it too. Now it had happened. The memory of a scent still lingered in Othello's nostrils. Ideas circled around his horns like swirling mist. Joy, anger, fury, a thousand questions and a tingling sense of embarrassment.

But Othello had learned to drive the swirling thoughts in his head away. Through the damp mist, he scented the air in the direction of the hay barn: nervous sweat and a sour smell of bewilderment. The flock was in the grip of disquiet. And rightly so: even Othello felt there was something eerie about the mist today.

Ritchfield still wasn't letting his sheep out of the dry barn. All the better, but Othello wondered what the lead ram hoped to gain by it. Did Ritchfield know who had come to their meadow last night? Was he trying to conceal the fact from the other sheep? If so, why?

The black ram briefly wondered which way to go. The least likely way, of course. He trotted toward the cliffs. Last night's rain and the misty air had washed away all the scents. Othello put his head on one side and used his eyes to look for tracks, the way a human would. He felt slightly ashamed of that.

Almost deaf, almost no sense of smell, he heard the familiar and always slightly mocking voice say inside his head. A voice from memory, accompanied by the rushing of black crow's wings. *If you want to know what the Two Legs know, you have to stop and think what they don't know. All that matters to them is what they can see with their eyes. They don't know more than we do, they know less, that's why it's so difficult to understand them, but . . .* Othello shook his head to drive the voice away. Good advice, no doubt about it, but the voice often said confusing things, and now he had to concentrate.

In one place the ground was not just soggy but positively churned up. By Miss Maple, probably. *He* would never have left a mess like that behind. Othello was looking for something less conspicuous. A little farther off he saw a stunted pine tree, the only pine growing anywhere far and wide. *Friendly evergreens, keepers of secrets, wise roots.* The pine tree attracted Othello.

He circled round the small tree until it seemed to lean over in shame before his eyes. Nothing unusual. Except for the hole, of course, but Othello didn't think much of the stories about the hole. The hole was right beside the roots of the pine and went down through the rock at an angle. Day and night the sound of the sea came through it, gurgling and glugging, mocking laughter from the depths. It was said that at full moon sea creatures came up through the hole to run their slimy fingers round the hay barn. But Othello knew that the shimmering lines you saw on the wooden walls of the barn when morning came were really slimy trails left by slugs. The other sheep knew it too, in their hearts; they just liked stories. On some days you could see three or four particularly bold young sheep assembled under the pine tree, listening to the sounds in the hole and giving themselves an enjoyable fright.

Now Othello looked down there too: steep, certainly, but not too steep for a human who could use his hands, and not too steep for a brave sheep. Othello hesitated. *Something that tastes bad the first time you chew it won't taste any better the tenth time,* mocked the voice. *Waiting feeds your fear,* it then added impatiently, as the ram still didn't move. But Othello wasn't listening to the voice. He was staring spellbound at something

53

dark and shining at his feet. A shimmering feather, black and still as night. Othello snorted. He turned his head in the direction of the hay barn once more, and then disappeared down the hole.

Mopple was out in the open air, breathing heavily and trembling. His sides felt sore, and there was a sharp, stabbing pain in one place. To calm himself down, he repeated the most difficult phrase he had ever learned: "Operation Polyphemus." George sometimes used to say it, and no sheep ever understood him. Mopple was one of the few sheep who could remember things he didn't even understand. After saying it he felt braver.

Mopple turned his head to look, not without pride, at the narrow gap through which he, Mopple the Whale, had just squeezed his way. But the wooden wall of the hay barn had already disappeared in a mist so dense and solid that Mopple felt almost tempted to take a bite of it. He controlled himself, and pulled up some grass instead.

The mist wasn't a problem to Mopple. You didn't see as well in mist, that was true, but then Mopple saw poorly anyway. He was more bothered by the fact that you couldn't pick up a scent properly if you had cool, grassy water drops inside your nostrils. But in general he felt safe in the mist, as if he were walking through the fleece of a gigantic sheep, fleece as light as a feather. Unperturbed, he went on grazing. Now he was sure that at least his first reason for getting out had been a good one. Mopple loved misty grass, clear-tasting as water, with all disturbing smells washed off it. He could look for Miss Maple later, and perhaps she'd be attracted over here by his grass-munching sounds anyway. He wandered back and forth at a trotting pace until he didn't feel quite so hungry.

Suddenly his nose came up against something hard and cold. Mopple jumped back in alarm with all four feet in the air at once. From where he was now, however, he couldn't see what had frightened him. He hesitated. Curiosity won the day. He stepped forward and looked at the ground. There lay the spade around which Tom O'Malley had assembled the human flock. It hadn't been driven into the ground deep enough; it had leaned to one side and finally fallen over. Mopple looked crossly at the spade. Human tools belonged in toolsheds and not on the meadow. But this spade didn't smell at all the way human tools usually smell, of sweating hands, annoyance, and sharp things. There was only a faint memory of human scent left around this spade; apart from that it smelled as smooth and clean as a wet pebble.

But if you tried hard enough to pick up that human scent you found the memory slowly, gaining a more distinct structure. Soapy water, whiskey, and vinegary cleaning fluid were all part of it. Mopple scented a short, rancid beard and unwashed feet. Almost too late, he realized that it wasn't the spade he was smelling now but a real human being moving through the mist right beside him. He raised his head and saw a figure, the white, misty shadow of a figure, moving sideways in his direction, like a crab. He lost his nerve and galloped away through the mist.

Running through mist is not a very clever thing to do. Mopple the Whale knew that. But he also knew he couldn't just stand still. His legs, which normally carried him unerringly toward wild herbs and fragrant carpets of grass, suddenly had ideas of their own. All the mist in the world seemed to have gathered inside Mopple's head, and he would have liked simply to forget it, he would have liked to be all legs, running away from everything: George, the wolf's ghost, Miss Maple, fierce dogs, Sir Ritchfield, his memory, and above all death. But one of his hooves was hurting from the unusual force with which his legs were hammering down on the ground. He tried thinking of something, anything, and promptly the most unpleasant thought of all occurred to him: the thought of what was bound to happen any minute.

Sooner or later he would come up against an obstacle. That obstacle could be the cliffs or the hay barn or George's caravan. *Please not the caravan,* thought Mopple. The idea of meeting a furious, ghostly George waving a nibbled lettuce stalk in the vegetable garden—the scene of Mopple's crime—scared him most of all.

Mopple the Whale bumped into something large and soft and warm. It gave way and toppled forward with a grunt. The smell was penetrating, and even before Mopple had finished investigating it his legs went weak with fear. He sat on his haunches and peered through the mist with eyes wide open. The grunt turned into a curse, words that Mopple had never heard before in his life, yet which he understood at once. Then the butcher emerged from the mist, first his huge red hands, then his rounded paunch, and finally his terrible, glittering eyes. They were looking at Mopple without haste; indeed they even seemed to be pleased with something. Without warning, the butcher flung himself on Mopple, as if to crush him with the sheer mass of his own flesh.

The next thing Mopple knew was that he must have managed to dodge him not just once, but several times. The butcher had repeatedly fallen in the mud; his elbows, belly, knees, and half his face were black with it. A few green blades of grass were sticking to his left cheek like whiskers, and through Mopple's shortsighted eyes the butcher looked like a very vicious, fat tiger cat. The parts of his face that weren't black with mud, especially his forehead and eye sockets, were red as a sheep's sore tongue. His neck was red too and curiously thick and swollen. Mopple was trembling all over, exhausted.

In the silence that followed, the butcher saw that Mopple was finished. One of his hands clenched into an enormous fist and slammed into the other, half-open hand. Then the outer hand closed around the inner hand. It was as if the butcher's arms were growing together into a ball of raw meat. The knuckles turned white, and Mopple heard a faint, nasty noise, a distant cracking, as if a bone were being slowly broken. The ram stared helplessly at the butcher, automatically chewing the last tuft of grass that he had pulled up in distant, happier times. It tasted of nothing. Mopple couldn't remember why he had been grazing, he no longer knew why any sheep in the world would want to graze as long as there were butchers around. The butcher took a small step backward. Then, all of a sudden, it was as if the ground had swallowed him up.

Mopple stood there chewing. He chewed until there wasn't a single fiber of grass left in his mouth. As long as he chewed nothing would happen. He felt silly, chewing with his mouth empty, but he dared not pull up another tuft of grass.

A few wisps of mist drifted past, and then—suddenly—there was a patch of clear air. A window, and Mopple could look through it. But he saw nothing. Mopple was standing on the edge of the abyss. He didn't wonder where the butcher had gone anymore. He took a careful step backward. Then another. Then Mopple the Whale turned and let the mist swallow him up again.

Up till now Mopple had always liked mist. When he was still a lamb the shepherd had stopped him suckling from his mother one day. He's getting fat too quickly, said the shepherd. From then on the shepherd himself suckled from Mopple's mother, using some kind of implement. The shepherd was fat too, but no sheep could stop him doing anything. Mopple was given mixed milk and water to drink. He enjoyed watching the milk and water mingle. The white milk spun threads in the water until a dense and delicate web had formed. That web was like the mist getting thicker and thicker, and it was a promise that Mopple would have a full stomach and everything was all right. But today Mopple had found out that mist wasn't the fleece of a gigantic sheep after all, or if it was, then that sheep was infested by vermin, butchers with hands made of raw meat that turned everything they touched into raw meat too.

Slowly, he began to wonder about the dreadful yells rising from the depths. They were yells that Mopple could feel right to the tips of his spiral horns. They hurt him in his teeth and his hooves, but he didn't try to run away from them. He knew now that you couldn't simply run away like that, not even to the other sheep, who were only a kind of mist themselves and could just as quickly dissolve into nothing. He'd seen sheep disappear before, all his foster brothers, his suckling companions, his friends when they were milk-fed lambs, and only the shepherd had ever come back, fat and cold.

Mopple looked at the ground and saw the grass, which was still as green as before. Perhaps he should hang on to the grass. Without taking his eyes off the ground, Mopple began to move. Carefully he put one hoof in front of another, following the grass wherever it might take him.

Othello was annoyed with himself. The hole had not been a problem, easy once you entrusted yourself to it. That was just like him. *Your problems aren't in your feet or your eyes or your mouth. Your problems are always in your head*, whispered the voice. Now Othello was sifting through his head as carefully as only a sheep chewing the cud can. He had already trotted some way along the beach without picking up any tracks at all. The sand moved beneath his feet, pleasantly soft, but sly and sluggish too. And now there was that yelling into the bargain.

It wasn't close enough to threaten Othello, but it was loud and nerve-racking. Who or what in the world could be yelling like that? The question interested him. In any other circumstances he would probably have turned round to take a look at the source of the yells, but what might lie ahead of him interested him more. He must be quite close to the village now. Othello knew it was time to get off the beach.

The ram looked up at the cliffs. They were less steep here, and soft and sandy in many places. Coarse sea grass grew where the wind had heaped the sand up into small dunes. It wasn't worth much as grazing, but it offered a good foothold. Othello climbed the slope. Once at the top, he saw more of the bristly sea grass and a narrow human footpath winding its pointless way through the dust. The sea grass stretched monotonously in all directions and told him nothing. *If you don't know what to do, you must either give up or let it alone*, mocked the voice. *It comes to the same thing.* Othello stood where he was. There were a number of paths a sheep could have taken here, but there was only one path that you could be sure no sheep would ever have chosen. Well, almost no sheep. Othello went on along the human footpath toward the village.

The path wound undecidedly this way and that a few times, and then he found a drystone wall and walked straight as a sheep's leg along beside it. The wall was so high that even if Othello got up on his hind legs he couldn't see over it.

That was a pity, because peculiar things were happening on the other side of the wall. Many voices were murmuring in a low, quiet tone, and it wasn't just the mist muting them. Othello felt that they were excited but had been made to hush. It was seldom that humans took the trouble to be quiet. It always meant something. Othello came to a small, wrought-iron gate; he pushed the latch down with one of his front hooves and the gate gave way with a squeal. The black ram slipped through it as silently as his own shadow and pushed the gate shut again with his head. Not for the first time, he was glad of those terrible times with the circus.

Othello thought he had arrived in a huge vegetable garden. It was so tidy that it looked like a garden: straight paths and square beds, and the smell of freshly turned earth and unnatural vegetation. Something must have been planted here, only it didn't really smell appetizing. Human forms were moving along the paths, taking small steps. They seemed to be coming from all over the place, but they were magically attracted to one point. Othello hid behind a stone that was standing on end. He felt uneasy, and not just because of the human beings: it was the smell. Othello now knew for certain that he wasn't in a vegetable garden. It might even be the opposite of a vegetable garden. A very old smell drifted with the mist along the gravel paths. Othello thought of Sam. Sam was a man who had worked at the zoo, and he was so stupid that even the goats made fun of him. But the zoo management had put Sam in charge of the pit which lay in the no-man's-land behind the elephant house. Even as a lamb Othello could understand why the elephants' eyelids always drooped and looked so red and heavy. Every animal in the zoo knew about the pit. When Sam came back from it the goats left him alone, and the eyes of the carrion eaters narrowed. When Sam came back from the pit, he smelled of ancient death.

It was the first time Othello had been to a funeral, but the ram behaved beautifully. Black and serious, he stood among the gravestones, munching a pansy now and then and listening attentively to the music. He saw the brown box roll up, and immediately knew by the scent who was inside.

Even before he emerged from the mist, he scented God swaying solemnly. God talked about himself, and fat Kate cried. Nobody seemed to be thinking of George inside the box. Except Othello.

Othello remembered when he had first seen George, through a great deal of cigarette smoke. Blood was trickling into his eyes. He was so exhausted that his legs were trembling. The dog beside him was dead, but that didn't mean much. There would always be another dog. Othello concentrated on staying on his feet and keeping his eyes open. It was difficult—too difficult. He just wanted to blink the blood out of his eyes, but once he had closed them they stayed closed. A few moments of heavenly blackness, and then the voice spoke up, rather late in the day. *Closed eyes mean death*, it said. Othello had no objection to being dead; all the same, he obediently forced his eyelids open and looked straight into George's green eyes. George stared at him with so much interest that Othello managed to hold on to his gaze until his legs weren't trembling so much. Then he turned to the door that the dogs came through and lowered his horns.

A little later he was lying in George's old car, bleeding all over the backseat. George was sitting in the driver's seat, but the car was stationary, and night pressed against the windows. The old shepherd had turned to him with triumph in his eyes. "We're going to Europe," he announced.

George had been wrong, though. They never had gone to Europe. Justice, thought Othello. Justice.

5

Cloud Kicks Out

The sheep had spent a horrible day. Never in their lives before had they felt so unloved. First the mist, then the feeling that something strange was moving through that mist, and in addition squelching sounds and a suspicion of hostile scents.

The winter lamb had enticed the two other lambs into a dark corner of the hay barn on some pretext or other, and then terrified them so much that they ran into the wall in their fright and hurt themselves, one on the head and the other on a front leg. Ritchfield saw nothing, heard nothing, and just stayed put. Then the yelling began, and finally even the old lead ram had to admit that there was something wrong. He looked relieved, because at last he had picked up some of what was going on.

The yelling was too much for the sheep. They raced out into the meadow and trotted through the mist, twitching their ears, too nervous to graze. They crowded together on the hill. Maude kicked out nervously and hit Rameses on the nose. In a sullen mood, they waited for the wind to drive away the mist and with it the silence. They even missed the crying of the gulls.

The wind rose around midday, the gulls began screaming

again, and Zora trotted over to the cliffs. She bleated, and soon all the sheep were standing as close to the abyss as they dared and gazing in amazement at the depths below. The butcher was lying there on a small patch of sand in the middle of a great many rocks. He was on his back, and he looked surprisingly flat and broad. Ritchfield claimed to see a red trickle of blood at the corner of his mouth, but they weren't feeling kindly disposed to Ritchfield today and didn't believe a word he said. The butcher had his eyes closed and wasn't moving. The sheep relished the sight. Then the butcher's left eye opened, and their good mood instantly vanished. It looked at every single sheep, and even high up there on the cliffs they felt weak at the knees. The eye was searching for something, didn't find it, and closed again. Cautiously, the sheep retreated from the cliff tops.

"He'll be washed away," said Maude optimistically.

The others weren't so sure.

"A young man always comes along the beach with his dog," sighed Cordelia. Several sheep nodded. They knew that from the Pamela novels. "The dog finds the person. The young man is enchanted and takes the person away," Cloud went on. She had always listened attentively. "At least he'll be gone then," she added. George had always told them, "The sea gives nothing back," as he threw boxes from the caravan over the cliffs at high tide. The young men, on the other hand, soon grew tired of the people they had found, even the fragrant Pamelas, so you could easily work out how soon they'd lose interest in the butcher with his sausage fingers.

"Let's get Mopple the Whale to tell the story of Pamela and the fisherman," said Lane. The others bleated in agreement: they loved the story about the fisherman because a gigantic haystack played the main part in it. Mopple told that story well, and when he'd finished they would stand in awed silence, imagining what *they* would do in the haystack.

But Mopple wasn't with them. They looked in the vegetable garden and in George's Place. George's Place was intact, and they felt ashamed of thinking Mopple capable of such a thing. The sheep fell silent, at a loss. Then Zora trotted back to the cliffs, tail wagging restlessly, to see if there wasn't a round blob of white wool on the beach as well. Luckily Mopple wasn't there, but the sheep's assumptions had been correct. No less than three young men were putting the motionless butcher on a stretcher. Zora shook her head at such foolishness. She bleated at the others, but no one dared watch the young men taking their heavy burden away. They remembered the butcher's eye.

Gradually it became clear that Mopple wasn't in the meadow at all.

"Perhaps Mopple's dead," said Lane quietly.

Zora shook her head energetically. "You don't disappear immediately just because you're dead. George was dead, but he was still there."

"He's turned into a cloud sheep," bleated Rameses excitedly. The sheep swiveled their heads to look up, but the sky was a uniform gray like a dirty puddle.

"He can't have disappeared," said Cordelia. "It's as if the world had a hole in it. It's like magic."

Heather scratched her ear with one hind leg.

"Perhaps he's simply gone away," said Maude.

"You can't go away just like that," objected Rameses. "No sheep can."

They said nothing for a long time. They were all thinking the same thing.

"Melmoth went away," said Cloud at last. Heather lost her balance and fell over sideways. The other sheep looked away.

They all knew the story of Melmoth, although no sheep liked to tell it and no sheep liked to hear it. It was a story that mother ewes whispered into their lambs' ears as a warning. It was a story without any kind of haystack in it, an impossible story, and it scared them all.

"Melmoth is dead!" snorted Sir Ritchfield. The sheep jumped. They had been speaking very quietly, and no one had expected Ritchfield of all sheep to catch what they were saying.

"Melmoth is dead," he repeated. "George went looking for him, with the butcher's dogs. George came back smelling of death. I was the only one waiting by the shepherd's caravan when the fifth night came. I waited for him and I smelled death. No sheep may leave the flock."

No one dared say anything in reply. Their heads sank one by one, and they automatically began grazing.

They would have liked to ask Miss Maple about Mopple, but Miss Maple wasn't there. They would have liked to ask Othello if there was anywhere to go beyond the meadow, because Othello knew the world and the zoo. But Othello wasn't there. Now they were confused. They wondered whether a robber was prowling around the flock and stealing the fattest, the strongest, and the cleverest of them. A robber without any scent. The wolf's ghost, for instance, or the Goblin King, or the lord, whoever he might be.

Sir Ritchfield decided to count the sheep. It was a tedious process. Sir Ritchfield could count only up to ten, and not always that, so the sheep had to stand in small groups. There were arguments, because some sheep would claim they hadn't been counted yet, while Ritchfield said yes, he had counted them already. All the sheep were afraid of being missed out of the count, because then they might disappear. Some of them tried to steal into other groups on the sly so as to be counted twice. Ritchfield bleated and snorted and finally came to the conclusion that there were thirty-four sheep in the meadow in all.

They looked at one another, at a loss. Only now did they realize that they had no idea how many sheep there really ought to be in the meadow. The figure so laboriously worked out was completely useless to them.

It was a great disappointment. They'd hoped they would feel safer after the count. George had always been so pleased when he had finished counting them. "Excellent," he used to say, although sometimes he just said, "Aha." In that case he would march off, either to the cliff tops to throw dried droppings at Zora, or to the vegetable garden to find a bold lamb pushing its neck through the coarse-meshed wire netting and putting its tongue out.

After he had counted the sheep George always knew what to do. The sheep did not.

Feeling frustrated now, Rameses head-butted Maude, who bleated indignantly. So did Heather. Zora nipped her hind-quarters. Strangely enough, Heather didn't react, but instead Lane, Cordelia, and the two young mother ewes all began bleating at once. Ritchfield's hooves were scraping up grass and earth. Lane nudged Maisie, the most naïve sheep in the flock. Maisie almost fell over with surprise, and then nipped Cloud lightly in the ear. Cloud kicked out and hit Maude's foreleg. All the sheep were offended, and all were bleating. Then they fell silent as if at a secret signal, all except for Sir Ritchfield, who was butting everyone and calling for order.

At that moment Othello came along the footpath. He looked at them with mild surprise, and trotted past them to the cliffs.

The sheep exchanged glances. Cloud licked Maude's ears apologetically. Rameses nibbled Cordelia's rump. The black ram looked down at the beach and the butcher-shaped imprint on the sand that the sea hadn't yet washed away. He tilted his head to one side. A moment ago the sheep had been full of questions, but suddenly none of them wanted to trouble Othello. It was enough to know that sheep who have disappeared can come back. They began grazing again with some enjoyment, for the first time that day.

Three men met under the lime tree. One was sweating, the second smelled of soap, the third was breathing stertorously. Their fear prowled around them with gleaming eyes.

"If Ham really snuffs it," said the sweating man, "we're done for and no mistake."

"Effin' madness!" gasped the one with the noisy breath. "What a crazy risk! George—well, who knows? But Ham lodged it all with the lawyer. It's all in his will. He's not making empty threats."

Their fear nodded agreement.

"What stupid fool went and did a thing like that?" groaned the sweating man.

"To Ham?" A waft of soapy air showed that the second man had made a sudden violent movement. "You think it wasn't no accident?"

"Sure and that's what I think," whispered the sweating man, perspiring harder than ever.

"Accident?" The rasping voice laughed. "Why would Ham fall off the cliffs? Sure-footed like he was! Why would he be up there anyway? I'll tell you what, someone lured him there, a whiff of violet perfume on a note and that stupid bastard Ham comes running."

"But he won't be snuffing it," said the sweating man. "Tough as old boots is Ham, always was, thanks be to God. His chances aren't so bad, the doctors say. They reckon he won't be walking no more, but what matters is he's alive."

"Maybe he'll have forgot it all. After an accident like that . . ." The soapy man's voice sounded optimistic.

"Ham'll remember," said the man with the rasping voice. "There mayn't be much gets into his head, but once it's in it don't come out so quickly. When Josh got him all boozed up the evening of George's wedding . . . remember?" Perhaps the men were nodding. Perhaps they were trying to grin. Of course they remembered. Josh had put glass after glass in front of Ham, and Ham, who usually hardly touched a drop, tipped 'em down his throat one by one. How they'd laughed! "Couldn't remember his own name. Didn't even blink when a fly settled on his eye."

"And Josh got his money for every single glass, and then more'n he'd bargained for . . . I wouldn't care for a walloping like that meself." The sweating man chuckled. He was getting on his companions' nerves.

"When Ham wakes up, sure and he'll remember," said the man with the rasping breath. "And so it all goes on again."

They said no more. Perhaps they nodded. Then they went away in different directions. Their fear smiled, it turned with an elegant movement, its mane billowed around the trunk of the old lime tree, and it followed all three of them home.

The lime tree was very old. It had once been in the middle of the village, and the villagers had danced round it. They had made blood sacrifices to it, and the tree had thrived and grown. Perhaps it had seen wolves; it had certainly seen the wolfhounds used by the new masters to hunt down game and cattle and

69

human beings. Today it stood alone, still thriving. Its trunk was taller than two sheep's lengths.

Mopple the Whale was standing behind that trunk. He had come there because he felt safe under the tree, it was like being in a barn. He hadn't run away when the men came. Mopple knew now that running away didn't work. He simply went on chewing, and memorized every word.

Mopple wasn't thinking of the three men or the butcher— certainly not the butcher! Mopple was thinking of their fear. The men hadn't noticed it, but he had seen every one of its few movements, as clearly as if the trunk of the old tree were transparent like water. It was bigger than a sheep and it ran on four legs. A huge, strong beast of prey with a silky coat and clever eyes. Mopple hadn't been afraid of that fear. It wasn't his own fear, after all.

A night bird sang. Evening was falling. Mopple thought of the other sheep and stopped chewing. Suddenly he wanted to be back with his flock so badly that the thick wool behind his ears began to itch. It was high time for another sheep to nibble the back of his neck—that was more important than strange beasts of prey and yelling butchers. Of course Mopple remembered the way he had come through the mist that morning, and his ears wagged happily up and down as he trotted home.

Mopple didn't arrive until dusk. He seemed more thoughtful than usual, and he seemed thinner. It was the different way he moved. Some of the sheep ran to meet him with welcoming bleats: his absence had made them realize how fond they really were of Mopple the Whale. He smelled particularly nice, the way only a totally healthy sheep with an excellent digestion can smell, and he knew the best stories. They bombarded him with questions, but Mopple was more silent than they had ever known him. A terrible suspicion hovered in the air that Mopple couldn't remember properly anymore. But no one dared to voice it. Mopple went to stand beside Zora, who nibbled the back of his neck in an absentminded way.

Darkness fell now, but the sheep stayed out in the open. They were waiting for Miss Maple. However, Miss Maple didn't turn up. Only when the round moon was high in the sky did the figure of a small sheep approach from the moors. A long, thin moonlight shadow trotted ahead of it. It was Maple, looking exhausted. Cloud gave her face a lick.

"Into the hay barn, all of you," said Maple.

The sheep crowded around her as they made their way into the barn. Moonlight fell through the narrow ventilation skylight on their expectant faces. Miss Maple leaned against Cloud and made herself comfortable.

"Where've you been?" asked Heather impatiently.

"Investigating," said Miss Maple. The sheep knew what investigating meant; they had heard the word in the detective story. During investigations the detective delves into other people's business and gets into difficulties.

Miss Maple told them how she had trotted along the road to George's house all by herself. Right through the village, where a car almost ran over her and a big red dog chased her. Then she had hidden herself under the gorse bush outside George's house and eavesdropped on a conversation through the open window. Maple's courage was quite astonishing.

"Weren't you at all frightened?" asked Heather.

"Yes," Miss Maple admitted. "It took me so long because I didn't dare come out of the gorse bush. But I heard a lot."

"I wouldn't have been frightened!" announced Heather, with a sideways glance at Othello.

Miss Maple told them how a great many people had come to see Kate from midday onward—not all at once but in small groups. They all said the same thing. How terrible it was. What a dreadful thing to happen. Now Kate must be strong. Kate hardly said anything, just "Yes" and "No" as she cried into a large piece of cloth. But then—very late in the evening—there was another knock, and it was Lilly outside the door. Kate stopped crying. "How dare you!" she said to Lilly. "I only wanted to say I'm sorry," Lilly whispered. "Well, at least *you* didn't have him," hissed Kate, and she slammed the door in Lilly's face. "Like an angry cat," said Miss Maple. "Just like an angry cat."

It didn't surprise the sheep. The Pamelas in those novels had often behaved in a bewildering and bad-tempered way too. They quickly lost interest in the story that seemed to have fascinated Miss Maple so much. After all, they had other worries.

"Did you have a nice day?" asked Maple, sighing, when she realized that no one was interested in her adventure anymore. The sheep looked embarrassed and told her what had happened during the day.

"He had one eye open," said Lane.

"The butcher was lying on the beach," added Maude.

"Mopple didn't tell us a story," said Heather, looking crossly at Mopple.

"He looked all flat," said Sara.

"We argued," said Cordelia.

"Sir Ritchfield counted us," said Rameses.

"Then the young men took him away with them," said Zora. Miss Maple sighed. "Let Mopple tell me about it," she said.

"Mopple wasn't here," said Cordelia. Maple looked surprised.

"And Othello wasn't here!" sighed Heather. Miss Maple looked inquiringly at Othello.

Othello told them about the strange garden and how George had been buried in a box. A murmur ran through the flock.

"They don't have a pit there, but the dead don't just decay either. It looks more like a garden, not a vegetable garden, but a garden anyway, and all very tidy. And do you know what they said about that garden?" Othello looked round at them, his eyes sparkling. "They said it belonged to God."

The sheep stared at one another in horror. Fancy planting dead people in your garden! They liked God less and less.

"It was him," murmured Ritchfield. Maple glanced at the ram. He looked old, much older than usual, and the great curves of his horns seemed too heavy for him.

"They weren't sad, those people," Othello went on. "Excited, yes, very excited, but not sad. Nervous. Black and talkative as ravens, and we all know what ravens eat." The sheep nodded, grave-faced. "The butcher wasn't there, and they were wondering about that. They won't be wondering about it anymore now." Othello thought some more. "Otherwise they were all there, Kate and Lilly and Gabriel, Tom, Beth, and God and lots of people we don't know. The thin man who came and found George, with the other three, is called Josh Baxter. He's the pub landlord."

They all looked at Miss Maple, but the clever ewe just rubbed her nose thoughtfully with one front leg. The sheep were disappointed. They had expected the hunt for the murderer to be more exciting, easier, and above all quicker. Like in the Pamela novels, where soon after every mysterious death an equally mysterious stranger would turn up, a man with a

73

thin, scarred face or cold and restless eyes. Generally he wanted Pamela for himself, but with a little practice it was easy to tell that he was the murderer, and two or three pages further on at the latest a handsome young man would kill him in a duel. But today's events seemed more like a real detective story, and George had thrown that book away without finishing it. They had been disappointed at the time, but now they wondered whether that hadn't been a better idea than racking your brains over it every day in vain.

"We must find out what sort of story this is," said Cordelia.

The others looked at her curiously.

"I mean, every story is about different things," Cordelia explained patiently. "The Pamela novels are about passion and Pamelas. The fairy tale is about magic. The book about the diseases of sheep is about the diseases of sheep. The detective story was about clues. Once we know what sort of a story this is we'll know what to look out for."

They looked at one another, embarrassed.

"Let's hope it's not a story about the diseases of sheep," bleated Maude.

"It's a detective story," said Miss Maple with conviction.

"It's a love story," Heather bleated suddenly. "Don't you all see? Lilly and Kate and George. It's *just* like with Pamela. George doesn't like Kate, he likes Lilly. But Kate likes George. And there's jealousy and death. It's perfectly simple!" In her enthusiasm Heather allowed herself to frolic like a lamb.

"Well, yes," said Miss Maple cautiously. "Only then Lilly ought to be dead. Not George. There'd have been a duel, and the rivals would have tried to kill each other. You don't fight the person you love—you fight whoever wants to take that person away from you. But," she added, seeing Heather's disappointed face, "I did think of that too. The story smells like it, in a way. Only of course that doesn't make sense."

"It *is* a love story," Heather repeated obstinately.

"Suppose George was one of the rivals?" asked Othello. "Fighting for Lilly? Or perhaps he was defending Kate."

Miss Maple put her head thoughtfully on one side, but she didn't seem to want to say any more about it.

Much later, when most of the sheep were asleep, Mopple, who for the first time in his life couldn't drop off easily, looked through the open door of the hay barn and saw the shape of a sheep standing motionless on the cliffs and looking out to sea: Maple. Mopple went to join her. They stood side by side in friendly silence for a while. Then Mopple told her about the horrors of the day, and Maple said nothing.

"It stretches on and on for a very long way," she said at last.

Mopple sighed. "Sometimes it scares me a bit. Looking out to sea for a long time—as long as Zora, I mean—I couldn't do that."

"I didn't mean the sea, Mopple," said Maple gently, "I mean all this. So many things happening. Hardly any humans ever used to come up here. Except for George, of course, but he wasn't really a human, he was our shepherd."

Miss Maple thought for a while.

"And suddenly there are whole flocks of them coming. Even slinking around in the morning mist. The butcher and someone else. Of course it all links up. Did they really lure the butcher here? If so, who lured him? And why? Why were the men under the lime tree afraid he'd die although they don't like him? We must keep our eyes open for everything, Mopple. You must remember everything."

Mopple raised his head. He was proud of being the flock's memory sheep. Then he remembered just why he had squeezed secretly out of the gap in the hay barn that morning.

"I've remembered something already," said Mopple. And he told her how he had been standing on the hill with Ritchfield, memorizing everything that Ritchfield saw. Almost everything. Ritchfield had seen the four of them going away again—Gabriel, Josh, Lilly, and the butcher. And he saw one of them lag a little way behind the others and bend over. Picking something up? Putting something down? Tearing up a tuft of grass? Then Ritchfield had to sneeze. Five times running. And when he'd finished sneezing he'd forgotten which of them had bent over and what that person was holding.

"He just forgot!" snorted Mopple pityingly. "After three breaths! Incredible! But he still knows he *did* forget something, and he's trying to intimidate me so I won't give it away." He put his head on one side. "I wouldn't have given it away either. I like Ritchfield. He's the lead ram. But I think it's a clue." He looked inquiringly at Maple. She was still looking out at the dark sea.

"A clue," she said thoughtfully. "But a clue to what? It's not like Ritchfield to go intimidating other sheep when they're telling the truth . . . Strange," she added after a while.

Then she seemed to come to a decision.

"Can you keep your mouth shut, Mopple?" she asked.

Mopple shut his mouth.

Maple told him about the hoofprint on George's stomach. "A sheep stood on George very hard," she said. "Or kicked him. Difficult to say which. The question is, when? Before his death? Perhaps. But not long before—the print was too clear for that. Which means . . ."

Mopple looked at her expectantly.

"Which means there was a sheep with George just before or after he died. Or *while* he died. A strong sheep, or a heavy one." She looked briefly at Mopple. "But why would a sheep kick George? Was there a struggle with him, like with the calcium tablets?"

Mopple thought of the calcium tablets and shook his ears.

"But the strangest thing," said Maple, "the strangest thing of all is that this sheep hasn't told us about it. Either the sheep has forgotten—"

"Ritchfield!" bleated Mopple. Then he looked embarrassed. After all, he had promised to keep his mouth shut. But Miss Maple was concentrating much too hard to notice.

"—or he doesn't want to tell us."

"Mopple," said Maple. She looked gravely at Mopple. "We have to think whether a sheep could have something to do with George's death. It's not only human beings who are behaving strangely, some of us sheep are too. Sir Ritchfield. Othello. He told us about the garden with dead people in it, yes, but we don't know what he was doing there. We know so little about Othello. We don't know what George used to do with him in the evenings behind the shepherd's caravan. We have to think hard about it all, Mopple."

Mopple swallowed. He kept his mouth shut.

When the two of them went back to the hay barn a little later, all the sheep were wide awake. There was excitement in the air.

"What is it?" asked Miss Maple.

The sheep said nothing for a long time. Then Maude stepped forward. The moonlight made her sheep's nose look alarmingly long.

"Heather has found a Thing!" she said.

77

6

Maude Scents Danger

And so began the eventful night that would have the sheep still bleating over it months later. It began with Heather standing in a corner, mute with shame, as the eyes of the whole flock were turned incredulously on her.

"A Thing?" exclaimed Mopple.

"A Thing?" breathed Cordelia.

"What's a Thing?" asked a lamb. "Can I have a Thing to eat too? Does it hurt?" The mother ewe looked embarrassed. How could you explain what a Thing is to such a young lamb?

"It . . . it's not really a Thing," murmured Heather. She had bent her head and was looking a little mulish. "It's beautiful."

"*Can* you eat it?" asked Mopple. When it came to Things, Mopple the Whale could be as stern as any other sheep.

"I don't think so." Heather's ears drooped.

"Is it alive?" asked Zora.

"I don't . . . Perhaps!" You could tell from looking at Heather that this possibility had only just occurred to her. "I was going to find out if it's alive. When the light falls on it something moves. It's as beautiful as water. I just wanted to have it so I could always look at it . . ."

"Heather!" Sir Ritchfield stepped forward. He held his head very high, and his horns, which had begun to grow their third curve, cast a reproachful shadow at Heather's feet in the moonlight. Othello gave him a strange look. Suddenly you could understand why Ritchfield was still the lead ram. "You can always look at everything really beautiful. The sky. The grass. The cloud sheep. You can catch the scent of lambs. See sunlight falling on fleece. Those are the important things. You can't *have* them." Ritchfield was speaking as he would have spoken to a very small lamb. He said what they all knew anyway, but the sheep were impressed.

"You can only have what's alive. A lamb, a flock. If you have something, it has you. If it's alive and it's a sheep, that's good. Sheep are meant to have each other. The flock is meant to keep together, ewes and lambs and rams. No sheep may leave the herd . . . so stupid, oh, such a stupid thing . . . I ought to have kept my mouth shut, oh, if only I'd kept my mouth shut . . ." Now Ritchfield was rambling. He looked right through Heather, muttering to himself. Heather made a defiant face again and was about to slip quietly away among the other sheep when a rusty voice spoke up from the darkest corner of the hay barn. A voice as brittle as a branch washed ashore.

"Having is bad," said the voice. "Having Things is bad." They all turned their noses to Willow, who was standing in the shadows behind the empty hayrack. Her old eyes glittered like two dewdrops. Heather's head sank to phenomenal depths.

"Mummy!" she murmured.

Normally mother ewes and their lambs stick together like sandy ground and sea grass. A mother ewe scolding her own offspring in public is unheard-of. But the only reason Willow had said nothing against Heather so far was that she didn't talk

79

anyway—or so the smarter sheep said. Willow was the second most silent sheep in the flock. The last time she had said anything was just after Heather's birth, when she made a casual and disproportionately pessimistic remark about the weather. None of the other sheep was sorry that Willow wasn't the talkative sort. She was said to have grazed a whole bed of bitter-tasting sorrel in her youth: there was no other way to explain her notoriously bad temper. But this time she hadn't been exaggerating.

"It's shameful," said Cloud.

"It's scandalous," said Zora, calmly pulling a single blade of hay out of the empty rack.

"It's undignified," said Lane.

"It's stupid," said Maude.

"It's human," said Ritchfield, who was wearing his stern lead-ram expression again. That said it all. Heather looked as if she might turn into some small scentless animal at any moment now.

Miss Maple pricked up her ears.

"What kind of a Thing is it, actually?" she asked.

"It's—" Heather stopped. She had been going to say "beautiful," but it was beginning to dawn on her that talking about Things in such terms wasn't right. She thought what else there was to say about the Thing that was good. "It has no end."

"Everything has an end!" sighed Sara.

"If something didn't have an end there'd be nothing else, not a sheep in the whole world," said Zora, who often occupied herself thinking over such problems on her rock.

The sheep exchanged melancholy glances.

But Heather was still defiant. "There are two signs on it, signs like in the books. Perhaps it isn't a Thing, perhaps it's a story.

And it's a bit like a chain, like Tessy's chain, only shorter and it doesn't have an end; you can look at it for hours and never see any end."

"And you *have* been looking at it for hours," bleated Maude. "Your nose smells of that human Thing. I picked the scent up at once."

Heather confessed everything. She had found the Thing in the meadow soon after George's death and let it enchant her. She had rolled a stone over it to keep it safe. Only today had she picked it up in her mouth and hidden it under the dolmen while Ritchfield was counting the sheep. She was sorry. She never wanted to see the Thing again.

The sheep decided to send an expedition to the dolmen immediately, to dispose of the Thing once and for all. They'd teach it where it belonged: in the world of Things, on the ground, far away from sheep. The expedition was an honorable affair, and they wondered who should be chosen to go. Cloud suddenly had her old trouble in her joints, Sara had to suckle her lamb, Lane had a sneezing fit. Surprisingly, Mopple turned out to be night-blind.

All the sheep were afraid of going to the dolmen by night, so soon after the dancing wolf's ghost had been spotted there. The expedition ultimately consisted of Sir Ritchfield; Othello; Miss Maple (who was very obviously curious about the Thing); Maude, who could never think up any excuses in time; and Zora, who was too proud to think up excuses. And Mopple had to go too. Colliding with a post inside the barn to convince the others of his night-blindness did him no good: Mopple was the memory sheep, Mopple had to be one of the party.

A mild, warm, moonlit night awaited them outside. You could see all the way to the cliffs from the shepherd's caravan, but the tangy nocturnal aromas dulled the sheep's powers of smell. Led by Ritchfield, they trotted to the dolmen. Maude stayed out in the open, so that her keen nose could instantly scent any wolf ghosts that might turn up. The rest of the sheep put their heads in to look under the capstone of the dolmen, Mopple and Zora from one side, the others from the opposite. Othello scraped up the earth with his hooves and uncovered the Thing. They couldn't see it at first because of the shadows they cast on the prehistoric tomb. A human smell rose to them, almost disguised by the scents of the night. The smell of a sweaty hand; metal; and an unidentifiable sharp, nostril-tickling scent. Maple persuaded Mopple to step back a little way, and as the fat ram retreated, offended, a broad shaft of moonlight fell brightly on the Thing.

Secretly, they had all been expecting something rather beautiful (or as beautiful as a Thing can be), but what they saw lying in the dust in front of them was just a kind of thin chain with a piece of metal on it. Sure enough, it didn't come to an end, because it formed a circle. But that was all there was to its endlessness. They stared scornfully at the human Thing.

"There really are signs on it," said Sir Ritchfield, who was embarrassed by the way he had lost his train of thought a little while ago. Now his good eyesight could regain him respect. "The first sign is sharp like a bird's beak pointing upwards," he added, "with a line through the middle of it. And the other one is like a stomach on two legs. That means it stands for one of the Two Legs. I think it's a bad sign!" Ritchfield looked resolutely at the rest of them.

Mopple wanted to throw the Thing off the cliffs.

Zora wouldn't hear of throwing it off the cliffs. She thought the cliffs were too good for a Thing like that.

Maude bleated in surprise, but no one took any notice of her.

Sir Ritchfield thought they should bury the Thing, although he didn't want to touch it personally.

Maude bleated again.

Mopple wouldn't have minded touching the Thing, but he didn't want to bury it and then maybe find himself grazing on top of it later.

Miss Maple surprised them all.

"We'll keep the Thing," she said. "It's a clue. It turned up after George's death. It may be something the murderer dropped. Well, like our own droppings, I mean," she added, when Sir Ritchfield looked at her blankly.

"It doesn't smell like droppings," objected Mopple.

Maude bleated in alarm.

Maple shook her head impatiently. "It occurred to me back in the barn just now. Human beings are attached to Things. Things attach themselves to human beings. If we keep a close eye on Things we'll find the murderer."

At this moment Maude squeezed her way in under the dolmen with the others, and seconds later a beam of light swept past them. Three people followed it closely. The beam of light came to rest on George's caravan and swept up the walls. It was looking for somewhere to hide.

"Switch that damnfool torch off," said a voice. "Bright enough to count grains of wheat out here, and Tom O'Malley has to bring a torch along!" The beam of light had found a gap to slip through, and suddenly disappeared.

"That's right, keep on shouting our names out! I'm wondering did we put these stupid stocking masks on for nothing?" complained another voice. The sheep knew that voice from the day before: Harry the Sinner.

Tom O'Malley chuckled. The sheep noticed that he didn't smell of drink. They'd almost failed to recognize him. "Hey," he said, "hey, why so jumpy? We're not doing nothing wrong. We're doing what's got to be done—for Glennkill!"

"For Glennkill!" murmured Harry.

"For my arse," said the voice they had heard first. The thin man called Josh. "Either we stop right here to sing 'Where Glennkill's Bonny Hills So Bright,' or we finally get that damn van open and look for the stuff."

No one opted for singing. The sheep were relieved. Three shadowy figures marched toward the door of the shepherd's caravan, two stout forms and a tall thin one. Metal glinted in the moonlight, and keys rattled. They rattled for a long time.

"It don't fit," said Harry the Sinner.

The thin man kicked the door three times. "Fuck George! That's it, then." He pressed his nose flat against the two little glass windows of the caravan. He was so tall that he didn't even have to stand on tiptoe to do it.

"Now what?" asked Tom.

"We need that grass," said Harry. "So we break the door down."

"Are you crazy?" said Josh. "I'm not doing that. That's a crime, that is."

"So disposing of evidence is legal, is it?" said Harry scornfully. "If they find the dope here it's all over. No Faerie Dolmen. No pony rides. No Celtic Cultural Center. No whiskey specialities. And you can stuff your seaside hotel!"

"Maybe there isn't any dope," said Josh.

"What else would it be in there? How did old George keep his head above water all this time? With his few pathetic sheep? You must be jokin'! Did he ever want to sell up? Laughed in

84

your face when you come along with your money, so he did. Here was this grand view just wasted on his sheep, and now he's dead at last, do we want Glennkill getting itself in the papers as a mecca for the drugs trade?"

The sheep's knees were shaking with indignation.

"Harry's in the right of it, Josh." Tom swayed back and forth a little, out of habit. "Old George was in the way of throwing sheep droppings at tourists, wouldn't let no one come up here, even fired a pistol off to scare us. And for why? He could've made a mint of money out of this land, so he could. But he was making a mint of money out of it already, that's what. Boats on the beach by night, the stuff gets took up to the caravan, he's off with it in his old banger next day."

Josh shook his head again.

But Tom had talked himself into a state of high excitement, and shouted across the nocturnal meadow, "And don't you go thinking George was no innocent angel. There's kids as saw him of an evening with a black ram. Now there's perverted for you! I hate to think what we might find in there, so I do!"

White faces appeared at the door of the hay barn. Every sheep in the meadow was now listening intently. And not just the sheep. Maude had been sniffing the air uneasily for quite a time. She couldn't smell the men with stocking masks on from here; the night-time scents, thankfully, had overlaid the nervous sweating of the intruders. But with every breath she took the suggestion of a human scent wafted past her: a smell of the digestion of cooked food, barely perceived. At first she had blamed the Thing. But the Thing was lying on the ground, and the human smell was seeping down from above.

She craned her neck up. She was certain of it—someone was lying on the capstone of the dolmen.

A master hunter. Maude knew that at once. The back of her neck tingled, and a memory that was not her own—of narrow, rocky ravines and lurking robbers—arose in her. *Wolf,* she thought, *wolf!*

When a sheep thinks *Wolf!* its proper course of action is to bleat and run away, but Maude stayed put. The enemy was too close, and now that she had identified him, his scent surrounded her on all sides. He wasn't coming closer, he was here already. She stood there as if hypnotized, helplessly breathing the air in.

It is surprising how easily fear can jump from sheep to sheep. Maude hadn't moved or made a sound. All the same, the other five sheep knew about the wolf at once. Maude's fast breathing told them how close the enemy was, and Maude's own scent had turned salty, with bitter undertones speaking of flight and ambush. Their hearts galloped to all four points of the compass. But since Maude didn't move, the other sheep stood motionless too. Maude was their warning sheep; she knew most about the danger. All the sheep would do as she did.

Maude was aware of her responsibility. Unable to run for it, she tried at least to scent the hunter on the roof above her as extensively as possible. The smell of smoke. A human being, that much was clear. He'd been eating onions not long before. Maude heard the man's stomach contracting around those give-away onions.

The thin man kicked the caravan door again. It made a small, frightened sound. Perhaps the beam of light was sitting nervously inside. The man on top of the dolmen tensed. At that moment Maude knew he wasn't hunting her, he was after the three men by the caravan. Maude gave off an aura of relief.

Over by the caravan, the interesting discussion of what exactly George and Othello did together had now come to an end.

"So do they search the caravan, then?" asked Tom. "Not them, they don't do nothing, devil a bit of it. No police inquiries, no questions. Hushed up, forgot, dead and buried, that's the way of it. All in league together they are, the police and the drugs boys. Bribed, every man jack of 'em!" Tom's voice held a trace of disappointment that no one had gone to the trouble of bribing him.

"So?" The thin man sounded annoyed. "So why do we have to break in here if no one's interested in the stuff anyway?"

No one replied. Harry halfheartedly kicked the door. It was quiet inside. Tom turned away from the others and was about to set off in the direction of the paved road. Then he froze.

"There's a car!" whispered Tom. The sheep had heard it long before. A big car without any lights on was purring along the road. It came to a halt and stopped purring. The three men scattered like chickens. Harry the Sinner doubled expertly back and forth a couple of times; the thin man bent his long back to run faster. The sheep were amazed. They had never before known how easily scared human beings could be. They themselves kept their nerve, in spite of the car. Then all three men galloped toward the hay barn, racing in past the startled sheep, and climbed the ladder to the hayloft.

The sheep spilled out into the open like milk drops to meet the man coming up from the paved road. But he took no notice of them. Nor did he seem surprised by the chaotic racing back and forth of bleating sheep in the meadow. He strolled toward the caravan at his leisure.

Only six sheep stood motionless under the dolmen. Maude had resisted the general mood of disaster. She was still concentrating on the wolf man above their heads. He had pressed himself flat against the stone. The onions inside him were churning wildly. He was breathing fast. Maude realized that the master hunter himself was frightened.

The man now beside the caravan didn't kick the door. He knocked. One short knock, two long knocks, another short knock. He waited. Soundlessly, he set to work on the lock. Now the master hunter's heart was beating like a sheep's when it has to swallow its calcium tablet. But he did not move. He *dared* not move. A faint, metallic click chirped in the air like a cricket's cry; but the door stayed shut. Finally the man turned and walked back to the path across the fields.

An engine hummed.

Silence.

7

Sir Ritchfield Behaves Oddly

Other things happened that night too, of course, but they weren't as spectacular as the events around the shepherd's caravan. The man on top of the dolmen disappeared silently, leaving nothing behind but a faint smell of onions. A little later the three other men emerged timidly from the hay barn. In trying to be quiet they made a lot of noise. They set off back to the village in silence.

The sheep watched these comings and goings, and stayed watchful for a while. They stood scattered at random over the meadow like perplexed blue clouds. Othello gave off the aura of a blue-black thundercloud. A gentle breeze softly fanned their fears away, but sleeping was out of the question all the same. They bent their necks and began to graze.

Grazing in the dark was surprisingly pleasant. Nocturnal insects in the grass chirped at them appetizingly, and everything smelled of wet herbs. Why had they let these pleasures escape them until now? It was George's fault. George had insisted that they must spend night after night in that boring hay barn, while the world outside was such an appetizing spectacle. George hadn't had the faintest idea of the art of grazing.

If anyone knew about grazing it was the sheep. Of course there were countless arguments on the subject, but that just made it more interesting. Miss Maple preferred sweet clover and flowers, Cloud liked grasses with dry but tasty seed clusters. Maude was wild about an insipid herb that the sheep called mouse weed. She was sure that it was good for your sense of smell. It was really the other way around: only a sheep with an outstanding sense of smell could even pick out the modest-looking mouse weed from all the tasty herbs that formed a carpet of scents. Sir Ritchfield liked the tempting look of large-leaved plants best, and if he took a mouthful of sorrel with them now and then by mistake, that didn't bother him. Sara hated the bitter flavor of sorrel. Lane loved aromatic, low-growing herbs like sheep's ear and sweet-wort; Cordelia, who didn't much care for bending, ate the tall oat grasses first. Mopple ate everything indiscriminately. When they returned to the other pasture after being away for some time, a mere glance at the fresh trails they left as they ate told you fairly accurately who had been grazing where.

Zora enjoyed this moonlit midnight grazing. It put her in a good mood: excited but philosophical, meditative and active at the same time. The ideal mood for stories. Zora was the only sheep who didn't just like listening to stories, but now and then made some up herself. Not complicated stories, little more than a couple of thoughts strung together. It wasn't so much what happened that mattered, it was how you looked at it. The stories helped Zora to understand how the world galloped around what happened in it. Zora was convinced that her stories were good practice for conquering the abyss beneath the cliff tops. She told herself a Mopple story. Stories about Mopple the Whale were definitely among her favorites. Mopple the

Whale wants to eat the herbs of the abyss, but Mopple the Whale doesn't like heights, thought Zora. It's not easy to concentrate on a story where the main thing is something that *doesn't* happen, but Zora had had a good deal of practice. Mopple was standing close to the top of the cliffs, only a little way from Zora's ledge. Of course he was pretending to be interested in the view. The wind was blowing off the land, so Zora could pick up Mopple's pleasant scent. She concentrated on the wind blowing through Mopple's fleece, sending little white ripples over it, pushing him toward the edge of the cliffs with gentle fingers and making him nervous. In Zora's story the weather was fine, of course. The gulls were crying, of course. Evening was beginning to fall. George was sitting on the steps of the shepherd's caravan smoking his pipe. Unbeknown to George, two tourists were walking along the beach, shouldering the weight of their huge backpacks. One of them spotted Zora on her ledge and pointed her out to the other. Mopple acted as if he had suddenly become fascinated by people with backpacks, and took another tiny step toward the abyss. The rest of the flock were grazing some way off. Othello stopped grazing. He was watching Mopple, obviously amused. Othello is clever, thought the Zora in Zora's story, not as clever as Miss Maple, maybe, but clever all the same. Othello notices everything! Those were Zora's thoughts in her story. She couldn't decide what Othello was thinking. Lane and Cordelia were grazing in the background. And behind Lane, far in the background, stood . . . Zora couldn't believe her eyes. Where the meadow met the paved road, there stood the butcher, smelling of nothing. There was just one eye in his face, in the middle of his forehead, and that eye was bent implacably on Mopple the Whale.

Zora shook her head. This wasn't the kind of story that helped a sheep to conquer the abyss. What was the butcher doing in her uncomplicated little story?

She looked up, and saw that she had emerged from her thoughts at just the right moment, for she was right on the edge of George's Place. High time to move away in a different direction. She looked critically at George's Place. It seemed smaller than before.

Just as she was about to turn, she noticed a sheep standing in the dark on the other side of George's Place, watching her. Normally Zora would have thought no more of it. She was logical about grazing: you had to concentrate and not let every little thing distract you. But something about this sheep looked strange to her. Maybe even slightly threatening. She raised her head, scenting the air, but the wind had veered round and told her nothing. She looked more closely. Curving horns. Sir Ritchfield. Zora was relieved. For a moment she'd been afraid . . . oh, she didn't know what she'd been afraid of. She bleated at Sir Ritchfield in a friendly tone, but he didn't reply. Ritchfield was hard of hearing these days, so she bleated louder.

Ritchfield turned his head and looked toward the dolmen.

"He's gone, hasn't he?" he whispered. Zora was surprised to find how soft Ritchfield's voice could be when he was whispering. Normally he snorted and bellowed, and the older he grew the worse it was. Zora wondered who he meant. The master hunter? George? She felt sure he must have meant George.

"He won't be coming back, will he?" Ritchfield persisted.

"No," said Zora. "He won't be coming back." She felt cold in the moonlit night. She wished for nothing more than to be back in the hay barn, crowding close together with a whole lot of other sheep.

"And that idiot Ritchfield stood by and didn't do anything," said Ritchfield almost cheerfully. Zora stared at him. She suddenly felt that she was looking down into an abyss deeper and wilder than the drop from the cliff tops. She closed her eyes, briefly, and when she opened them again Ritchfield had gone away. Zora peered round and saw him reappear beside the dolmen. She trotted after him.

"What do you mean, stood by?" she whispered to Ritchfield. He looked at her in surprise.

"What?" he bleated.

"What do you mean, stood by?" said Zora in a rather louder whisper.

"Speak up!" bleated Ritchfield.

Zora shook her head and trotted thoughtfully back to her ledge.

A little later Miss Maple in her own turn passed George's Place while she was grazing. Ever since they had put it out of bounds, George's Place had held a mysterious fascination for the sheep. Maple looked up and was about to turn away when she saw something terrible.

"Mopple!" she snorted.

A fresh trail of grazed ground, broad and shameless, led right through the middle of George's Place. At second glance Maple saw that she had done Mopple an injustice. Not all the plants had been eaten. Several nose-tickler flowers, slender and sweet-smelling, had been left standing amid the devastation. They tickled your nose as you ate them; they were among everyone's very favorite plants. It was unthinkable that Mopple had spared them.

Maple could not think which sheep in the flock didn't like

nose-tickler flowers. Oh, wait a minute; she once *had* noticed one who didn't. She tried to remember more clearly, but it was no good. She did not have a memory like Mopple's. If a sheep had grazed George's Place on purpose it was a serious matter. It must mean that the sheep who grazed there didn't want to remember George. It was a kind of insult.

Miss Maple looked around. Nothing striking to be seen. Most of the sheep were rhythmically pulling up grass as they moved over the ground. Miss Maple was no longer hungry, and the grass she had grazed at this unusual time of night felt funny lying in her stomach. She decided to put her mind more closely to solving the murder. But there were some practical things to be done first. She trotted over to the dolmen.

A little later the sheep saw her going toward the hay barn with the Thing in her mouth. She looked pleased and in high spirits.

"What are you doing?" asked Cloud.

"It's about time to think what to do when we've found the murderer," said Miss Maple. She trotted on to the barn door, and Cloud followed. Maple disappeared into the darkness, and when she came out of the hay barn again without the Thing, her eyes were shining.

"There we are!" she said.

The other sheep didn't seem particularly happy.

"She's got my Thing!" bleated Heather.

"Bad!" said Willow, the second most silent sheep in the flock, indulging in an unusual fit of loquacity.

Maple scrutinized her flock. The sheep were looking at her, very few of them in a friendly way. Cloud looked guilty, Heather jealous, Maude worried, and Ritchfield stern. Only Mopple absentmindedly grazed his way past them. Miss Maple

94

sighed. "I don't want the Thing for myself. It's for the humans. Have you ever stopped to think what will happen when we've found the murderer? Do you think lightning will strike him? We need evidence!"

"That's not evidence," bleated Maude. "It's a Thing."

"But maybe it could be evidence," said Maple impatiently. She herself had only a very vague idea of the part that Things could play in convicting the murderer.

"We won't find the murderer!" sighed Lane.

"We know George died of the spade. That's quite enough," said Sir Ritchfield, trying to calm things down.

"Very true!" bleated Maude. The spade was the only part of this murder story she really understood anyway.

"Very true!" bleated the other sheep.

"Let's stop all this investigating!"

"Let's stop all this thinking!"

Miss Maple looked at her flock in amazement. "But there are so many questions to ask," she said. "You collected them your-selves—some of them. Where's Tess? Who is the wolf's ghost? What was God looking for in the meadow? What's going on between Lilly and Kate? Why was Ham here? What does George have to do with drugs? What are drugs anyway? Who is the master hunter? Why was he here? There was a master hunter in our meadow and you don't even want to know why?"

"Right!" bleated Maude. "Just so long as he doesn't come back, that's the main thing." Some of the sheep bleated in agreement. "And if he does I'm sure to pick up his scent again!" added Maude, not without pride.

Mopple grazed past them again, beaming with contentment, living proof of the fact that earthly happiness existed and could be obtained by very simple means. The other sheep looked at him a little enviously.

"See that?" said Sir Ritchfield. "That's the way for sheep to spend their time. Grazing! Not asking questions! We can't find the answers. That was why George threw the detective story away. He realized you can't find out everything. You ought to see that too, Maple!"

Miss Maple impatiently scraped grass and earth up with her hoof. "But it happened," she said. "There must be an end to the story. If George had finished the detective story we would know how it ended. And I want to know. You want to know too, I know you're curious about it. You just don't want to bother your sheepy heads!"

"It's too much for us," said Cordelia, embarrassed. "So many human things that we can't understand. And there's no one to explain words to us now."

The others said nothing. Many of them were looking at the grass in front of their hooves as if they were planning to watch it grow. Others were looking for cloud sheep in the night sky.

"We ought to just forget it," said Cloud quietly. "It will be simpler when we've forgotten everything." Again there were bleats of agreement. Forgetting was a tried-and-true way for sheep to get over their sorrows. The stranger and more disturbing an incident was, the faster you needed to forget it. Why hadn't they thought of that before?

Maple looked at them incredulously.

"But if we forget everything there won't be any more stories," she said. "This is like a story, don't you see?"

No one replied.

"You don't want to!" she said, unable to take it in.

"We want to all right," said Cloud with dignity, "only not in the same way as you."

"Yes, you do," said Maple. "You just don't know it! There's a wolf out there. We don't know who he is, that's all. How are we to beware of him if we can't identify him? We don't even have a shepherd to look after us and you still think all's well with the world!"

They had never seen Miss Maple in such a temper before. Come to think of it, they had never seen Miss Maple in a temper at all.

"You wouldn't even notice if the wolf got into the flock. Do you remember the story of the wolf in sheep's clothing?"

It was the most frightening story they had ever heard George tell. Reminding them of it now, in the middle of the night, wasn't playing fair.

"Either you find the wolf or the wolf will find you. It's as simple as that! All stories have an end! It's no use throwing the book away in the middle of it just because you don't understand something!" Maple snorted. "If you don't want to find out what it is, I'll have to find out by myself!"

Cloud, who didn't like disagreements, looked at her, moist-eyed. "We need a shepherd," she whispered.

But Maple ignored her. She flicked her tail scornfully. Then she trotted off to stand under the crows' tree, as far as possible from the other sheep, and stared thoughtfully into the dark.

"Justice!" she bleated.

Only Othello answered her. "Justice!" he bleated back.

The other sheep looked at one another, downcast. Defiantly, they began grazing again. They wanted to show Miss Maple how wonderful a simple, nonthinking sheep life could be. Only

Othello, still lost in thought, went on bleating to himself. "Justice," he bleated quietly. "Justice!"

"What's justice?"

The winter lamb was there looking at Othello, with his small, shaggy body, his head that was rather too large for it, and his sparkling eyes.

"What's justice?"

It was really better not to get into conversation with the winter lamb, thought Othello. If the lamb opened his mouth it was usually just to make trouble.

"What's justice?"

All the same, Othello liked the winter lamb. He was exactly the kind of sheep who would have put the cruel clown at the circus off his stride.

"Justice . . ." said Othello. The lamb's eyes widened as the black ram spoke. "Justice," repeated the ram. What *was* justice? At the zoo, some of the sheep were taken out of the enclosure for the beasts of prey, although no one talked about it. They weren't the weakest or the most stupid. Just any sheep. That hadn't been justice. And then Lucifer Smithley had bought Othello for his knife-throwing act, because he was exactly what he was, black and dangerous-looking with his four horns. Because you couldn't see blood in the black fleece if Lucifer happened not to throw his knives with the diabolical accuracy proclaimed on his poster. That hadn't been justice either. Then Smithley suffered his stroke. That was justice all right, but afterward Othello was passed on to the cruel clown and his animals, and forced to perform silly tricks in the ring. That was *in*justice! Othello had lost his temper and the clown's ugly dog hadn't survived. *That* had been justice, but the clown had sold Othello to the knacker. Unjust! And the knacker took him to the dogfights. Unjust! Unjust! Unjust!

Othello snorted, and the winter lamb looked warily up at him. *Think of the snail's slimy trail in the grass, think of the time ahead of you,* warned the voice. The ram pulled himself together.

"Justice is when you can trot where you like and graze where you want. When you can fight to go your own way. When no one steals your way from you. That's justice!" Suddenly Othello felt very sure of himself.

The winter lamb cocked his overlarge head. Either derision or respect played around his nostrils.

"And they stole George's way?" he asked.

Othello nodded. "His way to Europe."

"But perhaps George wanted to steal someone else's way, and they fought. That would have been justice!"

Othello was surprised to find how well the winter lamb understood him.

"George would never have stolen someone else's way," he said.

"But suppose he did after all," said the winter lamb. "Perhaps he couldn't help it. Sometimes you have to steal because no one wants to give you anything. Who's to blame if no one wants to give you anything?"

"God is!" said Othello without even stopping to think about it.

"The long-nosed man? Why?" asked the winter lamb.

But Othello had trotted back into the past and didn't hear him. He was looking through fences, through more and more fences. And snowflakes. The first snow Othello had ever seen. But instead he had to trot after the clown to steal a handkerchief from his pocket. The clown stumbled, and the children in their warm caps and jackets laughed.

The kick the clown gave him when he finally got to his feet was not faked.

"Why does the sheep have to work at Christmas?" a child's voice asked. "It's unjust!"

A woman laughed. "Of course it's just. God made animals to serve human beings. That's the way it is."

Othello snorted angrily. That's the way it was! The winter lamb standing beside him snorted too, a comical imitation of his own anger. Then the lamb kicked up his heels cheekily and ran away over the meadow, leaping like a goat.

The horizon was rosy as a March lamb's muzzle now. Looking toward the village, Othello froze as he saw the black silhouette of a sheep. A few moments later other sheep appeared against the morning sky. And among the sheep, tall and clearly visible, was a figure wearing a slouch hat. Gabriel the shepherd was driving his flock toward their meadow.

8

No One Answers Zora

A white butterfly, a milk dancer, a piece of wind silk flew by. Silk was made from caterpillars, huge flocks of little crawling worms. Humans boiled the worms and stole their skin, sheep were shorn. Humans didn't mind whether they covered their own bare skin with worm juice or wool, so long as it was white, so long as it kept them warm. They all wanted to be as white as lambs, but they couldn't bear it, they came out in colors, they stank. They were still naked, though, that was the secret, the naked secret. Human beings stood naked before Things, delivered up to Things, betrayed by and betraying Things.

What had it been this time? A spade, wasn't that it? The memory made him shake—with laughter. A singeing sadness crept up his left hind hoof.

It was a fine day, and he was drowning in green. The fluttering white scrap above him had no chance against the green. The fragrant air wafted around him, the air singer willingly sank down. Green stretched all the way to the horizon. Green was the song of unreason. It grew without sense or understanding, urging all creatures to do the same. And they did. Green was the most beautiful commandment in the world.

Quietly, another voice had appeared on the horizon: the little red voice sang its way through the madness of the world. Only a fool would have ignored it. He straightened up, puffing for breath, and peered through the tall grass. The crow on his back flew up in the air.

A woman was coming down the road. She was concealed by a straw hat with a very broad brim that threw a sharp shadow right down to her neck, but she must be a young woman. She was carrying a suitcase with ease. Only a very young woman would have dared to wear such a red dress, red as the heart's blood from her shoulders to her calves. A fresh, strong scent went ahead of her, darkened by earth and healthy sweat. A scent to fall in love with.

She stopped and put her case down in the middle of the road. That wasn't clever. A car could suddenly come out of the green nowhere and splash her dress over the tarmac. He didn't run the risk of going on roads himself, but the woman was not bothered. She was tall and stood well above the green. Reason and fire. The grass would bow to her. She mopped her cheeks with a scarf wound around her right wrist. When she looked up at the sky, he saw her face. Only for a moment, before the sharp shadow fell over her eyes and nose in the direction of the red dress. She leaned down and took a road map out of her case. A stranger then, not someone coming home. Or could you come home to a strange place? Could you come home at all? She belonged here, mistress of the green. But what would the pale people say? The pale people sitting in the village, chopping up their memories?

She swore very well, like a drover. Then she laughed, a strange laugh. Penetrating as a bleat.

The woman picked up her case again with a vigorous movement. You could tell she had put it down to think, and not because she needed a rest. Then, unexpectedly, she left the road.

She almost found him in the tall grass. Fancy leaving the tarmac without fluttering her eyelashes or rolling her eyes! Most humans hesitate before stepping off their roads. They're suspicious, their feet are tender, as if the ground were full of holes to make them stumble, and their first steps are like walking through mud. The woman had left the road decisively, like a sheep following her nose. She was still following her nose now, clever as a sheep as she made her way toward the village. She hadn't let the road lead her astray. She'd make the pale people dance, swinging their spades in a big circle. Something to look forward to.

The sheep had always been sure that Gabriel must be an excellent shepherd, if only because of his clothes: in winter and summer alike he wore a cape of undyed sheep's wool. Some even said it was unwashed sheep's wool. Gabriel smelled as much like a sheep as a human can. Specially in wet weather.

Gabriel knew how to pay a sheep compliments. Not with words, as George sometimes did (though not often enough), but just by looking at the sheep with his blue eyes and never once blinking. That sort of thing tickled a sheep's soul and made it go weak at the knees.

The sheep had great expectations of Gabriel's abilities as a shepherd.

Not much had happened yet, however. Gabriel's dogs had briefly herded them together, and Gabriel had counted them without a single sound. Gabriel's dogs never barked. Ever. They just stared at the sheep, which was enough to make cold wolf fears chase up from their hoofs to the marrow of their bones.

Gabriel was standing outside the shepherd's caravan, as silent as the dolmen. His blue eyes looked at every single sheep, one by one, as if he wanted to find out something. Almost imperceptibly, he nodded his head once at every sheep. Most of the sheep were sure that it had been an appreciative nod. Gabriel had inspected them and approved of them. It was exciting. They were a little proud—until Othello ruined their good mood.

"He was counting us," he puffed in annoyance, "just counting us, that's all."

Unlike the rest of his flock, Othello had not been pleased to see the new shepherd. He stood apart from the others, thinking dark thoughts.

An old anger sparkled in Othello's eyes. He recognized an animal tamer at once: the same few gestures, the same boredom in the eyes. The same malice behind that deceptive friendliness. The cruel clown had been a tamer too, using sugar and hunger and stealthy torment. He had implanted anger in Othello, and Othello was surprised to find that anger still so fresh and intact after all this time.

But he would no longer give way to the anger just like that. He had learned to control his anger with patience.

It was the day when the clown didn't close the shed door straightaway but instead bent over the box of props, turning his behind to Othello. Hungrily, Othello put his nose in the hay, but his eyes never left the clown's behind for a moment.

He forgot the hay.

He lowered his horns.

At that moment he heard the voice for the first time. A strangely dark, soft voice which had many things hidden in it.

"Careful, black ram," said the voice behind him. "Your anger's already lowered its horns, you're seeing red, and if you don't watch out your anger will gallop away from you."

Othello didn't even turn round. "So?" he snorted. "So what? Why shouldn't it? He deserves it."

A crow fluttered past outside the window.

"But you don't deserve it," mocked the voice. "Who do you think you're turning your anger on? Not him, the man who grazes on fear, who drives terror into people. Your anger's turned on yourself, and once it charges you, you won't be able to stand up to it."

Othello merely snorted.

He kept his horns lowered and his eyes fixed on the clown.

But he didn't charge.

"So what?" he snorted again.

The voice did not reply.

Othello turned. A gray ram with mighty horns stood behind him. A ram in the prime of life, all muscles and sinews and grace of movement under the thick fleece. His amber eyes sparkled with goblin light in the dark stable. Feeling awkward, Othello looked away.

The clown emerged from the property box, slammed the stable door, and walked off. The world spun under Othello's feet in his disappointment. The strange ram nuzzled him. He smelled peculiar, of a great many things that Othello couldn't understand.

"There now," the gray ram murmured in his ear, "head like a drop of water on a branch, right? If your anger had galloped away he'd have known you, he'd have seen over your horns into your eyes, into your heart. This way he knows nothing. Everything he doesn't know is to your advantage. *Find their weak points.* The old game." Suddenly the ram looked amused.

Othello twitched his ears to get rid of all these words buzzing round him in the dark. But the gray ram gave him no time to get his breath back.

"Forget your anger," said the ram now. "Think of the snail's slimy trail in the grass, think of the time ahead of you."

"But I am angry!" said Othello, just for something to say.

"Then fight!" said the ram.

"How can I fight when he keeps me locked up?" snorted

Othello. Now that he had Othello's interest, the ram turned as monosyllabic as a mother ewe in a bad mood. "Nothing helps!"

"*Thinking will help*," said the ram.

"I do think," said Othello. "I think day and night." It wasn't quite true, because at night he usually fell asleep in a corner of the stable.

"Then you're thinking of the wrong thing!" said the ram, unimpressed. Othello said nothing.

"What do you think of?" asked the gray ram.

"Hay," admitted Othello in a small voice.

As he had expected, the ram shook his head disapprovingly. "Think of the way a mole's coat shines, think of the sound the wind makes in the bushes and the feeling in your stomach when you trot down a slope. Think of the way the path smells ahead of you, think of the freedom the wind is blowing your way. But never think of hay again."

Othello looked at the gray ram. His stomach felt peculiar, but not with hunger.

"Or if you want to keep it simple," said the gray ram, "think of me."

Othello thought of the gray ram, and his anger retreated behind his four horns where it belonged. The sheep in his flock were still looking at him with surprise.

"Gabriel was counting us," he told them grumpily. "He was only counting us."

Now that Othello said it, they thought so too, and they were disappointed. But their mood soon improved. If even being counted by Gabriel was such a friendly, mysterious process, they could imagine how exciting the really important things would turn out to be—things like his filling the hayrack, spreading straw, and feeding them mangel-wurzels. Most of all, they couldn't wait to find out what Gabriel would read aloud to them.

"Poetry," sighed Cordelia. They didn't know exactly what poetry was, but it must be beautiful, because Pamela in the novels often had men reading poetry aloud to her in the moonlight, and George, who never had a good word to say about Pamela herself, would stop being so angry and sigh.

"Or something about clover," said Mopple hopefully.

"About the sea and the sky and fearlessness," said Zora.

"Not about the diseases of sheep, anyway," said Heather. "What do you think, Othello?"

Othello said nothing.

"He'll read in a good loud voice, loud and clear, just the way it should be," said Sir Ritchfield.

"He'll explain lots of new words to us," said Cordelia.

They were getting more and more curious. What in the world *would* Gabriel read to them? They could hardly wait for the afternoon reading time to come.

"Why don't we ask *them*?" suggested Cloud. She meant the other sheep, Gabriel's own flock. Gabriel's dogs had herded them together at one side of the meadow, and Gabriel was busy putting a wire fence round them. George's sheep weren't sure what to think, because it made their meadow quite a bit smaller.

"Just where the mouse weed grows," grumbled Maude. The others didn't mind about the mouse weed. It was the general principle that bothered them.

On the other hand, they were glad that Gabriel's sheep wouldn't be running around with them, because they found them rather weird. Short legs, long backs, long and humorless noses, restless eyes, and peculiarly pale coloring. They didn't smell good either. Not unhealthy but nervous and lifeless. The oddest thing about them was that they had almost no fleece, just a curly, dense down on their skin. Yet you could see they hadn't been shorn recently. Why did Gabriel have sheep that didn't grow wool? What was the use of them?

How happy Gabriel must be now he had such a woolly flock as themselves at last. Soon he would send the other sheep away. Until then, they agreed, the best way of getting along with Gabriel's sheep was to ignore them. But now they were tormented by curiosity.

"I'd go and ask what he reads them," said Maude, "only my nostrils itch when I get too close to them."

They looked at Sir Ritchfield. As lead ram he could be expected to make contact with the strange flock. But Ritchfield shook his head. "Patience!" he snorted.

Mopple didn't dare, Othello suddenly seemed to have lost all interest in literature, and the other sheep were too proud to speak to the fleeceless flock.

Finally Zora volunteered. She had done a great deal of thinking on her rocky ledge, and believed that pride, however well justified, shouldn't prevent sheep from finding out as much as possible about the world. When Gabriel was busy with a roll of wire netting behind the caravan, she trotted off.

Gabriel's sheep were grazing. The first thing Zora noticed about them was how close together they kept, side by side, shoulder to shoulder. It seemed uncomfortable, grazing in such a cramped space. No one took any notice of Zora, although her scent must have reached them long before she did. She stopped just beyond the flock and waited politely for someone to speak to her. One or another of the sheep sometimes raised its head and looked nervously in all directions, but its eyes passed straight through Zora as if she were invisible. Zora watched them for a while in surprise. Then she lost patience and bleated loudly.

Their muzzles stopped grazing, their necks rose. Countless pale eyes stared at her. Zora was used to looking into an abyss. She stood in front of them as if she were standing in a cold wind, and faced them down.

Perhaps it was a test to see how brave she was. Zora waggled her ears briskly and playfully pulled up a few blades of grass. Nothing happened.

At the other side of the flock, a few of the sheep lowered their heads again, and a monotonous munching sound told her that they had gone back to grazing. But most of their eyes were still bent on Zora. She had to admit those eyes made her uneasy. There was a flickering light in them, the kind that sometimes played across the sky on days when the weather was very bad. On such days a sheep could hardly think clearly at all.

It was obvious to her that nothing was going to come of the other sheep. If anything was to happen here, then she, Zora, must make it happen. She took a glance back at her own flock, whose heads were turned her way. For a moment it seemed as if even her own sheep were looking at her oddly. But then she realized that wasn't true: Sir Ritchfield was standing on the hill, looking stern and attentive; Cloud, Maude, Lane, and Cordelia had crowded together and were watching her expectantly. A little ahead of them stood Mopple, looking hard in her direction. Zora knew that at this distance he couldn't make out much more of her than a black-and-white blur. She was moved. Suddenly it didn't seem difficult to speak to these strange sheep.

"Hello," she called. She decided to try some harmless subject. "Do you like the grass around here?" she asked. It occurred to her, too late, that this might be taken badly, as alluding to the fact that they were tucking into other people's grazing.

"The weather's not bad either," said Zora. The sky was gray and warm, the air refreshingly moist, and the meadow fragrant.

The strange sheep said nothing. A few of the heads that had been lowered to graze rose again. Perhaps they didn't care for idle chitchat. Who could say what intellectual books Gabriel might have read aloud to them?

"We could talk about how you get into the sky," suggested Zora. Gabriel's sheep did not respond. "I mean, it must be possible somehow," Zora said. "We can see the cloud sheep in the sky, after all. But how do you get there? Is there a place where you can just climb into the sky? Or do you just carry on grazing straight up into the air?" Zora looked at the sheep intently. Nothing. Or yes, a slight change. The unsettling flicker in the sheep's pale eyes was stronger now. "All right, I don't mind what *you* think about it. To be honest, I'm just about sure it's connected with conquering the abyss. But I certainly didn't come here to discuss that with you!" She decided to be straightforward. "It's about Gabriel. He's been your shepherd for a long time. We want to know what he reads aloud to you."

The sheep stared at her. Didn't they understand? That was impossible. No sheep could be so stupid. Zora snorted.

"Your shepherd, understand? Gabriel! Gabriel!" She turned her head briefly his way, and saw that he had almost finished getting the next roll of wire netting ready. Time to be off.

She turned to look at Gabriel's flock again, and saw that still nothing had changed.

A strange ram was standing right opposite Zora, only a few steps away. She cast him a last furious glance—and stopped. She saw that the strange sheep weren't so small after all. Rather short in the legs, yes, but long in the body and heavily built. The ram opposite her made a very powerful impression that reminded Zora of the butcher. She had meant to say something sarcastic and scornful by way of good-bye, but now she thought it would be better to get out, fast. The ram looked at her, and it seemed to Zora that the strange flickering had gone from his eyes. For the first time she felt that he was really *looking* at her. The ram slowly and almost imperceptibly shook his head.

Zora turned and galloped straight back to her rocky ledge.

Gabriel finished the fence around midday. He sat down on the steps of the shepherd's caravan, where George always sat to smoke a pipe. The fine tobacco fumes rose to the sheep's noses in a strange way. Behind the veil of smoke the real Gabriel was hidden, in a place where no sheep could pick up his scent. Even Maude had to admit that she could tell very little about Gabriel himself beneath those aromas of sheep's wool and tobacco.

The middle of the day was more peaceful than they'd known it in a long time. The mild sun, half covered by hazy clouds, was part of it, and so were the magnificent view of a spotlessly blue sea and the humming of the insects. But the best part was relief at knowing such an efficient shepherd was sitting on the caravan steps. And looking forward to Gabriel's stories when twilight fell.

When the man on the bicycle raced toward them, however, the peace and quiet were suddenly gone. The sheep didn't trust bicycles. They withdrew to the hill for safety's sake. But the man on the bike wasn't after them. He was making straight for Gabriel.

Once they were at a safe distance, the sheep calmed down slightly, and turned their nervous ears toward the shepherd's caravan. They recognized him as soon as he got off his bicycle and stood right in front of Gabriel. He had come with Lilly, Ham, and Gabriel and was the first human to examine George's body: Josh, the tall, thin man who had pressed his nose against the windows of the shepherd's caravan last night. He had the scent of alcohol on his fingers, and he also smelled of soapy water and unwashed feet. His aura was slightly rancid. Mopple hid behind the dolmen and peered anxiously out between the stones.

Braver sheep like Othello, Cloud, and Zora, feeling curious, trotted closer.

"Josh," said Gabriel, without taking his pipe out of his mouth. His blue eyes were fixed on the thin man. The sheep knew how he must be feeling at this moment. There would be a flattered expression on his face, and he'd be a little weak at the knees.

The thin man rummaged around nervously in his jacket pocket, found a key, and held it out to Gabriel.

"It's from Kate. She just found it in a packet of oatcakes, would you believe it?" said the thin man with a laugh. The sheep understood why he was so nervous. He had probably eaten the oatcakes.

"Kate thinks it must be in the caravan," said the thin man. "Because it's certainly not in the house."

"Right," said Gabriel. He took the key and put it down carelessly on the top step of the caravan.

"Gabriel?" asked the thin man. A magpie flew curiously over the roof of the shepherd's caravan. "Suppose we don't find it, then what?"

"So long as nobody else finds it either . . ." said Gabriel. His blue eyes were searching the blue sea while clouds of smoke wafted out of his mouth.

"Do you know what they're saying, Gabriel?"

Gabriel looked as if he didn't know and didn't want to. All the same, the thin man went on. "They're saying it's not in the caravan at all. They say it's all in the will."

"Then if that's right we'll find out on Sunday," said Gabriel.

The thin man made a nervous sound. Then he hunched his head down between his shoulders and walked back to the bicycle. After about three steps Gabriel called him back.

"By the way, Josh."

"Yes, Gabriel?"

"There's been enough nonsense going on around here, see? You want to make sure it stops. Now."

"Nonsense? How d'you mean, Gabriel?" Josh sounded alarmed.

"Well, like midnight expeditions to George's caravan, for instance. What's the idea? You'll only scare the sheep."

Cloud was touched. Even now Gabriel was thinking of them.

Josh didn't seem to want to discuss last night. "What sort of sheep are those anyway?" asked the pub landlord, looking critically at Gabriel's sheep and speaking very fast. "They look odd, they do. I never saw sheep like that before."

"A new meat breed," said Gabriel out of the corner of his mouth. His blue eyes were fixed on Josh. The two men said no more for quite a time.

Then Josh sighed. "You really know everything, right?"

Gabriel said something in Gaelic. The sheep wondered if he had a second tongue in his mouth for speaking that language.

"It couldn't be helped," said Josh. "Tom and Harry would have gone anyway, the idiots that they are. Find the grass, avoid scandal, keep the tourist trade going, same old story. As if *that* was it . . . They've no idea, that they haven't. So I thought I'd better be there than not, see what I mean? I gave them a wrong key so they wouldn't bring any tools, but they'd be sure not to get in."

Gabriel nodded understandingly, and Josh was obviously relieved. Talking seemed to come more easily to him now.

"You know something, though?" he said. "We wasn't the only ones. There was someone else around. A stranger. One of the drugs people, if you ask me. So there's something going on. If *they* find it before we do . . ."

The magpie flew back over Gabriel and Josh. Of course there was no saying whether or not it was the same magpie, but it described an elegant curve and landed on the roof of the caravan, chattering.

"They won't find it," said Gabriel. "They don't know anything about the cassette. They're just after their stuff. Anyway, I'm here now. You want to get the folks in the pub to calm down."

Josh nodded enthusiastically. The sheep knew just how he felt. It was his pleasure to do Gabriel a favor.

"Gabriel?" Josh had been on his way again but turned back once more.

Gabriel shifted his pipe from the right to the left corner of his mouth and looked inquiringly at Josh.

"You fixed all this really good." He waved his hand in a gesture taking in Gabriel, the shepherd's caravan, the sheep, and the whole meadow.

Gabriel nodded. "The sheep need a bit of looking after, at least until the will is read. They were really grateful to me in the management office—animal welfare, hygiene regulations, and that. And I'm saving on grazing for my own." He smiled an engaging smile. "And of course I can sit here," he added, slapping the steps of the caravan with his hand, "just as long as I like."

Josh grinned with relief. He nodded good-bye to Gabriel, mounted his bike, and clattered away in the direction of the village.

As soon as Josh had disappeared round the bend in the path across the fields, Gabriel's brown hand came down on the top step of the caravan. But it felt around in vain. The key was no longer there. It was clinking and shining at Gabriel from high up on the roof of the shepherd's caravan, in a magpie's beak.

In Gabriel's care, the sheep were more ambitious than they had been for a long time. They grazed conscientiously, taking long, straight steps, they craned their necks gracefully, they felt they were being "good doers," and even ate the dry, less-tasty grass with pleasure. When they rested in the shade of the old hay barn they held their heads high and watched Gabriel out of the corners of their eyes. Gabriel was running after a magpie, like a lamb frolicking in high spirits, chasing from bush to tree, from tree to shrub, back and forth all across the meadow . . .

9

Miss Maple Investigates

"Glendalough, for instance," said the strange woman. "This saint goes off there to live alone and be a hermit, and the moment people find out about it he can hardly move for pilgrims. The most popular place of pilgrimage in the Middle Ages, and why? Because human beings are herd animals. You have to make them believe everyone's coming here, and if they believe it, then everyone *will* come here. It's that simple." She took a bite of her buttered scone and smiled at the same time. Her dress was as red as autumn berries.

A whole basketful of buttered scones lay in front of her, neatly covered with a napkin to keep the flies away, but the sheep could smell them all the same. The woman dipped her scone first in softly whipped cream, then in red jam. She poured tea from a teapot into a plastic cup, added two brown sugar cubes, and then some more cream. The scones, jam, tea, sugar, and cream were set out on a huge, brightly checked picnic tablecloth. There was also a bottle of orange juice, some cream cheese, biscuits, toast, a little pot of mayonnaise, and a bowl of tomato salad with chopped parsley. The cloth itself covered a small part of the sheep's meadow close to the cliff tops, luckily spread over a place where the interesting plants had already been grazed. The bright colors alarmed the sheep. They were nervous anyway because after his summery dance with the magpie, Gabriel had left them to their own devices.

Aromas that they had never guessed at wafted over the meadow and tempted their nostrils. They kept a safe distance, but they squinted with undisguised greed at the basketful of scones and the tomato salad.

Beside the cloth sat Bible-thumping Beth, a black picture of uneasiness with slender wrists and a tidy hairdo, trying to make her full skirt take up as little space as possible. She wasn't eating anything, but sometimes her hand moved to her breast and closed around a small, glittering object there. When she did that the pot of mayonnaise wobbled.

"Belief," she sighed now. "Belief is never easy."

"Not your own belief, no. Other people's beliefs are—very easy." The strange woman laughed. Her second scone received its baptism of cream. "Do help yourself!" she said.

Beth silently shook her head. Her eyes wandered to the dolmen.

"You really ought to have some," said the woman. "They're good. You don't look as if you eat much usually," she added, glancing at Beth's thin, hairy arms.

"No," said Beth firmly, "I don't eat much usually. I live next door to a takeaway. If you see people stuffing themselves sense-less instead of thinking about the salvation of their souls, it spoils your appetite."

Unimpressed, the woman bit into her scone with relish.

"Do you know the really strange thing?" she went on a little indistinctly, because she hadn't finished chewing her scone yet. "Do you know just *when* people will believe everyone's coming here? When you persuade them it's an isolated place! That convinces them. Everyone's after isolation. If a place is isolated, crowds of people just have to come rushing to enjoy it."

Beth stared blankly straight ahead. The little pot of mayonnaise wobbled. Maude was thinking how unpleasant Beth smelled, both sour and sweetish. She smelled of long starvation and early death. She was spoiling Maude's pleasure in the aromas rising from the bright check tablecloth.

"I really don't understand why you're worried, though." It didn't seem to bother the red woman that Beth smelled nasty and was silent. "It's absolutely dreamy here. Anyone would feel good in this place."

"I don't," said Beth. "No one from Glennkill would feel good. Terrible things have happened here. I shouldn't just say so, I ought to convince you of it. But I do say so all the same. I'm not going to be intimidated anymore. The Lord is with me."

"Terrible things?" asked the woman, unfazed. "All the better! People just love terrible things. A saint tortured by heathens? Great! A heathen chucked into the sea by saints? Even better! When it comes to crime, you can hardly go wrong in the tourist trade."

The red woman had no problem with words. Cordelia listened to her admiringly: this woman was full of stories.

Beth swallowed. It sounded like a suppressed giggle, but anyone looking into Beth's face could guess that it must have been a desperately concealed sob.

The woman noticed, and turned serious. "You mean the murder? I'm so sorry, I didn't know it happened here." She put her half-eaten scone back on the picnic cloth.

"It did happen here," said Beth in a graveyard voice. The little pot of mayonnaise wobbled yet again.

"Was he a relation of yours? A boyfriend?" The red woman's voice sounded gentle now.

Beth shook herself. "Not a relation. Certainly not a boyfriend—he'd have laughed at the mere idea. He always laughed at me. But we were at the village school here together. It was a terrible death, a heathen death."

"I've read about it in the paper," said the red woman thoughtfully. "With a spade. Not nice. But you really don't have to worry that it'll make any difference to the tourists. Although an arrest would be a good thing, of course. Do they have a suspect yet?"

The red woman reached for the tomato salad. A soundless sigh went through the flock of sheep. They were more interested in the tomato salad than any of the other things on the picnic cloth. They had hoped the woman would overeat on scones and leave the tomato salad behind ungrazed. At present the outlook was not hopeful.

"Some say it was about money or drugs or even worse." Beth flushed red. "But that's not the worst of it. The worst of it is, there's someone going around here in Glennkill . . ." Her voice rose to a higher register, so that she didn't really sound like Beth anymore. The sheep jumped and twitched their ears nervously. "A human being like anyone else on the outside but a wild beast inside, eaten away by such sickness of the soul, such Godlessness, such despair . . ."

Beth stared into the eyes of the stranger, who held her gaze unflinchingly for a moment. Then the strange woman stuck her fork into the bowl of tomato salad and brought out a tiny whole tomato. The sheep had never seen such small tomatoes. Even the stunted tomatoes in George's vegetable plot (George had never been particularly successful with tomatoes) were giants by comparison. But they had an aroma just like a big tomato, a delicious aroma—and they were disappearing rapidly between the red woman's immaculate teeth.

Now that Beth had started to talk, there was no stopping her.

"You see, it's not an ordinary, logical sort of murder. Not the kind you see on TV, where it's all about money or power. I can just feel it. I distribute tracts, you see, wonderful writings about the Gospel, and if you do that long enough you get a feeling for what people are like. You may laugh at me, but I have that feeling."

Beth's voice, which didn't sound at all like Beth's voice anymore, trembled. But the woman's hand didn't as she raised her fork to her mouth, with *two* little tomatoes on it.

"I could tell you such things . . . this murder is to do with souls, I can say that much. It's a matter of guilt. Whoever did it knew what's right and what's wrong, but wasn't strong enough to do the right thing. It's so terrible when you don't have the strength to do the right thing, you feel like cutting your own weakness out of yourself with a knife. A knife . . . But the weakness is still there, and a time comes when you don't see any option but to destroy what's strong. Destroying what you can't achieve—that's the worst of human sins. God be with me."

Beth had spoken directly to the heavens, with her head raised as if she had entirely forgotten the red woman. But now the two of them were looking at each other again. The woman's eyes had narrowed; a fork with two more baby tomatoes was hovering in front of her red lips, forgotten. Beth's eyes were round and wide as a child's and she was smiling sadly. For a second the sheep forgot the tomatoes too. They had never seen Beth smile before. She looked pretty—or better than usual, anyway.

120

"I can imagine that seems strange to you, but I do have a feeling for these things."

The red woman shook her head. She was going to say something, but Beth didn't let her get a word in edgewise. A Beth who wouldn't let someone else get a word in edgewise was something entirely new.

"You see, I spoke to the police. I was the only one who did too. Imagine that: a whole village, and I'm the only one to ask the police about it. We'll all stifle in the silence here." Beth took a deep breath. "Well then, the police say George was poisoned first. He fell asleep peacefully. Then came the spade. When he was already dead, you understand? The question is why, and the CID from town probably don't think anything much of that. But I've been going from door to door with my pamphlets for years. I know what heathens the people here are at heart."

Two red lips closed round two equally red tomatoes.

"There's an old superstition, you know. If someone dies, you shouldn't come too close to the body for the first hour. They say the hounds of the Devil are on watch, waiting to swallow the dead person's soul. And George's soul belonged to the Devil, oh dear, yes! Can you imagine what horror that lost soul must have felt beside the body, with the spade? Can you guess what it takes to overcome that horror? You say the murder won't affect the tourist trade. But I can feel that Glennkill won't be able to live again until the black sheep has finally left our flock."

Beth rose abruptly, with surprisingly flowing movements. Othello gave her a nasty look. Once on her two hind legs, Beth lost that little touch of elegance as quickly as it had come.

"Well, if you have any questions—about the tourist openings,

I mean—then please come to the parish office. Open daily from ten to twelve, nine to twelve on Wednesdays."

She was going to turn, but the red woman gently took her by the sleeve. Her eyes were still narrowed.

"And suppose I have questions about George?" she whispered, looking up at Beth. In a deep voice. A husky, beautiful voice. A voice for reading aloud in.

Beth froze. Once again her eyes searched the spotlessly blue sky. When she finally looked down at the woman there was the hint of a smile on her lips.

"In that case," she whispered, "come and see me this evening. The blue house opposite the church. The takeaway is at the front. I live at the back."

Beth turned, and was soon only a sharply outlined black silhouette getting smaller and smaller against the background of the afternoon sky. The red woman, motionless, watched her go. The last tomato lay forgotten in the salad bowl.

Othello had got the last tomato. He stood there dreamily, watching the strange woman pack away all the rest of the fodder in her basket and stroll thoughtfully along the cliff tops toward the village. Envious sheep faces surrounded him. How did Othello always know what to do? Who had taught him to get on with humans so well? How did he know simply to stand there in front of the woman, not pushy but not shy, just as she was going to put the salad bowl back in the basket? The woman had laughed in her kind, husky, George-like way, and held the bowl out to Othello. And Othello had eaten the last baby tomato at his leisure.

Now the sheep were in a bad mood. None of them would have dared to do what Othello did, particularly with a woman who was a complete stranger, but they all begrudged him that tomato. Only Miss Maple was looking reflective. She even grazed her way right past an excellent patch of clover, which showed just how deep in thought she was.

"She's not stupid," murmured Miss Maple, more to herself than to any of the other sheep. "Beth's not stupid. She thinks too much of souls and not enough of human beings, but she's not stupid."

"The red woman isn't stupid either," said Othello, almost a touch too proudly.

"Oh no." Miss Maple nodded. "The red woman isn't a bit stupid."

"I'd never have expected George to have a child," said Maude. "You did smell it, didn't you?" Several sheep had now joined the interesting conversation between Maple, Othello, and Maude. They nodded. The family scent. Sweat and skin and hair. Unmistakably George's daughter.

"We don't know what it means," said Cordelia. To sheep, the identity of the ram who sired them is of no importance, but who knew if it was the same with human beings? There had been a father in one of the Pamela novels who locked up his daughter so that she couldn't run off with some baron.

"That apple-pie Pamela isn't her mother, anyway," said Cloud. Once again they looked at each other, baffled. What did it mean? And was it important?

"She did say something important," Miss Maple went on. "She's like George: she says important things in ways that a sheep can understand. She said humans are herd animals. I think she's quite right."

Miss Maple had forgotten all about grazing now and was trotting up and down, concentrating hard.

"They all live in the same place, in the village. They come to see the spade together. They're herd animals, like us, we're a flock. But why . . ."

Miss Maple stopped trotting.

"Why does it seem so new to us? Why didn't we know that humans are herd animals? The answer's simple!"

Miss Maple looked keenly at the sheep around her. From their expressions she could tell that the answer wasn't simple enough. But just as she was about to go on, Sir Ritchfield bleated excitedly.

"He left the flock! George left the flock!"

Miss Maple nodded.

"Yes," she said, "George must have left the human herd. He never belonged to their flock. Or perhaps he was chased away. He was always angry with the people in the village, we all know that. Perhaps his death is a *punishment* for leaving the flock."

The sheep were silent with horror. It seemed terrible to think of their shepherd leaving the flock.

"But the Devil's hounds!" whispered Cordelia. "He didn't deserve that."

Lane shuddered. "They must be terrible hounds if even humans are afraid of them. Perhaps the wolf's ghost was really one of the Devil's hounds."

Despite the sunny weather in the meadow, the thought of the wolf's ghost sent a misty fear creeping through the fleeces of all the sheep. They instinctively moved closer together. Cloud began bleating anxiously.

Only Maude made a mocking face. "The Devil's hounds don't necessarily have to be *big*," she said. "Not when you stop to think how small human souls are. No higher than a sheep's knee, I'd say—at the most. Even a very small dog could cope with them."

The sheep thought about the smallest dog they had ever seen. It was about the size of a large turnip, with a golden coat and a flat nose, and it had yapped at them from a woman tourist's arms. Was *that* what the Devil's hounds looked like? Or the wolf's ghost? They didn't have to feel afraid of dogs like that.

Miss Maple shook her head impatiently.

"The important part is that human beings *think* they have large souls," she said. "Beth was right. Humans have to think of the Devil's hounds as big and terrible. So why weren't they too frightened to stick that spade into George?"

The sheep considered this question and came to no conclusion.

Maple went on thinking out loud. "We know why no one heard George's screams. It was because he didn't scream. He was already dead when someone stuck the spade into him. That's why there was so little blood on the meadow."

The sheep were amazed. Now that Miss Maple said it, it was as clear as a pool of clean water in front of them.

Miss Maple flapped her ears to shoo away a few flies. "But that doesn't explain anything. Why would someone stick a spade in George when he's already dead?"

An awkward silence. How could a sheep find the answer to such a difficult question? Miss Maple was not discouraged. She trotted briskly back and forth again.

"Of course there are more possibilities now. Perhaps there are two different murderers—one who poisoned George, and another who *thought* he'd kill George with the spade. Or the spade was there to cover up for the real murder. But if you ask me," said Miss Maple, stopping to nibble a few daisies, "the spade looks like a stupid trick. Like something a couple of lambs might think up together. Perhaps the murderer was brave enough to use the spade because someone else was with him."

Later, when the other sheep had scattered and were grazing in the meadow, the lamb who as yet had no name stood rooted to the spot where they had conducted this conversation. Snuggling safely into Cloud's soft fleece, he had heard it all. At first it had been mostly the warmth he was after. But deep in Cloud's wool, he had begun to tremble. He wished he was brave enough to speak up again in front of all those old, experienced sheep. But would they have believed him? Would they even have listened to him? In the end he didn't dare.

He had wanted to tell them it was all wrong. He'd wanted to say that Miss Maple, the cleverest sheep in Glennkill and perhaps the whole world, had made a terrible mistake.

Because the wolf's ghost wasn't golden. The wolf's ghost was shaggy and gray. The lamb knew that they mustn't forget the wolf's ghost, because it was still out hunting through the wild hills beyond the meadow. In the evening, when the moon had risen but the sky hadn't yet turned pale, and everything gave off its deepest, truest scent, you could feel it, the way you could feel darkness, even with your eyes closed. The lamb thought how the wolf's ghost had spread its black wings on the dolmen, and heard its hoarse cry for the second time.

The other sheep grazed peacefully around him.

But anyone looking more closely could see that the peaceful atmosphere of the meadow was deceptive, and that slowly but surely a small group of daring sheep was assembling behind the shepherd's caravan, where Ritchfield couldn't see them.

These sheep were thinking of leaving the flock.

It was Miss Maple's idea.

She was absolutely determined to get into the village that evening and eavesdrop on the conversation between Beth and the red woman. But not alone—she didn't dare do that again. So she had summoned the bravest sheep in the flock: Zora and Othello, Lane who thought more pragmatically than any other sheep, Cloud because they always grazed together anyway, and Mopple the memory sheep.

So far, her proposal had not met with much enthusiasm.

"No sheep may leave the flock!" bleated Cloud. That said it all, she felt.

"But we're not leaving the flock," explained Maple. "If just *one* sheep goes off on its own then it's leaving the flock. That was wrong of me; I'll never do it again, no sheep can stand it." Maple shook herself. "But if several sheep go off, two or three of them, then they can't be leaving the flock. Because then they're a little flock of their own!" She looked triumphantly round.

"We could all go," bleated Cloud. "If we all go I'll go too!" She made a daring face.

Maple shook her head. "We can't all go. Beth's whole garden would be swarming with sheep. She'd suspect something."

They could all see that.

"It has to be only a very few sheep," Miss Maple went on. "Few enough to hide under bushes and in the shadow of the trees, and then if anyone does see them he'll think they've lost their way. We'll just trot off to Beth's house, listen to what they're saying, and trot back again. Easy!"

"So where is Beth's house?" asked Zora. "It could be anywhere."

127

"Next to the takeaway, near the church. And it's blue," said Miss Maple.

"But how will we find the takeaway? Or the church? We don't even know what a church is," said Lane.

The sheep prepared for a long and awkward silence, disappointed but also relieved that no one would have to go on this dangerous expedition now. After a suitable interval they'd go back to grazing.

Then Mopple the Whale, of all sheep, opened his mouth.

"They have chips in the takeaway," he murmured, lost in thought between two goes of chewing the cud. You could tell he hadn't really been paying attention. Only when he noticed the silence of the other sheep did he raise his head and look directly at Maple, who was looking back at him with shining eyes.

Mopple was the only sheep in the flock with any experience of fried potatoes. George had once offered him one of those greasy yellow sticks, just to prove that he wouldn't like it. Ever afterward Mopple had known what chips smelled like, even what they tasted like. And he would remember the smell.

Mopple in search of fodder: he would be their radar sheep. It was a dead cert of a plan.

10

Geraniums for Mopple

There was a small and uninteresting square in the middle of Glennkill, containing four neglected trees, a park bench, a marble column with an inscription on it, and a hedge that would make good cover for a sheep. The hedge cast two shadows: one was a dull shadow shown in golden light, the other was sharp and glaringly outlined.

On one side of the square stood a house with a pointed roof, lit up with gold by the floodlights. On the other shone the cold neon lighting of the takeaway.

Darkness lurked behind the takeaway.

And three sheep were lurking in the darkness.

Maple, Othello, and Mopple the Whale had set off at dusk to listen in on the conversation between Beth and the red woman. Mopple was looking cross. He had been promised chips to induce him to take part in this expedition, but then Maple and Othello had chased him rapidly past the door of the takeaway. Now he was staring through the window with them, obliged to watch Beth, inside, consuming a plateful of raw food—kohlrabi, carrots, radishes, celery—with a big red apple for afters. To see anything at all Mopple had to prop his front hooves on an upside-down bench under the window box and crane his neck. This unusual position was beginning to make his back ache.

Alarming sounds came from the street: the noise of car engines, men laughing, dogs barking. The yard where the sheep stood absorbed these sounds and flung them back and forth between the wall of the house, the other wall, and the blank side of the garage.

After finishing her supper, Beth stood up. She had left a carrot, three radishes, a stick of celery, and half the big red apple uneaten. Mopple felt hopeful again, but Beth carried the plate out of the room and came back empty-handed. She sat down in an armchair and busied herself with a string of wooden beads. She let the beads slip through her fingers, murmuring to herself. Ourfatherwhoartinheaven . . .

When determined footsteps finally passed the takeaway and came into the yard, Beth was so busy that she didn't even seem to notice. But the sheep knew at once who was purposefully coming round the corner, casting a clear neon-lit shadow on the ground. She still smelled of earth and sun and good health, even if those delightful aromas were now partly muted by cigarette smoke.

Mopple began squinting uneasily at the backyard for their escape route. But the sheep stayed put; they had rehearsed it in advance. If the red woman went no farther than the door, they were well hidden from sight here behind a bush of broom.

The woman knocked, and Beth jumped in her armchair. She quickly put the string of beads away, traced a sign in front of her breast with her right thumb, and hurried to the door. Then Beth inside the house and the woman outside the house both disappeared from the sheep's field of vision, and all they could hear was an indistinct murmuring. It was exciting. They had never seen a human house from the inside. Obviously going in and going out were not the same thing.

The door of the room opened and the red woman came through it, not red at all this time but wearing blue trousers and a green shirt, followed by Beth.

"Rebecca," said the woman as she entered the room. "Please call me Rebecca."

But Beth said nothing. The two of them looked at each other in silence for a while.

"You're not here to help the tourist trade," said Beth at last. "You're here because of George."

Rebecca nodded. "I want to find out as much as possible about his life. And his death. If I can give the tourist trade of Glennkill a boost at the same time, then that's fine by me." Her smile was ironic, but Beth did not notice.

"Why? Are you from the police? Goodness knows it's about time they did something at last."

Rebecca blushed. "No," she said, "I'm here for . . . for personal reasons."

Beth narrowed her eyes. "But you don't know anything about him," she said. "That doesn't leave very many alternatives."

Rebecca lowered her eyes, and said nothing.

"So you come to me about it!" Beth's voice was agitated, much as it was when she pressed the tracts into George's hands. "Me, of all people! I thought you were a respectable woman. I ought to send you away—with a copy of the Gospel, yes, but I ought to send you away. What do you want here?"

Rebecca was still smiling, but it was a much sadder smile now. "You'd probably call it forgiveness," she said quietly.

Rebecca's reply did, with the utmost ease, something that none of George's sharp remarks had ever managed: it left Beth thunderstruck. Rebecca's slim hands traced curving lines on a chest of drawers, while Beth stood like a weeping willow on a very calm day.

Mopple was getting bored. He reached his neck out, tasted one of the geraniums in the windowbox, and chewed noisily. Othello cast him an irritated glance. Mopple looked back innocently.

On the other side of the glass pane, Beth had turned white as a sheet.

"My God," she whispered. "My God." Then a new idea seemed to occur to her. She calmed down slightly.

"Tea?"

Rebecca nodded.

There was a bump outside. Mopple had leaned too far over in his quest for a geranium bud and lost his balance, and was now sitting on his behind.

Othello snorted. "Mopple, if you touch another petal I'm going to chase you all over the meadow tomorrow until you're as thin as an old nanny goat." Mopple stopped chewing and clambered to his feet again. Maple looked sternly at both rams. The three of them took up their observation posts in the shadow of the geraniums once more.

But Beth and Rebecca had disappeared. Instead, there was the clink of china.

"You won't find anything out," said Beth's voice. "Not by asking people."

"As scandalous as that?" asked Rebecca's voice.

"Unspeakable," said Beth's voice. "Unspeakable if only because no one really knows anything. The whole village has rotted away like an apple, if you see what I mean. From the inside out. Like an apple."

Mopple made a face. It had been a mistake, trotting off to this village. He was about to get down from the window box when Miss Maple discovered what had happened to Beth and Rebecca. They hadn't disappeared at all. They had just sunk into two low armchairs, and now the geraniums hid them from view.

"Look at that," said Beth. Something rustled on the tabletop.

"Oh," said Rebecca.

Beth laughed in a forced kind of way. "It doesn't get really interesting until I tell you where I found it."

Maple could stand it no longer.

"Mopple," she bleated quietly but as firmly as a lead ram, "go ahead, then, eat those geraniums. Eat us a hole through the geraniums. Quick." Mopple was the fastest eater in all Glennkill; a few geranium plants would be nothing to him. But Mopple didn't move. He stood between Maple and Othello looking as if he had indigestion.

"Mopple the Whale!" Miss Maple was angrier than she had been in a long time. Mopple looked at her unhappily and turned his head to Othello.

"Eat them," growled Othello through his teeth.

A short time later there was devastation where the geraniums had recently been growing and thriving. Beyond the devastation the sheep could see Beth and Rebecca sitting at the table. From inside the room, it looked as if Beth had planted three sheep's heads in her window box, but luckily neither of the two women thought of looking out of the window. They were far too deep in conversation anyway.

"You could call it some silly boy's trick," said Beth.

"Hmm," said Rebecca.

They both looked at the small bundle of straw lying on the

table between them. Someone had tied the straw together into the shape of arms, legs, and a head. Someone had stuck a twig right through the straw body.

"Do you know what the children used to call George? 'Goblin King'! Imagine that—where did they get it from? Such heathens! Only behind his back, of course. Oh yes, they feared him like the Prince of . . ."

Rebecca nodded. "And so you thought . . . ?"

"A silly boy's prank. It wouldn't have been the first time." Beth sighed. "I found this one morning last week on the steps of George's caravan. I never gave up hope for him, you know, even though he laughed at me. But he wasn't at home. He'd been away quite often lately. So I took the thing with me. I thought those kids and their nonsense about the Goblin King weren't worth bothering about."

"And now you think . . ."

"Now I think it was a warning, and it's my fault he didn't get it." Beth smiled sadly. "But never mind. George wouldn't have listened to me anyway. If there's one thing I know it's that George never listened to warnings."

They fell silent.

"Why was he away so often recently?" asked Rebecca. "What was he doing when he wasn't there?"

Beth folded her hands. "I wish I knew. He dressed well when he went away, in a suit and white shirt. He looked ten years younger, and a real gentleman. That makes people talk, of course, but I don't believe a word of it. I think he went up to town, to Dublin, to offices and banks and so on. He wanted to get away from here, you see, away from Glennkill."

"But someone or other didn't want him to go away?" asked Rebecca.

Beth nodded.

"Was he having an affair?"

Horrified, Beth shook her head. Rebecca raised her eyebrows. Then she asked, "Do you think it was about money?"

Beth laughed her forced laugh again. "I expect that's what they're all wondering here. Money is all they can think of. What heathens! Did George have money anyway? Normally I'd have said no; not the way he lived: a bit of land, a few sheep, a little house, and not much business. Most people here have more. Most of them earn quite well from the tourists, though of course they all complain. But then again, sometimes George did have things. Expensive things, really expensive. A watch—no one in all Glennkill could have afforded a watch like that, not even Baxter, the pub landlord, even though he's getting fat on the bed-and-breakfast business. Figuratively speaking, I mean. If you ever see him you'll know why I say figuratively speaking." Beth giggled like a schoolgirl.

"And George thought nothing of that expensive watch," she went on. "He wore it when he was sowing radishes." Beth's hands played with the straw doll. A furtive trace of something like admiration had crept into her voice.

"So now of course everyone's waiting for the will to be opened. It's going to be this coming Sunday, out of doors, a lawyer will come from town. George told the lawyer just what he wanted. Money is what interests these heathens. Believe you me, they've never waited for anything more eagerly, not even that feeble-minded sheep competition."

"The Smartest Sheep in Glennkill contest," said Rebecca, smiling too. "The ultimate tourist magnet. And now George goes and steals the show."

"They should save themselves the trouble," said Beth. "The

135

things they do to animals. It's ridiculous. But I have to be going now—off to spread the Word."

One arm of the straw doll had come apart, so it looked as if it were holding a tuft of hay in its hand. Beth's thin fingers expertly wrapped a single blade of straw around the tuft until the doll was mended.

Maple realized that she was feeling uncomfortable, from her hooves to the ends of her fleece. It was as if her ears were stuffed with wool, as if the glass of the windowpane between them and Beth was clouded over like smoke. She could hear and see, but she felt as if she were standing in fog. It took her a moment to work out where that feeling came from. She couldn't *smell* Beth and Rebecca on the other side of the pane. There was no scent to let her know if they were telling the truth about what they felt and what they feared. It was a ghostly, incomplete world. It must always be like that for human beings, with their small souls and their sticking-out noses. It meant distrust. Uncertainty. *Anxiety.*

". . . changeable, capricious," Beth was just saying. "I don't believe it. The human heart is a strange thing. It can cling to only one thing in life, and where it clings it stays, for good or bad."

The sheep were astonished. They had never heard Beth talk about anything but the "gospel" and "doing good works." She called everything else "idle chat." And suddenly she was just chatting idly away without pressing a single tract into Rebecca's hand. In this new and careless mood she was a bit like a lamb, bold and vulnerable at the same time. She must be very worked up indeed.

"Take Ham, for instance," said Beth.

Rebecca looked at her blankly. "Ham?"

"Abraham Rackham, the butcher," Beth explained. Her grave face twisted into a smile. "If you want to find out anything here, you have to understand the way the locals think. Abraham is too long a name for them, of course. More than two syllables in your name and it hasn't a chance."

She thought for a moment. "There are exceptions, of course. Gabriel. Funny, I never thought of that before. No one here would dare to call him Gabe."

"But *Ham*?"

"When you see him you'll see why. 'Abe' would probably have been normal, they're not very inventive around here. But we already have an Abe, and then those two 'hams' in the name, and his job. Oh, you should just see him!"

"What about Ham, then?"

"I'd start with him if I were you. He always acts so pious, as if he was the only man in the world who ever read the Bible. But people are afraid of him. And he himself—he's afraid too. In his butcher's shop . . . he has a CCTV camera. He's had it for ages, even when we only knew about such things from American movies. But why does a butcher's shop need a camera like that? They don't even have one at the bank. I think he's genuinely scared, which means he has something to hide. That's what I think. I did once tell him so, at the Christmas collection in church."

"And?"

"He went red. He was angry, embarrassed. And Ham's not a man to get embarrassed easily. I don't like to think what might be found in his slaughterhouse. God be with us!"

Mopple's stomach was making funny noises. Othello looked at him reproachfully.

Rebecca passed her tongue over her lips. "This is a strange

place. It's not the way I imagined it. I thought it would be peaceful here."

"It was peaceful once," said Beth.

"Not peaceful enough, obviously."

Beth shook her head. "I don't mean just before George's death. I mean much earlier. Years ago." Beth thought briefly. "Seven years ago. I spent six months in Africa, and when I came back it was all different. More superstition. Less of the fear of the Lord. And George was more affected than anyone, and after that he became more and more of a recluse. After that . . . oh, I don't know."

"So what had happened?"

"Nothing, of course," said Beth bitterly. "They were very keen to say that nothing had happened. But since then," and Beth leaned forward again, "since then they've been waiting for something to save them."

Mopple's knees began to tremble. He slid off the window box and stared glassily at the garage wall. His scent was suddenly as sour as fermenting rowanberries. Mopple rolled his eyes. Colic! Mopple the Whale, who could eat any amount of fresh clover on an empty stomach, had colic! Those geraniums must be vicious as a wolf!

Othello and Maple flanked Mopple, one on each side, to prevent him from lying down. Walking up and down was the only cure for that sort of colic. They had learned that from George.

"Keep going," whispered Maple. "Take another step, another step."

"And don't bleat, Mopple," muttered Othello.

Mopple stumbled forward, eyes glazed, but he didn't bleat. Maple and Othello helped him to walk up and down the backyard of the takeaway.

Then the door suddenly opened and a great drift of Beth's sour smell wafted out. It was as if she kept the essence of her scent indoors and took only a little of it with her when she left home. Rebecca's full, warm scent wove its way sleek as a ferret through this sour aromatic wasteland. Then she was standing in the yard. Mopple, Maple, and Othello just made it into shelter behind the broom bush.

"Thank you very much," said Rebecca to the desolate scent standing in the door frame. "That was a great help to me, especially what you told me last." She smiled mischievously. "And now I'm hungry. Do you think the takeaway will still be open?"

"Not in a place like this," said the voice in the doorway. "But I can give you a bite to eat. Bread and some salad?"

"Thank you very much, but no." Rebecca smiled again and took a couple of steps toward the street before turning.

"There's one thing I don't understand," she said. "You obviously don't think much of Glennkill. Why did you stay here?"

Silence from the doorway. Then, "Let's say for very personal reasons," breathed a voice that none of the sheep would have recognized as Beth's.

"George?" asked Rebecca, but the door was already closed. Rebecca strolled across the yard and disappeared round the corner.

And just in time, too, as Mopple was writhing in agony. They forced him to walk back across the yard, Maple whispering comforting words into his ear, Othello muttering threats.

After a while Mopple stopped.

"Come on, keep going!" bleated Maple. Othello nuzzled Mopple none too gently in the side.

"No!" said Mopple weakly.

"You must," growled Othello.

"No, I mustn't," said Mopple. "Don't you understand? It's over. I'm hungry!"

When the three sheep left the yard of the takeaway again, it was quiet in the streets. Mopple was still rather shaky on his legs, but he ate a few flowers planted by some unthinking human around the marble column.

Miss Maple set off back to the meadow, but after only a few steps she noticed that Othello wasn't following. The black ram had stopped and was standing beside the marble column like a small dark cloud. Maple bleated encouragingly to him, but Othello shook his head.

"I'll stick around here," said Othello. Maple flapped her ears forward, wondering why, but Othello just looked mysterious, and next moment he had disappeared into the shadow of the hedge. Miss Maple would have liked to follow him, but Mopple the Whale smelled confused, he smelled of streaming eyes and trembling knees, and she didn't want to leave him alone now. Together they trotted back toward the meadow.

Mopple's eyes were still a little glazed. Maple trotted along beside him more briskly than she had trotted for some time.

"That was interesting," she said. "Wouldn't you like to know what happened seven years ago too?" What an enormous length of time. Maple was the cleverest sheep in all Glennkill, but even she couldn't imagine seven years. She tried seven summers. No reaction. Seven winters? She could only really remember last winter, when George had nailed an old carpet over the door of the hay barn to protect them from the cold wind. There was a winter before that, and another before that one. Then the trail of winters was lost in the dark.

Mopple had been following his own train of thought.

"It was the butcher," he groaned.

"Why?" Maple looked at Mopple in concern. "Just because he has a CCTV camera? We don't even know what a CCTV camera is."

Mopple looked stubborn.

"No one likes the butcher," Maple went on thoughtfully. "All the same, those men under the lime tree were afraid he might die." She shook her head. "There's so much fear around here. Everyone's afraid. It's a wonder that George felt so little fear."

"But they tried to frighten him," said Mopple. "With straw." He shook his head at the thought of such human folly. There were plenty of terrible, horrible things in the world, but straw was surely not among them.

Maple nodded. "A warning." She had an idea, and stopped. Mopple looked questioningly at her.

"Mopple," said Maple, "if a small figure like that with a stick stuck through it was meant to be a little warning to George, could it be that George with a spade stuck into him was meant to be a huge big warning to someone else?"

Mopple looked blank, but Maple wasn't really expecting an answer. She was busy with her thoughts.

"The children were afraid of George. But why? What was so scary about George that so many people could be afraid of him? Mopple," she said, "please remember this. Goblin King."

"Goblin King," puffed Mopple.

11

Othello and a Case of Mistaken Identity

Othello had no difficulty in finding the house of God. It was the biggest in the village, tall and pointed, just as Cloud had said. Stealing up to God's house unseen looked to be more difficult. Unlike all the other houses, its façade was brightly floodlit. Only under the arched doorway was there a yawning shadow. Othello listened: somewhere in the distance a dog was whining and music was playing. He trotted briskly across the lighted yard. Two long sheep shadows trotted beside him, and a third, longer still and very pale, followed him. The four of them made hardly a sound.

In the shadow of the doorway Othello was alone again. He scented the air. Outside, it smelled of the street, cars, and a mild summer night; from inside cool, moldy, nostril-tickling scents came creeping out through the cracks and into the open.

No human being, no living creature at all.

Or was there?

When you start trusting yourself is the moment to stop it, whispered the voice in his head. Othello scented the air again.

One or two mice, maybe, certainly nothing larger. Only the door itself worried him. Taller and broader than any other door he'd ever seen. The handles were so high up that even if he stood on his back legs his front hooves wouldn't reach them. It looked as if giants lived on the other side of that door. God was tall, but not as tall as that.

Perhaps he could get a purchase on the handle with his teeth? He braced his forelegs against the door and stretched his neck. The door gave. Not much, but enough to tell Othello that it was open anyway and there was no need for him to use the handle.

He got down on all four legs again and lowered his head. The tall door was easily opened by his horns.

Listen.

Silence.

Othello put one front hoof on cold, shiny stone inside the house, and then the other. He was about to follow them up with a back hoof when the voice inside his head spoke up again.

Every way is really two ways, said the voice. There and back, thought Othello. *The way back is always the most important*, added the voice rather mockingly.

The black ram snorted impatiently. He was cross with himself. If the door would open to let him in, that certainly didn't mean it would be just as easy to get out again the other way.

Othello took a couple of steps back until his hindquarters were out in the light again, casting three long shadows. He lowered his horns, and raced forward. Attack—make impact—parry with raised horns. An elegant sequence of movements that would have earned him respect in any rams' duel.

The heavy wooden door swung wide open. For a moment Othello saw benches in the moonlight, tall pillars, a high dome. A circus ring?

The door swung back, wafting musty air before it. It swung out past the doorpost and back again. And out again. Back and forth. Now he was sure of himself: he'd be able to open the door from inside just as easily as from outside.

He waited in the shadow of the porch until all was silent once more. Then he went on waiting. His rage had given way to cold patience. Soon he would challenge God to a duel, for the pain, the suffering, and all the greedy and indifferent eyes in this world.

But when he was standing on the smooth stone floor, and the door behind him cut off the light, the place gave Othello the creeps. Too much here reminded him of the circus. The organ that could play cheerful music to accompany the most dreadful things; the empty benches for the audience; the platform. It had the props for the performance on it: a microphone, a rostrum, and a small bench. A fence of iron spikes, with burning candles. Othello could just imagine unfortunate creatures being driven over that fence day after day, for the amusement of the audience. No doubt what Cloud had witnessed was one of those performances. Othello was glad to have tracked God down. The show must not go on.

He trotted past the rows of benches. A thick red carpet muted the sound of his hooves. The red carpet was only for the human artistes. Woe to any animal who accidentally trod on it. But Othello couldn't care less just now.

Then he heard a sound, a small tormented sound, like a door that needed oiling. Or could it have been an animal? Or a human? Othello peered cautiously along the rows of benches. Thick dust danced in the moonlight before him. There was a framework behind the dust, and on it hung a human form, more dead than alive. Was that what had made the sound?

Othello shuddered: the helpless victim of a knife-throwing act! Yet it didn't look like an accident; whoever had thrown the knives had known just what he was doing.

When Othello came even closer, he realized that the sound couldn't have come from the human figure. Cloud was right— you couldn't smell any blood—and Othello suddenly understood why: the figure was made of wood.

Oddly enough, this didn't make him feel any better. He knew that humans could make things out of wood. But why they would *want* to make a thing like this was beyond sheepy understanding.

Somewhere in God's house a door creaked. Footsteps.

God?

The long-nosed man had appeared through a side door on the other side of the room, carrying a small, dancing light.

Soundless as a shadow, Othello glided past the benches and crossed a strip of moonlight to the wall. There was a wooden shed against the wall, with a heavy velvet curtain in front of it. Behind the curtain was a musty smell and a trace of fear. Othello hesitated.

The dancing light came closer.

Othello mounted a wooden step and disappeared into the shed. The folds of the curtain swung. Back and forth.

But the man walked past.

So he doesn't know everything, thought Othello triumphantly.

The four-horned ram didn't move a muscle. When the curtain had stopped swinging he looked cautiously around the wooden shed. A bench. A barred opening in one side, perhaps to air the boxlike shed. A transport crate for humans? That would fit the smell. People had been frightened in here.

From outside came a metallic sound. Not too close.

Othello decided to venture a glance. If you peered past the folds of velvet there was a fine view of the space outside.

The long-nosed man was standing on the rostrum, doing something in a desultory way to the fence with the candles on it. Now and then he looked at his watch. He was waiting for something.

For a while nothing happened.

Then there was the sound of creaking outside, and something dragging its way over the gravel, coming closer and closer.

God turned expectantly.

The big door swung open, sweeping over stone, caught on an uneven place in the ground, quivered with the impact. Light fell through the tall opening, not cold moonlight but the yellow glow of the floodlights outside.

Othello waited in suspense. A figure appeared in the light, as short as a child, but so wide that it could hardly get through the doorway. It was wheeling along like a strange hybrid of man and machine. A thickset black outline with a wreath of tangled hair, golden in the floodlights. Wheeling along soundlessly now, over the smooth stone floor, motionless but moving. For a moment Othello felt it was about to take off. He caught a bewildering scent of metal and bitter medicine, of oil and wounds healing over, and under that a smell he recognized.

"Ham." The long-nosed man smiled gently. "How good to see you recovering. How good to see you coming to me in your trouble." His hands dug into warm, fragrant wax. But not even the fragrance could drown out the stink of bitter sweat that he was suddenly giving off.

Suddenly Othello realized that God hated the butcher more than anyone else, more than he must have hated George. The butcher seemed to know it too. Child-sized, he wheeled past the long-nosed man without so much as looking up, making straight for the wooden figure.

"I haven't come to you," he said. "I've come to him."

The other man hunched his shoulders as if a sudden frost had fallen. He said nothing. So Othello discovered that God was afraid of the butcher too.

While Ham stared at the wooden figure in silence, the long-nosed man moved nervously around in a niche. He was waiting for the butcher to go. Othello peered cautiously out through the heavy curtains and waited too. Time went by, and Othello could smell the long-nosed man getting more and more nervous.

Finally the butcher's moving chair turned. It wheeled soundlessly to the doorway, out of the door, creaked and dragged its way over the yard, and was gone. Relief hung in the air like quivering mist. God went cautiously up to the door and looked out. He braced his whole weight against the door to free it where it had caught on the stone. When it had closed and the golden light was banished outside, the long-nosed man felt noticeably better. He was even humming.

His peculiar dress moved like water in the moonlight as he passed the rows of seats, on his way toward Othello's shed. Othello quickly withdrew his head, but God must have noticed something. He stopped right in front of the boxlike shed. The soft fabric rustled as his hand pushed the curtain back. Othello lowered his horns. The box shook, but no light fell in. God had gone into the other side of the shed, and Othello decided it was time to go. But as he turned, the boards creaked under his hooves.

"Ah," said the long-nosed man, "so there you are. Sorry you

had to wait. I only have to leave the church unlocked for an evening and in he comes." He laughed.

Othello didn't move a muscle.

"Do you want to make confession?" The voice sounded as glutinous and sticky as the resin oozing from pine trees.

Othello kept quiet.

"Only joking," the voice whispered through the grating. "I'm really glad you came. I was beginning to be afraid you wouldn't. But this is important, you see. I kept my mouth shut over George. I won't do it again. I have my conscience too."

Involuntarily, Othello snorted.

"Don't laugh!" wailed the voice outside. "Just leave Ham alone. I don't know if it was you lot up on the cliffs. If so it was an idiotic thing to do. But that must be the end of it, do you hear? If Ham dies it'll all come out—you ought to know that yourself. Anyway, Ham's no danger. Why would he suddenly do something now? He wasn't all that fond of George. He has his cameras and his butcher's shop and the TV; he's happy with that. No, there's no need for you to worry about Ham."

It was easy to tell from God's voice that he was very worried about Ham himself. That seemed strange to Othello, who had scented the depth of the long-nosed man's hatred for the butcher. He began thoughtfully chewing a piece of leather hanging loose from the upholstery of the seat inside the shed. He wasn't afraid of the man anymore. He was even looking forward to attracting his attention.

"With Kate around," said God, "it's safe enough. As long as Kate's here, Ham won't do anything to frighten the horses. Especially now she's a free woman again. He may even be glad that George is dead. So leave Ham alone, do you hear?"

Othello made a rasping sound, and the long-nosed man took it as agreement.

"Good to know you see it the same way," he said. Suddenly his face was very close to the wooden grating. "And as for that business with the grass . . ." he whispered.

Othello's head moved close to the wooden grating too, until it was only a few inches from God's nose. God's nose was twitching restlessly. Othello was surprised to hear him suddenly broaching such a sensible subject as grass.

But now the long-nosed man had stopped talking, and was staring through the grating with glittering eyes.

"Is that you?" he asked.

Othello kept quiet. Suddenly God shot out of his side of the box and pulled back the curtain in front of Othello. Moonlight streamed in. For a moment neither of them moved. Then Othello bleated, a terrible, aggressive bleat that echoed right through the room.

The long-nosed man gave a high, shrill scream. He ran past the rows of benches, stumbled and fell, got to his feet again, leaped over the iron fence and the candles with a single great, clumsy movement, and disappeared through the small door through which he had come. Pleased, Othello watched him go.

When Othello left God's house, two sheep shadows were trotting beside him again and one long, very pale shadow was trotting ahead of him. But the night birds in the trees saw something strange that disturbed the symmetry of the shadows in the light. For there was a fourth shadow, a shadow trotting along some way *behind* Othello. A very shaggy shadow with long, curved horns.

★

Like the clouds, calm and well fed as the clouds, smelling sweetly of their youthful multitude, they grazed the pasture in the first light of dawn. Guessing nothing of the night that had crept away over the grass. It still crouched under the dolmen, its stars like dead eyes among bones. No wonder they didn't twinkle. He knew that the dolmen had been built as a caravan for Death, with no wheels, of course, because Death can wait. You didn't need a spade to prove that Death was patient.

On the other side of the dolmen youth grazed, his own youth, with strong limbs and a sense of joy in its belly, but stupid, so stupid that you could almost feel sorry for it in its happiness. On the other side of the dolmen was the meadow that couldn't exist: the Way Back. He had looked for it all over the world, under smooth stones, on the far side of the wind, in the eyes of night birds, in pools of quiet water. All he had seen there was himself, and that would soon have been too much company for him—if he hadn't found the Way Back. It sat behind his ears laughing, so no wonder he hadn't been able to find it anywhere in the world. He had been carrying the Way Back with him all the time, but only in the tips of his fleece where the rain cooled it, where it tickled him but he didn't notice it. Too many parasites in his wool, and you couldn't be sure that the Way Back wasn't one of them.

The Way Back is always the most important, said the leaves. They said the same everywhere, and you had to believe them: they were the fragrant, breathing fleece of the world, even though it always grew away from you, in flight from the withered brown. But when the air began to smell of cold smoke, when swallow-flying time came and dark days, brown covered the ground all the same. Then you had to watch out in case it caught hold of your hooves and crawled up your legs like tiny spiders. His legs itched—it wasn't a good idea to think of the spiders. They tried to chill his heart and crawled into his nose. But the leaves were right. Even in swallow-flying time they whispered from the hedgerows, from the holly bushes, the ever-ravenous ivy in the under-growth, the little pine trees and his own shivering soul. The Way Back is always the most important. He believed them all. And he believed the crows who freed his fleece from parasites but left the Way Back unharmed. Black wings on his back, hoarse cawing and shiny eyes. For the swallows returned with the leaves too.

Now the Way Back had curled up, like a wood louse, into a single step to be taken. Beyond that step they were grazing, they were like clouds of wintry breath, warm and alive in an empty world. He saw the black ram among them, the ram with the angry soul and all the scars under his fleece. The black ram belonged here now. Who could fix it for someone to belong somewhere? George had known how to herd sheep together and then drive them apart better than any sheepdog. George should have herded him too with all the scattered sheep, right into the middle of the Way Back. But George had looked too deep below the dolmen, to stone and bone. He saw the one who was like a quiet pool of water, saw his belly hanging slack. But those horns wound like the Way, curving and proud as his own.

His soul galloped ahead.

But he himself still stood there, watching his soul go. No one had told him that the last step was the impossible one. Sadness, enough to make you howl at the moon the way his crows secretly did when they thought he wouldn't notice. There was no bridge to take him over that last step, no ford where the water wouldn't be so deep. He hadn't expected to drown at the last step. His horns bored into the passing night like screws. And yes, yes . . . there was a ford after all, you could build it with words, ancient words lovingly kept safe in the soul all those years, thought out like magic spells. Now he was looking for them. But his soul had grown so large, so bewildering and crowded, there were ways after ways after ways, all the ways he had ever gone, and he couldn't find the words anymore. He must, though. It must be done

151

quickly, because the fleecy ones were as ephemeral as wintry breath, and the silent shepherd already sat under the dolmen with his blue eyes gleaming. Day came up slowly above the sea and threatened to drive him away again, as it had driven him away those last four days. The fifth day. The fifth day was the day of the Way Back. He hesitated.

12

Rameses Intervenes

Miss Maple was the first sheep out in the meadow at dawn. She couldn't remember having slept at all. Something wouldn't let her rest. A dream? No, more like the memory of a dream, the memory of the half sheep. She felt as if that scent of a great many sheep were in the air again but strange and incomplete.

Gabriel's sheep, thought Miss Maple. But at the same moment she knew it couldn't be that. Gabriel's sheep were easy to scent, a flock of young ewes and rams one and two years old with no difference between them, a flat kind of smell. But these half sheep weren't all young. There were some very old rams among them; there were mother ewes and lambs; there were memories, experiences, ingenuity, youthful high spirits, innocence. A complete flock, only not really complete. Strange scent strands hung in the air.

Ritchfield was standing in the morning mist. On George's Place. For a moment Maple thought he was dead—not because he was standing there so still (that was nothing unusual in old rams) but because of the birds. There were three crows perched on Ritchfield's back, and what live sheep would put up with crows using it as a lookout post? Certainly not Sir Ritchfield.

153

One of the crows spread its wings and croaked hoarsely. It looked as if Ritchfield had grown short black wings of his own. A shudder ran through Maple's fleece.

She sensed something moving behind her and shot round, jumping up in the air with all four legs at once, as only a young lamb or a very frightened sheep can. Behind her, Sir Ritchfield stepped out of the mist. But Sir Ritchfield was standing on George's Place in front of her, too. Awestruck, Miss Maple took a couple of steps backward.

The two rams were facing each other like reflections on two sides of a puddle. Except that the black birds weren't reflected. Maple remembered from the fairy tale that the dead don't have reflections either. Both rams lowered their horns and approached each other. Their horns clashed together with a full, ringing sound. Then they both raised their heads.

"I did dare," said Ritchfield with crows.

"You did dare," agreed Ritchfield without crows. He suddenly looked bewildered. "No sheep may leave the flock," he bleated. "George came back smelling of death." He shook his head, distressed. "If only I'd kept my mouth shut! So stupid . . ."

And Ritchfield without crows turned and trotted briskly toward the cliffs. The other Ritchfield stood there looking at him with an affectionate expression in his eyes. As if at a signal, all three crows rose into the air together, and there was only one Ritchfield left in the meadow. A shaggy Ritchfield smelling like a flock of half sheep.

Miss Maple looked anxiously at the other, bewildered Ritchfield wandering along the cliff tops. She turned and ran after him.

★

Normally Cloud and Mopple were the first sheep out at pasture every morning, Mopple because he felt hungry earlier than the others, and Cloud because she was convinced that morning air made your wool grow.

"You don't think I'm just naturally as woolly as this, do you?" she asked.

"Yes!" bleated the lambs and some of the older sheep who always admired Cloud's superior woolliness.

Cloud felt flattered and rolled her eyes. "Well, maybe," she would say, "but you needn't think I don't do anything to make it that way!" And then those sheep who took any interest in the subject could settle down to listen to a long lecture about the benefits of morning air. Oddly enough, although Cloud's sermons were very popular, no single sheep ever left the fleecy embrace of the flock earlier than the others in order to improve its personal woolliness.

This morning Mopple the Whale was still sleeping off the stress and strain of his first ever attack of colic, and Cloud was all alone in the dewy meadow. Well, not really. Of course there were Gabriel's sheep, who had to be up early, since they didn't have a hay barn, and who disproved Cloud's theory of the natural woolliness of morning air.

To Cloud's great surprise, Sir Ritchfield was up and about too. He stood on George's Place grazing with dignity. Cloud indignantly fluffed herself up and faced Ritchfield.

"Do you know where you are?" she asked.

"Back," said Ritchfield, sounding emotional. He lowered his head to the still ungrazed plants on George's Place and nibbled carefully around some of the delicious nose-tickler flowers.

"You're grazing on George's Place!" bleated Cloud. "How could you?"

"Easy," said Ritchfield. "Over the hills, over the fields, through the old stone quarry, over the body, all through the world and back again. Mustn't get caught by the butcher. Easy, because the carrion eater fears the dead. Head in the wind, eyes open, mustn't shake the memories out of your fleece. Impossible. Simple when you come to do it."

Cloud stared at Ritchfield in alarm. There was something badly wrong with him. She bleated uneasily. Ritchfield didn't seem to like that. He went closer to her and whispered in her ear. "Don't worry, woolly ewe. This isn't George's place. George's place is under the dolmen where no grass grows, where the blue-eyed shepherd sits waiting. George's place is safe until the key comes back into the light of day, all warm. Who has the key?" he asked.

These remarks were obviously meant to be reassuring. Ritchfield's voice sounded gentle. All the same, Cloud fled toward the hay barn in confusion.

A little later the whole flock had gathered at George's Place. They were standing, at a respectful distance, around Sir Ritchfield, who made no move to leave George's Place himself. All these sheep seemed to bother Ritchfield.

"Sometimes being alone is an advantage," he said.

"What does he mean?" asked Heather. The other sheep said nothing.

"It doesn't sound at all like Ritchfield," said Lane at last.

"He smells strange," said Maude. "Sick. Or perhaps not sick, but not like Ritchfield. In fact not like a sheep at all. Or at least not like *a* sheep. Like a young ram with just one horn. *And* like an experienced mother ewe. *And* like a young sheep with a very thick fleece who hasn't seen a winter yet. *And* like

156

a very old ram who won't see another winter. Yet not just like any of them. Somehow or other—he's half." Maude was at a loss.

"He's running out!" exclaimed Mopple. "Ritchfield is running out!"

That must be it! The hole in Ritchfield's memory had got so large overnight that every possible and impossible memory was now running out of it.

None of the sheep knew what to do. Ritchfield was the lead ram, but of course he couldn't be expected to do anything about it himself. Maple had disappeared, Othello was nowhere to be seen, Mopple, the memory sheep, had hurried off to the other side of the meadow because he was afraid a hole in the memory could be infectious. Zora stared wide-eyed at Ritchfield for a moment and then fled to her rocky ledge. Finally Rameses took the initiative. He led the flock a little way from Ritchfield, so that the old ram couldn't hear what ideas they were discussing.

At first they had no ideas to discuss. No one knew how to stop up a hole in the memory. They couldn't even imagine what a hole in the memory was like.

"We must get him away from George's Place before he grazes it bare," said Rameses.

"How?" asked Maude. "He's the lead ram."

"He is *not* the lead ram, not anymore," said Rameses. "We just have to make that clear to him."

It was a suggestion, anyway. The confused sheep would have backed almost any suggestion with enthusiasm. Before Rameses knew what was happening, it was decided that he would make it clear to Ritchfield that his time as lead ram was now over.

The sheep pressed close together expectantly as Rameses hesitantly trotted up to Ritchfield. Rameses swallowed. He felt as if he had never seen Ritchfield look so majestic. He was about to murmur a respectful greeting when Ritchfield interrupted him.

"Straight-horned ram, short-horned ram," he addressed Rameses. It was true: Rameses had horns that were little more than two small points. "Spare your breath. Never mind making things clear. Don't you see how clear the day is? Clearer than all the days there are. My birds know it and rise early. Ritchfield knows it and is looking for his memories. It's clear that I'm not a lead ram. It's clear that no sheep in the world is going to get me off this lovely pasture if I don't want to go. But you," he said, looking the other sheep up and down as they stared with wide, bewildered eyes in the direction of George's Place, "you could do with being a whole lot clearer."

Without having said a single word, Rameses trotted back to his flock.

"He heard us," bleated Maude. It looked as if the hole in Ritchfield's memory had sharpened his hearing. They decided to be more careful with critical remarks in future. To be on the safe side, they trotted even farther from George's Place, all the way to the dolmen.

Othello had hidden in the shadow of the dolmen and was looking across the meadow at Sir Ritchfield with close attention.

"Othello," sighed Heather in relief, "you must drive him away from George's Place!"

Othello snorted with derision. "I'm not crazy, am I?" he said, and they could get no more out of him.

Othello's strange answer made the sheep feel even more uncertain. He knew the world, he knew the zoo. He knew something they didn't know. That was why he was standing motionless in the shadow of the dolmen. They thought some more.

"Ritchfield did say he was looking for his memories," said Lane optimistically.

"If it's a hole in his memory we ought to stop it up with more memories," said Cordelia. "You stop up a hole in the earth with more earth."

"But you don't stop up a rat hole with more rats," said Cloud.

"You could," Cordelia insisted, "if they were very fat rats."

A few minutes later they had a plan. They would make a memory for Sir Ritchfield so big and thick that it could not fail to stop up the hole. It was a large memory involving as many sheep as possible. They enticed Zora off her ledge again and persuaded Mopple to venture back into Ritchfield's vicinity. Mopple's girth could only help with the size of the memory. Othello alone firmly refused to join them.

"It has to be something really special," bleated Heather excitedly, "something no flock has ever done before."

Soon afterward all the sheep in the flock were lying on their backs in front of George's Place with their legs in the air, bleating for all they were worth. Ritchfield had stopped grazing and was inspecting them attentively. If they hadn't been making such an effort, they would have noticed how amused he looked.

"What's all this nonsense?" snorted Ritchfield's familiar voice all of a sudden. "Have you gone out of your minds?"

The sheep cast each other triumphant glances, as well as they could in that attitude. Sir Ritchfield sounded perfectly all right again. They scrambled back on their legs, quite flustered but proud of their success.

Ritchfield trotted over from the cliff tops. "Let's have some order around here!" he snorted. "Stand to attention! Can't you be left alone for two minutes together?"

Ritchfield was there on George's Place, beginning to graze around the nose-tickler flowers again.

The sheep's eyes looked blankly from one of the two Ritchfields to the other and back again.

"That's Ritchfield," whispered Heather, glancing at the Ritchfield who was bellowing demands for order from the cliff tops, "but that's Ritchfield too."

"No," said Miss Maple, who had appeared beside Ritchfield like an interested shadow, "*that* is Melmoth."

Melmoth's arrival had the flock in such an uproar as only the arrival of a genuine wolf could have caused. Melmoth was more than a ram who had disappeared: he was a legend, like Jack the Lad who had got away unshorn, or the seven-horned ram, a ghost who was roped in to teach refractory lambs the meaning of fear when all other warnings had failed. He was an example of what happens to a sheep who leaves the flock and gets too close to the cliff tops or who eats strange fodder and ignores the warning bleats of the mother ewes.

"Melmoth leaned over just like that, and he never came back," they said when an inquisitive lamb ventured too close to the abyss.

"Melmoth ate just as much woe weed as that, and now he's dead."

Melmoth had died a thousand whispered deaths; he was the bogey sheep of the lambs' education; and now there he stood before them, radiating strength and in the best of health. The mother ewes were wondering how they were ever going to make their lambs behave in future. And no lamb had been told more Melmoth horror stories than the winter lamb. Now he was standing back in the shade of the hedge, staring at Melmoth with a strange gleam in his eyes.

"Two Ritchfields!" sang out the other lambs, except for one, who kept quiet and snuggled into Cloud's white fleece.

They all realized that Melmoth was something special. Some of them called him "the one who got away scot-free," and didn't quite know whether they meant it as an insult or a mark of respect. But once Ritchfield had told him why no sheep were allowed to graze on George's Place, Melmoth met with a friendly reception at first.

"He's woolly," said Cloud appreciatively. "A bit shaggy, maybe, but woolly."

"He has a nice voice," said Cordelia.

"He smells . . . interesting," said Maude.

"He's going to leave us the nose-tickler flowers," said Mopple optimistically.

Of course the question of who was really the lead ram soon came up.

"We can't have two lead rams," said Lane. "Even," she added thoughtfully, "if they're both the same."

They would have liked to keep Sir Ritchfield as their lead ram, but a lead ram who couldn't be told from another ram at first sight struck them as an impractical proposition. Ritchfield had changed, too. He was more cheerful, more playful, almost as daring as a young ram. He didn't seem interested in being lead ram anymore, and most of the time he stuck close to Melmoth. They had never seen him so happy. Ritchfield had made a new rule. "No sheep may leave the flock," he said to anyone who would listen, "unless that sheep comes back again."

★

Very early, earlier than George had ever turned up in the meadow, Gabriel was back again. Without his shepherd's crook and without dogs. Even without his hat but with his pipe in the corner of his mouth. And with a ladder. The sheep were proud to be already at work. Gabriel would soon see there were no idlers among them.

But Gabriel didn't seem particularly pleased. Was it that he didn't like Melmoth? Yet Gabriel didn't even seem to notice the new ram in the flock. He cast a brief glance at his own sheep, who had already grazed half their fenced patch of pasture bare, and then marched off to the crows' tree with the ladder.

There were no trees at all on the meadow itself. Instead, two sides of the meadow had hedges along them, which were no serious obstacle if a sheep had really decided to get out of the meadow. But they hid the view of the lush green countryside beyond them, and so prevented the sheep from *wanting* to leave. "Psychological deterrents," George had called them.

Three trees still grew among the gorse in these hedges: the shade tree, where it was cool in summer; a small apple tree, which much to the sheep's annoyance dropped its apples when they were no bigger than a sheep's eye and as sour as Willow on her worst days; and the crows' tree, where birds lived, croaking from dawn to dusk, except at midday.

Gabriel put the ladder up beside the trunk and climbed to the lowest branch. Birds flew up out of it, plump and clumsy pigeons, shiny and mocking crows, black-and-white and furtive magpies.

Gabriel spent some time clambering around in the tree. The sheep watched him.

"He likes magpies," said Mopple. It was the first time he had said anything about Gabriel. Mopple the Whale was ashamed of the fact that all this business about Gabriel didn't matter to him very much. If it had been up to him, Gabriel and his strange sheep need never have come here at all. Now the peculiar strangers were grazing part of the meadow bare at alarming speed, and Zora kept looking uneasily at a certain ram among them. Gabriel himself didn't seem to be very useful either. What had he done for them so far? No mangel-wurzels, no clover, no dry bread, not even hay. He hadn't cleaned out the water trough, and Mopple thought it badly needed cleaning. Yesterday Gabriel had spent the whole time scurrying uselessly about the meadow. And today it was trees! Naturally the birds scolded and squawked. If *that* was what Gabriel understood by his duties as a shepherd, there were difficult times ahead of them.

The wiry figure hauled itself from branch to branch, higher and higher up the tree. Like a cat, Gabriel was peering into the birds' nests.

The sheep quickly got bored with it. If Miss Maple hadn't insisted that they must watch Gabriel closely they would soon have thought of something else to do. But as it was, they stared up through the branches until they felt dizzy from holding their heads at such an unusual angle. Even Melmoth was peering up at Gabriel with a strange birdlike gaze.

It was Sir Ritchfield who saw the important thing. Gabriel seemed to have found what he was looking for in one of the nests. Not only Ritchfield but Zora, Maple, and Othello too could see that Gabriel had a key in his hand. But only Ritchfield saw that it was *not* the key from the packet of oatcakes, the one that Josh had brought yesterday.

"Small and round," said Sir Ritchfield. "The key from the nest is small and round. And the key yesterday was long and thin." The sheep were amazed, particularly at Ritchfield. He was so proud of his observation that he didn't even notice he had been able to remember yesterday's key. Melmoth's presence was obviously doing him good.

Gabriel's memory seemed to be worse than Sir Ritchfield's. Perhaps he hadn't really seen the key properly yesterday. He climbed down from the tree again in high good humor. In high good humor he trotted back to the shepherd's caravan, and still in high good humor he put the key in the lock. He gave an angry little whistle through his teeth. When Gabriel's sheep heard that whistle, silent panic broke out among them for no apparent reason. They were still in a state of panic long after Gabriel had gone marching along the path through the fields and back to the village. George's sheep watched them uneasily, until their attention was caught by another sound.

Melmoth was standing beside the dolmen, chuckling.

The sheep noticed that Melmoth was not just one more sheep in their flock. They couldn't explain to themselves exactly why. Melmoth was a disruptive influence. When Melmoth grazed with them the flock could hardly manage to stay in formation. Instead, they scattered as if a wolf had broken in among them. They scattered at grazing pace, of course, which meant very slowly, almost imperceptibly. It began to feel eerie.

And then there were the birds. Not nice plump songbirds, but hoarse-voiced carrion eaters like crows and magpies. Melmoth let them do gymnastics around him and took them for rides while he was grazing. Of course the sheep weren't afraid of crows (except perhaps for Mopple), but they smelled too much like death. When they asked Melmoth about it he snorted with derision.

"They're just a flock like you, a small flock of black wings.

They keep watch and graze and scratch your coats. It's not their fault if they graze on death. They leave memory in peace. They're cleverer than their own voices. They understand the wind."

Crazy, thought a lot of the sheep, but no one dared say so out loud. Melmoth's language might be as strange as a goat's bleating, but he didn't give any impression at all of being confused. It was as if Melmoth's remarks went around what he wanted to say in strange lines; his remarks seemed long-winded but not crazy. Only Cordelia insisted that Melmoth's language was more *precise* than anything the other sheep said.

"He doesn't just talk about things the way he sees them, he talks about things the way they *are*," she would say when a small group of sheep had gathered somewhere to criticize Melmoth. Such little groups were assembling with increasing frequency— and secrecy. They quickly noticed that Melmoth had a positively uncanny way of picking up much of what went on in the meadow.

"The birds tell him," bleated Heather, and the sheep began keeping a wary eye on the sky. They watched Melmoth more closely than ever.

Melmoth grazed his way across the meadow like a lone wolf. There was even something wolfish about the expression on his face. It seemed to them as if Melmoth wasn't really a sheep at all. The boldest among them briefly remembered the story of the wolf in sheep's clothing, and shuddered.

And then there was a single lamb, a lamb who stood on wobbly legs watching Melmoth with wide, timid eyes. A little later a rumor began circulating through the whole flock, the rumor that Melmoth *was* a ghost after all. They knew from the fairy tale that the dead sometimes returned as ghosts to take their revenge. Whispers ran through the flock. "Goblin King," said the whispers, and "Wolf's ghost."

Othello was annoyed. He had been trying to track the old ram down for days. For years, in fact, since that rainy night at the circus when Melmoth had galloped past the rows of tents like the wind, while Othello watched through bars, and the cruel clown lay in the mud shouting for a light, Othello had always known that he must find Melmoth again. And now Melmoth had found *him*. Othello was not happy. Should he race joyfully to meet him, like Sir Ritchfield? Melmoth had taught Othello patience, taught him about fire and water, how to watch the slimy trail of snails, how to chase rage and fear back to the world where they came from. He had shown him how to watch thoughts. He had taught him how to fight. Melmoth's voice, accompanying Othello, had saved his life more than once.

But Melmoth had left him behind with the cruel clown. "Sometimes being alone is an advantage," snorted Othello angrily. Of all the things that Melmoth had told him, this was the only one he had never believed.

Othello had hidden from Melmoth as best he could, unable to come to any decision. Yes, Melmoth knew he was here, but for some reason the gray ram had decided to leave him alone. Did he simply not care about Othello—just one of countless sheep he had met in his lonely wanderings, submerged in a faceless flock in which Melmoth took no interest? Of all possible explanations, this one struck Othello as the worst.

But now he heard the anxious whispers of his new flock— his first real flock—and he began to feel real concern. Suppose it were true that George had once tried to hunt Melmoth down in a life-and-death struggle, as the flock was whispering? Then what? If there was one thing he had learned in his time with the circus, it was that Melmoth was capable of anything.

Miss Maple was thinking feverishly too. She didn't believe for a moment that Melmoth was a ghost. But might he not have something to do with George's death? What did Ritchfield know? Maple was sure that Ritchfield's strange behavior these last few days must have something to do with Melmoth.

When Melmoth had dozed off under the crows' tree, Maple couldn't stand it any longer. Moving with determined steps, she grazed beside Sir Ritchfield.

"Who'd have expected Melmoth to survive?" she remarked casually.

Ritchfield snorted with amusement. "I would," he said. "It was a twin feeling. That rainy night I knew he'd come back. After that I waited."

"But you didn't say anything to us," said Maple.

Ritchfield did not reply.

"And you always told us you could smell his death on George's hands," Maple insisted.

"I smelled death on George's hands, yes," said Ritchfield thoughtfully. "So it must have been someone else's death."

"Or a near death," said Maple. "Perhaps Melmoth got away more dead than alive. He must have been very angry with George . . ."

Ritchfield did not reply. Miss Maple pulled up a dandelion plant.

"You haven't told us anything," said Miss Maple, when she had finished chewing the dandelion leaves. "You intimidated Mopple because you thought he'd found out something about Melmoth. So that he wouldn't give anything away . . . Why?"

Ritchfield looked bothered. "It wasn't right to intimidate Mopple the Whale," he said. "But I thought . . ."

Miss Maple could bear it no longer. "You thought Melmoth might have something to do with George's death! Behaving so strangely, stealing secretly out to the meadow by night, and just after George's death too. You imagined that something terrible must have happened back then, the night after Melmoth's flight. Melmoth could have been carrying his anger around with him all this time, couldn't he? You decided to keep Melmoth's return secret."

Maple looked up confidently: a proper deduction, made from clues, just like in the detective story. She was proud of herself. From Ritchfield's downcast expression, she could see she had scored a bull's-eye.

"I wanted to help him," said Ritchfield. "Twin for twin."

"Twin for twin," snorted Melmoth, who had suddenly popped up on Miss Maple's other side. Maple looked from one ram to the other and back. Whichever way she turned her head, she always saw the same ram.

Melmoth looked keenly at Ritchfield. "Angry with George?" he snorted. "Magpie chatter. Howling wind. Lambs' drivel. Would you like to come with me into the night when you didn't want to come too? Would you like to hear a story?" He bleated loudly, so that all the sheep in the meadow could hear. "The story of the fifth night."

The sun had climbed high in the sky, and no wind was blowing off the sea. The only creatures who didn't seem to mind the heat were the flies, who buzzed tirelessly around the sheep's nostrils and crawled into their ears. So even the more skeptical sheep had an excuse to come in under the cool branches of the shade tree, quite by chance, to where Melmoth was resting on a soft cushion of old leaves, telling his story. Even the winter lamb peered out from behind the trunk of the shade tree, and as the other sheep were too lethargic to chase him away, he stayed.

All the sheep in George's flock found they had shivers running through their fleece that perfect summer's day. Melmoth told a story such as the sheep had never heard before, not just with words but with the wind in his wool and his trembling heart, and soon all the sheep were racing through the darkness with him.

And in Melmoth's story, it was bitterly cold.

13

Melmoth the Wanderer

Over stick and over stone, stick and stone, stick and stone, stone and bone, stone and bone, and bone, and bone, and bone. Melmoth's hooves hammered over the wintry ground. His heartbeat galloped on ahead of him. *Stick and stone.* The butcher's dogs were howling. The carrion eater himself came behind them. Melmoth and Ritchfield called the butcher "carrion eater" because he smelled of death, and they thought he was too portly to kill anything for himself. But now it looked as if the butcher had joined the hunters after all, and Melmoth was running for his life. *Stone and bone, stone and bone.*

"You wouldn't dare," Ritchfield had said, with all the superiority of the older twin. Melmoth just felt annoyed. He hadn't thought to ask if Ritchfield himself would dare. It wasn't about that, it wasn't about any of the other sheep, it was only about him. Melmoth had stopped grazing. He turned his head and looked at the place where the countryside began to roll gently away from the meadow, hill after hill after hill. "I would dare," he had said, looking straight at the derisive expression on Ritchfield's face.

★

Stick and stone, stone and bone. Melmoth couldn't remember when and where he had learned these words. They were simply the right words. They helped him not to think of the carrion eater. Even the butcher didn't matter. He just had to run on, over stick and over stone, with his legs flying and his breath steady. As long as he kept going, the butcher didn't matter. But Melmoth's breath wasn't steady anymore. There was too much cold air outside, and too little warm air in his lungs. *Stone and bone. Stone and bone*, on and on forever.

"Three days and three nights," Ritchfield had said, "or it doesn't count."

"No," Melmoth had said. "Not three."

Ritchfield snorted scornfully. "Or it doesn't count. Any suckling lamb can spend a night lost in the fields. Or two."

"Five," said Melmoth. "I'll be gone five days and five nights." He enjoyed the sight of Ritchfield's baffled sheepish face.

"Five days and five nights," he sang, "five suns and five moons, five blackbirds and five nightingales." He pranced around Ritchfield, kicking out in high spirits. For a moment Ritchfield looked worried. Then he let Melmoth's good humor infect him. "Five blackbirds and five nightingales," he sang too, and the next moment they were both romping merrily around the meadow. Neither of them thought for a second that anyone would go hunting Melmoth.

Over stick and over stone. Most of all over stone. So many stones. And they didn't make running any easier.

"Don't catch a cold," Ritchfield had said awkwardly. Melmoth flung his head proudly up. His eyes were sparkling. What did Ritchfield know about the dangers of being alone? Catching a cold was certainly not among them. Melmoth had thought about it for days, and had concluded that those dangers didn't exist. Just fantasies. Nightmares dreamed up by frightened suckling lambs, horror stories told by anxious mother ewes. What did the sheep do in the flock? They grazed and rested. What would he do without a flock? Graze and rest, of course. Anything else was just imagination. There were no dangers. Not a single one.

Walls of rock. The moon had come out from behind clouds in the sky, and Melmoth could see rock walls flying past to the right and left of him. Not very high, but too high and too steep for a sheep. *Stick and stone, stone and bone.*

Stone.

Now it was all over, and the walls of rock were closing around him into a cul-de-sac. He must climb those rocky walls. He must. There was a place that didn't look quite so steep to his left. A collection of detritus, a natural ramp. Melmoth stumbled up it. Things went quite well at first, but then little stone falls came loose, kicked away by his hooves. It was like trying to run across falling rain. Impossible. The carrion eater seemed to sense it too. There was a terrible shout as he called off his dogs. They weren't needed now. Footsteps shuffled through the silence. They shuffled fast. Melmoth was defeated. His fear was defeated too. In the last seconds of his life, Melmoth made up his mind to be a truly brave sheep. He would stand and face the butcher. Slowly and trembling, he climbed down the pebbly slope again. *Stone . . . and bone . . . stone and . . . bone . . . and . . .*

Bone.

A leg bone was sticking out of the pebbles he had dislodged in his flight. A bone inside a human leg.

Of course he had caught a cold after all, on the very first night, huddled into a prickly hawthorn hedge and hardly protected at all from the icy November wind. He hadn't slept that night. He'd just listened to the sounds all around him and longed for day. Things were in fact better in daytime, now and then anyway. Melmoth had roamed the gray-green, wintry moorland with his nose dripping, cautiously nibbling at tufts of coarse grass.

Around midday he found himself on a hill that offered a very good view to a sheep with good eyesight. Melmoth had excellent eyesight, and he immediately turned it on the blue strip of sea on the horizon. He pretended it was to get his bearings; secretly he was looking for white woolly dots. But he saw nothing, not even a cloud in the sky, whichever way he looked. He was alone all the way to the horizon. A ridiculous feeling of euphoria crept down from his head into his legs, and he strained his eyes even more, so as to see even farther in his isolation. When the euphoria began turning to panic, Melmoth galloped away through the empty hills, zigzagging wildly.

He clambered cautiously over the human leg, *bone and stone*, until he had firm ground underfoot again. What a relief. Melmoth disappeared into the shadows at the foot of the pebbly mound and listened. The dogs were panting and the butcher was breathing hard.

"He's in the old stone quarry," said the butcher. "We've got him now."

"Hmm," said a familiar voice. "Hmm."

Melmoth watched as two white clouds of light emerged from the darkness, saw the dogs' hot, steaming breath and the massive deep black figure of the butcher. Melmoth was trembling but only with exhaustion. He heard everything, everything. The whining of the dogs and their slobbering heartbeats, the clink of moonlight on the cold ground, a night bird's wings beating, even the velvety sound of the night itself slowly moving on. It was his fifth night—it should be the last.

The butcher had brought a light with him. Melmoth watched it darting around, climbing the rocky walls, coming closer and closer. The light hesitated for a moment at the foot of the pebbly ramp. Then it hopped its way up the slope, over stone and bone, without dislodging a single pebble. The light was a good hunter, leaping from the slope into the shadows, making straight for Melmoth. For a moment he stood blinking at the dazzling white. Then everything went black around him.

"Oh, shit!" said the butcher.

"What's the matter? Has something happened to him?" asked George, who was lagging a little way behind the butcher. "I told you not to go chasing after him like that, not at night, not when he . . ." George fell silent for a moment.

Then he said, "Oh, shit!"

Forcing himself to open his eyes, Melmoth gradually succeeded in fending off the blackness again. Now he could see what had happened. The light had swung away from him once more. It had gone climbing the pebbly slope again, and had fastened on that solitary human leg bone. Only now did Melmoth realize how unlikely it was to find a human leg in this place. It was pointing to the night sky, pale and hairless and smelling of death.

The light began shaking. The butcher took a couple of steps back. Only the dogs were still showing any interest in

Melmoth, who stood there in the shadow of the pebbly slope, breathing heavily.

"George?" said the butcher. His voice didn't sound at all terrible now. "Do you think it would be a good idea to . . . to leave?"

George's thin figure stood perfectly still in the dark. He shook his head.

"We've seen it. Not a pretty sight. I agree, I'd rather we'd just found Melmoth and nothing else, but it's too late, we have to go through with it now. Shit!"

"Shit!" agreed the butcher. He had taken a step back. "Will you pull him out?" he asked.

George half turned to the butcher, and Melmoth could smell that he wasn't angry anymore.

"Ham," he said, "you're a *butcher*. You do this kind of thing every day. Theoretically. I was hoping that you . . ."

"That's different. Completely different. My God, George, this is a *body*."

George shrugged. "Did you think you worked with some kind of fruit in your job?"

He climbed the slope, and more pebbles came away. He took his work gloves out of the pockets of his jacket and put them on. He pulled at the leg. A whole lot of pebbles came away as a large body made its way to the surface. Melmoth took a step back so that the stones wouldn't hit his own legs. *Stone and bone*.

The butcher made a sound rather like a lamb suckling: a wet, smacking sound.

"It's Weasel," said the butcher. "Weasel McCarthy!"

George, who until now had been tugging grimly at the leg, looked down. A second leg had emerged beside it, topped by a thin torso, two thin arms, and a surprised, dead, weaselly face. The arms and legs were at odd angles.

"Stiff," said George.

The butcher nodded. "After about eight hours. They have to be processed by then." He clapped his hand awkwardly to his mouth, as if to catch back what he'd said out of the clear night air.

George shrugged his shoulders again. "McCarthy was always a bit stiff," he said. Then they both looked as if they regretted having said anything.

The dogs were sniffing curiously at McCarthy. Melmoth could easily have made his escape at this point, but he was too tired. Listening to the velvety sound of night slipping away, he stood there in silence.

George bent over McCarthy.

"Well, not a natural death. Look at that, Ham."

Ham nodded, but he didn't come any closer.

"Suppose we just fetch the police?" he suggested.

George nodded. "If it was anyone else, yes, but not McCarthy. Think about it, Ham. There's something very wrong here. And like I said, not a natural death."

Melmoth couldn't see anything unnatural about McCarthy. A number of small wounds on the upper part of his body and his arms, some of them harmless, not much more than bruises. But there were some sharp stab wounds too, looking as if a knife had made them. The fatal injury was probably the one on the head, where thick, cold blood covered greasy hair. All perfectly natural.

"I can't see enough here! Give us a bit more light, Ham, will you? Over here, not back there!" George sounded annoyed.

"You're standing in the way," said Ham. "I can't shine the light through you. Move aside."

"I can't move aside!"

That was true. George was in the middle of the narrow slope, the only place where a big Two Legs like him had room to stand without falling over.

"Then he'll have to come down here!" panted the butcher. "There's nothing else for it."

George tried to pull McCarthy out of the heap of stones, but the body's stiff limbs resisted. George turned to Ham. "Don't just stand there, do something!"

The butcher sighed. He took George's gloves, put them on his huge butcher's paws as best he could, and climbed up the pebbly slope. A great many pebbles rolled down. He took hold of the corpse by one foreleg and one hind leg, with an expert grip, and heaved it up and then down to George's feet with a single movement. For a moment, the butcher moved as elegantly as a seal in the water. Something heavy clattered over the stones behind McCarthy.

"Here." The butcher pointed to the back of McCarthy's head. "Blow on the back of the head. With that, I guess." The butcher pointed to the thing that had clattered down after McCarthy. Melmoth cautiously searched the air for its scent— just a spade, the kind George used in his vegetable garden.

"Here's a nice piece of work! Why all this nonsense was necessary"—the butcher pointed to McCarthy's upper body— "I can't imagine. Just makes 'em nervous."

"It's unnatural." George shook his head. "A real murder. Who'd have believed it?"

The butcher looked at George in alarm. "We really ought to go to the police."

"Just a moment," said George. "Just a moment. We must think first. We've stumbled into a right old mess here. Think,

177

McCarthy of all people. What might that connect up with? Who would they suspect? Who'd have had a reason to kill McCarthy?"

"Josh, of course, for one. Sam, Patrick, and Gerry," said the butcher. "Michael and Healy."

George nodded. "Eddie, Dan, Brian, O'Connor, Sean, and Nora."

"Adrian and Little Dennis," said the butcher.

"Leary."

"Harry and Gabriel."

"You for another," said George.

"You too," said the butcher quickly. "Well, everyone, really. Except maybe for Lilly." The butcher waved his hand dismissively.

George bent over McCarthy again. "Just about anyone could have done it."

Ham nodded. "Some would've done it better, some worse."

"You'd have done it better," said George. "If we go to the police now, the first thing we'll have to prove is that it wasn't us. We need . . ." He pushed his cap back on his head. Melmoth knew that George was thinking hard when he pushed his cap back on his head. "We need an alibi. The only question is, when for? Can you say roughly how long he's been dead?"

"Hmm," said the butcher. "I keep them in the cold store, of course. But it's not what you'd call hot here either. So supposing he was a pig, I'd say at least . . . hmm . . . let's put it at four days. Only if you're lazy, of course, and don't process the animal at once, and then you're in trouble."

"And suppose he'd been in the warm for some time and he'd only just been brought here?"

"Even then," said the butcher. "At least three days. See these

178

bruises? Two days for them to come out, and as noticeable as this . . . three days, I'd say."

George's cap was pushed even farther back on his head. "Three days. Three days ago was Sunday. I was out at the caravan, thought I'd have a nice restful day for once. And you were probably sitting alone watching the telly?"

Ham nodded, embarrassed.

"A bad business, a very bad business," muttered George. "If we report this now they'll turn our homes over. And they'll search the whole caravan. That's all I need. Me, end up in jail because of McCarthy? Not likely! I say we leave him here. The next comer can find him!"

George turned and marched firmly off the way they had come. The butcher whistled to his dogs and followed him with long, hasty strides. Melmoth stood beside McCarthy and watched them go. Even in his deep and woolly weariness he was surprised. The carrion eater in flight from a dead body! Who'd have believed it? Melmoth watched his certain death trudging away again. *Trudge, trudge. Stone and bone. Trudge.*

The butcher stopped and turned. A deathly cold crawled over Melmoth's horns and into his head. He couldn't bear to die again today. First the fear, sour and steamy, then courage in the face of death, rigid but clear, then relief, soft and soupy, and now fear again. Melmoth knew he couldn't be brave a second time. Not now.

"What's the matter?" asked George. He had stopped too.

"I have this funny kind of feeling," said the butcher. "As if we'd overlooked something."

Melmoth froze.

George laughed bitterly. "If you ask me, we'd have done better to overlook a whole lot more."

But the carrion eater was on the move. Coming Melmoth's way. *Trudge, trudge, stone and bone.*

"There's something wrong," muttered the butcher. "Something doesn't fit. If I only knew what!"

Melmoth closed his eyes. This was the moment of final surrender to the carrion eater. Any moment he'd remember what was wrong, and then . . . Well, it wasn't much use keeping his eyes closed. *Trudge. Trudge. Over stone.* Melmoth could smell the hot, rancid scent of the butcher coming toward him.

"In the shop, in the shop," muttered Ham. "In the shop today, three pieces of pork loin for Kate, then Josh comes for his ten kilos of minced beef, he needs it for the pub, and there was twenty sausages for Sam's birthday—no, that wasn't it. Josh, Josh and his ten kilos of mince."

The butcher stopped again, so suddenly that George stumbled into him and swore.

"Damn it, Ham, are you off your head?"

But Ham was not to be distracted.

"And then there were the pickled pork ribs. Can't remember who bought those now. Maybe Dan. Or Eddie. And then there was someone else. But I'm sure about Josh. Josh told me McCarthy was in the Mad Boar yesterday, Josh was pretty sour about that, said McCarthy's plans had all passed the authorities, nothing to be done about it now. Yesterday, he said that was. *Yesterday.*"

George whistled through his teeth. It was the whistle he normally used to call Tess to round the sheep up. Tess was still quite young, and sometimes it didn't work, but Tess wasn't here today, and it worked even less well on the butcher's dogs.

"I can't make it out," said the butcher. "Who was drinking in the Mad Boar yesterday?" The butcher briefly shone the light on McCarthy. Its beam brushed past Melmoth. "Not him for one."

"Are you sure Josh said yesterday?" asked George.

The butcher nodded. "Yesterday. If you don't believe me, I'm sure to have it on the CCTV video."

"There's no sound on that, is there?" said George.

"Yes, there is," said Ham.

George raised his eyebrows, but the butcher went on, undeterred. "I did wonder. They ignore McCarthy for weeks, and suddenly there's three or four people talking about him. Well, I thought to myself, if it's all out in the open now . . ."

George struck his forehead with the palm of his hand. Melmoth knew that this gesture was kept for the big ideas in George's life. Like the idea of putting luminous paint on rats so as to see which hole they used for getting into the shepherd's caravan. Or the idea that it was Maple stealing the syrup from his bread. Or the idea that you could catch Melmoth by catching Ritchfield. Because Melmoth and Ritchfield went together like sandy ground and sea grass. When George struck his forehead with the palm of his hand, he was always right.

"It was them," said George. *"All of them."*

The butcher looked at him blankly.

"Who do you mean?" he asked.

"Well, exactly which of them I don't know," said George. "But a lot of them. A whole bunch of them. So many that all of them in the Boar yesterday are in it together. My God, Ham, think. They just decided to do it, the way they decided that the village hall needed a new roof. Those bastards. And they hid him here. Now they're going around telling everyone he was in the Boar yesterday. And once he's found a bit later, when the time of death can't be so easily established, they'll all have wonderful—well, alibis, dating from yesterday onward. Appointments with lawyers and doctors, trips to town. You only have to watch them over the next few days and you'll soon see."

"But . . ." The butcher waved his fat arms about helplessly. "You mean all of them? O'Connor too? And Fred?"

"I don't know exactly who actually did it, Ham," said George irritably. "But everyone who was in the Mad Boar yesterday was in on it, anyway. And probably some who weren't. I guess whoever really pulled the strings kept well out of that business with the pub."

"But suppose I'd gone to the Boar? I thought about it, sure I did. There was nothing on TV."

"Then McCarthy would only just have left. Or he wouldn't have turned up yet. Or they'd have seen him in the supermarket. Or at the playground, telling the kids about his bloody plans. If there's enough of them in it all together, it comes to the same thing."

"I just don't believe it," wailed the butcher. "I mean, they all buy my sausages. My chops. And they're *murderers* all of a sudden? I don't believe it."

"That's human nature, and you'd better get used to it," said George, but the butcher wasn't really listening.

"My joints of beef. How can I go on selling them joints of beef when I know for sure that they killed a man?"

For a moment Ham's breath hovered soundlessly in the cold air.

George suddenly froze. "Shut up, Ham," he growled through his teeth. Very quietly. When George was very quiet, it was important. But there was no stopping Ham now.

"They won't get any more meat from me, none at all!" he announced angrily.

"Ham!" George spat. Something about the expression on George's face made Ham stop. That soundless breath hovered in the air again. And there were footsteps. Footsteps on stone. Footsteps rapidly retreating. Then silence.

"Shit!" said George.

"Shit!" said the butcher.

Neither man said anything for a moment.

George sighed. "Well, now they know. We were okay up to this point. Now we really are in the shit."

The butcher's eyes widened. His scent changed to a bitter, sourish note: the carrion eater was afraid.

"George, you don't mean they'd . . . ? George, they like us. They didn't like McCarthy."

George shook his head. "They killed McCarthy just for a bit of cash. What d'you think they'll do with their own skins at stake?"

"The bastards." Ham clenched his fists. "Security, that's the thing! You have to safeguard yourself, you always have to safeguard yourself. I'm not going to make it that easy for them!"

You always have to safeguard yourself, thought Melmoth.

"But how, though?" the butcher went on. "We stumbled into this mess like idiots. Now they know. What's going to help us now?"

"Thinking will help," said George. "We have to find their weak points."

Find their weak points, thought Melmoth. *Thinking will help.*

"They don't have any weak points," sighed the butcher. "There are so many of them. You know how it is, George, one crow doesn't peck another's eyes out, and if there are so many of them all in it together . . ." He flailed his meaty arms about, at a loss.

183

"Don't panic, Ham. Think. There are always weak points."

There are always weak points, thought Melmoth. He would never have thought that George and the butcher could say so many clever things.

George pushed his cap back from his forehead again. "Hmm, well, we have a little time. They'd have to discuss it first. None of them will dare act alone."

"We're outsiders now," said the butcher. His voice was trembling. "Don't you see, George? There's no going back. Once you're out, you're out for good. Oh *shit*!" Now the butcher's whole large frame was trembling.

George put a soothing hand on his shoulder. It looked rather funny, because Ham was so much taller than George. "Ham, did you ever herd sheep?"

Ham shook his head.

"A flock of sheep can be herded because you know something about them. You know they'll stay together. They'll do all they can to stay together. That's why you can herd them. You can't herd a single sheep on its own. A sheep on its own is unpredictable. Sometimes being alone is an advantage."

Melmoth and the butcher were listening to George wide-eyed.

"If we're outsiders now, we'd better exploit the situation," George went on. "Find evidence. Your CCTV video—that's not a bad idea. And you sell newspapers in the shop too . . ."

Ham looked doubtfully at George. "Newspapers? Yes, but . . ."

"Good!" George nodded, pleased. "Are they in view on the video? Because then we can prove it—about the date."

Ham nodded, with his jaw dropping. What George was driving at seemed to be gradually sinking into him.

But George had been thinking some more. "Excellent," he

184

murmured. "Excellent. There are a lot of them. And a whole crowd together don't risk anything. We'll make sure the police find McCarthy right away. And you make copies of that video. Then we'll hide the cassettes. And if anything happens to us it will all get out!"

"If anything happens to us it will all get out," repeated the butcher. "Yes. Right! They'll soon find out what I'm like! I'll be at the lawyer's with all that stuff tomorrow. And my will. To be opened on my death!"

George nodded. "Only they'll have to know about it as soon as possible, or it'll do us no good at all."

"First thing tomorrow!" said the butcher firmly. "The first customer to walk into my shop will know!"

They turned again and walked off even faster than the first time.

But then George turned and beamed at Melmoth. "Melmoth," he said in a friendly tone. "Come here, boy."

Ham snorted crossly. "How can you stop to think about that animal now?"

"Because he's mine. My lost sheep. Which of us goes to church every Sunday, eh? Come on, Melmoth."

George was enticing him with his friendliest voice, the I've-got-a-slice-of-mangel-wurzel-here voice. Melmoth could scent that George didn't have a slice of mangel-wurzel there. All the same, he would have liked to go with him. Back to the flock.

But he couldn't.

No going back. Once you're out, you're out for good. That's what the butcher said.

Melmoth was alone. He must stay alone now.

Sometimes being alone is an advantage.

He retreated from George, step by step, until his hindquarters came up against a rock. George kept on coming. He took Melmoth's young horns in a friendly grasp with one hand, the way he'd done many times before. Melmoth fought against that grasp as he had never fought anything in his life.

In the end George gave up.

"Want me to help?" asked Ham.

George shook his head. "It's useless," he said. "He doesn't want to come."

Suddenly George had a knife in his hand. He came toward Melmoth again and took hold of the wool right beside his throat, looking for something. Melmoth stood perfectly still. Then George found what he was looking for: a narrow thread, buried deep in Melmoth's fleece. He cut it. A key clinked as it fell and lay on the ground, smooth and shining. George bent down and picked it up. He sighed.

Melmoth could remember the day when George had tied that key round his neck. "Because you're the wildest of the bunch," George had said. Not Ritchfield, who carried his horns so high, but Melmoth. It had been a great day for him.

George walked away without once turning back.

"Are you crazy, George?" cried Ham. "First we spend all day looking for the creature, now you just leave it there. What's the idea? It'll run off to join the first flock it can find. A sheep without a flock? No one ever heard of such a thing! It'll never make it!"

"Oh yes, he'll make it!" Melmoth heard George say as two pale cones of light disappeared into the darkness.

14

Lane Goes for Help

All was quiet now on the meadow in the evening. Pigeons wandered through the grass looking for insects, the sky was pale and rosy, the sea lay smooth as milk at the foot of the cliffs. Even the monotonous sound of Gabriel's sheep pulling up grass had stopped. Dull-eyed, they pushed with silent effort against the wire fence, where one of the posts had come loose from its fixings.

George's sheep took no notice of any of that. They were still sitting under the shade tree, marveling.

"You made it," said Cordelia admiringly. The other sheep were silent. Their hearts were still beating fast at the tale of Melmoth's adventures, the glittering knife, the carrion eater's scent, the howling of the butcher's dogs.

Melmoth was silent too. He looked a little as if he were still wandering through the stone quarry. In a strange way, he looked young again.

"Go on!" bleated a shaky voice. The winter lamb. Melmoth quickly turned his head.

"Go on with what, young grazer?"

The winter lamb, alarmed, hid behind the trunk of the shade tree.

"I mean, how does the story go on?" he bleated from that safe place.

"The story doesn't go on," said Melmoth. "A story always ends just when it comes to the end. Like a breath. Now. But life went on, over hills and dales, away from the roads, along salty beaches and shimmering rivers, in the misty mountains where the wild goats of Wicklow graze, passing through many flocks, like passing through snowflakes, all the way to the North Sea where the world ends, and on and on—and I just followed life winding endlessly away, like a mouse running through the grass."

"Then tell us about the North Sea!" bleated the voice behind the tree trunk.

But Melmoth wasn't listening.

"I always wanted the story to go on too," he whispered to a gleaming black beetle that had gone for a walk on a long blade of grass in front of his nose. "Into my own skin, back again, not with strangers out in the world. But I needed a shepherd for that, and the shepherd is dead." Teeth snapped, and the stout beetle, together with its blade of grass, disappeared into Melmoth's jaws. The gray ram chewed thoughtfully. Mopple wrinkled his nose.

"How do you know that George is dead?" Maple asked abruptly.

Melmoth stared at her in surprise. "How could I help knowing? My birds know, the air knows. The blue-eyed man brings his pale-eyed flock here. You've plundered the vegetable garden. The human flock goes trampling over the grass just as it likes. And besides," he added in amusement, "anyone who saw him like that in the night, with his quiet heart and loud blood and the spade through the middle of his life, anyone who saw him then could be fairly sure he was dead."

"You were there in the night?" bleated Cloud, all excited. "You saw who stuck the spade in George?"

Melmoth snorted crossly. "I didn't see that," he said. "Oh, if only I had . . ."

"But afterward?" asked Maple. "Just afterward?"

"The night birds hadn't started singing again yet. I found him before the carrion beetles did. I found him before all the warmth of life had quite escaped into the darkness."

"And then?" asked Maple intently. "What did you do then?"

"Walked around him in a circle three times to the left, walked around him in a circle three times to the right, three leaps in the air, like the wild goats of Wicklow when a wise goat among their numbers falls silent. Put my hoof on his heart. Difficult to say where the heart is in human beings. But you could tell with him. I'd have liked him to see me once again, just for a moment, so that he'd know I'd made it. One sunset too late, only one. Since the swallows last flew I've been hearing time pass by, trickling away like sand in the wind. Thought it was my time running out. Couldn't have known it was his." Melmoth looked sad.

Maple pictured his shaggy shape in the darkness, his glowing eyes, his fluid movements, several black-winged crows on his back. That solved the mystery of the hoofprint. She nodded. "The wolf's ghost." She saw it clearly before her.

The other sheep looked at her, troubled. They didn't like to think of the wolf's ghost—not even in broad daylight, when the sun was shining down on their fleeces and the gulls were screaming. Maude suspiciously scented the air on all sides.

The brighter sheep looked at Melmoth. Slowly it dawned on them: no wolf's ghost in the meadow, only Melmoth. Although "only" didn't seem quite right for Melmoth. They were all wondering privately whether they ought to be as badly frightened of Melmoth as they were of the wolf's ghost, or alternatively as little frightened of the wolf's ghost as they were of Melmoth. Or then again, the other way around?

Uneasiness came over the flock. Lane and Mopple, who had been resting comfortably on the ground up to this point, rose nervously to their feet. No one else moved. Ritchfield, who as lead ram was supposed to set an example in such situations, wasn't being much help to them this time.

All he said was, "Huh!"

Huh? Did that mean there wasn't a word of truth in the story of Melmoth and the wolf's ghost? Did it mean that more than one wolf's ghost was needed to upset Ritchfield? Did it simply mean that he just hadn't understood something properly?

They looked at each other, baffled. Finally their hunger came to the rescue.

While Melmoth was telling the story of that night in the quarry, not a single sheep had been grazing. They had been running away with him, hearts beating wildly, they had trembled, they had hoped. Now their main feeling was hunger. It was lucky that the Pamela stories hadn't been like Melmoth's, or they would probably have ended up a very skinny flock. Wolf's ghost or no wolf's ghost, the sheep began grazing with a hearty appetite. As they worked away, jaws munching, lips tearing up plants, nostrils and thoughts buried deep in the grass, their tension melted away like mist.

But then something moved in Cloud's fleece. The lamb slipped out. His legs were trembling, but he had a determined expression on his face. He looked around the meadow. Melmoth was standing only a few steps away, as if he were expecting him.

The two of them looked at each other.

"They say you're the wolf's ghost," said the lamb, still rather hesitantly.

"I'm Melmoth," said Melmoth.

"Then isn't there any wolf's ghost?" asked the lamb, wide-eyed. Melmoth lowered his shaggy gray face to the lamb. The corners of his mouth crinkled. The crows on his back cawed mockingly.

"But you saw him with your own round eyes, didn't you, little grazer?"

"I did see him," said the lamb gravely. "He wasn't like you. He was scary."

Melmoth snorted in amusement, but before the lamb could begin to feel silly, he turned serious again.

"Listen, little grazer, listen carefully with those nicely shaped ears, listen with your eyes, with your horns that haven't grown yet, with your nose and head and heart."

The lamb even opened his mouth too, so as to listen better.

"If you saw a wolf's ghost," said Melmoth, "then that's what you saw. I was with George that night, but who's to say I was the *only* one? He was a special shepherd lying there under the fleece of darkness. He walked through many worlds, he was a guest in many worlds. Now the pale ones dance in the village and the red woman has come. The silent black ones knock on the door of the shepherd's caravan in vain, and carrion eaters drop from the sky. Who knows who else danced around his dead body? Not you! Not I!"

"Cordelia thinks it's all a trick," said the lamb. "Cordelia thinks there are no such things as ghosts. But she doesn't believe that herself—she's afraid of them too."

"It's not a trick," said Melmoth. "You may believe Melmoth,

who has grazed in many worlds. Yes, there are ghosts in the world. Water-hole crawlers and hedge creepers, sea fingers and hay specters, they're only the most harmless. But when the Weeping Lamb cries out in the mist, the mother ewes can't help themselves. They have to go to him, you see; he pulls them in on threads, like a spider. And none of them ever comes back."

The lamb shuddered. "None of them?"

"None of them. And mind you never set eyes on the Red Goat. If a sheep sees the Red Goat, then a ram of that sheep's flock will soon die in a duel, and not even the wind can do anything to stop it. It's better for a sheep not to see the Red Goat. As for the Lone Mist, seducer of noses, it's better for a sheep never to smell that either, little grazer. A heavenly scent, like all good things at once—herbs and milk and safety, the scent of a ewe in autumn, the smell of victory after a duel—it tempts you and lures you and whispers in its velvety voice. But only *one* sheep in the flock can smell it. And the sheep follows that smell, over stick and stone, away from the flock without a backward glance, out into the moors, to a black lake in the bogs. A wicked little eye of a lake, staring at you . . ."

"And then?" whispered the lamb.

"Then?" Melmoth rolled his eyes. "Then nothing. No one has ever got beyond that wicked eye—at least, no one who trotted away again safe and sound. Only one sheep has ever escaped the Lone Mist."

The crows on Melmoth's back turned their heads, and their bright little eyes stared expressionlessly at the lamb.

"You?" whispered the lamb.

"Me?" Melmoth winked. "It's the story that matters, not the storyteller. Hear the stories, listen to them, pay attention to them, gather them up from the meadow like buttercups. There

192

are the Howling Hounds, Thule the Scentless, the Vampire Sheep, the Headless Shepherd . . ."

"And the wolf's ghost," said the lamb.

"And the wolf's ghost," agreed Melmoth. "Yes, you persistent little ghost watcher, there's the wolf's ghost too."

As if in confirmation, the crows on his back spread their black wings in the evening sunlight.

But Melmoth turned and trotted past Maude, who scented the air after him. He trotted past Cordelia and Maple, Zora and Sir Ritchfield, who had a conspiratorial expression on his face. Then Melmoth disappeared into the gorse hedge, and a moment later it seemed to the sheep as if they had only dreamed the strange gray ram.

But Ritchfield looked happy. "He's just gone for a stroll," he said. "He always liked the night. 'A shame to waste it sleeping,' he used to say. He'll be back. No sheep may leave the flock. Unless that sheep comes back again," he added, to be on the safe side.

After Melmoth had gone away the meadow seemed oddly empty to the sheep, mysterious like a calm, deep sea. They all crowded together on the hill and listened first to the silence and then to Miss Maple, who was busy investigating.

"Now we know why George left the flock," she said. "On the night Melmoth was telling us about, he discovered that his was the *wrong* flock. It had killed McCarthy. Imagine you're living in a flock, and one day you find out that the others aren't sheep at all—they're wolves."

The sheep stared at Maple in horror. Only the winter lamb bleated mockingly.

"But it was a secret," Miss Maple went on. "Wolves that

couldn't be identified just by their scent—wolves in sheep's clothing. And it wasn't to get out. I think it's what humans call justice when something gets out."

"Gets out of what?" asked Othello, who was beginning to take an interest in the case.

Miss Maple thought hard. "I don't know what it gets out of," she finally admitted. "If we knew what it got out of, of course we could just try to let it out."

"Justice!" bleated Mopple, who liked the idea of letting something out of somewhere. At least, it didn't sound danger-ous: a little kick against the right gate, or a push from Lane's clever nose, and the whole murder business would finally be over. But then he wondered why justice had been shut up in the first place. Was it dangerous? And dangerous only to humans, or to sheep too? Mopple kept his mouth shut and made a very sheepish face. He decided to opt for saying noth-ing and chewing the cud at such meetings in future.

"It's interesting to stop and think who was afraid in Melmoth's story—and why," said Miss Maple after a short pause. "George and the butcher were afraid of the body at first. We know that. A body tells you that death is somewhere nearby—and everyone's afraid of death."

Hesitant bleats of agreement. This subject of conversation was definitely too morbid for the sheep. However, Miss Maple went relentlessly on.

"But then," she said, "George and the butcher were even more afraid once they knew that the murderers knew that they knew."

The sheep looked at one another. Who knew what? Miss Maple made use of the general bewilderment to pull up a fat golden buttercup and chew it conscientiously. Then she went on.

"And why? Because the murderers are afraid too—afraid it will get out. That makes them dangerous—like dogs. Dogs who are afraid are twice as dangerous. Dogs who are afraid bite."

Suddenly a new idea seemed to occur to her. She looked at Mopple, who was still concentrating on chewing the cud.

"Mopple, what are you supposed to remember?"

"Everything," said Mopple proudly.

Maple sighed. "And what else?"

Mopple thought for a split second. Then he said, "Goblin King."

Miss Maple nodded. "Now we know why the children were afraid of George—even though he never hurt anyone. They'd learned fear from the older humans, like lambs. George was a danger to the older humans because he knew the secret."

The sheep, impressed, stayed silent. Miss Maple really was the smartest sheep in all Glennkill.

"But perhaps none of that has anything at all to do with George's death," said Zora. "After all, they left him alone for years—almost as long as a whole sheep's lifetime. Why now, all of a sudden?"

Miss Maple shook her head vigorously. "It must have something to do with it. The spade here, the spade there—it's too obvious. Spades aren't dangerous in the usual way. Ours spent years in the toolshed. So how come two people suddenly die of spades? Because that's what it was supposed to look like with George, even though he was really poisoned. Whoever murdered George wanted to remind someone of McCarthy."

"How about the butcher?" bleated Mopple, who had already abandoned his good resolution to say nothing and chew the cud. "The butcher knew about McCarthy too."

"The butcher," said Maple thoughtfully. "The butcher." It was

195

as if she were chewing on the word. "The butcher has safe-guarded himself. *That's* why no one kills the butcher! Was it meant as a warning to him—because they didn't dare touch him personally? On the other hand," said Maple, twitching her ears, "on the other hand it could be just the opposite. Perhaps someone wants it all to get out now. Perhaps he murdered George so that it *would* all get out at last. And now, after failing with George, he has his eye on the butcher. The village people are afraid of the butcher. We've heard that they don't want him to die, even though no one likes him."

"It *is* a love story!" bleated Heather defiantly.

"Not if the butcher comes into it," said Mopple.

But Miss Maple seemed to think that even the butcher could feature in a love story. "Why not?" she said. "The butcher seems to be interested in Kate, anyway. And he knew what happened to McCarthy back then. Perhaps the butcher stuck the spade in George to make it look as if the others had done it again. All of them together! No one would dare to give him away—because he's safeguarded himself."

All this thinking on Miss Maple's part was making the sheep dizzy. Wherever she put her sheepy nose, new possibilities came buzzing around like flies from the feeding trough. It seemed to be more than Miss Maple herself could cope with now. "We still don't know enough," she sighed. "We need to know more about human beings."

They all decided to recuperate from the strain of so much detecting in the hay barn.

After the hot day, it was musty and stuffy in the barn. The heat had hunted old smells out of all the corners and nooks and crannies. A young mouse who had died under the wooden planks last summer. George sweating as he forked hay through the hatch in the roof and down on them, a fragrant shower. A screw that had fallen out of his radio and still smelled the way it used to, of metal and music. Blood and the stinging ointment dripping from Othello's wound to the floor. Swallow's eggs under the roof. The smell of oil. The smell of many lambs. The smell of snow. Powder on butterfly wings.

All these smells scurried round the hay barn like inquisitive rats.

Sleepily, Maple listened to them. In spite of the heat she soon dropped off.

It was cool in her dream. She was standing beside a brook, and the brook was murmuring to her. Gurgling, humming, singing. The brook was saying that everything flowed toward the sea and nothing ever came back. But Maple didn't trust the brook. There was a large flock of magnificent white sheep grazing on one of its banks, and sometimes one of them crossed the brook. Every time it reached the other bank it was a black sheep. Black from head to hoof. Maple strained her eyes to see just how and when the change happened. The black sheep stared longingly back to the bank where the white sheep grazed, but the white sheep didn't seem to notice them until one of the black sheep took a run and leaped back over the brook. But it didn't turn white again. In mid-leap it turned into a large gray wolf. The white sheep scattered before it, running straight up into the sky. In her dream, Maple made up her mind to notice just how they did it, so that she could tell Zora later. But in her dream Maple also knew that she would never be able to bring the secret back past the moment of waking. An unnerving smell wafted down from the sky.

Maple woke from her dream with a start and was back in the dark heat of the hay barn. The smell of a flock of sheep!

Strange sheep, quite close! Only a moment later did she remember that Melmoth was back with them now. Melmoth who smelled like a flock of half sheep. He had probably returned from his nighttime stroll sooner than expected, Maple reassured herself. She wondered why Melmoth smelled so strange, different from all the other sheep she knew. Perhaps it was because of his wandering life. Melmoth had never lived the way sheep normally live, so why would he smell like an ordinary sheep?

It could be to do with the flocks he had met, flocks where he had felt good and stayed for a little while. So many different lives begun in so many different flocks. And none of them grazed to the end. It made Maple dizzy to think of it. No wonder Melmoth smelled like many different sheep.

Or perhaps it wasn't that at all. Perhaps Melmoth had met special sheep that he liked during his wanderings, and had brought them away with him as a memory, as a smell, as a grazing habit, as a voice in his head. Had Melmoth chosen himself a flock, a flock of ghostly sheep, which he was now leading along behind him on invisible scent threads?

This idea made her uneasy. She'd never get used to Melmoth's scent. No sheep could. As if to confirm that thought, she smelled the strange flock outside again.

And suddenly she was wide awake.

Not Melmoth! Nothing half sheepish, nothing mysterious and inexplicable. A young, shallow, greedy scent. Gabriel's sheep! Very close.

Maple bleated in alarm.

It was a penetrating bleat, and instantly brought the sheep back from their lush dreamland pastures to the night. Heads were raised everywhere, peering around. A little later George's flock was standing at the door of the hay barn, watching the goings-on in their meadow.

A closed phalanx of muscular necks and munching heads was moving toward them. Gabriel's sheep had somehow managed to break out of their fenced-in patch of the meadow and were now grazing toward the hay barn, close together, side by side, unstoppably. In the dark their bodies looked even paler, giving off a wan light. Now that they weren't herded in behind the wire fence anymore, you could see how many of them there really were, like one of those sputtering, buzzing machines that drove over the fields in autumn.

"Gabriel's no good at putting up fences," said Zora tartly. "He's a bad shepherd."

"What are we going to do now?" asked Heather.

"Nothing," said Cordelia. "Stay here in the hay barn. They won't come into the hay barn."

"But we can't let them graze our whole meadow bare!" Mopple was beside himself. "Where are we going to graze tomorrow ourselves? We must drive them off!"

"Do you see how many of them there are? How are we going to drive all those off?" asked Zora. "I wasn't even able to talk to them."

"But we have to do it somehow!" Mopple wasn't giving up. "They'll eat everything up. The hill. The clover on the cliff tops. The herbs down the cliff side, the herbs of the abyss."

"Not *all* the herbs of the abyss," said Zora proudly.

"George's Place!" Mopple suddenly bleated. "They'll graze George's Place bare!"

The sheep looked at one another in alarm.

"George's Place," whispered Cloud. "Everything we mustn't graze ourselves."

"The mouse weed," said Maude.

"Sheep's ear and sweet-wort!" said Lane.

"Milk-grass and oats!" said Cordelia. It turned out that the sheep had a remarkably good knowledge of the plants that grew on George's Place.

The thought of George's Place tipped the scales. It was bad enough if Gabriel's sheep were devouring what was really *theirs*, but to think of them devouring what was meant to be a memento of George too, the grazing they had voluntarily given up themselves . . .

"No!" Mopple was looking furious. "They're not going to have George's Place!"

And so it was decided that the sheep would defend George's Place.

Led by Mopple, the flock trotted over to George's Place. If Mopple the Whale wasn't afraid, then it couldn't be so very dangerous.

Once they had reached George's Place they stood around at first, uncertain what to do. How do you defend a meadow from grazing sheep?

But then Othello showed them how they could form a circle around George's Place, sheep next to sheep next to sheep, shoulder to shoulder, heads turned toward the strange flock. Othello himself stood in the middle of the circle. From there he could lend a hoof anywhere and help to keep Gabriel's sheep off.

"Now you just have to keep standing where you are," said Othello. "If they can't get past you, they won't graze George's Place bare. It's that simple."

It did seem surprisingly simple. At first.

When they saw the pale wave of sheep rolling toward them, however, they felt doubtful again. Some of Gabriel's sheep were already raising their heads and scenting the air in their direction. George's sheep tried to give a determined impression, without conspicuous success. A strange ram bleated something, then Gabriel's sheep trotted toward them. "Fodder!" they bleated.

Fodder! George's sheep looked at each other uncertainly. What did being a meat breed actually mean?

The first of Gabriel's sheep had reached the ring of defenders and were craning their necks in the direction of George's Place. What they scented there seemed to convince them. They began forcing their way through George's sheep as they would have forced their way through a hedge. Mopple bleated indignantly.

Now that they knew where the best grazing was to be found, Gabriel's sheep kept quiet, as if there was nothing else in the world to say. Inexorable as surging water, they came ruthlessly closer and closer to George's Place, with their sinister eyes and their blank, sinister faces. But for Othello, George's sheep wouldn't have held out for long. It wasn't just the confused pushing and shoving, it was the stress and strain too.

Suddenly Cordelia uttered an indignant bleat: a young sheep with short legs had managed to push her aside and break through the defenders. Othello immediately came galloping up and, in a single great charge, sent the intruder flying to the other side of George's Place and out again.

"This isn't going to work," he muttered.

George's sheep were forced to retreat step by step. Mopple alone still stood in his original defensive position like a rock among the breaking surf. He looked in alarm to all sides, where Gabriel's sheep were succeeding in pushing his own flock farther and farther back. Zora was looking stoical, but her back legs were already among the forbidden herbs. There were just too many of Gabriel's sheep. Suddenly Othello came up beside Lane.

"Lane, run," he told her. "Find Melmoth. Bring him here!"

"Find him where?" Lane was a sheep who knew what mattered.

"I don't know," snorted Othello irritably. "Anywhere!"

It didn't sound exactly promising, but Lane was glad she didn't have to stand around like part of a living hedge anymore. She could run. Lane was the fastest sheep in the flock. Without a word, she pushed her way through Gabriel's sheep and galloped off. Othello filled the gap she had left in the ring of defenders, moving in between Heather and Miss Maple.

"But how will Melmoth get them away from here?" asked Heather. "He's not their lead ram. They won't follow him."

"No, they won't follow him," said Othello. "They'll run away from him."

Maple snorted incredulously. Even Heather looked skeptical.

By now Gabriel's sheep had discovered that it was simpler to stand sideways and lean their whole weight on the defensive ring. George's sheep groaned.

Then Zora lost patience. She nipped an intruding sheep sharply on its nose. The sheep bleated in alarm. The strange sheep raised their heads, and for a menacing moment nothing at all happened.

Then the pushing and shoving, the pushing back and resistance went on. At least they had had a moment to get their breath back. But the sheep who had been nipped had sounded so hurt that none of George's sheep felt like trying violence again.

Then—all of a sudden—Gabriel's sheep stopped shoving. They just stood there, listening to the darkness. Their flanks rose and fell, quivering with strain—or perhaps with something else. All around them, circling ever more closely, a dark body was hunting through the night.

Later, none of the sheep could remember exactly what had happened. It had been a sequence of flight and breathless panting, of crowding together and scattering, of blind excitement and tense expectation. There was never any panic, never a sense that there wasn't any way out. There was always another step to be taken. Somewhere out there, someone was herding them in a masterly manner.

After a short time—it could only have been a short time, because their breath was coming clear and their hearts thudded only with excitement—all the sheep were back where they belonged: George's flock in the hay barn, Gabriel's flock behind their wire fence.

On top of the cliffs, her eyes shining with admiration, stood Lane, the fastest sheep in the flock, looking dreamily into the night.

15

Zora Learns Something About the Grim Reaper

Next morning the sheep trotted out into the meadow early to look at George's Place by daylight. They were pleased: George's Place was unharmed, and even the trampled grass around it was beginning to revive. Gabriel's sheep were back where they belonged behind the fence, and not one of them had ventured through the gap a second time. George's sheep felt proud of themselves. They waited expectantly for Gabriel to arrive. He'd see what his own sheep had done, and so at last he'd realize what kind of sheep he'd brought here to join them: just a set of useless mouths to feed.

It was quite late by the time Gabriel turned up. Even the bumblebees who didn't like early morning were out and about, and lizards were basking in the sun on the drystone wall beside the gate. They disappeared like dark lightning when Gabriel finally appeared in the meadow. Beside him walked a man with quick, restless eyes, carrying a black bag. They both stopped in front of the shepherd's caravan.

"It'd be useful to be able to get in," said Gabriel. "I could leave my stuff in there. And maybe spend the night now and then."

"That's right," said the man, with a wealth of meaning in his voice, and he blinked his quick-moving eyes, "very useful, that'd be. Interesting too. Let's have a look."

The man took several tools out of his bag.

A magpie landed on the roof of the caravan and put its head inquisitively on one side.

The man set to work on the door of George's caravan with his metal implements. Soon he was sweating. The sheep could feel the heat of the new day too. It wasn't comfortable, it was the brooding heat before a storm.

After a while the man straightened up again, and wiped the sweat from his brow with his shirtsleeve. The flies buzzed.

"Sorry," said the man.

"Meaning?" asked Gabriel.

"Meaning I can't open it with a couple of tools, just like that. You'll need plenty of time and a specialist."

"I thought you were supposed to be a specialist, Eddie."

"Not with this kind of thing. Yes, I did once learn, but when you only kind of do it on the side, along with the farming . . ." Eddie shrugged his shoulders.

"What's the problem?" asked Gabriel.

"The lock's the problem. A security lock. You don't just make a second key. You have to call the firm and give a secret code before they'll tell you how to do it."

"Ah," said Gabriel.

"Look, Gabriel. We both know why you want to get in there. Your stuff could go somewhere else. Why not just break the door down, and if it's wrecked, so what? I mean, it's ridiculous, fitting a lock like that to a door like this . . ."

"So I could get in?"

"You could get in, easy."

"But people would see?"

"People would see."

"How about the windows?"

"Same thing. Getting in, no problem, but people would see."

Gabriel nodded. "That'll have been his idea. We'll let it alone."

For a moment the man looked at him blankly. The sheep could feel how much he wanted to get into that caravan. Almost as much as Gabriel himself. Once again they realized how different George had been from all other humans. He hadn't been interested in anything but his sheep. The rest of the humans weren't interested in anything but the shepherd's caravan.

Eddie's face cleared again.

"Scared, are you? Of them, the drugs mafia. If they can make sure the police don't search that caravan it must be important to them. So there's something in it after all . . ."

"I'm not scared," said Gabriel. He was lying. Scent trails of fear made their way out into the air even through Gabriel's woolen jacket, steeped as it was in tobacco smoke from his pipe. "I just don't want any unnecessary talk. Seems like I'm alone there, though." He looked sharply at the man.

"A little more talk in the right place might not have hurt," said Eddie. "The way things are, everyone's doing whatever occurs to 'em."

Gabriel looked at the man a little like a lead ram watching a young ram frisking about, almost courteously.

"What d'you think of this, then?" Gabriel put his hand in his pocket and brought out another shiny metal object.

The man whistled through his teeth.

There was a strange expression on Gabriel's face. For the first time since the sheep had known him, he looked tense.

Eddie noticed.

"You don't find a thing like that just lying in the road," he said. "Where'd you get it?"

"Fell from heaven," growled Gabriel.

The man shook his head. "That won't do, Gabriel. D'you know what's going on in the village? In the Mad Boar? They sit there drinking and waiting. They talk about anything and everything, they even laugh at O'Malley's jokes. Only of course they don't talk about this—this here. They've a right to know what's going on here."

"Nothing's going on," said Gabriel. He looked hard at the man with his blue eyes. "I'm taking good care there's nothing going on."

The sheep flapped their ears incredulously. A whole lot had been going on here the night before, and Gabriel had been the last person to do anything about it. They began admitting to themselves that they were disappointed in Gabriel.

The man sighed. "Okay, so it's the key to a safe. But not a safe you can just get by mail order. A very good one. Expensive. Really expensive, I mean. Maybe it has a combination too. Maybe it needs several keys. But it's sophisticated, anyway."

Gabriel nodded, as if he'd known that all along. "About how big would a thing like that be?"

Eddie shrugged his shoulders. "Hard to say. Big as a microwave? Big as a fridge? Don't depend on size, not as far as I know. The advantage of the big ones is you can't just carry them off. But you can't blow up the little ones without blowing up what's inside too. All depends what you want it to do."

He was looking curiously at Gabriel. Gabriel just looked indifferently at his sheep, as if he'd known that all the time himself.

"Thanks," he said. "There you go, then."

But Eddie wasn't to be so easily shaken off. "It's nearly noon," he said. "Tell you what, I'll just eat my lunch here."

"As you like," said Gabriel absentmindedly. He had spotted the gap in the wire fence now, and he began looking for another piece of wire netting and a fence post under the shepherd's caravan.

"You're lucky they didn't run off," said Eddie.

"Well trained," said Gabriel.

"You know how to handle *animals*, I have to give you that."

The sheep were indignant. Well trained! But for a small miracle, Gabriel might now be searching all the vegetable gardens of Glennkill for his wonderful sheep. It was only thanks to Melmoth that they were still behind that wire fence and dared not come out.

While Gabriel repaired the fence, his sheep cast greedy glances at George's Place.

"They're hungry," said Eddie, with his mouth full.

Gabriel nodded with a touch of pride. "Yes, they eat a lot, but they're good doers on it. You have to fatten 'em up."

Gabriel marched over to the little toolshed behind the shepherd's caravan and rummaged about in it. When he came out again he had a scythe in his hand.

George's scythe. The sheep knew that curious tool made of wood and metal, but they didn't know what it was for. "People who keep sheep can spare themselves the use of a scythe," George always used to say as he polished up the blade with a red and white rag. Only out of conscientiousness.

Gabriel did not spare himself the use of the scythe. He did not spare *them* the use of the scythe. He began grazing at the foot of the hill, on the side facing away from the sea.

The sheep fell silent. This was the first time they had seen a human out at pasture, grazing. It was a terrible sight. In Gabriel's hand, the strange implement turned into a gigantic iron claw that passed through the grass with a hostile singsong note. Strange noises hissed over the meadow, like the sound of sharp-beaked birds flying low. Wherever the scythe had passed grass blades lay flat on the ground, offering no resistance. Gabriel was grazing, but at the same time he didn't want the grass. It was a picture of senseless destruction. The good smell that rose from the dead grass made things even worse.

The sheep felt cold in spite of the summer sun. Mopple began trembling slightly, somewhere between indignation and horror.

Apart from the wicked swish of the scythe there wasn't a sound to be heard. Gabriel's sheep themselves had stopped bleating "Fodder!" and were watching Gabriel with hunger in their pale eyes.

"Why don't you go for to reap that bit?" asked the man. "The grass stands much higher over there." He pointed to George's Place.

The sheep held their breath.

"Better not," said Gabriel. "If the others don't graze it, could be there's some kind of poison in the soil. All I need is for my sheep to die off now, just when they're nicely fattened up."

"You certainly know your way around animals," said the man. "Better than I know mine around locks." Gabriel gave him a black look.

A point came when Gabriel the grim reaper was satisfied with his work of destruction. He stuck a single long grass blade between his teeth where he usually put his pipe, and strolled over to the shepherd's caravan to fetch the wheelbarrow. Eddie was sitting on the caravan steps. He had finished his sandwiches long ago. Gabriel took no notice of him. He wheeled the grass over to his sheep and threw it over the fence to them. The sheep had struck up their bleating of "Fodder!" once again, and they bleated until the last of them had their noses stuck in the dead grass.

Then calm descended. Gabriel went back to the caravan, where Eddie was still sitting on the steps. They looked at each other long and hard.

"So you're just planning to wait for that will to be opened on Sunday?" asked Eddie.

Gabriel nodded. Eddie abruptly stood up, took hold of his bag, and marched off in the direction of the village.

It took the sheep some time to get over their experience with the scythe. No one still claimed that Gabriel was a good shepherd.

"He's not a shepherd at all," said Heather. "We ought just to ignore him. He doesn't look at us either."

A good plan. Soon afterward the rear ends of several sheep were turned toward the shepherd's caravan. They had decided to graze straight past Gabriel, demonstratively showing their contempt. George would have been indignant, but Gabriel didn't even seem to notice. However, one of Gabriel's sheep was watching them with interest. It was the powerful ram that Zora had seen before. He had stopped stuffing himself with the mown grass, and was looking hard at George's sheep.

Zora was the first to notice him. She had made up her mind never to speak to Gabriel's sheep again. She had come to that decision for the first time after her failure to strike up a conversation, and for the second time last night, when Gabriel's sheep had swarmed all over their meadow like pale caterpillars.

But this one ram interested her. He was older than the others and more intelligent, or so it seemed to Zora. Besides, she could scent an abyss somewhere between his pale eyes. She began grazing in his direction as unobtrusively as possible. She grazed past him once, then a second time. His eyes followed her, but nothing else happened. Zora decided to have a third try, closer to the wire fence.

This time she succeeded.

"Fodder," said the ram. "Death." He had a beautiful voice, gentle and melodious, which didn't suit his short-legged, sturdy body. It was the voice of a very elegant sheep.

"Yes," said Zora sympathetically. "Your grass is dead. He cut it down. With a scythe."

The ram shook his head. "We are fodder. He is death. Run away!"

"Gabriel?" she asked. "He's death? Nonsense, he's a shepherd. If not a very good one."

The ram shook his head again.

"We are meat," he said.

Zora gave him a funny look. Something in her began to tremble. The abyss was there, somewhere in front of her, but she couldn't see it yet. She could only scent it.

"Meat is fodder," the ram went on.

Zora shook her head. "Grass is fodder," she said.

In frustration, the ram banged his hornless head against the wire fence. A metallic sound rang out across the meadow. Gabriel glanced at them briefly.

"Grass is death," said the ram, with emphasis. "Grass *brings* death." He looked at Zora almost pleadingly. Zora wondered whether the ram was simply round the bend. She had never heard a sheep mention meat before. She was about to turn away and give up Gabriel's sheep for good as a hopeless case when two little words came drifting up to her out of the abyss. Meat breed, thought Zora.

The air was suddenly very oppressive. Zora uneasily breathed in the heat of the approaching storm. The ram looked at his own flock, still mindlessly feeding their faces with the mown grass.

"They eat. They get fat. They die," said the ram. "And I . . ." He lowered his head and said no more. Zora braced her hooves against the ground like a mountain sheep, to help her cope with the scraps of words whirling up to her from the abyss. Mopple, she thought, they get fat, a meat breed . . . under the knife . . . good doers . . . nicely fattened up. Suddenly the mists parted, and Zora could see the abyss gaping before her. It was the deepest abyss of her life.

The strange ram was looking at her expectantly. He could tell from Zora's wide eyes that she had understood, and he looked relieved.

"Run away!" he repeated.

"Why don't you warn *them*?" asked Zora, trembling. "Why don't *you* run away? Yesterday, for instance—instead of attacking George's Place?" As soon as she had said that she regretted it. The ram looked sadder than she had ever seen a sheep look before.

"Fear," he said. "Fences and fear. Fences made of fear. They're young, they don't understand, they're meant not to see it. The mother ewes forget. Every year. They *want* to forget. His fences are high. His dogs are fast." He was looking across the meadow at Gabriel with an empty expression in his eyes.

Zora understood. Her own eyes were moist. The bravest sheep she had ever met stood before her. A sheep who looked down into the abyss all alone, day after day.

"You'll turn into a cloud sheep," she whispered quickly. "Just wait, it'll be easy for you. I'll soon see you up in the sky."

Then she couldn't bear it anymore and galloped away, right across the meadow. Where could she escape to? Her rocky ledge? The abyss dropping to the sea seemed as nothing to her now. She was ashamed before both the strange ram and herself. But then she remembered how he had spoken to her: it was a warning. A message. She must warn her flock.

"He's crazy," bleated Heather.

"He said *what*?" asked Cloud.

"He said they were going to die," repeated Zora impatiently. "He said Gabriel is going to kill them. Soon."

"He's crazy," Heather said again. "Gabriel is a shepherd. He looks after them—better than he looks after us."

"You said just now he wasn't a shepherd," Maude pointed out.

"No, I didn't," bleated Heather snippily, and she marched off with her head held high.

"Why would Gabriel kill them?" asked Sara incredulously.

"For their meat." Zora realized why the strange ram couldn't make his flock understand about the abyss. Even her own flock wouldn't believe it—although they were so much cleverer and more intelligent than Gabriel's sheep. "He gives them grass to fatten them up quickly. And then . . . well, it all makes sense. They're a meat breed because they get fat fast. Like Mopple. He's from a meat breed too. George said so. 'Under the knife,' he said back then. Please, just believe me."

"Is all this what the strange ram told you?" asked Cordelia.

"No," admitted Zora. "Not straight out. But he was afraid."

The other sheep said nothing. They felt sorry for the strange ram, but could they believe his story?

Zora saw from their faces that they weren't convinced. "Please," she said. "I just know I'm right!"

"Hmm," said Miss Maple. "That would explain why they're not very woolly. Do you remember how surprised we were to see Gabriel going around with such unwoolly sheep? If it wasn't their fleeces at all he wanted . . . yes, that would explain it."

Zora gave Miss Maple a grateful look. The others were thinking over Zora's theory again. If even Maple, the cleverest sheep in all Glennkill and perhaps in the whole world, was interested in the idea, well then, incredible as it sounded, there might be something in it after all.

Then Mopple, of all sheep, attacked Zora.

"I don't believe a word of it," he bleated. "That ram is out of his mind. Yesterday they wanted to graze George's Place, now they're trying a different way of scaring us. I ought to know. I'm from a meat breed. Did George ever try to make *me* go under the knife?"

"George was different," objected Zora. "He wanted sheep with plenty of fleece, as woolly as Norwegian sheep."

But there was no stopping Mopple now. "Being a meat breed means something quite different," he bleated. "Being a meat breed means . . ." Head on one side, Mopple sifted through his memories. But nothing came to him. "Something quite different," he obstinately repeated.

And now he had definitely convinced the others—of the truth of Zora's theory. If even Mopple the Whale, with his magnificent memory, couldn't think of any other explanation, then Zora's story must be right.

Panic broke out.

Maude bleated "Wolf! Wolf!" and raced over the meadow in

a zigzag course. Lane and Cordelia buried their heads in each other's fleeces. The mother ewes, bleating in alarm, called to their lambs.

"We're his flock now!" wailed Rameses. "We're done for!"

"He's going to kill us," whispered Cloud. "He's like the butcher. We must get away from here!"

"We can't get away," said Sara. "This meadow is our pasture. Where would we go?"

Mopple looked indignantly from one to another. "Do you really believe her?" he bleated. "Do you really believe her? Will I be killed too?"

"You'll be the first!" snorted Zora, who was still furious that Mopple hadn't believed her.

Even Miss Maple could think of no way out. She glanced anxiously at the shepherd's caravan to see if Gabriel was already whetting a knife.

"The rams must know about this," she whispered.

The sheep looked around for their most experienced rams. Ritchfield and Melmoth were playing a game of catch-the-sheep like two suckling lambs, and Othello was still keeping well out of Melmoth's way. But when he noticed how upset they were he came trotting over.

"Wolf!" bleated Maude.

"The strange ram," breathed Cordelia.

"He's going to kill us all," bleated Mopple in resigned tones. "Me first!"

It was some time before Othello had the story straight. He too was alarmed. Othello knew the world and the zoo, but he didn't know any sheep from a meat breed.

"We ought to tell Melmoth," he said. "Melmoth knows his way around."

They glanced at Melmoth. He and Ritchfield had gone on to fight a play duel. Just for fun, Melmoth had let Ritchfield defeat him, and was rolling about in the grass like a puppy.

"Are you sure?" asked Cloud.

With his heart thudding and a queasy feeling in his stomach, Othello trotted over to the hill. The moment of truth. In a way he was relieved. For days now he'd been looking for a reason to face Melmoth at last.

In another way, the idea of looking into the big gray ram's eyes again after so long embarrassed him. Melmoth knew him better than his own shadow. He had seen all the mistakes of Othello's youth, all the stupid things he'd done—and he had criticized them mercilessly. Othello's own embarrassment annoyed him. After all, *he* wasn't the one who had stolen secretly off by night from the cruel clown's animal trailer, without a word of good-bye except for that single, silly remark.

"Sometimes being alone is an advantage," snorted Othello angrily. It had *not* been an advantage. Being alone had hurt— a single sheep along with four dogs, two ferrets, and a white goose. Sheep weren't made to be alone. Sadness spread between Othello's horns, and something like pity for Melmoth, who had spent his whole life trotting through loneliness, in his heart of hearts alone in every flock. Now something that had always seemed unimaginable to Othello had happened: Melmoth had grown old.

He bore his old age as Othello had never seen any other sheep bear it, but all the same it was unmistakably the weight of the world that made the gray ram's beard grow so long now. Othello wondered how a duel between the two of them would turn out these days, and was horrified. It was an idea he had never before dared to entertain. When they met for the first time, Melmoth seemed to know nothing of the stony weight of life. His hooves hardly touched the ground, every one of his movements was a picture of controlled power.

And there was he, Othello, with his four ridiculously young horns and bewilderment in his heart. Fight? *He*, a sheep? Fight *dogs*? "I don't know how to fight," he had bleated in his defiant young voice.

"No," Melmoth had replied, "but that doesn't matter. Fighting isn't something you know how to do. Fighting is something you *want* to do."

A question of wanting, like everything in a sheep's life. Admiration for Melmoth rose now from Othello's horns, admiration for the will and wisdom that had carried him through loneliness so long. Othello stopped abruptly, feeling awkward again.

Melmoth was lying in the grass right in front of his hooves, still acting the part of pathetic loser in the play duel. Amber goblin eyes twinkled up at Othello as if from very far away.

"Shadow caster," said Melmoth. "Better to cast a shadow than stand in the shade. But being in the shade isn't to be despised either, not on a hot day like this."

Melmoth turned his head to Ritchfield, who was standing a few feet away, still surprised by his victory in the play duel.

"I know a new game," said Melmoth. "Who's afraid of the big black sheep?" Gracefully, Melmoth sprang back to stand on all four hooves, and turned to Othello again.

"Who's afraid of the big black sheep?" he asked Othello. His eyes looked serious; it seemed impossible that only a few seconds ago they had been twinkling mischievously. "A great many dogs are, if you ask me, and several sheep if they're clever. And of course the man in black. Not me, certainly." Melmoth looked hard at Othello. "But the black sheep himself—what is he afraid of?"

So that was their reunion. A familiar sense of bewilderment spread through Othello. He explained what Zora had found out about Gabriel.

"We ought to escape," he said. "If you lead us we can make it."

"All of you? So many?" Melmoth's eyes skimmed the sheep like the flight of a crow. They were standing expectantly, looking up at the hill. "Sometimes being alone is an advantage."

"They won't go alone," said Othello. "Not one of them."

"Then they'll have to stay here," said Melmoth briefly.

"But . . ."

"Better that way," Melmoth went on. "Escape? From the blue-eyed shepherd? From the grim reaper? Not worth the effort." He glanced at the sheep again. "They just have to learn a few things, learn to teach the blue-eyed shepherd how to dance—and how to feel afraid."

16

Mopple Looks Sinister

A little later Othello had assembled the flock around the hill. It was the first time they had seen the black ram putting his heart into something like that. All the same, they still weren't sure. It was one thing to get used slowly to Melmoth's strange scent, admiring him for his adventures and his courage. Letting him teach them things was something else again. After all, Melmoth talked almost like a goat, and every suckling lamb knows that goats are crazy.

Melmoth had placed himself on top of the hill, where they could all see him. A hot wind was blowing through his shaggy fleece, making the wool ripple like trembling gray flames. His horns shone in the sunlight.

"Who is your worst enemy?" asked Melmoth.

"The butcher!"—"Gabriel!"—"The master hunter!"—"The wolf!" bleated the sheep in chorus. There had been so many enemies recently that they hardly knew how to choose among them.

"The abyss," said Zora philosophically.

"Wrong," said Melmoth. "*You* are your own worst enemy! Stout and lazy, cowardly and scared, thoughtless and simple-minded—that's you!"

Well, now it was out at last: Melmoth was definitely crazy. A waste of time to listen to him while Gabriel was whetting the knife. And yet—none of them dared turn their backs on him.

"Disbelief," said Melmoth. "That'll do to start with. You shouldn't believe what you don't understand. You should understand what you believe. My friend Othello, the four-horned, black, bold-eyed Othello, will help you to understand."

Othello trotted up the hill to join Melmoth, who signaled to him with his eyes. Othello began to graze. The sheep watched him for a while impatiently, because they weren't supposed to be grazing themselves.

"What you see is a sheep grazing," said Melmoth after some time. "Lost in thought as he hunts the green grass down, dreamily roaming the meadow. And now"—here Melmoth signaled to Othello again—"you see a sheep paying attention to his grazing, tense as a cat about to spring, all his senses spying through the grass, feelers out in all directions, all the way up to the sky."

Othello grazed with fervor. The sheep looked at him enviously.

"What's the difference?" Melmoth suddenly asked.

They thought about it.

"His ears," said Zora. "They twitched more often."

"He's lowered his horns further," bleated Lane.

"He's not wagging his tail as much," said Heather.

"His scent," bleated Maude vaguely. You could seldom go wrong with scent.

"Wrong," said Melmoth. "Wrong, wrong, and wrong again."

"His nostrils?" said Sara. "His nostrils are distended."

"Wrong," said Melmoth.

"His fodder," bleated Mopple. "He's eating different things. More clover. Less oat grass."

"Wrong!"

"There isn't any difference," said Maple.

"Wro— right," said Melmoth, looking at the sheep with sparkling eyes. "You're learning that the sheep who pays attention sees but is not seen. The only ones who can make sure you pay attention are yourselves. If you forget about it, you're your own worst enemies. Because there is a difference after all. When he pays attention, Othello survives."

"But Gabriel—" Sara began, but Melmoth interrupted her.

"Paying attention will help you to track down the Two Legs' hairless thoughts. Noisy hypocrites, scent deceivers, but there's nothing they can do if you pay attention."

Melmoth studied the sheep's faces to see if they had understood him. Thanks to George's explanations, however, the sheep had had plenty of practice in looking intelligent, and Melmoth realized that he couldn't find out what they were thinking so easily.

When most of the sheep had given up hope, the practical part of the lesson began. The first exercise was to glare at a large round stone with as much attention as they could.

"But stones aren't dangerous!" Heather objected.

"Don't fool yourself!" growled Melmoth. "If a stone flies at your head it can kill you." Melmoth chuckled, as if at a very good joke. Heather jumped away from the stone in alarm.

"The whole point is that we think the stone isn't dangerous," Melmoth explained. "Every lamb pays attention once it realizes its own skin is at risk."

The sheep stared at the stone with concentrated attention, and if the stone hadn't been a stone it would surely have melted under their piercing gaze like a patch of snow in spring. While the sheep were paying attention to the stone, the heat of the day broke in a mighty storm above them. The stone was wet with rain and shone in the lightning flashes. Thunder rolled, and the sheep were drenched.

Heather was the first to lose patience. "I don't want to pay attention anymore," she grumbled. "I want to learn to herd sheep like you. I want to learn to be dangerous."

"You won't be able to herd anyone until you can herd yourself," said Melmoth. "And you're dangerous already—a danger to yourself. Once you've learned not to be a danger to yourself, you'll be a danger to everyone else. Simple, isn't it?"

That afternoon not all the sheep learned what Melmoth described as "the art of paying attention, nostril broad, wide as the sky," but all the sheep learned something. Maude learned that she could sleep with her eyes open in broad daylight, Mopple learned that it was possible to go a whole afternoon without grazing, Sara learned how to shoo flies away by twitching and jerking various muscles without moving her ears, and Heather learned to keep quiet. Melmoth was pleased with that for a start.

Later, in the fragrant air washed clean by the storm, he began setting them practical exercises. They were to walk right along the cliff tops, paying attention to every step. Melmoth supervised this exercise from Zora's ledge. Later, he sent the sheep to steal Gabriel's dripping-wet shepherd's hat from the steps of the caravan, where he had left it when he ran into the hay barn for shelter from the cloudburst.

The sheep learned faster than they understood. They realized that if they watched everything with the amount of attention required by Melmoth, they had very little time to feel afraid.

Of course not everything worked. During one of Melmoth's mock attacks, Mopple was paying attention so hard that he forgot to swerve aside and was run down. Heather choked while grazing because she was paying so much attention that she swallowed the wrong way.

As evening came on, Melmoth taught them something very unsheeplike. He taught them not to let themselves be herded.

"But that's impossible," bleated Lane. "It just happens. It's in your legs."

"It happens because you let it happen," said Melmoth. "They can herd you only because you can't herd yourselves. Forget the flock. Forget the dogs. Herd yourselves."

The sheep practiced not letting themselves be herded until twilight fell. Melmoth had taken over the role of sheepdog and galloped around them, bleating frantically, a whirlwind of mock attacks, feints, and sudden withdrawals. Their job was simply to stand still.

They felt exhausted, some from instinctively running away, others from heroically standing still.

"Will we soon be finished?" asked Maude.

"Finished with what?" Melmoth looked guilelessly at Maude.

"Finished with all this learning stuff," bleated Sara.

"No!" said Melmoth.

"Then when *will* we be finished?" groaned Mopple. His sinews were aching and his back was stiff. Oddly, he didn't feel hungry.

"Well-rounded ram," said Melmoth, "look at Melmoth who has traveled the world in search of the knack of paying attention, and believe him when he tells you there hasn't been a day in his life when he didn't learn something—or a night either."

Mopple groaned. Now they could forget about their usual good night's rest too! He prepared for another set of stressful lessons. But Melmoth hadn't finished yet.

"On the other hand," he said, "you can learn while you're grazing. And even in your sleep. You'd better go on learning while you graze now."

The sheep were quick to agree that grazing in the evening twilight was an excellent method of learning. Later, they trotted off to the hay barn to go on learning in their sleep. But although they were tired as they had seldom been before, they found it difficult to drop off. A drizzle was rustling through the leaves of the hedges in the darkness. They stood there exhausted, thinking about strange rams and wandering sheep, stones and shepherd's hats, meat breeds and wire fences, all mixed up together. An owl hooted, and even that made them nervous. Then something crunched near the door. The sheep crowded together in a corner, but it was only Melmoth appearing like a black shadow in the doorway of the barn.

"You're not learning," he said. "You're not asleep. What's wrong?"

"Fear," said Maude.

"Fear," bleated the other sheep.

"Fear," said Melmoth. "It's not in here. It's there outside, isn't it?"

He was right. Somewhere outside were Gabriel, the butcher, and all the world's meat eaters.

"You must drive it away," said Melmoth. "It's an exercise. You'll find out how useful paying attention is."

And once again Melmoth gave them exercises to do.

Sara, Cloud, and Maude were to stand in the dark black shadows under the crows' tree, listening to the birds thinking their night thoughts. Rameses, Lane, and Cordelia must go to the hole under the pine tree and listen to the cold sea in the depths below muttering threats to the cliffs. Zora was to stare

224

at the sky and imagine it didn't go up and up, but down into a sky-wide abyss. Heather was to stay in the hay barn by herself and pick up the scent of silence in the nooks and crannies.

And Othello, Maple, and Mopple were to go into the village, find the butcher, and watch him until they weren't afraid of him anymore.

It was still drizzling. Raindrops ran like beads down the windowpane. Caught inside each drop was a trembling spark of light from the room on the other side of the pane.

Miss Maple, Mopple, and Othello peered through the raindrops. Inside, God and the butcher were sitting at a table together. Between them stood a brown bottle and two glasses of golden liquid.

Ham had propped his chin on his huge butcher's paws and was staring at God.

God dipped his nose into his glass of liquid.

"All just vanity," he said, "*female* vanity. They dye their hair, they wear those tight-fitting clothes, and we're not supposed to notice. It's not right, so it isn't."

"Kate doesn't dye her hair," said Ham. "All natural, and what a color too!"

"Not right," said God. "And it makes me feel so bad. It torments my soul. It makes me feel so *bad*, understand?"

"Listen here," said the butcher. "If I'm drinking with *you*, just imagine the bad state *I* must be in."

God nodded understandingly. "You don't think I like you, do you? You've made my life hell for years, you have, and all because of that . . ." He shook his head sadly.

"But I have to tell someone, see?" said the butcher. "Or I'll go crazy." His voice sounded oddly thick and slurred. Perhaps it was just because of the glass pane between them. "If George was still alive, I'd have gone to him. George could keep his mouth shut, you have to give him that. Not that it did him much good in the end, poor devil. And you'll keep your mouth shut too, old friend, you *will* keep your mouth shut, whether you like it or not."

The long-nosed man smiled wryly. "Frailty of the flesh. D'you know what it's like telling folk about heaven day after day, knowing all the time you're expected down in hell? Expected, did I say? I get visits from the folk down there *in person*."

"You think I fell off those cliffs all by myself, do you? Just like that? You think old Ham is getting shaky on his feet?" Ham glared angrily at God.

This was not the reaction that the other man expected. For a moment he fixed his eyes on the butcher. Then he nodded his head several times with great emphasis, looking like a huge turkey as he did so.

"Straight from hell they come. Terrible, they are. Weeping and wailing and gnashing of teeth for all eternity, and all because of the sins of the flesh. We have to repent of them. It's meet and right and our bounden duty."

Maple and Mopple looked at each other. It seemed as if the long-nosed man had understood what was wrong with the butcher's job. Meat, and right? The butcher himself, naturally, remained unimpressed.

"I mean, they was only sheep," he said. "I'd never have slaughtered a horse. Nor a donkey neither. Donkeys, well, they have a cross on their backs. In their coats. Carried the Lord on Palm Sunday, a donkey did. *That's* a sign. But sheep? That's what they're for. Bred for it and all that. You don't need to have a guilty conscience, I told myself. A nice clean death, and off into the shop window. Simple as that. But then, then . . ." And Ham's sausage fingers drummed a wild rhythm on the table.

God said nothing. A small, clear drop was hanging from his nose, quivering like dew in the wind. Ham's fingers stopped drumming. For a moment it was so quiet that the sheep could hear the rain on the windowsill, fine and nervous like scurrying mice. Then Ham reached for the bottle and filled his glass to the brim with golden liquid. The bottle glugged. Ham shook his head.

"George," he said, "now he was different. Gave 'em names. Funny names. Talked to 'em. Never got on properly with no one else. Once he comes to me and he says, 'Melmoth's gone. Three days ago. That's long enough, we'll take your dogs and track him down.' I thought at first he meant some kid or other . . ." The butcher shook his head, laughing. "Crazy. But he was all right, was George, better 'n the rest of 'em put together."

"George?" The long-nosed man had grabbed the brown bottle jealously and was staring at the butcher. "You don't believe that, do you? We'll never know for sure what he got up to in that caravan, but I can tell you one thing: it wasn't only sheep he dealt in, right? Huh!"

God rolled his eyes. He took a deep draft from his golden glass, and coughed. His eyes popped out from between their lids, all moist.

"George. Always making trouble for me. No respect. Not a God-fearing man. And d'you know the worst of it? Once they finally get me down there, I'll be seeing him again. Don't think it's just chance, do you? He's set them on me. Avenging demons. Why doesn't he set them on the others? They're all deeper in than me. I only kept my mouth shut, that's all. But no: of course he bears me a grudge. Know when I saw the first one? At his funeral! The mourners left sharpish. Anyone could see they had better things to do than watch George put underground, so I'm just . . . well, it comes to the same thing now, I'm just looking at one of those magazines, only for a moment, and then I hear something. I look up and there it is, a skull grinning at me right over George's gravestone. Tall as a man, but the head, the head was the head of a . . ." God's unsteady voice disappeared into his glass and came out shortly afterward as a hoarse whisper. "The head of a ram! Looked me straight in the eye! A black ram! With four horns!"

Ham nodded vigorously. "A white ram it was," he said. "Came at me. Pushed me off the cliff top. Huge, it was. Strong as a boar. Wild, too. Is that normal, now? I mean, they're only sheep. And now that one. Bright white, shone in the mist. I'll tell you one thing, that was no normal sheep. But why? I've been seeing him ever since, wondering why."

The butcher drank deeply from his own glass. God blew his nose in a handkerchief.

"I could have coped with that," he muttered. "I burned that magazine and I prayed. But then, very next day, that new tourism woman came to see me—we found one at last—and I was to show her round. Well, I only looked at her—and I suppose even that was too sinful for them. Anyway, up comes a demon at the window. In the shape of a ram again. Not a black one, no, a gray one, with huge great horns and black wings. Tall as a man standing upright. Of course I sent the woman straight off again, I sent her to Beth. I can tell you, I'll never be able to set eyes on a sheep again without cold shudders running down my back."

The butcher tipped the rest of the golden liquid into his mouth and looked sympathetically at God.

"Me neither," he said. "I've thought and thought about it. They told me I only spent one night in hospital, but it felt like weeks. I thought the whole time: Kate. Well yes, I never could forget her even though she up and married George. That's why I bought the CCTV camera, so I could look at her again in the evenings, see her coming to buy her turkey breast. And . . ." The butcher stared dreamily into space. "Thou shalt not covet thy neighbor's wife . . . but I never touched her, never, you have to believe me. So what else was there? I didn't even join in that bad business with McCarthy, and he did me more harm than anyone. The only reason I can think of is the slaughtering. But someone's got to do it." The butcher slammed his empty glass back on the table.

"And now it's all avenged," whispered the long-nosed man. "Every sinful thought, every single one. Even in church. Think of that, in the house of God! I was in the confessional . . . there was something I wanted to discuss with Gabriel. He came along, we spoke. And then . . . oh, the horror of it, Ham, the horror. All of a sudden the confessional was full of this hellish stink. The voice changes to a terrible bleating, I pull the curtain back and . . . and instead of Gabriel I see the *black ram*, with his jaws grinding away. Seven-horned, like the Beast of the Apocalypse!" He sobbed.

Ham put his fingertips against each other, a vault of thick, pink ribs, and spoke in a very matter-of-fact tone.

"Either it was wrong to slaughter them," he said, "and I'm guilty, in which case this here is just." His hands touched the wheelchair. "Or it was right, and this here is an injustice crying out to heaven. Now it doesn't say anywhere that it's wrong, not in the whole Bible, there's not a word about it; they slaughter animals in the Bible too."

"Vengeance," breathed the long-nosed man, shuddering. "Vengeance is mine, saith the Lord . . . *that's* what I ought to have told 'em back then over the McCarthy business. It was up to me. Too late. Vengeance—and now it's up to them down there." God's hand gestured miserably in the direction of the floor.

"There's only two ways about it," said Ham. "Either I turn vegetarian, like Beth, or I show them you don't play around with me like that. A white ram. Yes, yes, just a dumb animal, instinct and all that. So I tell myself sometimes. But then I'm only a dumb animal too. Everything we see, it's kind of just like—I mean, in a way like masks, know what I mean? There'll be something behind them. I don't know what, but I know it was a white ram. I can get hold of him. I'll pay him back for it!" Ham leaned his hands on the table as if he were going to get up. But he raised himself only a little way from his peculiar chair, and then collapsed back into it, sighing.

Suddenly something moved beside Maple. Gravel crunched. Mopple the Whale had retreated from the windowpane and was eyeing the garden gate.

Maple looked at him sternly.

"Melmoth said only until we weren't afraid anymore," said Mopple, trying to look fearless.

"But it's important," said Maple. "Maybe they'll talk about George. Maybe we'll find out something about the murder. And you're the memory sheep."

At that moment there was a crash inside the butcher's house, a harsh, cold sound with a frightened echo. Mopple jumped.

"There," said Maple encouragingly. "Something's happened. Come on, you'll have to remember it!"

In the darkness, the slats of the garden fence looked like sharp teeth, and the garden gate creaked with a hostile sound in the wind. Suddenly the lonely way back through the night didn't seem such a good idea after all. Mopple pushed his way back into the safe place between Maple and Othello and stared bravely through the pane.

Inside, the bottle had fallen over, and liquid was gurgling as it ran out. The long-nosed man was clutching his glass. Ham was staring, fascinated, at the puddle spreading on the tabletop, as dark as blood.

"It's not about your wretched little soul," he said in a very quiet voice. It sounded more dangerous than anything they had heard the butcher say before. "Sin or no sin, do penance and the Lord will forgive you— Don't you believe any of the stuff you spout every Sunday? I'm not interested in your stupid chastity. It's because you didn't mind about Alice afterward, that's the bad part. And I'll make you sweat for it as long as I can!"

The sheep could see how the butcher's anger was taking God's attention away from his glass again. He sat up straight.

"*She* left *me*," he said soberly and sadly. "Not the other way around, no. What wouldn't I have done for her? Anything! Even now I see her in every woman I set eyes on. That's my fate. That . . . that witch."

The butcher's hands clenched into fists. The joints cracked menacingly. Mopple nervously twitched his ears.

"Witch? All my sister asked for was a little honesty!"

In the face of the butcher's cold fury, the long-nosed man slumped back in his chair again.

"You don't know all I do for you," he wailed. "D'you think they've never thought of getting *you* out of the way? Who persuaded them not to? With the tongues of men and of angels? Me! And then one of those smart fellows worked out how

useful it would be if your chain was found at the scene of the crime. Kate's gold chain." He grinned. "Thank the Lord he confessed to it. I went straight off to find the thing."

"You mean Josh," said Ham, sounding almost bored.

God raised his eyebrows in surprise. "You know?"

"All I know is I still had it on when Tom called me to the pub. And then, when we came back from George's body, it was gone. Obviously someone wanted to pin something on me. Who else would it be? Josh, that rat. Doesn't like me, don't ask me why." The butcher shook his head thoughtfully.

"You should never have thrashed him like that after George's wedding," said God.

"Well?" the butcher snarled at him. "Did you find my chain?"

"No," admitted God. "But I tried to."

"Just because you know that if something happens to me it will all come out," said the butcher scornfully.

"Then go ahead and do it!" The long-nosed man was trying a bold approach again. "Nail my love letters to the church door. If anyone's even interested now, after so many years."

"Believe you me," said Ham grimly, "they'll be interested."

God sipped nervously from his glass.

"I don't envy you, listening to confessions week after week," muttered Ham after a while. "The stuff they must have to tell you! A spade! Who'd dream up such a thing . . ." He shook his head.

God leaned far over the table, so far that it looked as if he was about to topple forward, and stared at Ham. While the butcher had slowly collapsed back in his wheelchair, God seemed quite alert again.

"No one's said anything. *No one*. Not a word. Not even in the confessional. McCarthy, oh yes, I've heard all about that!

232

But George—not a word. They thought about it, yes. But no one says they did it."

Ham shrugged his shoulders, as if that didn't particularly surprise him. But the other man was getting more agitated with every word.

"This silence, Ham, it makes my blood run cold! Even before God they won't . . . I really wish they *would* confess. This isn't like them, you know. They were always mad keen to unload their guilty consciences on me. Perhaps . . . I mean, that with the spade is *sick*."

A crafty look came into his eyes.

"Wait a minute," he said, "how come *you* were back at the scene of the crime again? On the day of George's funeral?"

Ham made a face. Apparently he didn't like to think back to that misty morning. Eyes glazed, he stared out of the window, straight into Mopple's brown eyes.

"Because I wanted my chain back," he growled. "I had the same idea as you—even without confessions. That idiot Josh. And when the police didn't turn up to see me, I thought it must still be there . . ." Ham's eyes fixed on something, and he fell silent.

God laughed. "And Josh must have been looking for it too at just the same time—remorse and so on. He didn't find anything either. Seems to be a jinx on this whole thing, and in my opinion . . ."

God fell silent too when he saw the frozen horror on Ham's face. Following the butcher's gaze to the window, God too froze. He turned very pale, and his left hand went to his chest.

"There he is!" shouted Ham. "I'll get him now!"

With a skillful movement, Ham turned his wheelchair and raced it to the door. God was staring in amazement at the black

233

rectangle, where for just a moment three sheep's heads had been visible, bathed in reddish light.

Mopple, Maple, and Othello trotted back to their meadow in the drizzle. They had good reason to feel pleased with themselves. If they hadn't entirely banished their own fear, at least they had scared God and the butcher.

Othello trotted proudly ahead. He had impressed God with his four horns; the whole thing was worth it for that alone. Even Mopple trotted through the night with his head held high. Melmoth was right! With a little attention and a fearless sheepy gaze, you could really terrify human beings.

Deep in contemplation of his newly discovered abilities, Mopple had set a brisk pace and was now trotting shoulder to shoulder with Othello. He was about to fall a couple of timid steps back when Othello turned his head and looked at him.

"So *you* pushed the butcher off the cliffs?" he asked.

Mopple raised his head. Ah, to think of the way he'd attacked the butcher in the mist . . . strong as a boar! With a little attention, a sheep really could do anything . . . But then his memory switched in. Mopple was the memory sheep. He had remembered everything.

"No," he sighed. "He was chasing me through the mist. And then he fell."

Othello snorted in amusement, but his face was friendly.

"Quite an achievement, all the same," he said.

They looked round for Miss Maple, who had dropped a little way behind. Now and then, lost in thought, she stopped to eat a few leaves from the hedges along the path over the fields. The rams waited patiently.

17

Cordelia Knows Some Useful Words

Long ago, before Miss Maple had ever seen a winter, George used to have a slice of bread and butter with maple syrup for breakfast every morning. He always ate his breakfast out of doors on fine days, publicly and before the envious eyes of his sheep. First he put a little folding table up in front of the steps of the shepherd's caravan. Then he made coffee. Then he fetched the plate with the slice of bread on it, already spread. Then he had to go in again to speed up the coffee machine. While he did that, the bread lay unsupervised in the sun. All the sheep would have liked to eat it. But only Maple could count up to fifty. As soon as the coffee machine started gurgling because George had hit it with the palm of his hand, she was off. One to fifteen: Maple stole over to the caravan; fifteen to twenty-five: she peered in through the caravan door, to be on the safe side; twenty-five to forty-five: she very carefully licked the syrup off the bread, so carefully that not the faintest mark of a sheep's tongue was left on the butter (it was also important to leave a very thin layer of brown syrup so that George wouldn't notice anything); forty-five to fifty: she ran back to the other sheep and hid behind the woolly body of her mother, who found the whole business embarrassing; fifty-one: George came out of the caravan with a steaming mug of coffee and began his breakfast.

One day the coffee machine went wrong, and when Maple reached thirty-five there was George, standing in the doorway with his arms folded. That was the day when George gave her a name even before her first winter. The other sheep were a little envious, and her mother was as proud as if she personally had stolen the syrup from the bread. Maple herself pranced around the meadow until sunset, the youngest lamb ever to have been given its own name.

By now it was clear to all the sheep that Miss Maple really must be the cleverest sheep in all Glennkill—and perhaps in the whole world. So in spite of being so tired they went on paying attention when Maple, Mopple, and Othello told them what they had seen and heard God and the butcher discussing in the village. It was about meat again, and the fear of the knife that they had worked so hard to overcome revived. But Miss Maple wanted to broach another subject.

"God said something important," she remarked. "He said no one had told him anything. He thinks that's sinister, and I'd say he's right. If they'd done it as a flock, they'd feel safe and tell him. Like with McCarthy. God didn't give them away then, so why would he do it now? He didn't like George."

"Perhaps they forgot?" suggested Cloud.

Mopple the Whale shook his head. "Humans don't forget so easily. George still remembered in spring who'd been gnawing the trees' bark in autumn. McCarthy has been dead for seven winters, almost the whole of a sheep's lifetime, and they still remember that." It was obvious that Mopple felt respect for human powers of memory.

"No, it's nothing to do with their memory," agreed Miss Maple. "I think they're keeping quiet for some other reason. I don't think it was all of them together, like with McCarthy. They're not acting like a flock who have all grazed a place bare. They'd stick together then, crowd into one place, and wait. But that's not what they're doing. They're running about in confusion. They suspect one another. They all want to find out something about the others. Josh comes to see Gabriel to find something out. Eddie comes along. Gabriel watches when Josh and Tom O'Malley and Harry steal into the meadow by night."

The sheep bleated in surprise.

Miss Maple snorted impatiently. "We should have found out much earlier. Then we wouldn't have fallen for him so long. Gabriel is the master hunter!"

Gabriel, the master hunter? By now they thought Gabriel capable of any dreadful deed. But how had Miss Maple found out?

"It ought to have struck me straightaway," Miss Maple explained. "If only because Maude couldn't pick up his scent at once. Only Gabriel can disguise his scent, under the smell of damp wool and smoke. And what's more—" Miss Maple looked all round energetically. "What's more, he knew those three were in the meadow. He said so to Josh. He even knew that they'd made us nervous. How could he know that if he wasn't there?"

"But why would Gabriel hunt other humans?" asked Cloud.

"Perhaps he wanted their meat," said Mopple. "Humans aren't particularly woolly."

"No sheep may leave the flock," bleated Ritchfield.

Maple nodded. "I think Ritchfield is right. Gabriel is their lead ram. He doesn't want them running all over the place. He wants them to stay in one place and keep still—like his sheep. But they aren't doing that, and when Gabriel noticed that three of them had gone off, he went after them."

"He's not a very good lead ram," said Heather.

"No," agreed Miss Maple. "He can't keep the flock together. That's why he's sitting here watching the shepherd's caravan. There must be something important in there. Something that mustn't get out, whatever happens."

"Justice!" exclaimed Mopple.

Miss Maple put her head on one side. "Perhaps. It's a very important question. What do all those people want from the caravan? Eddie, Gabriel, Josh, Tom, and Harry? What are they looking for?"

"Grass," said Zora. "Tom said they were looking for grass."

That seemed to the sheep *too* sensible. Humans didn't normally have such reasonable aims.

Mopple made a skeptical face. "There's grass all over the place here. The whole meadow is full of grass—at least where *they* haven't grazed it bare," he added, with a dark look in the direction of Gabriel's sheep. "Why would they go looking for grass in the caravan when they only have to bend down?"

They had to admit that Mopple was right. Even humans could be expected to show a tiny amount of sense. It was an appetizing subject of conversation. Several heads bent to rummage about for tasty grass blades in the straw of the hay barn.

"I don't think they all want the grass," said Miss Maple, when her head came up from the straw again with a long seed head in her mouth, "whatever it may be. I think it's much more important to Gabriel for *nothing* to get out. Not even grass."

Mopple stared enviously at Maple's seed head. "But why?"

"Gabriel is the lead ram," said Miss Maple. "I think he was

already the lead ram back when they murdered McCarthy. He knows that George and the butcher made sure they were safe. If anything happens to them it will all get out. And now something *has* happened to George. Naturally they're all waiting for it to get out. And I believe they think it will get out of the shepherd's caravan."

The sheep gathered at the door of the hay barn and looked doubtfully at the shepherd's caravan, asleep like a stout stone in the darkness. Until now it had always seemed to them harmless, and the only thing ever to get out of it had been George himself.

"I don't know . . ." said Cordelia.

"Whatever it is, it won't get out," said Lane. "Nobody can open the door. Gabriel tried, and so did Eddie, Josh, Harry, and Tom O'Malley. And the man with the quiet car."

"But why do they want to open the door when none of them wants what's inside to get out?" bleated Heather. It was not a bad question.

Miss Maple twitched her ears. "Even if they can't get into the caravan, they must still be afraid that someone else may be able to, and that person will discover their secret. But if they get into the caravan themselves, they can find the evidence and destroy it forever."

They stood there for some time, wondering, thinking, or simply chewing the cud. Just as it looked as if all this thinking might end in a comfortable doze, Miss Maple woke them up again with a start.

"Imagine if it was only one person who killed George," she said suddenly. "Who could that person have been?"

Slightly shocked, the sheep bleated wildly in confusion. Gabriel and the butcher were their favorite candidates.

"Hmm," said Miss Maple. "Have you noticed something? A little while ago no one would have thought it of Gabriel, because we liked him. And now he's a suspect, because we don't like him anymore. Perhaps we're making a mistake. The murderer could be someone we like."

"If he's the murderer, we wouldn't like him anymore," said Heather firmly.

"But perhaps we still like him *now*. Or her," said Miss Maple.

"Rebecca?" bleated Cloud, shocked.

"What do we know about her—except that she smells nice?" said Miss Maple. "She simply turns up after George's death. She acts as if she'd come just about the tourist trade, but that's not true. She's trying to find out things about George."

"She wants to find the murderer too," said Othello.

"Or to make sure the murderer isn't found. She asked if there were any suspects. Perhaps she just wants to know if there's anyone on her trail."

It didn't sound improbable. Beautiful daughters often caused their fathers' deaths in the Pamela novels. All the same, none of the sheep could get around to liking this theory.

"She gave me the last tomato," said Othello. A number of the sheep looked defiantly at Maple. Was a woman who could do a thing like that capable of murder?

But Miss Maple was not to be moved. "She doesn't come from here. She's not afraid of anything getting out. She doesn't even know that something could get out. And do you remember what Beth said about the spade, the body, and the Devil's hounds?"

" 'Can you imagine what horror that lost soul must have felt beside the body, with the spade?' " said Mopple.

"Exactly." Miss Maple looked at Mopple the Whale approvingly. "But Rebecca doesn't come from here. She has no idea about the Devil's hounds. She certainly wouldn't have felt horrified."

"Well, she's brave. So what?" snorted Othello. "That doesn't prove anything."

"You're right." Miss Maple sighed. The sheep could see how tired she was. "No, it doesn't prove anything."

Deep in thought, she began trotting up and down the confined space of the hay barn. Some of the sheep bleated indignantly when she pushed them aside or bumped into them, but Miss Maple didn't seem to hear them.

"The small puzzles are solving themselves," murmured Miss Maple. "One by one, like buds opening. Now we know why the butcher and Josh were out on the meadow in the mist— because of the Thing. We know who bent down and what he put there: it was Josh leaving the Thing. We know who the wolf's ghost is—and who the master hunter is. But what about the big puzzle? What about the murder? Why doesn't that fit?"

She trotted briskly toward Sara, who managed to get out of her way at the last moment.

"Though perhaps not everything has to fit. Perhaps it's a mistake to think that everything always has to fit together. In that detective story it was all supposed to fit, and then it got tangled up, and George threw the book away. Perhaps the answer is that many things simply don't fit. Things that we think are connected, but really they don't have anything to do with each other."

Miss Maple had stopped.

"We must concentrate more on the big puzzle," she explained. "The big puzzle . . . is . . . the spade!"

Then Miss Maple said nothing for a long time. At first it

241

looked as if she were thinking very profoundly about something. But soon afterward deep and regular breathing gave away the fact that the cleverest sheep in Glennkill had dropped off to sleep.

Next morning the sea was growling, and yellowish light made the hatches in the roof of the hay barn glow like cat's eyes in the dark. But the birds were singing their morning song outside, carefree as ever. Finally a dissonant bird, far away at first, then coming closer and closer, joined their chorus.

Peering out of the hay barn, the sheep saw Gabriel sitting down on the steps of the shepherd's caravan again. He was whistling.

The sheep looked at their new shepherd through the light morning mist.

"We have to get rid of him!" said Heather.

No one contradicted her.

"But how?" asked Lane.

They watched Gabriel sitting on the steps, as firmly rooted as a pine tree on top of the cliffs, surrounding himself with pipe smoke. It was impossible to imagine a sheep—even a whole flock of sheep—doing anything to shift him.

"Fear," said Zora. "We must make him feel afraid."

They thought of what made *them* feel afraid: large dogs, noisy cars, the stinging ointment, wolves' ghosts, the scent of carnivores. None of those things seemed likely to drive Gabriel away.

They looked at each other blankly.

"Pay attention," snorted Melmoth suddenly. "If you'd all been paying attention, you'd have found out what Gabriel's afraid of long ago. What do human beings do when they're afraid?"

Miss Maple widened her eyes. "They put up fences," she said.

All heads turned to look at Gabriel's sheep, who were staring through the wire netting hungrily again.

"What can happen to them behind that fence, with all the fodder Gabriel throws to them every day?" bleated Heather bitterly.

"They could be ill," said Melmoth.

"We don't want them to be ill," said Zora. "They have a hard enough time as it is."

"If they fall ill they could pass it on to us!" bleated Mopple in alarm.

Melmoth winked in a conspiratorial way. "And suppose *we* fall ill?"

All of a sudden Cordelia's head was full of words. All the mysterious names she had learned from George had broken out and galloped wildly through her thoughts: prophylactics, foot rot, meningitis, Creutzfeld-Jakob . . . the book about the diseases of sheep had been full of strange words. And they all meant something.

A short time later the sheep had a plan.

They disappeared into the hay barn to rehearse. When they trotted out into the daylight again quite a while later, they themselves were rather bemused by the terror they had conjured up in the dim light of the barn.

Now they'd teach Gabriel to be afraid.

But Gabriel wasn't sitting on the steps of the shepherd's caravan anymore, he was grazing again. The cold song of the scythe rose above the meadow, and the grass fell down at Gabriel's feet. The sheep shuddered. They decided to wait until Gabriel had finished. Then, suddenly, the wind brought them not just the swish of the scythe and the scent of dead grass.

There was something much more terrible in the air blown from the village by the morning wind. They galloped up the hill and stood there, watching the butcher wheel his chair bumpily along the path through the fields and then right across the meadow to Gabriel.

The scythe sang a loud song, and the butcher's wheels made almost no sound in the grass. It was possible that Gabriel really hadn't noticed anything yet. At least, he didn't look up from his work.

The butcher was sweating. He watched for some time as the blades of grass flung themselves into the dust before Gabriel.

Then he said, "For all flesh is grass."

The scythe stopped in midair. Gabriel turned to the butcher and smiled his winning smile.

"The other way around," he said. "All grass is as good as flesh once I've fed it to the creatures there."

The sheep cast meaningful glances at one another. As if he had sensed it, the butcher suddenly turned in the direction of the hill and narrowed his eyes.

Gabriel looked at the butcher long and hard. "What brings you here, Ham?" he asked cautiously.

Ham was sweating from his laborious ride through the grass, and his hair, which had looked so nice and golden in God's house, was gray and sticking to his forehead. He looked nervously to all sides.

"Are you coming to the opening of George's will under the lime tree today?" he abruptly asked Gabriel. "At twelve noon. I just wondered if you'd heard of it."

Ham wheeled himself a little closer to the shepherd, until he was sitting directly opposite him, looking up inquiringly at him from below.

Gabriel shook his head. "Ham. People have been talking of nothing else for almost a week now. *Everyone's* heard about it. And everyone will come—everyone who has the use of his legs," he added, glancing down at Ham. "Everyone who's not dead yet. Except for Father Will, of course. He'll be showing he's not interested in worldly things. Won't miss a golden opportunity like that. You didn't come to ask me about the opening of the will. What do you want, Ham?"

Ham passed his sausagelike fingers over the wheels of his chair in embarrassment.

"I wanted to warn you," he said quietly.

"Warn me?" Gabriel's eyes were narrowed. "What could you want to warn me about, Ham?"

"Them." Ham cast a quick glance in the direction of the hill. His eyes passed nervously over the flock until they found Mopple. Mopple bleated uneasily. The paying-attention method didn't work nearly so well when the butcher wasn't behind a pane of glass.

"The sheep?" Gabriel lowered his scythe. "Oh, come on, Ham, we're alone here. Never mind the veiled allusions. If you want to threaten me you can go about it openly."

"Threaten you? Why would I want to threaten you, of all people? You've no idea! You're one of the few decent people around here. I want to warn you."

"About the sheep?" asked Gabriel.

"About the sheep," Ham agreed. "You probably think I'm crazy. I think so myself quite often. I wonder if something happened to my head when I fell. But that's not right, because it happened before that. The ram was there first! Don't you see? He was there first! It's his doing!" Ham pointed to the hill with one fat finger. "You think they're harmless animals and you can do what you like with them. That's what I thought too. Ha!" The butcher laughed bitterly.

"So?" said Gabriel, sounding irritated.

"I was wrong," said the butcher. "They know just what's going on around here. You ask Father William. They chased us yesterday! Specially that fat one. He's a devil, he is!"

"The one at the back trying to hide behind the gray ram?"

"Exactly!" Ham mopped some drops of sweat from his brow with a handkerchief. Gabriel had just been staring at the sheep after looking the way Ham's finger was pointing, but now something else seemed to occur to him. He narrowed his eyes again.

"You were talking to Father Will yesterday. *You?* Talking to *Will?* Well, signs and wonders will never cease!"

Ham nodded. "A sign. Yes. But what of? It's for sure I'm not putting up with it. Look at them! There was three of them yesterday. I tell you, those are no normal sheep! See the way they're putting their heads together? They're planning how to trick you."

The sheep looked at one another in alarm.

Gabriel shaded his eyes with his hand and looked at them again.

"I do believe you're right," he said to Ham.

A sigh passed through the flock. Now Gabriel knew. He wouldn't disappear. *They* were the ones who'd disappear from the meadow. For all flesh was grass, and that was because all grass was as good as flesh. And that meant meat. Meat was right, God said. Gabriel had admitted it himself.

Ham looked up at Gabriel in surprise. "Really?" he asked. "You believe me?"

Gabriel nodded calmly.

On the hill, sheep's heads sank into the grass, resigned to their fate. Only Maude still persisted in staring at Gabriel and the butcher. "Let's try it, all the same," she bleated.

"They're certainly not ordinary sheep," said Gabriel. "Unusually unprofitable, that's what they are. Old breeds. Not good doers, don't have enough lambs. What George planned for them is a mystery to me."

Ham was awkwardly twisting his waistcoat button. "Maybe you'd sell me one of them? The ram at the back there?"

"The dangerous one?"

Mopple was rigid with terror. But suddenly the butcher lowered his eyes.

"You don't believe me," he said, resigned. He didn't seem to want to talk to Gabriel anymore.

The butcher turned his chair and wheeled it away from Gabriel. Gabriel watched for a while as he made his laborious way back through the grass. Then the shepherd made a trumpet of his hands and shouted after Ham.

"Hey, Ham," he called. "Are you coming to the Smartest Sheep in Glennkill contest the day after tomorrow?"

But Ham didn't turn to him. Sweating and panting, he just wheeled the chair faster through the grass, making for the path across the fields.

As soon as Ham had turned off along the path, Gabriel began grinning. Now he'd finally got the old bastard's measure. Right round the bend! He shook his head and raised his scythe again. But something distracted his attention. One of George's sheep had stumbled and fallen on the grass. A Blackface sheep. Gabriel's grin broadened. Old domesticated breed! Sure-footed! The things folk claimed! The sheep picked itself up with difficulty. After a couple of steps it fell over again. Behind it, a second sheep stumbled. A fat ram was rubbing his head on the wall of the hay barn as if possessed. Gabriel's grin froze on his lips. His blue eyes suddenly didn't look like ice anymore but like meltwater, murky and unsteady. The scythe fell on the grass.

"Shit!" said Gabriel. "Scrapie. Shit, shit, shit!"

The sheep were still reeling about, picking their way through the grass with shaky, unnaturally high stepping movements, long after Gabriel had stopped looking at them. They were having fun. Gabriel had whistled up his dogs at once. He tore a gap in the wire fence that he had put up with so much trouble only a few days before. The sheep now witnessed a masterly display of the art of herding. Within a few seconds Gabriel's dogs had driven his sheep out of the enclosure in perfect order, without panicking a single one of them. A few minutes later, a cloud of dust on the path through the fields and the empty wire-fenced enclosure were all that was left to remind anyone of Gabriel and his sheep.

"We won't be seeing him again," said Heather happily.

"Oh yes, we will," said Maple. "We'll be seeing him again at noon today, when the shadows are short. Under the old lime tree. Maybe it will come out then."

18

A Lamb Cries in the Night

"The last will and testament of George Glenn," said the lawyer. "Drawn up and signed this thirtieth day of April, nineteen hundred and ninety-nine, in the presence of three witnesses, one being a sworn lawyer, namely myself."

The lawyer looked round. A pair of curious eyes gleamed behind his glasses. Not only were the villagers of Glennkill keen to know what would happen next, so was the lawyer. The atmosphere under the lime tree was like the air before a summer storm: ominous and expectant. The suspense was terrible. Silent, oppressive heat, a thunderstorm brewing in their heads.

"To be publicly read on the Sunday following my death, or one Sunday later, at twelve noon under the old village lime tree of Glennkill." The lawyer looked up at the canopy of leaves above him. One leaf had floated down and landed on his immaculately tailored shoulder. He plucked it off and turned it this way and that in front of his eyes.

"Undoubtedly a lime tree," he said. "But is it the village lime?"

"Yes, yes," said Josh impatiently. "That's the village lime. You can get started."

"No, I can't," said the lawyer.

"You can't?" asked Lilly. "You make us all come here and now you aren't going to read us the will?"

"No," said the lawyer again.

"What's the idea?" asked Eddie.

The lawyer sighed. Suddenly a watch glinted on his wrist. A very fine watch, like the one George had worn for working in his vegetable garden. "It's exactly eleven fifty-six. Believe me, I'm right." That was meant for those present who had looked at their own wristwatches. "I can't help you before twelve."

The humans began muttering. Annoyance, indignation, nervousness, and even a little relief crept into their insectlike voices.

Led by Othello, the sheep ventured closer. They had set off all together when the time of short shadows began, to see if the Will and Testament would reveal anything. The murderer, or at least an important clue. No one took any notice of them. Othello had drummed it into them that they must creep up to the humans as quietly and naturally as dogs. But even if they had galloped up to the lime tree bleating at the tops of their voices, hardly anyone would have noticed. The human beings were much too busy looking at their watches.

The church clock struck twelve. "Now!" the people under the lime tree whispered. But the lawyer shook his head. "It's fast. You want to put it right next chance you get."

Another angry mutter. Then the humans fell silent one by one. Yet again Mopple saw fear padding through their ranks with its mane blowing in the wind, rubbing around the landlord Josh's legs like a cat, sending its cold breath down Eddie's back, grinning as it sniffed at Kate's black dress.

Then a muted murmur rose from the humans again. Rebecca

had joined them, her dress like a drop of blood against the mourning black that most of them wore. All eyes followed her, one pair after another. Othello could see exactly what was going on: Rebecca was a feast, and the men were grazing.

The lawyer let his watch disappear again under a white cuff. He cleared his throat to get the villagers' attention back.

The sheep were all agog. This was the first time in ages that they'd had anything read aloud to them. And George himself had written the will.

"To my wife, Kate, I leave my library, including seventy-three trashy novels, one detective story, a book of Irish fairy tales, and a book on the diseases of sheep, as well as everything else that the law considers her due."

The lawyer looked up. "You can keep the house," he said, "and you'll get a small annuity too." Kate nodded, gritting her teeth.

"To my daughter, Rebecca Flock—" A whisper ran through the crowd. George? Daughter? A little something on the side? Adultery?

"—I leave my landed property, consisting of pastures in Glennkill, Golagh, and Tullykinree."

Othello looked at Rebecca in her bright red dress. She was like a poppy standing among the black- and gray-clad villagers. She had gone very pale, and her lips were compressed. No one was taking any notice of her. Kate sobbed. Ham looked at her with concern.

"So that's it," someone or other said.

"No," said the lawyer, "that's not it."

Mopple could positively see muscles tensing under the people's black clothes. Would it get out now? But if so, what was it? Mopple prepared for flight.

"To Beth Jameson I leave my Bible."

Bible-thumping Beth, sitting in the third row, began sobbing uncontrollably with her hand over her mouth.

"To Abraham Rackham I leave my Smith & Wesson with its silencer, being of the opinion that he will need it." Ham sat there in his wheelchair. His eyes were moist. He nodded grimly.

"I know what you are thinking now," said the lawyer. "Not all of you but enough."

"How can you know that?" Lilly asked him.

"I'm quoting," said the lawyer. The expression on the villagers' faces was blank. The lawyer sighed again. The sheep sympathized with him. Even they knew what "quoting" meant. Roughly, anyway. It was something like "reading aloud."

"And I have considered it for a long time," the lawyer went on, "but I won't do it. Just go on living your lousy little lives."

The lawyer looked up. "I expect you can make more of that than I do."

"Is that all?" asked Josh, with perceptible relief in his voice.

The lawyer shook his head, cleared his throat, and leafed through his papers.

"The rest of my fortune, amounting at the present time to the sum of"—and here the lawyer mentioned a number that the sheep had never heard before—"I leave to . . ."

The lawyer was taking his time. His clever eyes glittered through his glasses as he observed the people of Glennkill under half-closed lids. They had gone very quiet. In the middle of this silence, Kate burst into hysterical laughter.

"I leave to my sheep so that they can go to Europe as I promised them."

Kate went on laughing in the silence, an ugly laugh that penetrated the sheep's fleeces like cold rain. Ham blinked hard, as if the same rain were falling on him too.

"Is that some kind of a joke?" asked Harry the Sinner.

"No," said the lawyer, "it's perfectly legal. I shall administer the money. Of course the animals will also need an authorized representative to go with them to Europe as their shepherd. That representative's rights and duties are clearly set out in the will."

"So who is it, then?" asked Tom O'Malley, in suspense.

"That," said the lawyer, "hasn't been decided yet. I am to use my own judgment in appointing one, preferably now. Does anyone present happen to want the job?"

Silence.

The lawyer nodded. "Of course you need to know what it would entail. I have prepared some details here." And he handed printed sheets out to the villagers.

Lilly giggled. "'The sheep are to have stories read aloud to them for at least half an hour a day'? Who'd do a thing like that?"

"The authorized representative," said the lawyer. "All the conditions will of course be checked by a third party, namely me."

"'None of the sheep may be sold, none of the sheep may be slaughtered'? 'In breeding them, a dense fleece is to be the prime concern'?" asked Eddie. "Not what you'd call economic."

"It doesn't have to be," said the lawyer. "You'll see the representative's salary at the bottom of the page. Every time one of the sheep dies it will be decreased by a certain amount, but it still appears to me a handsome figure."

"And when they're all dead?" asked Gabriel. "Of an epidemic, for instance?"

"In that case there will be a small final premium in recognition of services rendered, and all further payments will lapse."

Gabriel stepped forward. "I'll do it," he said.

"Very good," said the lawyer. "Any other offers?"

The people of Glennkill looked at one another nervously. They looked at their printed sheets and then back at Gabriel and the lawyer. Some of them seemed to be thinking feverishly. A strange light had come into their eyes, and suddenly there was a faint smell of sweat in the air. Expectant. Hungry. But they looked at Gabriel, standing beside the lawyer with his hands in his trouser pockets, and they kept silent. Like with a lead ram, thought the sheep. When the lead ram has taken something on, no other sheep would dream of disputing it with him.

But then one sheep did dream of it.

"Are you sure there's no one else?" asked the lawyer. There was a touch of disappointment in his smooth tone.

"I'd like to do it," said a warm voice. A good voice for reading aloud in.

"Excellent," said the lawyer, looking at Rebecca almost with a touch of gratitude. Pale but beaming, she was standing next to Beth. The sheep were relieved. With Gabriel, they wouldn't even have wanted to go to Europe.

"And who's going to decide which of them it will be?" asked Lilly. "You?"

"The heirs, of course," said the lawyer.

"The sheep?" asked Ham breathlessly.

"The sheep," the lawyer confirmed.

"Then we'll have to go up to the meadow," said Gabriel. His blue eyes were laughing at Rebecca.

"I don't think so," said the lawyer. "It appears to me that the heirs are already among us. A black four-horned Hebridean ram, a mountain Blackface, a merino, and the rest Cladoir with some Blackface crosses—the last Cladoir flock in all Ireland. An

old Irish breed of sheep. It's a shame they're not raised anywhere else these days."

The humans turned, first just in surprise. But then they
looked down on George's flock with undisguised hostility.
Gabriel examined the sheep with a critical frown on his
brow.

"Sheep? *Those* sheep?" gasped Ham, who had been sitting in
the front row in his wheelchair. Now that they had turned he
was suddenly in the back row, he couldn't see, and he had no
idea what was going on. No one took any notice of him.

The herd of humans and the flock of sheep faced each other.
The humans' eyes ran over the sheep like lice running over
their coats. The three rams had retreated slightly, but they had
no intention of running away.

"Good," said the lawyer. "Then we'll see."

"See what?" asked Lilly, with some derision in her voice.

"I'm not exactly sure myself," said the lawyer. "Since my new
clients can't talk we'll have to try some other way. Would you,"
he said, turning to Rebecca, "please stand here, and you," he
said, turning to Gabriel, "over there, please? Good."

He turned to the sheep.

"George Glenn's sheep," said the lawyer, who was obviously
enjoying himself, "who would you like to accompany you to
Europe as your shepherd? Mr. . . . ?" He glanced at Gabriel.

"Gabriel O'Rourke," said Gabriel, between gritted teeth.

"Or Ms. . . . ?"

"Rebecca Flock," said Rebecca.

A murmur ran through the crowd. Even the lawyer raised his
eyebrows. Kate began laughing hysterically again.

"Mr. Gabriel O'Rourke or Ms. Rebecca Flock," repeated the
lawyer.

The sheep's eyes moved silently back and forth between the lawyer and Rebecca.

"Rebecca!" bleated Maude.

"Rebecca!" bleated Lane, Cordelia, and Mopple in chorus. But the lawyer didn't seem to understand them. The sheep, confused, fell silent. How could they let him know what they wanted?

"Nothing's going to come of this," someone said in an undertone. "Give 'em to Gabriel. He at least knows how to get along with sheep."

The villagers began to turn hostile toward Rebecca.

"She couldn't tell a sheep from a powder puff," someone murmured.

"Slapper," chirped a woman's voice.

But a simple, captivating melody sang its way through the angry whispers. Gabriel had begun murmuring in Gaelic. Once it would have totally enchanted the sheep, and even now Gabriel's soft voice had an undeniable charm.

Othello took a step forward while the flock kept close behind him. He looked briefly at Gabriel with glittering eyes. Then he calmly turned and trotted over to Rebecca. Gabriel cooed away in Gaelic like a demented pigeon, but it did him no good. One after another the sheep clustered round Rebecca.

Maude began bleating again.

"Rebecca!" she bleated.

"Rebecca!" bleated all the other sheep.

"Excellent," said the lawyer. "I call that a unanimous vote." He closed his briefcase. "George Glenn's sheep," he said very politely, "I hope you have a good time in Europe."

★

Silently, as if in a dream, the sheep trotted back to their meadow. There was a lot they had not understood, but one thing they knew: Europe. A huge meadow full of apple trees awaited them.

"We're going to Europe," said Zora in a daze.

"With the shepherd's caravan. And Rebecca," added Cordelia.

"It's . . ." Cloud took a deep breath. She had been going to say "wonderful," or "amazing," or simply "great," but all of a sudden she couldn't think of words anymore. She felt a little frightened.

"It's as if George had tipped out sugar beet and bread in front of us at the same time," said Mopple with a wise look on his face. "And apples and pears and concentrated feed."

"And calcium tablets," said Lane.

Joy came over them, slowly but intensely.

At this very special moment, Zora retreated to her rocky ledge to meditate, while Heather leaped in the air. "We're going to Europe," sang the lambs, and anyone grazing close enough to Ritchfield could hear him quietly humming along. But most of the sheep rejoiced in silence as they grazed, and only at second glance could you see the gleam in their eyes.

Othello was the happiest of all. Now he would be able to put into practice all the things that George had taught him behind the shepherd's caravan in the evenings: how to lead a flock, how to keep your nerve while on the move, how to lead the others forcefully but cautiously past obstacles—or over them. "I've been waiting just for you," George had always told him when, yet again, he had done everything just right. "With you, Europe will be child's play." And now they were going. Not with George, unfortunately, but Rebecca wasn't to be sneezed at either.

"Justice!" bleated Othello contentedly. "Justice!" Then he fell silent. Europe would be wonderful, but all the same, all the same . . . Suddenly the black ram raised his head.

"It never got out," he snorted.

The sheep stopped in the middle of their rejoicings and looked at Othello. He was right. The will had been full of splendid things, but they still didn't know who had murdered George.

"It doesn't matter," bleated Heather happily. "We're going to Europe and the murderer will have to stay here. He isn't dangerous anymore."

"It ought to get out, all the same," said Mopple bravely.

Cordelia nodded. "He read aloud to us. He made the will so that we could go to Europe. *He* ought really to have been coming with us."

"We mustn't take it lying down," said Zora. "He was our shepherd. No one can just kill our shepherd like that and get away with it. We ought to find out *before* we go to Europe. Justice!"

The sheep proudly raised their heads. "Justice!" they bleated in chorus. "Justice!"

Miss Maple stood in the midst of them, and her inquisitive eyes were sparkling.

Toward evening Rebecca came up from the village. George's daughter: their new shepherdess. She came on foot, carrying a small suitcase. Her face was paler than the whitewashed side of the shepherd's caravan. She put her suitcase down on the grass and climbed the steps to the caravan door.

"I'm going to live here now. Until we go to Europe," she explained to the sheep. "I'm certainly not staying in that village any longer."

She shook the door for a long time, tried levering the windows open, even fiddled around in the keyhole with a hairpin. Then she sat down on the top step of the caravan and put her head in her hands. George sometimes used to sit there just like that, motionless and solitary as an old tree. It seemed to the sheep almost uncanny. They realized Rebecca was sad. Melmoth began humming into the wind.

Rebecca raised her head as if she had heard him, and started whistling a tune. It fluttered through the air defiantly, reeling about like a butterfly on its first flight.

She didn't notice the black figure that had appeared at the side of the meadow. The sheep twitched their ears nervously. Then the wind turned, and told them it was only Beth, coming into their meadow. Beth, looking for good works to do. She glided toward Rebecca, silent as a ghost. Rebecca sat there whistling and didn't even turn her head.

"I'm sorry," said Beth. "Those heathens!"

Rebecca whistled.

"You won't have any luck with that door," said Beth. "Eddie says it's a safety lock. You'll never open it."

Rebecca was still whistling as if Beth wasn't there at all.

"Come back with me," said Beth. "You can sleep at my place."

"I'm never going into that village again," said Rebecca in a calm voice.

They said nothing for a while. Then Rebecca asked, "Who was Wesley McCarthy?"

"What?" Beth came out of her thoughts with a start.

"Wesley McCarthy. I've been through the newspaper files, you see. Of seven years ago. When you were in Africa. Wesley McCarthy was found murdered in the stone quarry. An anonymous caller phoned the police to report it. No suspects, no arrest, nothing. It went out of the headlines at once. I think that's what you were looking for."

"Wesley McCarthy!" Beth clutched the glittering pendant that hung round her neck. "*Weasel* McCarthy, that's what they called him."

Rebecca raised her eyebrows.

"There was a lot of talk at the time. No one knew where he came from or what he was doing in Glennkill. But he had money. He bought Whitepark and did it up. He lived there quietly for some time, so we thought. He was popular back then. Later, of course, everyone claimed to have had a funny feeling about him from the first."

"So then?"

"Well, it seemed all right to start with," said Beth. "All the drinkers in the Mad Boar hung on his every word when he told them how he came by the money. Apparently he began as a small farmer and then . . ." She laughed derisively. "People began pressing their money on him for investment abroad. And the first few even saw some of it back." She shrugged her shoulders. "Well, you can guess the rest."

Rebecca nodded.

"But that was only the start," said Beth. "He bought up land, bit by bit. Right here next to the meadow, and then almost everything all the way to the village. It all belonged to him back then. He paid well, and people really didn't have any choice, because they had no money left. No one asked what he was going to do with the land, not at first, anyway. And then it was too late."

"Too late for what?"

"There was to be a slaughterhouse here. The biggest abattoir in Ireland. When I set off for Africa they were frantically

discussing ways to stop it—citizens' action groups, petitions . . .
And when I came back: nothing. Whitepark was empty, and I
never heard that he was murdered until today."

"What's so bad about a slaughterhouse?" asked Rebecca.

Beth smiled sadly. "Did you ever see one? The stink! The
animal transports! It would have ruined all of them. The tourist
trade would have been done for, all the bed-and-breakfast
places, the Mad Boar—but the farmers wouldn't have had a
market for their meat either. That's how people are around
here, you see. Complain as they might about McCarthy barg-
ing his way in, they'd have gone to buy meat where it was
cheapest."

"So that was it," said Rebecca. "I don't think I want to hear
the details. Not now."

She looked up at Beth's black scarecrow figure. "I came here
because I wanted to know everything about him. Particularly
why he was murdered only just before . . ." She broke off and
rubbed the bridge of her nose with her forefinger. It was a
gesture the sheep knew well from George.

"He wrote me a letter," she added, "and I took my time
answering it. Let him stew, I thought." She swallowed. "I'm sure
we'd have been reconciled."

"I think so too," said Beth.

"Really?" asked Rebecca.

"Really," said Beth.

"And now I know a little about the life he lived, outside
that . . . that village. This is the first time I've admired him."

As if they had heard a sound, they both turned their heads to
the beautiful sunset sky above the sea. For safety's sake, the
sheep looked the same way, but they couldn't see anything
special.

"What will you do now?" asked Beth after a while.

Rebecca shrugged. "Count sheep. What about you?"

"Pray," said Beth. "I'll pray for you here and now."

But then she didn't do anything after all, just stood with her eyes closed, casting a long, straight shadow in the evening twilight. Crickets chirped. A white cat stalked along the stone wall by the gate with its tail in the air. The first night birds began to sing while the sheep grazed the soft evening grass. Melmoth went on humming until a magpie flew down from the crows' tree and perched on his back.

It didn't stay there long, but flew on again, up to the roof of the shepherd's caravan. It had something in its beak that shone like fire in the sunset light. This something dropped from the magpie's beak and landed, clinking, on the top step of the caravan.

Rebecca quickly rose to her feet. The door of the shepherd's caravan creaked, and Beth opened her eyes. Rebecca was laughing, almost in high spirits.

"Wow," she said. "If only I'd known it works as well as *that*! You must bring me a few of your tracts sometime."

Beth clutched the glittering little pendant on her breast. Her knuckles were white.

"Come in," said Rebecca, from inside the shepherd's caravan.

But Beth moved away from the door, shaking her head vigorously. The sheep were nervous too. Was something going to get out now? But nothing came out of the shepherd's caravan, any more than it had come out of the will.

"I ought to go back," said Beth. "If I may offer you a piece of advice: don't put a light on this evening. I'll say you've gone away."

She turned abruptly and marched back to the village, thin and upright, as she had done so many times before.

Rebecca and her case disappeared into the shepherd's caravan. The sheep heard her turn the key in the lock. They put their heads together.

"Do you think she's gone to sleep?" asked Cordelia.

"She smelled tired," said Maude.

"She can't go to sleep," said Heather, a little stubbornly. "It says so in the will. She has to read aloud to us. She's a bad shepherdess."

"Read aloud, read aloud!" bleated the sheep.

Then they fell silent. Melmoth had come up to them, shaggy and mysterious as ever.

"Nonsense," he said. "Don't you understand? The story is here. The story is us. The child needs the key."

"But she already has the key," said Heather.

Melmoth shook his head. "George's red lamb needs *all* the keys," he insisted.

"You mean the key for the box under the dolmen?" asked Cloud.

"Yes, under the dolmen," Melmoth agreed. "Who has the key?"

"I do," said Zora proudly.

"Ah, the sheep of the abyss." There was a note of respect in Melmoth's voice. "Who else?"

No one answered.

Melmoth nodded. "Carried away into the air with mischievous pleasure, brilliantly hidden until the human cat came. We must hurry."

"You want me to *give it up*?" Zora looked indignantly at Melmoth.

"To the shepherdess. As you did to George the shepherd."

"I never gave it to George just like that," said Zora. "He used to wait for it on the edge of the abyss."

"George knew. Rebecca is a lamb. She doesn't know anything. We have to guide her to the milk," said Melmoth.

Zora made a sulky face.

A little later Rebecca came out of the caravan. A lamb was crying outside, and the sound went to her heart. When she put her foot on the steps of the caravan, she saw something glittering there. It was not like fire—the sun was too low for that now—but more like spilled blood. She bent down. A key on a string. Shrugging, she put it in the pocket of her skirt. Today was not a day to wonder about anything.

The lamb was still crying, and she followed the sound under the dolmen.

The sheep watched expectantly as Rebecca came upon the hidden box. Othello had scraped the earth up first, to make it easier for her to find. Rebecca laughed and took the key out of her pocket to open it. As she knelt to remove a small packet from the box, a good smell rose from the nape of her neck.

She bit through a piece of string with her teeth. There was a crackle of plastic. Something dry crumbled in her fingers.

She sniffed it. The sheep sniffed too. It smelled . . . strange. Appetizing. Mopple knew at once that you could eat it.

"Grass!" said Rebecca out loud. "Any amount of grass!"

The sheep looked at each other. So *that* was the mysterious grass the humans were so keen on. Each of the sheep had carried a small packet like that, tied under their bellies and buried deep in their fleece, when George drove them to the other pasture for a few weeks. "We're off over there again," George had announced every time. "Operation Polyphemus." If only they'd known then that those little packets, tied with string and smelling of nothing, contained grass . . .

Now it was up to Rebecca. Would she give them any of it? Apparently not. Rebecca held her skirt out like a kind of red bag and shoveled everything she could find under the dolmen into it. Many, many small packets came to light, and a larger, squarish package. And a file of papers.

Rebecca carefully carried it all back to the shepherd's caravan in her heavily laden, bunched-up skirt. She remained out of sight for a while. Then she was suddenly out on the steps again, with a glowing point of light in front of her lips.

Sweet, heavy smoke wafted over the meadow. It made the sheep sleepy. But suddenly Rebecca was very talkative.

"So I'm supposed to read aloud to you, sheep," she said. "I'll read aloud to you as no one ever read to you before. And I know what I'll read, too. Let's see if you like it . . ."

Her footsteps unsteady now, she climbed back into the caravan and came out again with a book in her hand. She opened it somewhere in the middle. The sheep knew the book had to be opened at the front first, and only as it was read aloud did the sheets of paper slowly move from one side of the cover to the other. Some of the sheep bleated in protest, but most of them were too tired to get upset about this small deviation from the rules. They were being read aloud to again at last, anyway. Their young shepherdess couldn't be expected to get everything right straight off.

Rebecca began to read.

"'Catherine Earnshaw, may you not rest as long as I am living! You said I killed you—haunt me, then! The murdered *do* haunt their murderers, I believe. I know that ghosts *have* wandered on earth. Be with me always—take any form—drive me mad! only *do* not leave me in this abyss, where I cannot find you! Oh, God! It is unutterable! I *cannot* live without my life! I *cannot* live without my soul!' "

The moon disappeared behind a dark cloud, and the only light falling on the pages now came from the little glowing point between Rebecca's lips. The sheep stood around the caravan, fascinated. In the light of that glow, she looked as the sheep had always imagined the Siamese pirate would look in *Pamela and the Yellow Buccaneer*, narrow-eyed and melancholy. She closed the book.

"That's too sad," said Rebecca. "I don't need a book to tell you sad stories, sheep." She was silent for a while, blowing sweet smoke over the meadow. Then she began again in her reading-aloud voice, but without a book.

"Once upon a time there was a little girl who had not one daddy but two. A secret one and a . . . an unsecret one. She wasn't supposed to see the secret one, but of course they did see each other all the same, and they were very fond of each other. The little girl's mother, the beautiful queen, didn't like that, but there was nothing she could do about it. No one could do anything about it. But one day the girl and her secret daddy quarreled about a stupid thing, and the girl did all she could to make him angry, even when it hurt her too. After that they didn't speak to each other for a long time, not a single word. At last a letter came for the girl. It said that her daddy was planning to travel to Europe, but first he wanted to see her. The girl hid her joy, and kept him waiting. So he waited himself to death."

It wasn't a bad story, but nothing like as good as what Rebecca had read them first. However, the sheep didn't mind. They suddenly felt so tired that they could hardly listen anymore. All but one of them.

Mopple the Whale had no time to feel tired. Ever since

Rebecca had found the grass under the dolmen he had been obsessed by the idea of tasting it. This was his moment. Rebecca was sitting in the dark with her eyes half closed, humming quietly to herself. Beside her, forgotten now, lay an open packet of the grass. Quick as a flash Mopple was beside her with his nose stuck inside the packet. Quick as a flash he had swallowed the contents. By the time Rebecca noticed, Mopple was licking the last crumbs off the steps of the caravan. Rebecca began to laugh.

"Pothead," she said.

Mopple chewed guiltily. He was disappointed by the grass. It smelled much better than it tasted. It didn't taste anywhere near as good as the grass in the meadow, or even as good as hay. Human beings had a very poor sense of taste. Mopple lowered his nose and once more resolved never to eat anything unfamiliar again.

The little glowworm in front of Rebecca's face went out.

"Time to sleep," she told the sheep, curtsying to them before disappearing inside the shepherd's caravan. This time they didn't hear the key turning in the lock.

A clear night wind carried the smoke away, and the sheep felt less sleepy again.

"She's polite," said Cloud approvingly. The sheep nodded, all except Mopple, who had fallen asleep on his feet in the middle of the meadow.

The others didn't want to sleep yet. All today's excitement had left them short of time to graze. They decided to stay outside a little longer, fulfilling their daily quota of grazing work and keeping Mopple company, since he was sleeping like a dormouse and wouldn't be woken.

Night had fallen, the stars were twinkling, and somewhere an owl was hooting for all it was worth. Somewhere a lonely toad was croaking. Somewhere two cats were playing the game of love.

And somewhere the purring sound of a powerful car engine was coming closer. Lane raised her head. The car stopped at the gate to the path through the fields. No lights. A man got out and steadily crossed the meadow to the shepherd's caravan. Just outside it he stopped, and sniffed the air. Then he climbed the steps and knocked on the door. Once, twice, then once again.

19

Maple and a Lovers' Meeting

Nothing moved inside the shepherd's caravan. The man put his hand on the door handle and pressed it down, opening George's creaking door without a sound.

He closed it behind him without a sound too.

Soon after that, a pale, flickering light came on behind the caravan windows.

"Did you smell it?" asked Maude. "The metal? He has one of those pistols too, like George." She shuddered.

"But he doesn't have a target!" said Rameses. The man wouldn't be able to do much with his gun without a target.

"Perhaps he wants George's target," said Lane thoughtfully. "Perhaps he wants to take it away."

Othello looked uneasily at the caravan. "We ought to find out what's going on in there."

The sheep moved closer to the caravan. Maple and Othello began grazing under the only open window.

"Why should I tell you that?" said the man's voice, so softly that you couldn't hear any emphasis in it. A sparse kind of voice.

Rebecca said nothing, but the sheep could hear her breath

coming fast and irregular. Something made a noise inside the caravan. A heavy object fell to the floor.

"So you've found it," said the man. "Congratulations."

Then, after a while, he added, "Where?"

Rebecca laughed softly. "You'll never believe me."

"Oh, I'll believe you," said the man. "George was one of our best. Our specialist for the Ireland and Northern Ireland consignments. Full of ideas and never a single incident."

Rebecca laughed again, louder this time, and choking slightly. "All that, just for grass?" she asked, in a hoarse, toneless voice, quite unlike the one she used for reading aloud. Othello looked anxiously up at the window.

"Mainly grass. Sometimes cigarettes. Sometimes other stuff. Whatever was in demand on the market."

"You're telling me that because you think it makes no difference now, am I right?"

"I'm afraid so," said the man. "I mean, you have the file too. Do you know what you could do with the information in that file? It would be a severe blow to our firm."

"But I won't do anything with it," said Rebecca.

"I believe you," said the man.

Rebecca did not reply.

"I believe you," the man repeated after a while. "But unfortunately that's not good enough." He hesitated. "I'm sorry."

"Would you mind putting that light of yours out? It's dazzling me."

"Yes, I would," said the man. All the same, the pale light behind the windows of the shepherd's caravan went out. Maple cautiously scented the air. A strange storm was raging in there: heavy, oppressive, violent. A storm that could send the cloud sheep galloping over the sky.

"Don't you think that's a little unprofessional?" asked Rebecca after a while. "I have a proper job now, as a shepherdess. Well paid. And all I have to do for my money is take the sheep touring Europe. I've nothing against your business, nothing against you. The last thing I need now is more problems. I won't say anything. Ever. To anyone."

"It would be unprofessional to take the risk," said the man.

"Leaving another corpse in this meadow would be unprofessional too."

"Not very. We know the investigating police inspector. He's incompetent. And very cooperative. What do you think of this one: illegitimate daughter with dubious past breaks into caravan by night, finds a pistol there, plays about with it, and shoots herself by accident? Or out of grief for her beloved father. People like that kind of thing. Or out of a sense of guilt . . ."

"In her nightie?" asked Rebecca.

"What?"

"Well, it's not exactly the right outfit for breaking and entering, I'd say—in case you hadn't noticed."

"Hmm."

"And what's more, that's not George's pistol. If your story is supposed to convince anyone, you'd need this one."

The sheep heard the man take a noisy, startled breath.

"Careful. Put that down this minute. That's no gun for a lady."

"And I'm no lady," whispered Rebecca. "So get out."

Something inside hit the wall with a bang. Rebecca gave a little scream. The man swore.

Then all was quiet inside the shepherd's caravan again. Very quiet.

"Damn," said Rebecca at last.

271

"Don't let it bother you," said the man. "It was worth a try, I suppose."

A foot began tapping rhythmically on wood.

"Would you really have shot me down, just like that?" asked the man, with a note of respect in his voice.

"Why not? What you did to George . . ."

"We had nothing to do with that. You can believe me there. Definitely. For sure. A great loss to the firm."

Rebecca breathed slowly out. "Do you know who it was?"

"No," said the man. "No one in our line, anyway. So theatrical—almost a ritual murder. That's not how we work. We don't need that kind of intimidation."

"You don't?"

"We don't."

Silence. The foot tapped faster.

"Is there anything I can do for you?" said the man. "Do you have a last wish?"

"A last wish?"

"Well, yes. Whatever. A glass of water? A cigarette?"

Rebecca laughed again, in a strained way. "Where do you think you'd find a glass of water here? You've never done anything like this before, have you?"

"Yes. No. Well, no need to let that worry you."

Rebecca sighed. It was a sigh that Othello could feel to the tips of all his four horns. Melmoth had appeared beside him. They were both looking intently up at the half-open window.

"Damn," said Rebecca. "Why now? Why now, of all times? What can I do to convince you I'm no danger to you?"

"You're putting other ideas into my head," said the man slowly. "Sounds tempting, but I'm not *quite* that unprofessional."

"What? You think *that's* what I meant?" spat Rebecca. "What are you after, anyway? You just break in here, and . . . and I suppose you think I'll do anything you like just because you have that pistol!"

"No," said the man, surprised. "That bit was *your* idea. I mean, it never even entered my head!"

"I see. Really?"

"If you think I *need* that kind of thing . . ." The man sounded angry too now.

Silence, for quite a long time.

Then, suddenly, both of them laughed at the same moment.

Then silence again.

"Okay," Rebecca laughed. "Then we'll just have to pass the time some other way. Sit down."

"Hmm," said the man.

"I could tell you stories. Like Scheherazade in the Thousand and One Nights."

"I wasn't really planning to stay quite that long," said the man. "On the other hand . . ."

Silence billowed out of the window of the shepherd's caravan, dense and heavy as hot breath.

The sheep looked at one another. Perhaps it was getting interesting in there after all.

As if at a signal, Maude and Heather started bleating.

"Stories!" they bleated. "Stories!"

It was some time before Miss Maple had restored peace and quiet.

"Even if they *are* telling stories in there," she said, "how do you expect to hear them if you're kicking up such a racket?"

But the sheep didn't get to hear any stories. No more was said inside the caravan. The sheep were not surprised: they were familiar with this situation from the Pamela novels. When the mysterious stranger—and without a shadow of doubt, they had one of those here—was left alone with a woman you could expect the story to trail off into nothing. The man and the woman stopped talking at some point, and that was the end of the chapter. You never found out what happened next. It was a mystery to the sheep, because something had to happen. Human beings didn't simply disappear. Usually they turned up again in the next chapter, alive and well. All the same, there were these gaps in the stories.

The sheep did what they used to do when George reached such places: they grazed patiently until the story went on. Only Maple raised her head once to scent the atmosphere inside the shepherd's caravan, just for safety's sake. Stormy but clear. Rain dripping fragrantly on leaves. Reassured, Maple lowered her head to the grass.

Much, much later, when even Miss Maple was bored with watching the shepherd's caravan, the door slowly opened. The man came out and looked at the moon shining down for a little while.

"A lovely night," he said. Rebecca had appeared beside him on the steps of the caravan. She had picked up the skirt of her nightie to make a bag of it. One shoulder strap had slipped down, baring a moonlight-blue shoulder.

Rebecca was humming to herself. The two looked at each other, and Rebecca stopped humming.

"I smoked one joint," she said apologetically.

The man waved a hand dismissively.

Rebecca chuckled. "And there's a whole packet missing. One of the sheep ate it. The fat one there."

"Looks like a ram," said the man. "Expensive animal. But we can live with that."

The man began fishing the packets out of the bag that Rebecca had made of her skirt and stuffing them in his coat pockets. He counted as he went along.

". . . twenty-one, twenty-two, twenty-three. Less one packet of sheep feed, and that makes the delivery complete. The file. Yes, everything's there. What's that?" The man was holding the rectangular package.

"I should think it's a videocassette," said Rebecca. "You don't know about it?"

"Never heard it mentioned," said the man, as he stowed the rectangular package in his pocket too.

He carefully took Rebecca's hand between his thumb and forefinger, raised it slowly like something very heavy and fragile, and kissed her fingertips without a sound. Then he turned and went back to his car without saying good-bye. The purring engine moved away.

Only when the car was out of hearing did the sheep relax. The quiet man had made them uneasy. But now everything was back in order again—in better order than it had been for a long time. George's daughter was sitting in the shepherd's caravan, Gabriel and his voracious sheep had disappeared, and Europe awaited them.

Unfortunately this happy state didn't last long. It was one of those nights when all sorts of people kept invading their meadow. This time a small, plump figure was making its way clumsily and noisily around the caravan.

Then Rebecca was suddenly standing in the doorway with George's gun in her hand.

Lilly uttered a short, sharp scream.

275

"What's the idea?" asked Rebecca wearily. "What are *you* doing here now?"

"I just wanted . . . I thought . . ." Lilly was staring as if hypnotized at the pistol. "I wanted to think about George a bit."

Rebecca shook her head. "I suspect not. I think you wanted to get in there." The pistol pointed briefly at the door of the caravan and then back at Lilly. "And I want to know why. And after that I really would like to get some sleep."

Lilly struggled with her fear for a moment. Then she gave in. "I just wanted the receipt," she said. "So that they can't hold anything over me. The receipt, that's all!"

She fell silent for a moment, but went on talking in a hurry when Rebecca made an encouraging movement with the pistol.

"I sometimes work at the Lonely Heart Inn," she said. "Only now and then. When . . ." She stopped.

Rebecca looked at her in annoyance for a moment, but then suddenly nodded. "All right. What about the Lonely Heart Inn?"

"Well, the customers there, they don't just come to . . . you know what." Lilly's hands fiddled with her hair. She was embarrassed. "They like to smoke something too. And I knew George, and George was a good place to go . . . so I always bought from him. Only the landlady is so . . . so suspicious. And greedy. She wants a receipt. With my name on it. And I just forgot it, that wretched night. And then he was dead. And if they find it, they'll have a hold over me. Everyone here's been waiting for that."

Rebecca lowered the gun, and Lilly calmed down a bit.

"You were here?" asked Rebecca. "On the night when George was murdered?" She whistled through her teeth, exactly like George when something struck him as remarkable. "If that gets out, and you go on slinking around here, you'll soon have more hanging over you than just a receipt for a bit of grass."

Lilly made a face. "Ham says so too. Says they'll pin something on me if I don't watch out. But I need that receipt."

"You mean Rackham? The butcher?"

Lilly nodded. "He must have seen me when I came back from visiting George. But he says I needn't worry. He knows I don't have anything to do with it, he says. He has evidence. Although he hates me really. Because of Kate."

"Ham's the only one who saw you? And then he had that accident, falling off the cliffs. You must have really strong nerves if you're still worrying about a receipt."

"But I need it," said Lilly obstinately.

"And you can have it if you'll tell me exactly what happened here between you and George that evening," Rebecca promised.

Lilly looked at her indignantly. "Nothing happened! Nothing at all! Everyone thinks it did, and they'll say anything they like about me too. But George was a good man. You could still talk to him like a decent human being. I bought the grass, and we chatted for a bit. That was it. That was all."

Rebecca sighed. "And what did you talk about?"

Lilly thought. "About the weather. What lovely weather it had been these last few weeks. Weather fit for a new departure, he said. He was in a good mood, really cheerful. I never saw him like that before. He said I'd have to buy the goods somewhere else in future. He gave me a phone number. And then he suddenly . . . I think he almost cried."

The sheep could tell from Lilly's face that a new and unwelcome thought had just made its way into her brain.

"Oh shit!" she said. "I've forgotten the phone number too."

"You can have the phone number," said Rebecca.

"Really?"

"Did George say what else he was planning to do that evening?"

Lilly wrinkled her brow. "Go to the Mad Boar for a Guinness. That surprised me, because he never usually went to the Boar. Never ever! He said he wanted to take one more look at the people there. And then he was going to say good-bye to someone."

"Who?"

"I don't know. He didn't say. It was an old story, he said, and he laughed a little."

"Right." Rebecca disappeared up the steps of the shepherd's caravan and came back with a scrap of paper.

"'Received from Lilly Thompson, the sum of three hundred euros for woollen goods.' And the phone number's on there too."

Lilly happily stuffed the paper down her neckline, and looked gratefully at Rebecca.

"Now get out," said Rebecca. "And if you meet anyone else on the way here, tell them to turn back. Because the next person who disturbs my sleep gets shot right away."

Lilly nodded, alarmed. Then she tottered back toward the gate. When she was halfway over the meadow the sheep heard one of her sharp little screams again. Lilly had trodden in a pile of sheep droppings.

The sheep thought it best to go back into the hay barn. Who could tell what might make Rebecca feel that her sleep had been disturbed?

"What about Mopple?" asked Zora. "We can't just leave him standing all alone in the meadow."

There was still no waking Mopple, but the sheep discovered that he could walk in his sleep. It worked if Othello and Ritchfield pushed him with their horns from behind, while the rest of the flock struck up a bleat of "Fodder!" in front of him.

Before they went to sleep they thought a little more about Europe.

"It will be lovely," said Maude. "There will be apple trees everywhere, that's for sure, and the ground will have mouse weed growing all over it."

"Nonsense," said Zora. "Europe is on the edge of an abyss, and everyone knows mouse weed doesn't grow in an abyss."

"How big do you think Europe is?" asked Cordelia dreamily.

"Oh, big," said Lane with conviction. "A sheep would have to gallop like the wind for a day and a night to cross the whole of Europe."

"And there are apple trees everywhere?" asked Maisie, marveling.

"Apple trees everywhere," Cloud confirmed. "But with real apples on them, red ones, sweet ones, yellow ones, not like ours here."

They were in a mood of happy anticipation. Impatiently, the sheep bleated for Europe.

Othello spoiled their fun.

"It's not that simple," he snorted. "Not even in Europe. It's not like that anywhere. It will be dangerous and strange too. A sheep will have to be as watchful there as anywhere else in the world. Maybe even more watchful."

Sir Ritchfield agreed with him. "There's nowhere in the

world where only apple trees grow. You always have prickly gorse and sorrel too, thistles and spew weed. There's a cold wind in your wool and sharp stones under your hooves everywhere."

Ritchfield was wearing his official expression as lead ram and looking sternly round. The sheep lowered their heads. Their most experienced rams were probably right. No apples without bitter sorrel. Nowhere without danger.

When Ritchfield saw all those disappointed faces, he thought it his duty as lead ram to add a word of encouragement.

"We can look forward to Europe, all the same," he said. "Only not as a lush dream meadow, but like a . . . a . . ." Ritchfield couldn't think of a comparison.

"Like being shorn?" asked Cordelia. "It twitches and nips you and everything goes round. But afterward you feel light and cool."

Sir Ritchfield looked gratefully at Cordelia. "Exactly. Like being shorn."

The sheep fell asleep, one by one, with pleasantly cool thoughts of a summer shearing in their minds. Mopple did something he had never done before: he made snorting, snoring noises in his sleep.

Gradually these snoring sounds became more rhythmic, more metallic. Now and then there was a little bang. Miss Maple tore her eyes open with difficulty. Gray light fell into the hay barn through the skylights. It must be early morning. The snorting suddenly turned to rattling and clattering. Stones sprayed through the air. These sounds were strangely familiar to Miss Maple. She had heard them every morning, almost all her life, when George's car turned off the road and into the path across the fields.

When she had made her way through the door of the

hay barn, George was already sitting on the steps of the shepherd's caravan. Miss Maple trotted closer, curious. On seeing her, George raised his head and grinned.

"Get to work, you lazy creature!" he said.

Miss Maple obediently put her head down in the grass. Now that George had so unexpectedly come back to them, she was happy to do as he wanted. But George didn't seem to be pleased with her.

"Get to work," he repeated. This time it sounded more serious. Miss Maple realized that he didn't mean the work of grazing this time, but something else. She flapped her ears, at a loss.

George saw that she wouldn't get any further on her own, and let out a long-drawn whistle. "Round up the flock" was what that whistle meant. But instead of Tess, the spade suddenly shot around the corner of the shepherd's caravan. As spades go, it made a very good sheepdog. It came quite close to Maple and then put its nose down in the grass. The two nails fixing the blade to the handle suddenly looked very much like eyes: lively, watchful eyes. Maple bleated uneasily, but the spade would not back off. It inched its way closer, bit by bit, with those nail eyes always turned on Miss Maple.

The spade was scenting the air in a terrible, noseless way, its thin wooden back bent as if to spring. Suddenly Miss Maple was afraid. She made for George in search of help, but he was cold as frozen ground.

"Why are you dead, George?" she asked. Her words rang out over the meadow, loud and echoing like human language. George would understand every one of them. Miss Maple thought it was wonderful to be understood like that by a human.

"I cannot live without my soul," said George.

It wasn't a satisfactory answer, but it was the only one she was going to get from George now. As he spoke, George changed, though you couldn't really see what was different. But a sheep could smell it. When the last word had left his lips, dragging along like a lazy wave, there was only an empty husk left on the steps of the shepherd's caravan.

At that moment the spade leaped up in a single, perfect arching movement, its metal nose making straight for Maple . . .

Suddenly Miss Maple was wide awake.

"I know!" she bleated at Cloud, who had snuggled close to her in her sleep.

"You know what?" asked Cloud sleepily.

"All of it!" said Miss Maple. "I know all about George's murder!"

20

What Maisie Knows

A little later all the sheep except for Mopple were on their hooves again, still half asleep but in good spirits. Miss Maple was the cleverest sheep in all Glennkill. And now she knew all of it! The sheep would rather just have been told the murderer's name; but Miss Maple didn't seem to know where she should begin.

"I'd never have thought of it if it hadn't been in the book," she said. "What a good thing George said in the Last Will and Testament that she has to read to us."

The sheep couldn't make head or tail of this. They were getting worried: Maple really did seem to be very worked up.

"She'll read aloud to us again," said Cordelia soothingly. "She must. It says so in the Last Will and Testament."

"But we know enough already," said Miss Maple. "She read just the right bit out loud. Do you remember what she read to us? Exactly, I mean?"

In search of help, the sheep looked at Mopple the Whale. But he was sleeping a rock-solid sleep. When Zora nipped his rear end quite hard, he didn't even twitch his ears.

Miss Maple waited patiently until all attempts to wake Mopple had broken up in frustrated bleating.

"Think about it," she said.

The sheep obediently thought about it.

"There was something about resting," said Maude. "She read that aloud."

"And there was the bit about the abyss," said Zora.

"And about the way the murdered *do* haunt their murderers," said Cordelia, with a shudder.

"Exactly," said Miss Maple. "It's like a trail through the grass, do you see? Why the spade, we wondered, if George was dead already? What was it for?"

Miss Maple let her flock think about that for a little while and then, losing patience, answered the question herself.

"The murderer was afraid of being haunted. The idea of the spade was to prevent that. How could George haunt his murderer if the spade was pinning him to the ground of the meadow? That's what the murderer must have thought. But"— and she paused for effect—"but he was wrong."

Things were getting exciting now. The sheep crowded closer together.

"Because the murder victim can haunt his murderer in *any form*. It says so in the book. George didn't need his own form anymore, so he could choose anything he liked. And we all know what George liked."

"Us," said Heather proudly. "He liked us better than human beings."

"Quite right," said Miss Maple. "That means George is haunting his murderer in the form of a sheep. So now we just have to think who is being haunted by sheep."

That was easy.

"God!" bleated Lane, Cordelia, and Cloud in unison.

"Quite right," said Miss Maple.

"But," said Zora hesitantly, "wasn't that Othello?"

Maple nodded. "Once, yes. In the graveyard. But he mentioned a gray ram too. Imagine George in the form of a sheep—he could easily look like a gray ram."

"I'd love to see him like that," said Cordelia.

Miss Maple shook her head. "I don't think it would work. Probably only the murderer can see him."

The sheep sighed. They would have been so happy to welcome George into their flock.

"But why?" bleated Heather.

"That's just the way it is," said Cloud soothingly.

"No!" Heather obstinately shook her head. "I mean why did the long-nosed man murder George?"

All eyes were turned on Miss Maple. Yes, why?

"The book tells us that too," she said. "It says, 'I *cannot* live without my soul!'" She looked at her flock with sparkling eyes.

"So what?" bleated Heather.

"That reminded me that dying and souls have something to do with each other," explained Miss Maple, concentrating much too hard to mind about Heather's interruptions. "When you're dead your soul has to leave your body. Because the body smells bad after death, and the soul's sensitive nose can't stand it. And then the soul is vulnerable. We heard about the Devil's hounds. Someone wanted George's soul before it fell into the jaws of the Devil's hounds. The murderer wanted George's soul for himself."

Miss Maple took a deep breath. You could almost see her thoughts galloping through the hay barn, out into the meadow, up to the dolmen, on to the abyss, and back again, to and fro, following mysterious patterns.

"We heard how scared God is about his own soul. Dreadfully scared. So it would be only logical for him to try to get hold of a replacement soul . . ."

The sheep thoughtfully put their heads on one side. They hadn't looked at it that way before. Feeling sure of herself, Miss Maple waggled her ears and went on.

"The spade itself gave something away. What do you think of when you think of a spade?"

"A spade, of course," said Cloud.

Maple sighed. "What else?"

"Mouse weed!" said Maude at once.

The others looked at her.

"Why mouse weed?" asked Zora.

"Why not?" said Maude. "I often think of mouse weed."

"But mouse weed has nothing to do with it," said Heather.

"She didn't say it had to have something to do with it," said Maude, offended. "I can think of mouse weed whenever I like."

"But it doesn't mean anything," said Heather.

"It means a whole lot!" Maude looked at her flock with eyes that sparkled angrily. "I'm going to think of mouse weed all night now! Just letting you know!"

Maude closed her eyes and thought very hard about mouse weed. The other sheep went on wondering about the spade.

"A vegetable garden!" bleated Zora.

That was obvious. George had dug the vegetable garden with his spade. He used it to dig up weeds and trace straight lines on the soil. He drew narrow furrows with the handle, and scattered seeds or planted seedlings in the furrows. The spade and the vegetable garden belonged together.

Miss Maple nodded, pleased. "Exactly. I was sure the spade meant something. God's garden—do you remember about that? It was a clue. The vegetable garden where dead people are planted with a spade. The long-nosed man dug holes with a spade and shut the souls up in them. He didn't want just one extra soul, he wanted a large supply of them."

The sheep were amazed. Suddenly it all fit together the way chestnuts fit perfectly into their husks. Miss Maple really was the cleverest sheep in Glennkill.

"But . . ." someone in the back row bleated shyly. The sheep turned their heads. Maisie! Maisie, of all sheep! Curiously, and with just a touch of malice, the sheep pricked up their ears to hear what Maisie knew.

"But it can't have been God," bleated Maisie excitedly. "He said George was a lost soul. If he thought George had already lost his soul anyway, there wasn't any point in taking it away from him."

Maisie twitched her ears.

The other sheep looked at her crossly.

But Miss Maple was not offended. After all, what mattered to her was the truth, and it seemed that she didn't know the truth yet.

"I'm sure it's about his soul," she said. "It must all fit together somehow or other."

"Beth doesn't have a soul," Maude suddenly bleated. She had quickly got bored with thinking of mouse weed.

Although the sheep had never thought about that before, it immediately made sense. No one who smelled as dead as Beth could have a good nose. If you had a good nose you couldn't stand it.

Miss Maple stood perfectly still for quite some time. Not even the tips of her ears twitched. She stood the way very old rams stand, lost in thought and completely motionless.

"But Beth wanted a soul more than anything," she said at last. "Because you can't really live without your soul. It says so in the book."

Othello raised his head. The other sheep could see from his eyes that he had understood something.

"She came to George's caravan year after year," Miss Maple went on. "She brought him books, because she knew George liked books. She hoped George would begin to like her so much that in the end he'd give her his soul."

"But George didn't do it," said Rameses. "George burned those tract things."

"Exactly," said Maple. "That was clever of him. Then Beth started saying something about good works and how George's soul was in danger. She wanted to take it away with her to somewhere safe, where the soul could do good works."

"She wanted to take it to God?" asked Heather curiously.

"That was just an excuse, of course," said Miss Maple. "Beth wouldn't really have taken the soul to God. She'd have kept it, and George would never have seen it again."

"But George didn't go along with that," said Lane, relieved. "George began working in the vegetable garden. With the spade."

"That was clever too," said Miss Maple. "Because that way he could do his own good work. Beth had no excuse for taking his soul away anymore."

The sheep remembered: Beth had turned up in front of the caravan steps so often, talking about George's soul. They'd always fallen for it, never suspecting anything. "Like a fox," said

Cordelia, "a fox who finds an injured lamb. And prowls around it in smaller and smaller circles until it's so weak that it doesn't defend itself anymore."

"But George wasn't weak," said Othello proudly. "He kept defending himself."

Miss Maple nodded. "And Beth kept waiting. Sometime or other, she thought, sometime or other . . . And then—do you remember what I told you? It's all to do with the spade! I just didn't understand how it all fits together at first. The spade means the vegetable garden. It means that George defended himself. It means that Beth couldn't get at his soul."

Miss Maple paused for a moment.

"But then she found out that George was going away to Europe, taking his soul with him. She'd waited all those years, like a spider in its web. She had to do something if her waiting wasn't to have been in vain. And we all know what she did."

Impressed, the sheep said nothing. Except for Zora.

"But what about the murdered haunting their murderers?" asked Zora. "Beth wasn't haunted by a sheep."

Maple thought.

"That's what it looks like," she said after a while. "But it wasn't really like that. We've even seen Beth being haunted twice, with our own eyes."

The sheep thought, but for the life of them they couldn't remember anything. And Mopple, the memory sheep, uttered nothing but snoring sounds.

"You have to remember that we probably can't see the ghostly sheep," said Miss Maple. "Only the murderer can see it. But we were watching Beth when she saw the ghost. Once at that picnic. Remember how Beth looked at the place where George died? She was so scared she couldn't even eat anything."

The sheep did remember. Lack of appetite in view of all the delicious things on the brightly colored picnic cloth was an infallible sign that Beth really had been scared.

"The second time was when Rebecca opened the door of the shepherd's caravan. We were all waiting for something to come out. But Beth *saw* something come out."

They remembered how Beth had stared at the door wide-eyed with horror.

"You think . . . ?" asked Cloud.

Maple nodded. "Beth saw George's ghost. She almost gave herself away once. Remember how she said she couldn't live here again until that black sheep had left the flock? What could Beth have against Othello? She must have been talking about George's ghost."

This time there could be no doubt about it. Miss Maple had found a watertight solution to the mystery. The sheep, much impressed, were silent.

"Do you think she got it?" asked Cordelia after a while.

"Got what?" asked Zora.

"George's soul," said Cordelia.

"Well, if she did, she'll have to give it back again," said Sir Ritchfield sternly. A soul was the opposite of a Thing. It was something that helped you to discover the world. Something very valuable and very important even if, as in the case of humans, it was only a very small soul.

Miss Maple shook her head. "She hasn't got George's soul. Just look at her. She looks like someone who's lost something that mattered to her and will never find it."

She was right. The sheep breathed a sigh of relief because George's soul had escaped Beth. But did they have justice yet?

"Justice!" the winter lamb suddenly bleated into the silence. No one chased him off.

"Justice!" Othello agreed.

"Justice!" bleated the other sheep.

"But how?" asked Lane.

"It's her fault George is dead," said Cloud. "It would be justice for her to be dead too."

That sounded like good sense.

"It wouldn't be difficult," said Othello. "Maybe we can't do it just the way she did, with poison and a spade. But we could push her off the cliffs, for instance."

"Not the cliffs," said Zora.

"But she said she wasn't afraid of death," bleated Heather. "Remember? She kept saying so. And we want her to be afraid!"

The sheep bleated. They wanted Beth to be afraid! That would be justice. These last few days *they* had been afraid of the terrible things happening in the meadow.

"We could pretend to be ill again," suggested Cordelia. "It worked well with Gabriel."

But somehow it seemed to the flock as if the diseases of sheep were not the way to frighten Beth.

Miss Maple trotted up and down in the dark. "It must get out. They're *all* afraid of that. We must make sure it gets out. Not out of the shepherd's caravan, out of our heads. All the humans have to know. That's justice."

"But they don't understand us," said Cloud.

"It's difficult," Miss Maple admitted. "We could get them to understand something if they'd only pay attention to us. The only thing they pay attention to is the caravan."

"Except for the butcher," Sara objected. "The butcher pays a lot of attention to sheep now." None of them, however, wanted to communicate with Ham.

Lost in thought, Miss Maple trotted up and down for a long time.

Then she stopped. "There *is* one thing that makes human beings pay attention to sheep!" Miss Maple looked around her, beaming. But the only sheep who seemed to be pleased with her brain wave was Miss Maple herself. During her long period of cogitation the others had fallen asleep, one by one.

"It could work," said Miss Maple.

They had woken up early, but stayed in the hay barn to keep Mopple company in his deep dormouse sleep. The morning sun fell through holes and cracks, painting shimmering golden signs on the sheep's backs. They were in good spirits. "If they're looking for that smartest sheep, they're sure to be watching sheep closely."

They liked the idea. Secretly, they had always been interested in the Smartest Sheep in Glennkill contest. There were rumors that the sheep who took part were fed shamrock and apples and admired by all the human beings. George had never let them join in. "That's all I need," he said once, when the conversation got around to the contest. "Those drunks on the jury sitting in judgment on my clever sheep."

Now George was dead and couldn't tell them what to do anymore. "We'll do it," bleated Sir Ritchfield. His eyes were sparkling as he looked forward to some action.

"But how?" asked Cloud. They put together all they'd heard about the Smartest Sheep in Glennkill contest.

"It's total rubbish," said Maude.

"It's a tourist trap for when there's nothing else on offer," said Heather.

"It's in the Mad Boar," said Sara.

That was a start, anyway. The sheep knew the pub from their expeditions to the other pasture. They noticed the Mad Boar every time they passed because of the smell of whiskey and beer, and also because of the eyes that inevitably popped up on the other side of the windows, watching George until he and his sheep had disappeared around the bend in the main road.

"We'll just go along," said Zora boldly. "The others must get in somehow or other."

The others! Other sheep! The whole place would be full of sheep—very clever sheep. They could learn a lot from those sheep. Perhaps they'd all join up into a particularly large flock afterward. Sara waggled her ears happily, Zora took deep, appreciative breaths of the cool morning air, and Cloud lay down on the straw with a contented sigh.

"But when is it?" asked Lane. They knew that the contest took place only once a year. And a year was a long time, from one winter till the next.

"The day after tomorrow," said Mopple. Mopple the Whale had woken up and was looking at them bright-eyed again.

"How can you know?" asked Heather.

"Gabriel said so to the butcher when the butcher was trying to warn him about us," said Mopple.

The day after tomorrow, then! Two sleeps, and it would be the day of the contest. Not much time to prepare.

Only Miss Maple looked skeptically at Mopple. "But we've already slept once since then. It's not the day after tomorrow anymore. It's tomorrow."

"The day after tomorrow," Mopple obstinately repeated.

"It's changed," Miss Maple explained. "It changed in our sleep. It's only tomorrow now."

"But I remembered," said Mopple. "Once I've remembered something it doesn't change."

"Yes," said Miss Maple. "Yes, it does."

Mopple the Whale withdrew into a corner and began noisily chewing a mouthful of straw.

"We just need a trick," said Heather enthusiastically. A sheep needed a trick to appear in the Smartest Sheep in Glennkill contest.

"What's a trick?" asked a lamb.

Silence drifted down in the hay barn, gathering around their hooves like snow in winter. Somewhere, very far away, they could hear a cow mooing. A car hummed along the road, no louder than an insect. A little mouse scurried about in the hayloft, its feet pattering like raindrops on the rough dry wood. A large brown spider stole soundlessly through a forest of sheep's legs.

"Perhaps there's a trick in the toolshed," said Cordelia after a while.

"Even if there is," said Zora, "we wouldn't know what the trick looks like."

"We could take all the things we don't recognize out of the shed," said Heather, who was desperate to get to the contest at any price.

They trotted inquisitively off to the toolshed, and Lane pushed back the bolt with her muzzle.

The door swung open, and old air wafted out: aromas of oil, metal, plastic, and many other unpleasant smells. The sheep looked hopefully into the toolshed. It was a tiny place, so small that not even a single sheep would have fit into it entirely, but it was stuffed full of things.

The scythe. The shepherd's crook. The shearing machine, a little can of oil, the toolbox, the rat traps, seeds for the vegetable garden. The seeds didn't smell bad at all. A mug full of screws, a small rake, a flea collar for Tess. A tin of rat poison that George had bought once in a temper and then never used. The red and white rag, the chamois leather for the windows. All of them things that the sheep knew. They knew exactly what George had done with them—and it wasn't tricks.

Lane, who was standing in front, turned to the other sheep.

"Nothing here," she said.

Suddenly they heard a chuckle behind them. Melmoth. It was as if he had suddenly turned into a completely different animal. He was standing on his hind legs, marching up and down like a Two Legs. His movements were awkward, strange, pointless, and wrong.

"What's that?" breathed Cordelia.

"That," said Othello, who had got up on his own hind legs too, "is a trick."

When the sun was high in the sky, and Rebecca came groping her way out of the shepherd's caravan barefoot to stretch like a cat, the sheep were still discussing the matter.

Nothing they could do seemed to be a trick. Grazing, running, sitting on a rocky ledge, jumping, thinking, remembering, eating. None of those was a trick.

"What about listening?" asked Heather.

Othello shook his head impatiently. "It has to be totally pointless," he explained for the hundredth time. "Pointless and obvious. Like walking on your hind legs. Or holding a cloth between your teeth and waving it. Or rolling a ball."

"Why would a sheep want to roll a ball?" asked Maude.

"See what I mean?" said Othello.

"They think sheep are smart because they do pointless things?" Cloud flapped her ears, incredulous.

Othello snorted. "We don't have to understand it. We just have to know about it."

Melmoth nodded approvingly.

"We don't have a ball," said Lane, who was a very pragmatic sheep.

"I don't think we know any tricks," said Zora calmly. "Luckily."

Some of the sheep hung their heads, but Miss Maple wasn't to be discouraged.

"That doesn't matter," she said. "We only want them to pay attention to us. We don't want to win."

"I do," said Heather.

Miss Maple ignored her. "If we can get in there, they'll pay attention to us. And then perhaps we can get them to understand."

"Understand what?" asked Maude.

"That Beth killed him with poison, and then she still wasn't happy, she wanted his soul too. And she stuck the spade in him so that his ghost wouldn't haunt her," Rameses explained.

"They'll never understand all that," groaned Mopple.

"Make it simpler!" said Miss Maple.

"That Beth is George's murderer. First with poison. Then with the spade," said Heather.

"Simpler still!" said Miss Maple.

"Beth—murderer—George," said Zora, feeling unnerved.

"That's it," said Miss Maple. "If we're very lucky they might understand that."

The sheep looked at one another. Three words, such simple words—and it would be difficult to make human beings understand them . . .

They looked round to Miss Maple for help, but she had disappeared. Instead, the sheep heard strange scratching noises from one corner of the hay barn. A moment later Miss Maple was back among them again, with a grubby nose and the butcher's Thing between her teeth.

Miss Maple had a plan.

21

Fosco Knows His Way Around

Inspector Holmes stared into his Guinness, feeling frustrated. At any other time the sight of it would have cheered him, but not here. This was what you might call a duty Guinness, which spoiled any enjoyment of it. Here of all places, in this God-forsaken dump Glennkill! Here at this stupid sheep contest, jammed in between tourists and the locals in festive mood. He didn't like the atmosphere. Relaxation was all very well, but the people here were too relaxed by half. Although probably it just seemed that way to him because he wasn't having fun himself.

He never ought to have joined the police, not with a name like his. They had a Watson in Galway, and no one ever left him in peace either, but Holmes . . . Stupid remarks were the least of it. All the most hopeless cases landed on his desk. *With* stupid remarks. It wasn't his fault that he had the worst success rate in the entire county, and no prospect of improving it. Not with cases like this one. George Glenn. Right at the start he'd known: if it wasn't the family who did it, I'll never find out the truth. The family consisted of that pretty plump redhead, who of course had an alibi. Then all that stuff about the legacies. He had made up his mind just to arrest the heirs. Better than no arrest at all, he'd told himself. He could always let them go again later.

But now! He could hardly arrest a flock of sheep. To be honest, by now he hated the sight of sheep. So of course the Smartest Sheep in Glennkill contest was no place for him.

A wooden platform had been erected in the middle of the big hall in the Mad Boar. No steps leading up to it, only ramps. All for those animals. Behind it stood the shepherds with their champion sheep, so worked up that it was hard to say which of them was giving off the most penetrating stink. Or perhaps that was the tourists: many of them had cycled here in the summer heat, and you could smell that, naturally. What was he doing here? Did he expect the murderer to give himself away while under the influence? Did he expect the sheep to supply the crucial clue? No, really he just didn't want to be back in the office with a filing cabinet full of unsolved cases. Better to go on investigating a little longer.

Now all was quiet. Quieter, anyway—of course the sheep were still bleating merrily away. Not particularly smart of them. A thin man climbed up on the platform. If that was the landlord it didn't say much for the food in this place; the inspector would sooner have bought a meal from the fat man in the wheelchair. Hadn't the pair of them been among those who found the body? Yes, right. Baxter and Rackham.

Taciturn fellow, that Baxter, he'd thought when he questioned him. But now the landlord was holding forth to the spectators for minutes on end. St. Patrick . . .Yeats and Swift . . . tradition . . . tradition . . . Glennkill's pride in its sheep. Enough to make you sick! And he'd finished his Guinness.

At last the skinny landlord had finished and the contest began. Now it was really quiet; even the sheep had stopped bleating.

In the midst of this silence, a knock on the front door was heard. A minute ago it wouldn't have had the faintest effect, but now all eyes went to the door. There didn't seem much point in knocking on the door of a pub. But no one in the hall moved. More knocking. In fact it really sounded more like someone thumping on the door with a hard object. Only at the third knock did the man with the big nose take pity on whoever was knocking. He'd talked to him too. Father . . . Father something or other, the parish priest.

The priest went to the door and opened it, smiling. Only priests knew how to smile that way: he'd never seen a smile like it on anyone else's face. But even as the inspector was thinking this, the holy smile slipped. Froze. Twisted in amazement. The priest's horrified face stared at what was waiting for him outside.

When the door finally opened they felt like running away again. They'd never have thought there were so many people in the world. More than had come to their meadow, even more than had come to the lime tree. And the stink! The smells of individual humans had merged into a vast, collective aroma, greasy and smoky, pungent, rancid, monstrously alien. The stink settled like oil around their nostrils, depriving them of the ability to scent anything.

In addition, dense cigarette smoke lay like fog over the human faces above them. Its acrid smell drifted into the sheep's faces and made tears come to their eyes. They couldn't rely on their hearing anymore either—it was as if some strange veil had come down over them. Somewhere music was playing, muted as if by the leaves of a hedge, and a few feet were tapping under the pub benches. Nothing else.

The people stared at them in silence. God, after opening the door, had taken a couple of steps back, his jaw dropping right open, then collapsed into a chair, and was now clutching his chest. Othello took a step forward into the middle of the narrow aisle between the rows of tables. The others kept close behind him. They would all have preferred to race away from this dreadful cavern at top speed—but it was the only thing they could think of to do. At first all the sheep had wanted to be in the Smartest Sheep in Glennkill contest, but most of the flock had stayed behind after the vote finally went to just four sheep—Miss Maple, Mopple the Whale, Zora, and Othello. By this time fear had obliterated all pride and anticipation in Mopple, in Zora, even in Miss Maple. Othello was their lead ram; all they could do now was let him lead them.

Head held high, he strode past the rows of tables, showing not the slightest sign of fear. Right behind him came Zora, then Miss Maple, and bringing up the rear, stout and nervous, Mopple the Whale, with the cloth firmly held between his clenched teeth. That stinking rag was their most important stage prop.

When they had gone halfway into the hall, one of the humans shouted something, and an infernal racket broke out. The human beings were clapping their hands, shouting, and roaring. The sheep moved even closer together, pushed along by Mopple the Whale, whose vulnerable position had filled him with panic. Mopple's head was now resting on Maple's rear end, Maple's on Zora's, and Zora was pushed right up to Othello.

"What's that?" she whispered in fright.

"Applause," said Othello calmly. "It means they like us."

"That noise?" asked Zora, but Othello had already moved on, and Mopple was shoving Zora and Maple from behind.

The clapping and shouting didn't stop. It pursued them right through the hall, and when Othello finally led them up onto the platform it became unbearable.

The black ram stopped and turned to the human beings. The sheep finally had a bit of room, but they were suddenly bathed in dazzling light. Mopple, Maple, and Zora took their chance to get Othello between them and the human hordes again. Shoulder to shoulder, they trotted round and stood in close formation behind him. Othello bowed his head down to the floor three times.

"I wish they'd stop it," said Mopple indistinctly, through the cloth held in his teeth. "Make them stop it."

But Othello did nothing at all. He just stood there, looking calmly out over the sea of human heads. The other sheep peered uneasily to all sides. There was a second ramp at the back of the platform which led down to a corner where the other sheep and their shepherds were waiting. It looked calm and peaceful, dark and safe. That was where they wanted to be. Othello showed no sign of moving yet. He was waiting for something. Gradually the volume of noise decreased, and then it died away altogether.

Othello got up on his hind legs.

The noise began again, louder than ever. The humans were roaring.

"See?" said Othello, without turning round. "It's dead easy. When we do something they make a noise. When we don't do anything, they don't make any noise."

"Then we'd better not do anything," said Mopple the Whale.

"It's not at all dangerous," said Othello, when he was down on all four legs again. "They're the audience." So saying, he turned and led his miniflock down the second ramp and into the corner with the other sheep.

There was a low fence around this corner, with a small gate in it. Othello opened the gate with his front hoof, led his sheep through it, and closed the gate with his nose. The other sheep were tied up to the fence. Their shepherds were sitting at a table in the middle of the fenced area, staring open-mouthed at the newcomers.

"You were right," Zora whispered to Miss Maple. "People really do pay a lot of attention to sheep here."

They felt better again in the company of the other sheep. Othello led them to a quiet place between a stout gray ram and a brown ewe. They waited to see what would happen next.

The applause had gradually turned to an excited murmur. Compared with the racket just now it was almost refreshing. A strange man wearing glasses pushed his way through all the humans crowding curiously around the fenced-off shepherds' corner. When the shepherds saw him they mobbed him.

"Against all the rules!" shouted one.

"Why didn't anyone tell us? Why aren't they listed on the program?"

"Get them out of here at once!"

"What's the idea? You told us no one could enter more than one sheep. If I'd known I could have brought along Peggy and Molly and Sue—then you'd have seen something!"

"They haven't been entered." The bespectacled man smiled. "To be honest, I haven't the faintest notion where they come from. Or where their shepherd is."

The shepherds looked at one another in silence. Then one of them said, "Their shepherd won't be coming."

"How can you be so sure?" asked the bespectacled man.

"He's dead," said the shepherd. "Those are George Glenn's sheep."

"Oh." The bespectacled man looked confused.

"They should be thrown out," shouted a sturdy, red-faced farmer.

The sheep were horrified. All that trouble, just to be chased away from the pub when they were so close to achieving their aim?

"It's not that simple," said the bespectacled man. "Don't you hear the audience? The tourists? They *like* those sheep. If we turn them out, what do you think will happen?"

"I couldn't care less," growled one of the shepherds. "Rules are rules."

"No." The bespectacled man shook his head. "Why should we deprive the audience of its fun?"

"Fun?" shouted the red-faced farmer angrily.

"Look, we'll let them perform outside the contest," said the bespectacled man soothingly. "At the end, when no one's really watching anymore."

The shepherds sat down at their table again in a bad temper, giving George's sheep black looks.

Wide-eyed, Mopple, Maple, and Zora watched the strange things going on around them. Children's hands pushed through the fence, offering them sweets, bread, cake, even ice cream. Not even Mopple dreamed of touching this fodder. For the first time in his life he had no appetite. Perhaps it was also because the rag he had put down on the straw beside him was still giving off its horrible smell.

The music was very loud now. This time it didn't come from a small gray radio set but from a troop of people who had marched up onto the platform and were doing things with a strange set of tools. The music made the sheep's hearts beat faster, as if they were galloping. The human beings gawping around the fence had taken out small box things and were aiming flashes of lightning at the sheep. Maple blinked. She was the cleverest sheep in all Glennkill, but at that moment she made up her mind that no one must ever find it out.

In search of help, Maple, Zora, and Mopple looked round at the other sheep. The brown ewe on their right was nervously munching a piece of straw. Maple was about to ask her a question when she noticed the stout gray ram scrutinizing her.

"You lot aren't particularly clever," said the ram, his eyes glittering. "Just walking in here, as if it were summer pasture. Taking part in this contest at all. I wouldn't call that smart." He winked at her mischievously.

"The others are taking part too," said Mopple the Whale.

"The others aren't particularly smart either," said the stranger. The two rams looked hard at each other. Mopple had never before met a sheep who was fatter than he. He immediately felt respect for the gray ram.

"You're taking part yourself," said Miss Maple, offended. After all, coming to the Smartest Sheep in Glennkill contest had been her idea. "So I suppose that means you're not particularly clever either."

"Wrong," said the gray ram. "I am Fosco. All the others are here for the first time—they've no idea what's coming to them. Except for the dappled ram there: he's been competing as long as I have. But he has no idea either. He forgets the whole thing again every year. It would be crazy to take part a second time."

"Oh, you're crazy, are you?" asked Miss Maple.

"Wrong," said Fosco. "I am Fosco. The others take part. I *win*."

Maple was about to ask another question when the music stopped. The bespectacled man had climbed up on the wooden platform. "Ladies and gentlemen, here we are at last. The traditional Smartest Sheep in Glennkill contest will open in a few minutes' time. One by one, the cleverest sheep in Glennkill will do their tricks for you, then you will use your voting papers to decide on the winner. And of course there's a prize to be won as well. For you, it will be a week of culinary lamb specialities at the Mad Boar. For the sheep—well, it'll be the same!"

The human beings roared their approval.

"Only joking," the bespectacled man went on. "Of course the smartest sheep in Glennkill doesn't go under the knife itself. There's a pint of Guinness and a wreath of shamrock waiting for the winner. Then it will go on tour and show off its skills in all the pubs of Ballyshannon, Bundoran, and Ballintra."

The bespectacled man didn't do any spectacular tricks, but he was applauded all the same.

"The shepherd will receive a small mark of appreciation to the value of two hundred euros. So let's have a round of applause, please! I now declare the Smartest Sheep in Glennkill contest open!"

The humans in the hall obediently made a lot of noise.

Othello glared at the bespectacled man. Zora flapped her ears, and Mopple swallowed. The remark about lamb specialities had left a nasty taste behind.

Fosco winked at them. "He says that every time. Take a look at me. Would you say I look like a lamb speciality?"

"Off we go," announced the bespectacled man. "Let's hear it for Jim O'Connor and Smartie."

"Oh wow!" chuckled Fosco. "He's going first! Just watch this!"

The sheep craned their necks. The red-faced farmer had stood up and was leading the dappled ram to the platform by his halter. Gradually the audience fell silent.

The farmer bowed to them. "Smartie, the only footballing

sheep in the world," he said. He put a mottled black-and-white ball down on the floor in front of Smartie.

Fosco turned to George's sheep. "He's supposed to nudge the ball along with his hoof. I'm only telling you because you'd never guess it from his act."

Smartie conscientiously sniffed the ball all over. Then he rubbed his head on one foreleg. The farmer looked at him with an expression showing that he was perfectly confident of victory. Now Smartie swung his foreleg back and forth, and stared at the ball again as if he'd just seen it for the first time. He was in no hurry. A few whistles could be heard from the audience. The farmer was getting impatient. He went over to Smartie and pushed the ball a little too hard with his own foot, sending it rolling over the platform. Smartie trotted after it and tried to bite it. In doing so he only pushed the ball farther on. The ball bounced off the platform, and without a moment's hesitation Smartie jumped off after it, landing on top of the first of the tables where spectators were sitting. Glasses clinked, and the humans at the table bleated in protest.

The sheep rolled their eyes at such nonsense.

"Look at him!" chuckled Fosco. "He's been doing the same silly trick here for years. The only bigger fool in his flock is the farmer himself."

Smartie, the only footballing sheep in the world, earned only halfhearted applause. The bespectacled man smiled apologetically as he climbed up onstage again. "Simon Foster and Einstein, defending his title," he announced.

"That's me," said Fosco. "They think my name is Einstein." There was a conspiratorial twinkle in his little eyes, as if being called by the wrong name was a particularly clever move on his part.

Fosco's farmer was tall and strong and even stouter than Fosco. He was holding a bag in one hand, and his other hand was in his pocket. The two of them walked calmly out onstage. For his girth, Fosco was surprisingly light on his hooves.

The farmer didn't say a single word. He took a bottle of Guinness and a glass out of his bag, poured the Guinness into the glass, and put it down on the floor in front of Fosco. Fosco took the glass in his teeth and raised it. Next he tipped his head back and gulped down the contents of the glass. Applause. Fosco put the glass neatly back on the floor again. The farmer took a second bottle out of the bag. He still hadn't taken his other hand out of his trouser pocket. A third bottle followed. The humans roared their approval. At the fourth bottle, they rose from the benches chanting, "Einstein, Einstein," over and over again, in chorus. The farmer himself—still working one-handed—drank the fifth bottle. Then he took his other hand out of his pocket and waved to the audience with both hands. Amid thunderous applause, sheep and shepherd marched back into the corner. The other shepherds looked enviously at them. Fosco was tethered next to George's sheep, and the farmer sat down again.

"So that's how you win?" asked Miss Maple. "By *drinking*?"

"Wrong," said Fosco. "By drinking *Guinness*. From a glass. That's what they all do themselves. So of course they're convinced it's the cleverest thing anyone can do. That's why I win. Every time."

"But it's not a difficult thing to do," said Zora.

Fosco was unmoved. "That just shows how smart I am. Why would I do something difficult when I can win with something easy?"

"And why do you want to win?" asked Mopple, convinced by now that they could really learn a lot from Fosco.

"For the Guinness, of course," said Fosco. "Didn't you hear, the winner gets a Guinness? And then he does his trick again in the other pubs. And he gets more Guinness. And then of course there are the weeks of training before the contest." His eyes were shining.

Next came Jeremy Tipp and Wild Rose. George's sheep craned their necks again curiously, but Fosco shook his head. "Nothing worth mentioning," he said. "They put the good turns on first this time. You can forget the rest of it. You might as well not watch anymore."

But the sheep did watch. Wild Rose ran around in circles and changed direction when the shepherd whistled. Another sheep jumped clumsily over small obstacles. A massive ram kept nodding his head when his shepherd gave him a signal. At another signal he bleated. His shepherd talked to him all the time. Surprisingly, this act went down well. Saddest of all was the performance of the brown ewe, who didn't even have a name. Once onstage, she was so frightened that she lost her sense of direction and couldn't run through the little obstacle course that her shepherd had set up. She stood still in the middle of the platform. When the shepherd hit her with a stick, the brown ewe raced across the stage in panic and fell off the other side. A few people clapped even at this.

Fosco remained grimly silent.

The bespectacled man came up on the platform again. "And now, ladies and gentlemen, our surprise guests: Peggy, Polly, Samson, and Black Satan."

"He's gone and thought up wrong names for us," bleated Zora indignantly.

Othello snorted too. "Do I *look* like a donkey?"

"Never mind," said Miss Maple. "Here we go! Just do everything the way we discussed it, and remember what Melmoth taught us."

And now George Glenn's sheep had trotted up onto the platform, into that dazzling light, to ensure that justice got out at last.

The people in the hall were looking expectantly at them. The babble of voices slowly subsided into a muted murmur. At last it was quiet enough in the room for the sheep to hear their own breathing again. Then—suddenly—there was a loud bang. A chair had fallen over. Next moment a door slammed. The humans turned their heads in surprise.

A murmur ran through the hall. "What was that, then?"

"Father William," someone replied. "No idea what's the matter. He just shot out of the door as if the Devil himself were after him."

Although the others hadn't noticed, a queasy feeling was spreading between Othello's horns. Was it the audience? He sensed all eyes on him like ticks in his fleece, just the way he had felt them the first time Lucifer Smithley dragged him into a circus ring. Othello waited for the voice in his head. It would say something soothing or something provocative or something to make him think. Anyway, the voice would send the queasy feeling away.

But Othello heard nothing. He listened to his front right horn. He listened to his front left horn. He listened to his back left horn and finally to his back right horn. Nothing at all. Othello was so surprised that he stopped still. The voice had gone away! For the first time he was alone. Shivers ran through his fleece. Somewhere among all those spectators, panic lay in wait for him. But just as it was about to leap on Othello, he felt a gentle nudge against his hindquarters. It was Zora's velvety nose reminding him to go on walking as he pulled himself together. After all, he had defeated the dog in the end. He had defeated many dogs. He had faced God, and God had run away from him. He was now the lead ram. And today, on this special day, he was death.

Sometimes being alone is an advantage, Othello thought, and he set his black hooves firmly on the platform.

Zora was relieved. After that moment's hesitation, Othello had started moving again. At last. The long wait had started her thinking, and today, onstage at the Smartest Sheep in Glennkill contest, Zora wanted, just for once, to think as little as possible. But it was too late. Zora thought of what the man with the glasses had said. Lamb specialities. She thought of the strange ram. All flesh was grass. They grazed sheep's flesh like grass. Meat was right. That was why they'd laughed. That was why there was the butcher. Zora looked at all the faces of humans who wanted to win the lamb specialities. She saw an abyss that had always been there, right in front of her, although she had never guessed at its existence. The seagulls were silent. For the first time in her life Zora felt dizzy.

She peered in all directions. Then she saw a small, perfect cloud sheep floating in the air a few paces away from her. It had risen from the pipe being smoked by a young man in the second row. Zora knew that it wasn't really a cloud sheep, but it reminded her of what the abyss was there for: the abyss was there to be overcome. Sure-footed, she climbed upon the platform behind Othello. Zora was the shepherd today.

Miss Maple trotted along behind Zora and Othello, in good spirits but feeling the tension to the tip of every hair in her fleece. It was her plan. Would the human beings understand the show they were putting on for them? The sheep had understood it, all of them, the whole flock. Some had even galloped up the hill in a fright during rehearsals, because the act thought up by Miss Maple and the others had seemed so real. Maple thought optimistically that human beings, on their good days, weren't much dimmer than sheep. Or at least, not much dimmer than *dim* sheep. But would the humans believe them? And if so, then what would happen? Miss Maple looked forward to seeing what justice looked like. She stepped up onto the wooden boards and blinked fearlessly down at the spectators. Miss Maple was the wolf.

Mopple the Whale trotted after the others, with the rag between his teeth again and taking rather short breaths. The smell of the rag was the reason they had to be short, quick breaths. Apart from that, Mopple was feeling surprisingly good. He knew what he had to do. He had remembered everything. When he made his entrance, even the dimmest sheep in the meadow had realized what part Maple was playing, who the murderer was. Horns held confidently high, hooves treading carefully, Mopple stepped up onstage—and froze.

For there in the front row, only a few paces away and with his hands clamped on the arms of his wheelchair, sat the butcher.

22

Mopple Is Important

Tom O'Malley was inspecting his Guinness. These last few days hadn't been so bad: people had wanted to talk to him because he had a story to tell. What a difference it made when people wanted to talk to you.

If anyone had asked him what he liked best about Guinness, the colors would have occurred to him first. Black that could often be a dark red or a brown too. Tom had once seen a horse that was brown like that Guinness brown. And the luscious sweet, white, creamy head on top was irresistible. Although he hadn't drunk quite so much of it these last few days. Suddenly everyone wanted something from him, even though he could hardly remember anything. Just his foot meeting something soft, and a nasty fright.

Odd that now, just when people had stopped asking him so much about it, he was beginning to remember again. It had taken him a long time to understand that the spade really went right through George. *Right through him!* No wonder he was back in the Mad Boar now tipping Guinness down his throat.

At least I never saw his eyes, he thought. If you don't see the eyes you're still okay.

For the third time in his life Mopple was at very close quarters with the butcher, staring into his eyes. The butcher stared menacingly back. Without a glass pane between them now, without any mist—just a little smoke. Mopple turned and trotted back toward the ramp. Justice was all very well, but the butcher was the butcher.

Silently, Othello barred Mopple's way.

"The butcher," panted Mopple. "He'll kill us all. Me first."

Othello shook his head. "He's one of the audience too. The audience never does anything."

Mopple squinted uneasily down at the butcher, but Othello seemed to be right. The butcher wasn't moving. Only his big hands opened and closed around the arms of his wheelchair. Heart thudding, Mopple went back to the side of the stage where Maple and Othello were waiting to make their entrance, while Zora had already trotted to the middle of the platform.

First she had to get the humans to understand what it was all about. George. Zora began by imitating George's position at the time. She lay down on her side and made her legs go rigid.

A few of the audience applauded, but no one was really scared.

Imperceptibly, Miss Maple shook her head. They still didn't get the idea. Zora stood up and tried again, this time with a much more spectacular death scene.

As Zora's forelegs slowly gave way under her, while she bleated dramatically, Mopple curiously inspected the humans. So those were the audience. And indeed, they weren't doing anything. But what was going on at their tables was far from uninteresting. He saw any amount of glasses of Guinness, small dishes of human fodder, and strange bowls full of ash. Auto-

314

matically, Mopple sniffed the scent of the human fodder. Most of it smelled inedible, but over there in the middle of the first table a sweet, promising scent thread wafted through the smoke. Mopple looked round at Zora, who was now lying on her side with her legs twitching. Plenty of time before he made his own entrance.

Mopple the Whale took a step toward the ramp. Those were the audience. If even the butcher wasn't doing anything, just think how harmless all the others must be! While all eyes were turned on Zora, who was just drawing her last breath, Mopple put his rag down at the side of the stage and stole down the ramp, stopping right in front of the table with the delicious smell.

Up onstage, Zora leaped to her feet again. This time they must have understood. Now it was time for the murder itself.

With long, straight, George-like steps Zora stalked across the meadow, an expression on her face that said: get to work, you idle animals. Then she pricked up her ears: an idea. George left the steps of the shepherd's caravan to pay Beth a visit. Maple was standing on the other side of the platform, calm as a wolf, waiting.

They greeted each other. Maple looked friendly. She nuzzled Zora with her nose: Beth wanted to make George do something. But George didn't want to. He shook his head impatiently. At this point Zora's eyes flashed with amusement, as George's had done so often. By now an idea had occurred to Beth. Maple uttered a friendly bleat, inviting Zora to take some refreshment. Unsuspectingly, Zora dipped her nose in the invisible, unwholesome puddle and drank her fill.

As she did so, she squinted surreptitiously at the audience. The humans were sitting there, blank-faced, and only Ham seemed to be really upset. Had they seen through Beth's plan?

315

At home in the flock, there had been alarmed bleats of "Don't do it, George!" at this point. But it was already too late. George had drunk the poisoned water. For the third time that day, Zora performed a dramatic death scene onstage.

There it was. A little piece of cake with a fork sticking into it. Mopple had had good experiences with cake, not quite such good experiences with forks. He hesitated.

That was a mistake. The human on the other side of the piece of cake had noticed him.

"Hey!" he shouted. "Shoo, shoo!" And he made sudden movements with his hands that would normally have frightened Mopple.

You're the audience, thought Mopple the Whale, and he stretched his neck out to the cake.

The human snatched it back from in front of Mopple's nose with a surprisingly quick movement, and held it high above his head, where Mopple couldn't reach it.

At the same moment Zora's legs twitched in the air for the last time, and then she lay still.

Also at the same moment, Tom O'Malley looked up from his Guinness for the first time in quite a number of minutes, saw the shadowy outline of a long shape with a metal implement sticking in it, saw a sheep behind it—dead?—wasn't that the black-faced sheep he'd seen sitting right above the abyss?—and beside that one a black four-horned ram—George's sheep—his foot struck something soft . . .

"George!" howled Tom. Under the table Cuchulainn, Josh's old sheepdog, whom he had kicked in the side by mistake, howled too.

George's name hung in the air for a long time, while the

other sounds gradually died down. Something changed in the atmosphere of the hall. It was as if the wind had blown cold air into the Mad Boar and extinguished a few of the lights.

"You sit down, Tom," said Josh in the silence. It sounded stern. "You're pissed. Just you sit down again."

But Tom had no intention of sitting down. He pointed to the stage.

"The—the sheep! They're . . . they're trying to tell us something about the murder!"

"That's not funny," growled a second voice.

"Sit down," Josh repeated.

His face pale, his nose bright red, Tom looked round the hall.

"You sit down again," said Josh's stern voice for the third time. "You've had one too many."

He was right. Tom had certainly had one too many. He dropped back on the bench and patted Cuchulainn's head comfortingly. Pissed again. The hall was going round and round. Yet only a second ago everything had been perfectly clear. The sheep—it had to mean something. But probably it just meant he was pissed. Yet again. Hopelessly.

By now death itself, in the shape of a black ram, had appeared onstage. Othello's entrance was not strictly necessary. No one who had seen Zora die could doubt that she was dead. But Mopple, Maple, and Zora had insisted that Othello must go to the Mad Boar too. Othello knew the world, he knew the zoo. They wouldn't have dared to go there without him.

So now Othello and Beth were watching the body, both of them greedy for George's human soul. The time came when Beth didn't want to wait around anymore. Miss Maple pushed Zora back to the meadow on the other side of the platform. It

317

was the only part of her scene that didn't look deceptively genuine: for Beth to be able to move the body at all, Zora herself had to help, using her powerful leg muscles. (At this point they had been interrupted during rehearsals by excited cries of "He's alive! He's alive!")

But George Glenn was dead when the sheep launched into their grand finale. Once she was in the meadow again, Zora lay there on her back, rigid. For want of a spade, Maple stamped on her chest with one front hoof. It was a breathtaking effect that had given Zora a few bruises in rehearsals. Death in the shape of a black ram with demonically sparkling eyes was still prowling around the body.

Down in the audience, Mopple the Whale let his piece of cake go and scurried back to the stage. Suddenly he was glad he hadn't eaten it. His stomach felt peculiar, shallow and queasy. Mopple was important. Now came the third and most difficult part of their performance, the scene about Beth. Mopple dutifully picked the smelly rag up in his teeth again and positioned himself close to Miss Maple, just in time.

They had thought hard about the best way to depict the murderer. Finally Mopple the Whale had come up with the idea of the scent. Of course there had been discussions, more particularly between Mopple and Maude, about the size of souls, about Things, and about the ability of humans to pick up any scent at all. But Mopple had won the day. "Humans have noses," he said, "large noses, right in the middle of their faces. They must pick up some kind of scent with them. And Beth— well, anyone is bound to pick up *her* scent! Anyone with a nose!"

So they had set to work. Maude discovered a very faint,

sourish smell on the rag in the toolshed which was not unlike Beth's scent. To make it stronger, they had buried the rag overnight in dirt, they had covered it with chewed sorrel next day (as senior lead ram, Sir Ritchfield had taken on the arduous task of chewing the sorrel) and then they had wrapped it around a recently deceased shrew found by Heather, and left it there for some time. The result was breathtaking. Of course, it didn't smell exactly like Beth, but the similarity was close enough for the sheep to identify her without any doubt. It must be good enough even for human beings with their poor sense of smell.

Mopple dramatically shook the rag, and clouds of sharp, pungent murderer scent wafted through the room. That was the most difficult part. They had the scent, and they had the Thing. It was a chain with a glittery pendant on it, just like Beth's. The most lifelike idea would have been for Miss Maple to hang the Thing round her neck. They'd tried that, but every time they tried it the cross and the chain instantly disappeared into Maple's thick fleece and couldn't be seen at all. So now Miss Maple took the Thing between her teeth—it had been hidden inside her mouth up to this point—and went to the front of the stage with it. She carried the little cross up and down in front of the audience. Mopple kept close behind her with his smelly rag.

Down in the audience, something stirred. A murmured curse. A clatter. A glass clinked as it fell to the floor.

The butcher came thundering up the ramp, with the wheels of his chair flashing in the spotlights.

Once up on the platform he hesitated for a moment. His eyes wandered back and forth between Mopple and the thing in

Maple's mouth. Then he shot toward Mopple the Whale. Mopple didn't waste a second. He turned and galloped down the ramp at the back of the stage, the rag still held tightly in his teeth. The butcher was hard on his heels. He could move with amazing speed in that wheelchair. The other sheep watched from the platform as the butcher chased Mopple through the hall, down one aisle, and up the other aisle again.

None of the sheep could say whether it was sheer desperation or a brain wave that finally led Mopple to turn into a narrow pathway left free between two rows of tables. As might have been expected, the butcher thundered after him. But it now turned out that although Mopple the Whale was a fat sheep, he was still thinner than the butcher in his wheelchair. While Mopple raced on along the pathway unimpeded, the butcher got stuck after going a few sheep's lengths. The sheep prepared to hear bloodcurdling curses, but in astonishment Ham just watched Mopple go and silently laid his hands in his lap.

Mopple the Whale, weak at the knees, returned to the platform, where he felt safer among the other sheep. He had lost the rag somewhere in his flight.

Mopple cast a nasty glance at Othello. "The audience!" he snorted. "They never do anything! Huh!"

Othello looked embarrassed.

They studied each other in silence: the villagers of Glennkill and George Glenn's sheep. No one applauded. Mopple, who was feeling brave again, was disappointed: he had been secretly hoping for applause. Perhaps for even more than applause. During the show, and under the attentive gaze of human eyes, he had started to wonder what one of those Guinnesses tasted like.

The sheep blinked through the tobacco smoke. Zora looked

uneasily all round. Smoke filled the hall like an unpleasant fog, and somewhere in that fog a beast of prey was preparing to pounce.

But no beast of prey pounced. At first a few voices were heard in the back rows, where the tourists were sitting. Questions, quiet laughter. Someone stood up and pushed Ham back to his place. Soon the whole hall was humming like a beehive. The moment when everyone's attention was on the sheep had passed, and still justice hadn't put in an appearance.

The bespectacled man who had called Othello "Satan" climbed up onstage again. The sheep fled down the ramp at the back to get away from him. Once there, they regrouped to watch.

"Let's hear it for Peggy, Polly, Samson, and Black Satan, who have just shown us that even sheep know something about the modern drama," said the bespectacled man. "Give them a big hand!"

At best the applause was halfhearted, but the sheep had a feeling that it was more for the bespectacled man than them.

"Ladies and gentlemen, you have just seen the most talented and clever sheep in Glennkill do their turns to win your favor. Now it's up to you to . . ."

Right at the back of the hall, something moved. Beth came slowly walking down the central aisle past the audience. In her hands, as tenderly as a mother ewe, she held the rag that Mopple had dropped. Beth had unfolded it, and even through the dirt the sheep could see the pattern of two red signs on a white background.

Beth made straight and undeterred for the stage, as if following a secret scent. She walked so calmly and held herself so upright that it was a pleasure to watch her.

321

She stopped in front of the stage.

The bespectacled man looked down at Beth.

"Excuse me, please," said Beth, "but I'd like to say something."

"Does it have to be now?" the bespectacled man hissed down.

"Yes," said Beth.

The bespectacled man shrugged his shoulders.

"Ladies and gentlemen," he said, raising his voice again, "there will now be a brief intermission for a charity appeal."

His hand sketched a gesture of invitation, but Beth didn't join him on the platform. She simply sat down on the edge of the stage and smoothed out her skirt and the piece of cloth she held.

"George," she said. "I want to tell you something about George."

From then on it was so quiet in the hall that you could have heard a pin drop. Neither the bespectacled man nor the sheep had really mastered the knack of getting everyone's attention; Beth did it with the utmost ease. Yet she didn't do any tricks, she just sat still on the edge of the stage and spoke. Sometimes she swung her legs a little, sometimes her fingers carefully stroked the piece of cloth.

The piece of cloth seemed to be important to her, although it stank. At first she didn't talk about George at all, but about herself.

"I gave him this," she said. "Long, long ago. It was so easy. I sat up for a whole night embroidering it. I knew in advance just what it would look like. And in the morning I felt as if I could float in the air, do anything, say anything. It was . . ." Beth hesitated for a moment, perhaps to recover her voice, which had grown quieter and quieter and was now in danger of fading away entirely. "It was good."

Some of the people began to murmur.

"And then the moment came, and I didn't say anything after all, just put the handkerchief in his hand without a word. He looked at me as if he didn't understand, and I couldn't say anything or do anything. Ever again. When I saw it again just now, I realized that *that* was the big mistake in my life—not the other thing."

The sheep could see a shudder run from the nape of Beth's neck down her spine and into her limbs.

"The Sunday before last, late in the evening, there was a knock on my door. I was still awake, so I opened it, and there was George. I started telling him something about the Gospel, like every time we saw each other. I always talked about the Gospel."

Beth sadly shook her head.

"But this time it was different. "Beth," he said, very gently. "Stop that. This is important." I went weak at the knees because he said it so gently. So I stopped, and he came into the room. It was almost the way I'd imagined it back then. But of course he had something quite different in mind.

" 'I've come to say good-bye,' he said.

" 'Of course,' I said, and I smiled bravely. At least, it seemed to me it was brave, but now I know it was cowardly. 'Of course. Europe calls!'

" 'No,' he said. 'Not Europe.'

"I understood at once. It was almost good that I understood what he meant so quickly. Then he told me why he'd come to me. I don't remember exactly what we said after that, except that I begged him again and again not to do it. But he was stubborn. He was always so stubborn."

Beth's thin fingers traced the lines on the dirty piece of cloth.

"'But you were looking forward to going to Europe so much,' I said.

"'Yes,' he said, 'I was. I'd still like to go in a way. But I'm afraid, Beth. I can't do it. It's so late now!'"

By this time Beth was trembling so much that her fingers couldn't follow the lines on the cloth anymore. Now her two hands were clutching each other in search of help, clasping and stroking to calm themselves down.

"I couldn't give him the courage to go on. And then I even helped him do it the way he wanted. When I thought that otherwise they wouldn't bury him . . ."

Beth's voice had lost its way in a wood and stopped for a moment, trembling.

"I'd have gone with him, but he didn't want that. 'In an hour's time in the meadow,' he said. 'I'll have it over with by then.' And I went, in the pouring rain. He was dead already. If I can't do that for him, I told myself—well, what's it all worth?"

Beth smiled, with tears in her eyes, and the sheep were surprised. But then the smile seeped away like rain in the sand.

"Oh," she sighed, "it was hell. And the days afterward . . . everything about it was wrong, such a sin, and yet, and yet . . ."

"Why?" asked a hoarse voice from the front row, almost a whisper but clear and distinct in the tense silence.

For the first time since she had begun talking, Beth looked up.

"Why . . . like that?" croaked Ham even more quietly.

Beth looked at him, irritated. "I don't know why. But it absolutely had to be the spade. 'That'll give them something to think about,' he'd said. I couldn't persuade him not to do it. It was terrible."

Ham shook his head. "Not the spade—George."

"Is that so hard to understand?" said Beth. Suddenly she looked angry in a vulnerable sort of way—like a young mother ewe defending her first lamb. "When I gave him the handkerchief I felt the same. Sometimes your hope is so great that you can hardly bear it. So your fear is even greater. He'd waited for Europe too long. Perhaps . . . perhaps he simply didn't have the courage anymore to see if he could really do it."

"But . . ."

However, Beth didn't let him go on. "And is that so surprising? Was I the only person around here to notice how lonely he was, always alone, just him and his sheep? Of course he always laughed at me, but I noticed him moving away from everything, step by step, moving on and on toward something black."

The sheep glanced uncertainly at Othello. Their lead ram was looking baffled.

Beth sighed.

"It's been going on so long! Seven years ago, when I came back from Africa, it was really bad. I don't know what had happened at that time, and I don't want to know. But since then he didn't get on with anyone here, or with God either. At first I thought it might be something to do with me, with my absence—but that was vanity.

"I said so much to him! But he wasn't really listening. And the one thing I always wanted to say I never did. It's quite easy now."

It sounded as if Beth and George had been talking about George's death. But how could George have known he was going to die? And why didn't he run away if he knew about it?

What Beth was saying made no sense. They understood the words—they were simple words, words like "life" and "hope" and "alone"—but they could make hardly anything of what Beth meant by them.

A point came when the sheep gave up. It was such a strain concentrating on the words when they couldn't understand their sense. After a while Beth's voice was just a quiet, sad melody to them.

Baffled, they trotted back into the dark to join the other sheep in their corner.

"So who *did* murder George?" Mopple asked at last.

No one answered.

Then the sheep heard a snort. Fosco was standing behind them. His eyes were shining almost too brightly, and his breath smelled peculiar.

"George," said Fosco.

None of them reacted to this strange echo.

Then Zora asked, very slowly and carefully, "You mean George murdered George?"

"Exactly," said Fosco.

"But George is dead," said Zora. "George was murdered."

"Right," said Fosco.

"George murdered *himself*?"

"Right," said Fosco again, suddenly looking very impressive and gray.

"She's telling lies," bleated Mopple, who had carried the smelly rag all the way to the Mad Boar to clear up the murder of his shepherd. "She just doesn't want to admit that she did it."

But the sheep could tell by the scent of it that Bible-thumping Beth wasn't telling lies. Not in the least.

"Is that crazy?" asked Zora.

"No," said Fosco. "It's suicide."

Suicide. A new word. A word that George couldn't explain to them anymore.

"They sometimes do that—humans, I mean," said Fosco. "They look at the world and decide they don't want to live."

"But," bleated Mopple, "living and wanting to live are the same thing."

"No," said Fosco. "Sometimes it's different with humans."

"That's not specially clever," said Mopple.

"No?" asked Fosco. There was a glimmer in his eyes like reeling glowworms. "How would you know? I've been here several years running. If there's one thing I've learned, it's that it's not easy to say what's clever and what isn't."

No one contradicted him. The sheep were silent again for a while, digesting what they had heard from Fosco. Out in the hall Beth had stopped talking, and the humans were bleating with agitation.

Zora raised her head.

"What about the wolf?" she asked.

"The wolf is on the inside," said Fosco.

"Is it like an abyss?" asked Zora. "An abyss inside you?"

"Mm, like an abyss," Fosco agreed.

Zora thought about it. Falling into an abyss—she could understand that. But falling inside yourself?

She shook her head. "This isn't something sheep can understand," she said.

"No," said Fosco. "No, it really isn't anything sheep can understand."

Miss Maple had been silent for a long time with her head on one side, thinking. Now she flapped her ears, baffled.

"Well, it got out," she said at last. "Let's go home."

The sheep said good-bye to Fosco, who could understand such dark things and was rightly crowned the smartest sheep in Glennkill year after year. They trotted to the way out at the back that Fosco had shown them. First Othello, then Zora, then Maple, and last of all Mopple the Whale.

Just as Mopple, with a sense of relief, was about to slip out into the open air behind Maple, a meaty hand came down on the door and closed it gently in front of his nose.

Mopple was imprisoned inside the evil-smelling pub. He froze.

Beside him sat the butcher, pale-faced, his eyes narrowed to slits. The wheels of his chair smelled of rubber. Mopple looked in all directions. This time there was no escape.

Mopple sat down on the cold stone floor with the sheer shock of it. He was in a trap.

"You," said the butcher in a dangerously quiet voice. "You . . . ?"

Mopple the Whale trembled like grass in the wind. All flesh was grass.

Ham's hand waved clumsily in the air. Mopple flinched back. For a moment he feared the hand might come off the butcher's arm and leap at him.

But Ham just nodded to him, almost respectfully. "Now I understand," he said. "Now I know I deserved all this. Should have noticed what a bad way he was in. He didn't have any other friend—nor me neither."

Wide-eyed, Mopple stared at the butcher. The butcher's great paw in front of his nose had now clenched into a fist.

"But I didn't," said the butcher. "I just looked away. Ignored him. George took that kind of thing to heart."

328

The butcher's paw shook slightly, and then was carefully withdrawn. Mopple felt dizzy.

Suddenly the door in front of his nose was open again.

The butcher said no more, but he was watching Mopple with bright eyes. His hands lay limp and lifeless on his thighs.

It was some time before Mopple realized what the butcher was waiting for.

Then Mopple the Whale was in the open air again, dazed. Out there dark had fallen. Dense, velvety night air, incredibly sweet and clear, streamed into his nostrils.

Inspector Holmes watched, stunned, as his case solved itself on the stage of the Smartest Sheep in Glennkill contest. Suicide. And the business with the spade had been that gray-haired woman's doing: he'd never in his life have thought of that, but in retrospect it didn't seem to him at all implausible. A lonely old man, eccentric, marriage failed, daughter gone—the usual kind of thing. You could never really understand it, though.

A quiet throat-clearing sound nearby brought him out of his thoughts.

A man in dark clothes had appeared next to Holmes. Discreet was the word for him. One of the sort you couldn't describe accurately five minutes later.

"My border collie's name is Murph," said the man.

"Oh Lord," said Holmes. "I might have known it. What do you want now, then? Don't I keep quiet enough for you?"

"Silent as a stone, inspector, silent as a stone. We're really impressed by your masterly inactivity."

"What do you think of all that?" asked Holmes, jerking his chin in the direction of the stage, where the gray-haired woman had just stopped talking.

The discreet man shrugged. "Nothing to do with us. Nothing much to do with you either, am I right? Look, how would you like a genuinely successful investigation for once? A successfully solved case of your own?"

Suddenly there was a videocassette on the table next to the inspector's Guinness. His glass was already half empty again.

"Take that away with you," said the man. "It'll tell you all about that man McCarthy. Could do your career a bit of good."

By the time Holmes had finally stowed the unwieldy cassette in his pocket, the man had long since disappeared. So what? He wouldn't have answered any questions anyway. Holmes stared at the table, where a beer mat promised that Guinness would bring you fame and fortune. There was a strange feeling in the pit of his stomach, and it wasn't just to do with the Glenn case.

It was to do with his own life, with the police station, and with his certainty that he didn't want to go back there again. He left his glass of Guinness half full.

23

Heather Is Right

"Perhaps it all really did just seem like a trick to him, the spade and all the upset in the village. Perhaps it seemed easier to him when he thought of all the confusion he'd be creating." Rebecca sniffed.

The sheep had gathered round the shepherd's caravan the way they did in the old days, but there were no more Pamela novels now. Instead Rebecca read big, rustling newspapers with very thin sheets. The wonderful thing about the newspapers was that they contained stories about George, about Beth, even about their own appearance at the Smartest Sheep in Glennkill contest. Another wonderful thing was that Rebecca sometimes knew more than the newspapers said, because she had talked to Beth (who had left Glennkill now to spend the rest of her life on an island doing good works).

The story the sheep liked best was called "Sheep Bring the Truth to Light." There had been a picture too, showing the platform in the Mad Boar and on it Maple, Mopple, Othello, and Zora—all of them small, gray, and without any scent, but unmistakable. Rebecca had held it right in front of their noses so that they could see it properly, and Mopple had tried to eat part of the newspaper. After that she let them look at the pictures only from a safe distance.

There was a picture of George with an unknown lamb in his arms, standing on the grass and looking very young and adventurous. (Cloud claimed to be the lamb in the picture, but the others didn't believe her.) Beth, in a summer dress, young too and bright-eyed. "A Deadly Romance," said the story that went with it. "Corpse Desecrated for Love" also showed Beth, but old, the way the sheep knew her, with a high-necked dress and a very serious expression.

Rebecca thought about Beth a lot. "She's been quite different since that evening," she said. "I think she's the most romantic person I know."

"That evening"—as the sheep understood—was the evening when four of them had taken part in the Smartest Sheep in Glennkill contest. They proudly raised their heads. They had done something vital that evening, even if they weren't exactly sure just what it was.

The suicide business remained a mystery to the sheep. They couldn't understand why George should have done such a strange thing—George, of all people, who usually said things in a way that a sheep could understand.

"Right up to the end, he probably didn't know what he was going to do himself," said Rebecca. "Sometimes that helps me—imagining that up to the last he thought he'd really go to Europe. But then he went on a different journey . . ."

She swallowed and passed her hand over her wet, reddened eyes. Rebecca's eyes had often been red recently.

"But I know it can't have been so simple. He made his will first, so that whatever happened *you* could go to Europe. He was a good shepherd . . . he took Tess to the animal shelter.

He . . . he wrote me the letter." Rebecca wiped a single tear from her cheek with her hand. She stared right through Mopple, who was standing in the front row of the sheep, hoping for a chance to nibble on that newspaper. An absent expression had come into Rebecca's eyes. She lowered the newspaper. Sometimes it seemed as if their new shepherdess suddenly forgot about reading aloud to them when she was in the middle of it. Then they had to drive her back to work.

Heather and Maude bleated, a loud and penetrating bleat, and then Rameses joined in too.

Rebecca looked up and sighed. She opened the rustling newspaper again and went on reading the story of "The Lonely Shepherd and the Wide, Wide World."

The Glennkill stories in the newspaper gradually became shorter and more boring, and Rebecca went back to the book that had already impressed the sheep when she first read aloud to them. Now, in the light of day, the sheep could see what a lovely picture it had on the cover: lots of greenery, a brook, mountains, trees, rocks.

But of course it was about humans again after all. A little uneasily, the sheep followed the adventures of a small flock of humans living on the moors. Their experience of newspapers had given the sheep a great respect for the written word in general.

"If sheep and humans can get into books so easily, then something can come *out* of books too," said Lane, and Rameses and Heather began watching the new book suspiciously when Rebecca left it on the caravan steps after reading aloud. No one wanted to be suddenly taken by surprise by that wolflike Heathcliff out of the book.

But the book kept quiet.

Toward the end it even got romantic, with two ghosts wandering at liberty over the moors at last, the way they'd always wanted. The sheep thought of George, and hoped that his own soul was wandering on some green meadow now, perhaps with a little flock that he'd found somewhere.

One day Ham came wheeling himself along the path through the fields. The sheep fled uphill in their usual panic. From there, they watched what was going on by the shepherd's caravan. Rebecca and the butcher greeted each other.

"I hope she's not going to sell us," said Mopple.

"She's not allowed to!" bleated Heather. "It says so in the will!" All the same, the sheep looked hard at the two humans.

Rebecca and the butcher seemed to be getting on well together. The sheep never took their eyes off the butcher. He looked to them serious, wrinkled, and not nearly so dangerous now. Luckily, as a salty wind was blowing off the sea, they couldn't catch his scent.

Heather came to the astonishingly bold decision to go and look at the butcher at close quarters. The amazed glances of the other sheep followed her downhill.

" . . there's connections," said the butcher. "Connections everywhere. Transmigration of souls and all that. I read a lot these days so as to understand the connections, know what I mean?" He turned his head and looked Heather straight in the face, half awkwardly, half curiously, and very respectfully. Perhaps he also nodded his head slightly, as if in greeting. Heather was so surprised that she forgot to look fearless and just stared at the butcher in amazement.

Rebecca shrugged her shoulders. "Why not? They were with

him for so long. I can well imagine that there's a little bit of George in the sheep . . ."

Heather gave the butcher a pert look and then trotted back to the others. A respectful flock of sheep awaited her. The butcher and Rebecca shook hands and then, to everyone's relief, the butcher wheeled himself back toward the paved road. Life could go on.

And so it did. The sheep went to work as usual at dawn, and grazed until late in the afternoon. Then they assembled round the caravan to be read to. Then there was more grazing until they went back to the hay barn. A well-ordered life for sheep.

They liked to think of George, and were grateful to him for the will. "He was a good shepherd after all," said Cloud.

The sheep respected George's Place. None of them would have dreamed of nibbling the herbs and grasses that grew there, yet inexplicably George's Place grew smaller and smaller.

"It's because everything has an end," explained Zora.

One morning, when the other sheep were still asleep, a round white blob slipped out of the protective embrace of the flock and made its way over to the cliffs. Mopple the Whale stood in front of Zora's rocky ledge for a long time, thinking. Then he took a step forward. And another. Zora could do it. A third. Melmoth could do it too. Four. Five. He had looked the butcher in the face. Six, and Mopple was on Zora's ledge at last. He carefully lowered his head to taste the herbs of the abyss.

More often than before, small groups formed as the flock grazed to exchange tales of their experiences.

"It was a trick," said Cordelia.

335

"No sheep may leave the flock," said Sir Ritchfield. "Unless that sheep comes back again."

"Sometimes being alone is an advantage," said Melmoth snidely.

"It *was* a love story," bleated Heather, waggling her ears in triumph.

24

Zora Sees a Cloud

Rebecca closed the book with a bang. That was new. The Pamela novels had been printed on soft, thin paper, and would never have made such a good bang. Nor would the newspapers. Willow, who had gone to sleep in the back row, opened her eyes and then silently turned her back to the shepherd's caravan. The others looked expectantly at Rebecca.

"That's the end," Rebecca explained. "We'll start something new tomorrow."

The sheep looked disappointed. What would happen to Heathcliff and Catherine as they wandered over the moors together? Why didn't the book go on to say how the moors smelled when a shower of rain had swept over them? The story must go on somehow!

But Rebecca just sat on the top step of the caravan, and obviously had no intention of reading on. Her hand gently patted Tessy's head, and Tess wagged her tail very slightly. You could see it was the first wag of her tail for a long time.

One morning Rebecca had brought Tess back in a car. Tess had strange, sad eyes. She didn't go racing over the meadow as usual. She didn't leap around the caravan looking for George either. Tess disappeared in Rebecca's shadow and followed her red skirt everywhere, like a very young lamb following its mother.

"Time to sleep," said Rebecca.

The sheep looked at one another. The sun was still high in the sky, the shadows were no longer than two galloping leaps, and they hadn't finished their daily work of grazing and chewing the cud. Back in the hay barn? At this time of day? Never! Moreover, Rebecca had read aloud to them less than usual. They stared obstinately at their shepherdess.

"Mo-o-ore!" bleated Maude.

"Mo-o-ore!" bleated the three lambs.

But Rebecca was not to be moved. Anyone could see she was George's daughter.

"The story's over," she said. "That's it for today."

Maude could scent the determination in Rebecca's face, and fell silent, but the three lambs went on bleating. Rebecca raised her eyebrows.

"Next time I'll read aloud from *The Silence of the Lambs*," she promised. Then she rose from the steps of the caravan.

The silence of the lambs, that sounded promising. The mother ewes in particular hoped something would come of it.

"Go to sleep," said Rebecca. "We're off to Europe tomorrow. Very early. I don't want to see any sleepy faces."

And so saying she disappeared into the shepherd's caravan with Tess at her heels.

"Tomorrow!" bleated Heather.

"Europe!" breathed Maisie.

"It's good that we're going to Europe," said Cordelia thoughtfully, "but it's a pity it means we must leave here."

The other sheep nodded in agreement.

"If we could go to Europe and stay here at the same time," said Mopple, "then we could graze in two places at once."

They thought a little about the wonderful possibilities of double grazing.

Then Melmoth suddenly raised his head as if he had heard a call. His eyes were moist and shining. He began to prance about.

"Come over to the cliffs with me," he said. "I want to tell you a story about saying good-bye." The sheep willingly went with him. When Melmoth told them something, it was like a strange wind caressing their faces, a wind spiced with vague presentiments and mysterious scents. They followed the gray ram over to the cliffs.

Suddenly the crows on their tree began to caw, a blood-curdling sound, the cry of carrion crows. Instinctively, the sheep looked for the dead animal that must be the cause of all this uproar. But they couldn't see anything.

When they turned round again, Melmoth had disappeared. Just like that. They looked under the dolmen, in the hay barn, and behind the shepherd's caravan. They looked in the hedge and under the shade tree, although Melmoth had been standing on the cliffs and couldn't possibly have galloped over to the hedge in such a short time. He must be hiding somewhere, with his story about saying good-bye. But Melmoth was nowhere to be found.

Then Zora bleated in surprise. She had tipped her head back, and was staring bright-eyed up at the sky. A single dark gray storm cloud was hurrying past up there, driven over the sea by moody winds.

"He's turned into a cloud sheep!" bleated Mopple.

"A cloud sheep!" bleated the other sheep excitedly. One of their flock had made it!

"Do cloud sheep come back?" asked a lamb after a while.

Othello tore his eyes away from the beach and turned to Mopple, Maple, Zora, and Cloud, who were still looking up at the shaggy gray cloud with mingled veneration and sadness. Othello wondered if he ought to tell them. Of course Melmoth hadn't turned into a cloud sheep; something much more mysterious had happened: he had simply climbed down the steep tunnel through the rock under the pine tree and gone away. *Sometimes being alone is an advantage.*

Othello decided not to tell the others. They wouldn't have understood it better, they'd have understood it worse. The more he knew about Melmoth, the less he really understood. And always he had the uneasy feeling that Melmoth understood perfectly. Understood himself, understood Othello, all the sheep—even the shepherds. Either that or he was just crazy.

Othello shook his head to get rid of the sadness. But shaking his head didn't help, nor did scraping his hooves.

What helped him was the wind.

For the wind brought with it—who knew from where?— a leaf, and laid it carefully in front of Othello's hooves. A golden leaf. Autumn gold. Swallow-flying time. The time of scents, mating time. Once again he turned back to the meadow, where Mopple, Maple, Zora, and Cloud were gazing reverently at a gray cloud. But he saw none of them. What he saw, scented, felt with all seven senses and several brand-new autumn senses too, were three dazzling beauties with white fleeces and intoxicating scents. And a rival, young and strong but inexperienced.

Othello looked forward to trying his strength against the

rival almost as much as to what would follow the duel. His hooves impatiently scraped up earth, and the blood flowed through his veins faster than usual.

Then the wind turned, carrying away the scents of Zora, Cloud, Maple, and Mopple. Othello calmed down. Once again he looked down at the beach, where Melmoth had imperceptibly turned into a wandering gray dot surrounded by the darker gray of the water. From this distance, if he hadn't known better, Othello would have taken him for a small wave, a drift of spray, a little foam on the vast expanse of the sea. But Othello didn't see a gray wave. What he saw was a mighty rival moving away from the flock—his flock.

And Othello was content.

A Note of Warning

The sheep of Glennkill are exceptional sheep. Ordinary sheep don't tolerate either alcohol or drugs. I must ask my readers not to tempt sheep to take any narcotic substances. If you really want to give a sheep something nice, try bread or genuine grass.

Acknowledgments

Thanks to M. E. Frensch, S. O'Donovan, my family, Florian O., Chloë H., Laura von O., Renate G., Ortwin D., Stefanie W., Sonja T., Stefanie S., K. La Storia, and A. Bohnenkamp. Special thanks to Louise C., Tanja K., and Martin S.

Very special thanks to Orla O'Toole, for our conversations at Leenane Sheep & Wool Centre (Connemara, Ireland) and for inspiring insights into the eventful lives of sheep.

For their help and enthusiasm, I would like to thank my agent, Astrid Poppenhausen; my German editor, Claudia Negele; and my English editor, Jane Lawson.

Many thanks to M., for great contributions and all kinds of everything.

About the Author

Leonie Swann was born in 1975. She took degrees in philosophy, psychology, and communications from Munich University, spent some time in Paris and Ireland, worked in journalism and public relations, and is currently preparing a doctorate in English literature. *Three Bags Full*, her first novel, is being translated into six languages.

JUN   2001

Connolly Branch Library
433 Centre Street
Jamaica Plain, MA 02130

BOSTON PUBLIC LIBRARY

3 9999 05919 428 0

JUN 2007

Connolly Branch Library
433 Centre Street
Jamaica Plain, MA 02130

No longer the property of the
Boston Public Library.
Sale of this material benefits the Library.

WITHDRAWN